CONTENDER

THE CHALLENGER

TARAN MATHARU

CONTENDER
THE CHALLENGER

Hodder
Children's
Books

HODDER CHILDREN'S BOOKS

First published in Great Britain in 2020 by Hodder and Stoughton

1 3 5 7 9 10 8 6 4 2

Text copyright © Taran Matharu, 2020

The moral rights of the author have been asserted.

A CIP catalogue record for this book is available from the British Library.

ISBN: 978 1 444 93899 9 (hardback)
ISBN: 978 1 444 93900 2 (trade paperback)

Typeset in Garamond by Avon DataSet Ltd, Bidford-on-Avon, Warwickshire

Printed and bound by Clays Ltd, Elcograf S.p.A.

The paper and board used in this book are made from wood from responsible sources.

Hodder Children's Books
An imprint of Hachette Children's Group
Part of Hodder and Stoughton
Carmelite House
50 Victoria Embankment
London EC4Y 0DZ

An Hachette UK Company
www.hachette.co.uk

www.hachettechildrens.co.uk

To my readers, for all your support.
This book could not be written without you.

ONE

There was blood in the water. Cade heaved on his fishing line, dismayed at the wriggling mass that churned beneath the surface. His catch, a flat silver-bellied fish, emerged half-eaten, flopping glassy-eyed to the shoreline of the river.

It had been this way with every cast, the shoals of small fish descending on any other that showed distress, stripping flesh as it twisted on his line. Twice before, he had pulled in little more than a skeleton, though even the scraps that hung off the bone were worth keeping.

Still, the silver fish was prize enough for the hungry boy, and there was no time for another cast. Beside him, Quintus pointed at the sky, warning of the setting sun. Together, they pushed their ragged haul into their wicker basket and stole away into the undergrowth, keeping to the shadows.

It was a curse that the fish only began to rise at dusk, when the insects descended. The insects whined about their heads, but Cade did not slap at them. By now, he could tell by their sound which would simply sup on the salty sweat on his skin, and which would sting him for the blood beneath. This time, there were few of the latter.

The boys caught sight of the waterfall not far along the river. It was always a risk, leaving the clearing beyond the Keep. But their fruit-heavy diet was taking its toll. Cade's stomach churned at the sight of figs, and their attempts to trap the rodents that frequented the orchards on top of the mountain had not met with any success.

These same rodents were the reason for their unvaried meals, having eaten up most of the ground vegetables the Romans had left behind. What was left they had set aside, fenced off and replanted for next season, painful as that had been. It amazed Cade how much food eight people could consume in such a short time, and now it was fruit, fruit and more fruit.

Quintus caught his attention, and spoke, giving him a thumbs up at the same time.

'Good trip.'

Cade smiled and nodded, still amazed at the boy's progress. Quintus's English had come along in leaps and bounds, and Cade had become used to his unique diction. Cade's Latin was returning too, swimming back from the recesses of his memory. In fact, all the contenders were practising it, with Amber and the other girls already having studied it at school.

They'd had little to do in the three months since the battle. Three months of staring at the timer, waiting for the Codex to speak. No questions, cajoling or even threats had succeeded in breaking its silence. It was the great weight that hung above them. That and the timer, ticking down inexorably.

Relieved to be home, the pair hurried down the black tunnel that led them back to the Keep. The fish stew they would have that night was one of the few things Cade had to look forward to. Yoshi had turned out to be an excellent cook, limited though he was by their paltry stock of ingredients.

'Any luck?' Amber called as they ducked out of the tunnel.

'Some,' Cade said begrudgingly.

Amber sat alone, cross-legged upon the cobbles. The girl was prodding at their small communal fire, and Cade was again struck by how strange it seemed to see her in school uniform.

'Guys,' Amber called. 'They're back.'

Cade set the basket down and grinned as the others emerged from the Keep, their usual lethargy interrupted by the news of the fishermen's arrival.

'Wanna whip this up?' Cade asked Yoshi, seeing his friend rub his hands together at the sight of the wicker basket.

'You have no idea,' Yoshi muttered. 'Hand it over.'

Without waiting for a response, the boy lifted each fish one by one, grimacing at the sorry state of the first pair; they were mostly skin and bone. Grace shook her head at the sight, but lay a hand on Yoshi's shoulder as the boy dropped them back in with disappointment.

'The bones are still good for a broth,' Grace said. 'My mum makes one that'll blow your socks off.' She wrinkled her nose. 'Shame we don't have any chilli.'

Yoshi nodded mournfully, but Scott rolled his eyes.

3

'I'd eat a week-old hot dog out of a wrestler's jock-strap if it meant an end to all these figs,' he said. 'Cook it however you want, just leave some for me.'

'Gross,' Bea muttered, and Trix gave the boy a glare.

The twins looked sickly pale, and not just from Scott's joke. They had all lost weight over the past three months, but then the twins had been slight to start with. It was another source of worry for Cade, though none had broached it with them.

The only silver lining was that the contenders had all been given time to heal from their wounds. Perhaps too much time. Cade stared up at the light from the windows of the top floor of the Keep, where the Codex and its glowing timer had settled since his conversation with Abaddon.

The timer had begun at four months. And now, they had a little more than one left, ticking away like a bomb. Far, far more than they had been given before the qualifying round.

It scared Cade, this extra time. Scared everyone. As if they were supposed to be preparing. As if somehow, it would make up for the halving of their numbers. Four school girls, three delinquents, and . . . Quintus.

Thank the heavens for Quintus. It was he who knew how to replant the crops, how to protect against the vermin. How to grind the wheat in a bowl to make flour pancakes. He had even brought down a pterosaur with his sling, though the wily creatures now knew to stay away.

So here they sat in limbo, waiting. Though for what, they didn't know. Only that it would be cruel and violent, with unimaginable consequences.

4

Such thoughts were ever-present at the back of Cade's mind, but now they swirled to the forefront as he watched his friends around the fire. He knew them now. Cared about them. Their three months of healing had been more than merely physical.

He knew the joyride that landed Scott in jail had been a cry for attention following his mother's death. Knew Grace prayed every night to the small crucifix around her neck. He learned Bea and Trix had never spent a night away from their parents. That Yoshi's greatest frustration was the Keep's lack of music, while Amber's was the lack of chocolate.

His frustration mounting, Cade's feet moved unbidden to the Keep. They carried him up the stairs, and he tried to forget the pooled blood and bodies that had once littered the floors, the sight of which had turned a safe home into nothing more than a shelter from the wind and rain.

He walked on, past the empty rooms, to the round table at the very top. To the ominous glow of the timer, and the Codex that was its source. He stood, his fists clenched, as the numbers flashed and changed.

36:22:58:26
36:22:58:25
36:22:58:24

'Is this fun for you?' Cade asked. 'Watching us scratch out an existence here?'

His voice felt strange in the empty room. Like he was talking to himself.

'Some game master you are,' Cade said, layering his words with as much contempt as he could muster. 'I'm sure it will be great fun to watch us all butchered when our four months are up. Fun for you, and your so-called Pantheon.'

The Codex's lens stared back, silent and impassive. Cade ploughed on.

'I bet they'll be super impressed with the eight half-starved teenagers you offer up as a challenge.'

Something moved within the floating drone, so minutely, it was almost imperceptible. A gear, twitching. A circuit sparking. Something.

'I hate to think of all those remnants you left in the jungle. So carefully curated, selected from the very best of human history. Never to be used. Just to rust and rot once we're dead. We're the last, right? Nobody else will use them.'

Nothing. He tried again.

'So this is Abaddon's swan song for Earth. Going out with a fizzle, not a bang. Eight trussed lambs, ready for the slaughter. I thought you would have something better planned.'

Silence.

Cade tried not to let his frustration show. He turned, letting his anger dissolve into thoughts of fish stew.

Then . . . a voice.

'Do not presume to know my stratagem, foolish little child.'

Cade's breath caught in his throat, his stomach twisting. Slowly, he turned, and jumped to see the Codex hovering before his face. The room, once bright with the timer's glow, now fell to darkness.

'Oh, come now, is this not what you wanted?' the voice said. 'My attention? Be careful what you wish for, boy.'

It was a deeper voice, rasping and cruel. Not girlish like last time. But then, Abaddon's last form had been to put him at ease. That was no longer the intention.

'Call the others,' Abaddon commanded. 'It's time to play.'

TWO

It was amazing what fear did to the body. Cade's hunger, once ravening, had fled, leaving only a sick feeling in his stomach. And as the others hurried up the steps behind him, their laboured breathing matched his own.

All the bravado of the past few minutes vanished. Suddenly, the interminable waiting seemed far better than this, where a sadistic, immortal being dictated their fates. Told them the manner of their deaths in no uncertain terms.

The others arrived, and as they trooped into the dark room, none spoke. They only shuffled around the walls as if the Codex were a viper, and the drone in turn swivelled its gaze to follow them. Terror hung heavy in the air, almost palpable.

'You are ungrateful,' came the voice. 'Like an infant who spits up their mother's milk.'

The voice tutted. It was a strange sound, coming from a machine. Cade was not sure Abaddon even had a tongue. Each word was measured, weighted. The sounds, the tones, the inflections – all contrived. It was unnerving.

'Did I not give you time to heal?' Abaddon went on. 'To prepare yourselves for the challenges ahead? Instead, you dissolve into self-pity, and let yourselves waste away. And you presume to blame me for your incompetence.'

Despite himself, Cade felt a twinge of guilt. But what else could they have done? Piled more rocks onto the wall?

'You owe your very existence to *me*. As does your species, and the very planet you crawl on. Have some gratitude.'

There was no response to be made. And yet the Codex went quiet, as if waiting for them to speak. The silence dragged on, and then:

'Thank you,' Amber said. 'You're right.'

The Codex snapped to her, the lens twisting behind the translucent exterior.

'Amber Lin,' Abaddon said. 'You surprise me. I had intended you to be no more than fodder for my pets in the jungle. Yet here you stand.'

Amber lifted her chin.

'I'll play your game,' she said. 'We all will. But you can't ask us to master it if we don't know the rules.'

The lens twitched.

'Very well,' Abaddon said. 'But I would advise that you not let go of the bliss of ignorance so easily, as your canonical Adam and Eve once did. Your rude awakening may be as painful as theirs.'

'I think we'd rather know,' Amber said, crossing her arms.

The Codex edged backwards. The room flashed with light. And they saw it.

A two-dimensional pyramid appeared in the empty space before them. It consisted of twenty-one blocks: six on the bottom layer, five on the next, then four, three, two and one. A red line separated the third row from those beneath it.

'What is that?' Cade breathed.

Abaddon's voice echoed in the room.

'Each block represents a corresponding planet, ruled by one member of the Pantheon.'

The left-most block on the row of three pulsed, and a symbol revolved slowly upon it. A skull. A human skull.

'That's us. Earth.'

Us.

There was no 'us', and it sickened Cade that Abaddon somehow imagined themselves on the same team. Yet there it was. The game board, so to speak.

'To reach the top, each planet's representatives must battle their way up the leaderboard by attacking planets above or adjacent to them. They must also defend against attacks from below and adjacent. The winners of these battles switch places with the losers.'

Cade could not help but move closer, his eyes widening at the simplicity of it.

'Your predecessors saw the wisdom of remaining on the edge of the leaderboard,' Abaddon said. 'Placed as you are, only the planet to Earth's right and the two planets below can attack. But it also limits you in your path upwards – you must defeat the planet directly above you to do so, while if you were in the centre of the leaderboard, you could choose between two.'

'And what is the red line?'

It was Grace who spoke this time, her arms also crossed in anger.

'Excellent question, Grace,' Abaddon said, and Cade could hear the pleasure in the entity's voice. 'It is your line in the sand. Fall beneath it and . . . Earth is wiped clean of life. I start again.'

Cade stared at the leaderboard in horror. If they lost a single attack from below . . . it was over for them. Over for everyone.

'We reserve the positions above the red line for the older, more advanced planets,' Abaddon went on. 'Those with space-faring civilisations in particular.'

Cade's sudden fascination did little to dispel the fear that pulsed through him.

'Can we be attacked at any time?' Cade asked.

'Fortunately for you, no,' Abaddon replied. 'Members of the Pantheon agree on a time and place for each battle, as well as the rules that must be followed by both sides. If we cannot agree terms, the rest of the Pantheon vote on the dispute, to decide what a fair match might be. It's my job to negotiate for you, and choose who and when to attack.'

'And we have no say in this?' Cade demanded. 'We're just pawns?'

'That's a very good way of putting it.' Abaddon chuckled darkly. 'Well done, Cade.'

Cade closed his eyes, wishing it would all go away. Suddenly, he wanted to go to sleep. Close his eyes, let his worries fade away. His favourite time of the day was waking up, and those few brief seconds before he remembered where he was.

'Now, our next battle was agreed some time ago,' Abaddon went on. 'But since I was not sure how many of you would survive my qualifier round, it was a difficult battle to negotiate. In the end, it came down to a vote from my brethren. And I must confess, the rest of the Pantheon do not like humans much.'

The voice paused, as if relishing the dread across their faces.

'The question of how many contenders would survive was neatly solved by my own proposal. A duel. One-on-one. Two combatants, fighting on open ground.'

Somehow . . . this seemed better. It was an ugly picture, but it would only put one of them in danger.

'You may not use firearms, nor explosives or flammables. Other than that . . . the only rule is it's a fight to the death.'

There it was. The fate of the world, hanging on a single bout.

'And if we lose?' Amber asked, her voice shaking. 'What happens to the rest of us?'

'You'll find out.'

Silence.

'Who fights?' Scott blurted, then covered his mouth.

'I had not decided until a few minutes ago, Scott,' Abaddon purred. 'But now I have a clear choice.'

Slowly, the Codex turned towards Cade.

'After his little tirade, it seems that Cade is the one with the most fight left in him. And it's an apt punishment for a petulant, ungrateful child.'

The lens hovered closer, until it filled Cade's vision.

'Lucky you.'

THREE

Darkness. And then, light.

36:22:47:17
36:22:47:16
36:22:47:15

'*Contenders have been granted access to higher Codex functions,*' the Codex intoned, back to its bored robotic voice.

Cade had almost missed the damned thing. Almost.

'He's gone,' Grace muttered, steadying herself against the wall.

'No,' Cade said. 'He isn't. He's watching us.'

Bea hugged her sister tight. 'Does he have nothing better to do?' she said, her words muffled in Trix's shoulder.

'I don't think this is all he does,' Cade said, staring at the Codex. 'If what he told me in our first conversation is true, he's capable of doing a thousand things at once. Imagine a being infinitely smarter than us, but deranged by a million

14

lifetimes of boredom. We are just a small part of this attention; a toy to pass the time.'

Abaddon's parting words were only hitting him now, like a creeping ice in his chest that seized his lungs and would not let him breathe.

He hunched over, then slid to the floor, his back against the wall.

Grace knelt beside him, rubbing his back.

'It's going to be OK, Cade,' she whispered.

But it wasn't. He was no fighter. He wasn't even a grown man. Yet now, he would fight to the death against the champion of an unknown enemy. And the weight of the world, more literally than ever before, lay across his thin shoulders.

It was hard to breathe.

'We can do this,' Yoshi said, crouching down. '*You* can do this. How many vipers did you kill in the qualifier round, huh? Ten? Twenty? It'll be a walk in the park.'

Cade shuddered, remembering the baying, howling mass of monstrosities they had faced before.

'We're not fighting vipers,' Cade whispered. 'This is going to be the best another world has to offer. Their greatest fighter.'

'We have over a month,' Yoshi said. 'We can practise. Train.'

'Practise for what?' Cade muttered. 'A sword fight? A wrestling match? Will it wear armour? Will it fly? Is it capable of speech, or strategy? We don't even know what I'm fighting!'

Yoshi had nothing to say to that.

'We'll figure it out together,' Grace said. 'You're not alone in this.'

15

'Until I *am*,' Cade whispered. 'One-on-one, Abaddon said.'

'Codex, show us the leaderboard again,' Amber snapped.

The pyramid flashed up once more, the timer still ticking away above it. Cade could hardly lift his eyes. He dry-heaved, but his empty stomach did little more than clench, leaving him choking like a beached fish.

But he saw it all the same. Earth's block and symbol pulsed, and in the lower left corner a second block pulsed in tandem with it. They were being attacked from below. A loss meant . . . the end.

A second bout of nausea sent black clouds across his eyes, his eyebrows knitting as he heaved a second time.

'Is that who we're fighting?' Amber demanded.

Instead of speaking, the lower block detached from the pyramid, floating outwards. Its symbol was also a skull, though shaped so strangely he could not identify it one way or the other.

'What can you tell us about them?' Amber asked. 'I thought you could only show us information originating on Earth.'

'*I may also display information catalogued by prior contenders,*' the Codex intoned. '*But only that which has been captured on film, or written while present on Acies. There is no guarantee that this information is accurate.*'

'Acies?' Grace asked.

'*The name that the prior contenders gave to this world.*'

A memory swam to Cade's mind. A book, written in Latin code, had been found in what they assumed was the old Roman commander's chamber, not too far from the old-timey projector. Perhaps that knowledge was somehow available through the Codex.

'Tell us about the creatures,' he managed.

Above the block, a set of three-dimensional figures appeared, spinning gently. They were in miniature, standing beside a projection of a human silhouette.

'Prior contenders named this species Hydra,' the Codex said. *'It is made up of three male phenotypes, and a single female queen. The queen's form has never been recorded in detail, so I will only provide images of the males.'*

To Cade's surprise . . . he recognised the projections. He had seen them before, in grainy black and white, not too far from where he saw them now. These were the self-same monsters the Romans had been fighting in the film clip on Louis Le Prince's projector.

All three sported heads of similar appearance, with an elongated skull in the shape of a conch shell, studded with black eyes. This ended in a squid-like mouth, formed from grasping tentacles that had a sharp beak and teeth nestling within the central maw. With each iteration, from smallest to largest, the number of tentacles increased, and the head's spiked, sea-shell formations became more jagged.

'Mother of God,' Scott whispered.

Cade stared, his eyes dancing from one figure to the next. His eyes could not help but focus on the raptor talons on each foot, each bigger and sharper than the last.

'The first phenotype is the male in its youngest form. These sterile, larval-stage workers make up around two thirds of all Hydras.'

The smallest of the trio of holograms pulsed. It was the size and shape of a plucked turkey, with two feet, small nubs in place of arms and a kangaroo-like tail. It stood no taller than a turkey too, though it looked more agile and far deadlier, with tentacles that could latch around the face as easily as a face-hugger from an *Alien* movie.

The next largest pulsed in turn.

'The second phenotype is the male in its adolescent form. The tail retracts, and the vestigial arms become front paws. Also sterile, they make up around a quarter of all Hydras, suggesting a high attrition rate for larval workers as they age.'

It had a four-legged body similar in form and stature to a hairless leopard's, with talons no less dangerous and a musculature to match. The claws on its back legs were akin to those of the raptors he had fought three months earlier, and Cade could imagine them ripping through the cloth of his uniform like rice-paper, as its forelegs and tendrilled mouth wrapped about his shoulders. He shuddered at the thought, but the Codex gave no respite, moving to the next projection.

'The third phenotype is the alpha male in its final form, one reserved for the most aggressive adolescent males that survive the constant warring between herds. These fertile, mature males protect the queen, and earn the right to mate with her. It is the alpha male you will duel.'

If the first two had scared him, this third specimen struck horror into Cade's heart. It stood taller than eight feet, with a tailless, humanoid physique that rippled with muscle. Long arms tipped with three-fingered claws emerged from an upright body, and thick armoured plating adorned its chest.

Long grasping tentacles seemed to reach for him, and he could see the concentric rings of teeth within, circling a beak large enough to crush a skull.

The prehensile feelers were capable of wrapping around his head like many boa constrictors, crushing the life from him – if the sharp beak and terrible talons of its feet and claws didn't do the job first.

This was the creature he would fight. And it would tear him to pieces.

FOUR

If the Codex had information about the queen, Cade did not hear it. Overwhelmed, he had slumped to the side, and the others had helped him from the Keep and out into the fresh air.

But he already knew what the queen looked like. Had seen one in the projector all those days ago. A veritable giant, larger than an elephant, though the image was too unfocused to make out much more.

It didn't matter though; the Codex had informed them that he would be fighting an alpha, so knowing more was largely irrelevant. In truth, Cade didn't want to know. Perhaps Abaddon was right. Ignorance was bliss.

Now, they sat beside the fire. The red moon hung low in the sky as they ate their meal, savouring the rich broth that Yoshi had made. A small glimmer of pleasure in their new, violent world. And through some combination of pity, the fact he had caught the fish himself, or that they thought he needed to build his strength, Cade was given a double helping.

He scraped the bottom of his bowl, aware of the others' ravenous eyes upon him. They would fish more the next day. It was just a shame they had only one hook, found between the cobbles in the mostly empty armoury. Perhaps they could make a new one. Quintus was pretty handy at that sort of thing.

'So,' Cade said.

He stopped, unsure of what to say next. Fortunately for him, Scott was rarely at a loss for words.

'No firearms or explosives, huh,' the boy said. 'Like we've got many of those lying around.'

It was a poor joke, but his words sparked something in Amber's eyes.

'No . . .' she said. 'We don't.'

She looked to Cade, and cocked her head to one side.

'Why tell us not to use something we don't have . . . unless it's a hint. I mean, Abaddon doesn't *want* us to lose, right?'

Cade shrugged.

'Who knows what that psycho is thinking. Maybe he can't wait to wipe us all out, start from scratch again.'

Amber pursed her lips.

'How did we win the last battle?' she asked. 'Because you found swords. Because you found *us*. You had the *Witchcraft*. You had Quintus. Maybe we aren't allowed to use explosives and such, but there *will* be other weapons we might use.'

Cade looked up. It seemed obvious, but in his despair he had hardly considered it.

'I have a sword,' Cade said, thinking aloud. 'A good one. I can't imagine a better weapon to fight with. But maybe something long-range?'

He gave it more thought. This battle was David vs Goliath, in more ways than one. He had a sling-stone after all. But looking at that behemoth, with its armour plating and rubbery tentacles . . . would a stone really do much before it hit him like a freight train? A bow, or javelin might be a better option.

'I don't think it's weapons that you need,' Bea said quietly.

Cade caught her eye, and saw the worry there.

'I want you to survive it,' she muttered. 'And you have no protection. Your clothes might as well be wrapping paper.'

'Well, don't sugarcoat it,' Scott said.

'We have some hockey pads in our van,' Trix said, ignoring him. 'It's somewhere out there in the jungle. Maybe we can find it.'

'My goalie helmet is pretty good,' Grace said, catching onto the idea.

'Seriously?' Yoshi asked. 'No offence guys, but this isn't a field hockey game.'

'You have a better idea?' Amber asked.

Yoshi raised his hands.

'All I'm saying is, one of those claws will punch through your plastic helmet like it's orange peel.'

Cade shuddered, and Yoshi grimaced an apology.

'Sorry man. Just trying to help.'

Cade forced a smile in return. Yoshi was right, though it pained him to admit it. But they were onto something. He had no chance without armour – not unless he killed it from a distance, and he was sure it would charge right at him.

Back when they had fought the vipers, there had been no time to search for new artefacts in the jungle, and he had been sure that the previous contenders had picked everything nearby clean. Indeed, there had been a supposed flotilla of Roman ships out there, if he remembered correctly.

Now though, with the benefit of time, it might be worth exploring what else was nearby. Even some rusted old Roman armour would be better than what he had now.

'Codex!' he called.

He turned to the Keep, and the Codex floated down from the window to hover beside him.

'Show me the map again.'

The Codex obeyed wordlessly, and together they stared at the bird's eye view of the caldera, a ring of brown mountains looped round a circle of green. In its epicentre, a smaller circle of blue delineated a sea or lake.

'Woah,' breathed Yoshi.

Cade realised that not all of the contenders had seen the map – there had been no time before the qualifier round, and the Codex had been unresponsive since.

'Here,' Cade said, pointing to the glowing blue dots scattered across the map. 'These are remnants that we and previous contenders have identified.'

'What are remnants again?' Scott asked.

'Objects, creatures and even people from Earth,' Amber explained.

'Seriously? Shouldn't the whole thing be covered in moving dots?' Scott asked. 'There must be thousands of animals out there.'

23

Cade shook his head.

'The blue dots aren't live,' he said. 'Look.'

He stood and walked over to the map, pinching with his fingers to zoom closer to a location, a patch of grey-brown squares among the green.

'Hueitapalan,' Cade said. 'The Mayan city where Quintus found me. Look.'

He tapped a cluster of blue dots beside the pyramid he had once summited.

'Remnants identified as the swords named Nagamitsu, Kunitoshi, Tak—'

'That's enough,' Cade said.

'But aren't those here?' Scott asked, nodding to the swords they now carried at all times. 'How can they be there?'

'The Codex only shows us where an object was scanned, when it was scanned and what it is,' Cade said. 'It doesn't tell us where it is *now*. Nor does it tell us where *everything* is. Only things the Codex has scanned in the past. Which means if we or the previous contenders haven't scanned something with the Codex, it won't show up as a remnant on the map.'

Scott groaned.

'Just when I was getting my hopes up.'

Cade shrugged.

'It's still a lot better than nothing,' he said, zooming out on the map again.

He let out a low whistle as he swiped his finger about, able to examine it with more than just a hurried few glances for the first time.

'The last contenders kept busy,' Cade said. 'They came across a lot of remnants.'

'I don't know if that's a good thing,' Grace said.

Cade turned to look at her. 'What do you mean?'

'If the old Roman contenders found it . . . it means they might have brought it back here. And there's *nothing* here. Who knows how many remnants they took with them when they marched off to war.'

She was right. Cade's stomach twisted with disappointment.

'So even if we do find some useful remnant of the map and trek our way through the dinosaur-infested jungle . . . there might be nothing there?' Yoshi asked. 'The Romans might have just scanned it there, and then brought it back with them?'

'Right,' Cade said, trying to keep the frustration from his voice. 'But it's a hell of a lot better than running around in there like headless chickens. At least we have something to aim for.'

At least.

FIVE

They decided to leave the remnant search for the next day, the emotional lows of the day taking their toll. They all retired to their respective rooms, but Cade knew he would not sleep that night. Instead, he headed for the Orchards above the Keep. There was something he had to do. Something he'd put off doing for a long time.

It was a long walk up the mountainside, one that wasted precious calories he had just consumed. But some things were worth doing.

At the top, Cade was amazed to see that so much had changed in so short a time. How eight people could burn through hundreds of fallen fruit, and even most of the ripe ones that had hung from the branches.

Their supposed goldmine of food was almost gone. Who knew how the Romans had sustained themselves for so long, and in such great numbers. By hunting, most likely.

Cade trudged through the trees, heading for the place he had hardly allowed himself to look at each time he'd made the journey here over the last few months.

Graves. He wouldn't know they were there but for the crosses stuck into the ground, the rows of dug up earth now dusted with grass. Four crosses. Simple things of bound twigs and twine. Less than they deserved.

The others had chosen well – it was a beautiful place. A small patch of untended land, at the cliff's edge. Beyond, the green blanket of jungle could be seen, illuminated by the expanse of stars above.

It was guilt that had kept him away. Guilt that he had told them this was a place worth fighting for. Worth dying for. But that was not his gravest sin. He had convinced them that victory was possible. That they were fighting for humanity itself.

Now, he knew better. The game was unstoppable. Even if they did climb to the top of the leaderboard and were allowed to go home, the game would go on. Some other group of lost souls would replace them. Perhaps they would arrive home, only to be burned from existence a few days later – that next batch of contenders failing where Cade and his friends had succeeded.

In the best of scenarios . . . the deaths of Eric, Spex, Jim and Gobbler had only delayed the inevitable.

Cade knelt in the grass, resting a hand on the grave closest to him. He did not even know whose it was, though those who had buried them did. He had never thought to ask.

A slow tear worked through the grime on his face.

'Did you want to be alone?'

Amber's voice cut through his thoughts. He wiped his

eyes and turned towards her.

She stood, hesitant, in the dappled shadows of the fig trees, her face half-cast in moonlight.

Cade forced a smile and drew his knees up to his chest. He did not answer, but she took it as an invitation, settling beside him on the grass, looking out at the jungle beyond the cliff's edge.

They sat in silence, the only sound the soft soughing of the breeze, coupled with the echoing crash of the waterfall far below.

'Did we make the right call, coming back here?' Cade asked.

With each word, it felt like a weight was lifted from his shoulders. That question had sat like a lump in his throat, suffocating him. As if in the asking of it, he would acknowledge that guilt, that unsure regret that he had allowed to fester inside him.

'Of *course*,' Amber said.

It was not the answer he had expected.

'These four,' Cade said, gesturing at the shallow humps of the four graves in front of him. 'They died because we came here. Because I told them to.'

He felt Amber's soft hand on his shoulder, and somehow that touch broke the thin dam inside of him, the one that had held back a flood of tears.

Cade did not sob. Only took a deep, shuddering breath as his eyes streamed, and the beauty of the world in front of him blurred.

Amber's hand squeezed his shoulder, yet when she spoke,

there was steel in her voice as well as sympathy.

'You did not force them to come here,' Amber whispered. 'Look at me, Cade.'

Cade raised his head, meeting her gaze.

'You gave them a *chance*,' Amber whispered. 'A *choice*. One they made willingly.'

'But it was the wrong one,' Cade whispered back. 'At least for them.'

'Don't you dare say that,' Amber said, and her tone was like a slap that jarred him from that spiral of despair. 'You're allowed to feel sorry for yourself. You're allowed to be scared. But I won't let you take their deaths on your shoulders.'

Her finger jabbed out at the dark jungle.

'You think we'd have lasted this long out there?'

Cade shrugged, and wiped his face a second time.

'I'm alive right now because of what you did. Me and the others. And countless souls, back on Earth. Leaders make hard choices. Sometimes, you don't get to save everyone.'

Cade swallowed, hard. She was right.

She stood and kicked a loose pebble out into the darkness.

'I'm going with you tomorrow because *I* think it's the best choice – just like these four did before. Not because you told me to. And if I die out there, that's on me.'

She pressed her hand into his shoulder once more, then she walked back towards the path down the mountain.

Cade stared out into the jungle. Soon, they would be venturing deep into it. And here he was, feeling sorry for himself.

He set his jaw and pressed his fingers into the soil.

'You died for this,' he whispered. 'Died for us. For the world. I'll not let it be for nothing.'

Cade stood and wiped the tears from his eyes. The time for grieving had come and gone. Now was the time to fight.

SIX

Cade made the long slog down the mountainside, and by the time he had reached the bottom he was damp with sweat. Mixed with the grime from his fishing expedition, he felt gross.

So, he headed to the baths, hoping a long soak in the cool waters of the bathing pool would help clear his thoughts.

Passing through the yawning doorway of the Keep, he crossed the atrium and descended the stone-cut stairs and into the cave-like chamber below, taking the time to light a single torch at the bottom with flint and steel.

They were trying to conserve their torches, since their own attempts at making them had failed, and their supply of old Roman ones was running out. But he allowed himself the indulgence of it on this night. He was sure the others would understand.

A sudden movement made him jump, and he spun round with his heart in his mouth. He spotted something hovering just above head-height a few paces behind him.

31

'Codex!' He sighed. 'You scared the crap out of me.'

It looked like after its long hiatus, the machine had taken to following him again.

Beyond the Codex, a shadow moved, and Cade realised the machine was not alone. Quintus padded out of the gloom, a look of concern across his face.

'Sorry, Quintus,' Cade said, pitching his voice louder, as he always did, for the boy's benefit. 'I should have made sure you understood it all.'

'No problem,' the boy replied, repeating the phrase he had learned from the others. He trotted past Cade and dive-bombed into the pool, fully-clothed.

Cade grinned and followed, stripping as he went. By now, the boys were used to bathing together, after the girls had their turn.

The echo of rushing water surrounded him as he slid into the dark pool, placing the torch in a holder beside it. He shuddered briefly beneath its chill, letting himself acclimatise. Quintus gave him a smile, while Cade racked his brains, trying to think of the simplest way to explain.

'We fight those monsters?' Quintus asked, before Cade could speak. 'The ones like the *polypus*?'

He wriggled his fingers in front of his mouth, mimicking an octopus.

Cade shook his head, even as he laughed. Somehow, Quintus had a way of making everything seem better. They had become closer since the battle. And though the others made time for the near-deaf, Latin-speaking boy, it seemed it was Cade he trusted best.

'No, Quintus. I will fight one monster. The big one.'

Quintus frowned, watching Cade's lips closely.

'We don't fight together?'

He motioned at Cade and himself, mirroring his meaning with his hands, as he did with almost everything he said.

'Just me. One against one.'

The legionary, usually so positive, sank deeper beneath the water, staring across the pool. He shook his head.

'Not fair,' Quintus said.

Cade looked down.

'Not fair at all,' he agreed.

Silence reigned, but for the echoes within the cavern.

'That is why you need *armatura*,' Quintus said finally. 'Arm . . . armour? For the fight?'

Cade nodded.

'We will go into the caldera,' he said. 'To search for . . . *armatura*. Do you know where *armatura* could be?'

Quintus considered the question for a moment.

Cade didn't hold out much hope. He and Amber had spent many hours with Quintus in the days following the battle, scratching out drawings with sticks in the dirt, searching their memories for half-forgotten Latin. He had told them everything he had known, which was not much.

Quintus's own legion and those that had been there before had both marched off into the desert, barely a day after Quintus had arrived on Acies. They'd been armed with traditional weapons, no guns to speak of, and their number included cavalry and mercenaries. They took catapults with them, and loaded wagons, though what the wagons contained Quintus didn't know.

Whatever campaign they had set out on, they had intended it to be a drawn-out affair. It was why those that had been left behind, like Quintus, had waited so long before they abandoned the Keep.

The Romans left behind had spoken only of battling monsters from the underworld, and winning. Just as Zeus and his siblings had overthrown the Titans, so too had a new Pantheon overthrown *them*. And these new gods, these beings of unimaginable power, had tasked the Romans with protecting the Keep.

Beyond that, Quintus had been ostracised by those left behind, for his deafness, and for his unusual appearance – the mismatched eyes, set more widely apart than other people's. Most of them were soldiers from another, earlier time in history, and had considered Quintus a bad omen. What he knew he had overheard, and he overheard very little. It was why he had been one of the first to abandon the place.

'No,' Quintus said finally. 'They left nothing. Even my gladius, I stole before.'

Cade sighed. So, no help there.

'Did the old contenders go to the jungle often?' Cade said.

Quintus smiled.

'They hated jungles,' he said. 'Only hunted for food, near Keep. And sometimes . . .'

The boy thought for a minute.

'They said, sometimes they go deeper,' he said, searching for the words. 'To hunt for . . . remnants?'

'Yes, remnants,' Cade said, leaning closer.

'They sent . . . *exploratores?*'

Quintus made a flowing motion with his hand, as if taking a meandering path.

'Explorers,' Cade said, and Quintus nodded, closing his eyes as if mentally noting the word. The boy was *good* at languages.

'Many men went,' Quintus said. 'None came back. Only . . .'

He gestured to the Codex.

'That came back. Alone.'

Cade nodded, both pleased and worried at the news. That the armed explorers had not returned did not bode well for their upcoming expedition. But it *did* mean that it was possible the Roman explorers had not intended to bring back the remnants themselves, only discover them and return to the Keep. Smaller items may have been taken, sure. But transporting back a full set of armour, across rugged terrain crawling with prehistoric monsters? They would have to be mad to do that.

And yet, that was exactly what he intended to do. If the others could be convinced, that is.

He dipped his head beneath the water, as if the cold might shock some sense into him. But when he emerged, no alternative presented itself. This was the game . . . and he would play it.

'Come on then, Quintus,' Cade said. 'Let's get some sleep. I have a feeling we're going to need it.'

SEVEN

They sat around the table, bleary-eyed and apprehensive. It was morning, and they were on the top floor. A basket of figs lay forgotten at the table's edge, barely touched despite their hunger. Their very lives depended on what they would learn in the next few minutes.

'Codex, bring up the map,' Cade said, speaking first when he realised nobody else would. 'Make it big.'

Immediately, the screen appeared, beyond the table where all could see. There was no glare from the morning light of the window, and Cade had a sudden, mad fantasy of watching films on it. But the timer, ever counting down, brought him crashing back to reality.

He went to get up and manipulate the map with his fingers, then thought better of it.

It's artificial intelligence, right? I can just tell it what to do.

'Codex,' Cade said, after a moment's contemplation. 'Roughly how far is the city of Hueitapalan from the Keep?'

'*Approximately ten miles,*' came the reply.

Cade scratched his chin, where an itchy fuzz had begun to grow. The jungle was thick and dangerous, but it might be possible to get as far as the ancient city by river, floating down on a raft until the rapids and paddling for shore in good time. They could travel on foot from there, with Quintus as a guide – he would know the area well.

There were other branches the river took, tributaries they could float down. Risky if there were more rapids, but perhaps worth it, considering the creatures that inhabited the jungle.

Still, they would need to return by foot, since the raft would not float upriver, and he imagined they would move no faster than half-a-mile an hour when hiking through the jungle. He made some quick calculations in his head.

'Show me all the remnants within twenty miles of the Keep,' Cade said.

A blue ring flared across the map's surface, and the view zoomed closer to encompass its edges. There were fewer blue dots within the space than Cade had hoped. They would have to go farther afield for any others.

'Twenty?' Scott groaned. 'How long will that take us?'

Cade grimaced.

'We might make five miles a day, on foot,' he said. 'So four days there, four days back. But if we take a raft down the river we might save a day or so. Call it a week's trip.'

'I wish we still had the *Witchcraft*,' Grace murmured, and Cade felt a flash of anger, remembering Finch's betrayal. Who knew how many more of them would have survived if they'd had access to the boat's fuel. Or how much of a difference an extra fighter would have made.

'If we find Finch out there . . .' Amber said, cracking her knuckles.

Cade nodded in grim agreement, though he wasn't sure exactly *what* they would do if they did find him.

Pushing the thoughts from his mind for now, he leaned closer and examined the remnants.

'Remove all remnants that are known not to contain weapons, armour, vessels or vehicles,' Cade instructed. 'Ignore the Roman ships nearby. And also the ones that I have seen before.'

A few of the glowing dots disappeared, and Cade felt a twinge of guilt.

'Summarise what remains,' Cade said.

'*Remnants are: Spearhafoc, a Benedictine monk and artist who vanished with the gold and jewels for the crown of King Edward the Confessor.*'

'Nice,' Scott said.

'Yeah, like gold is going to help us right now,' Yoshi retorted sarcastically.

'*Gold and jewels can help you.*'

Cade stared at it.

'How?' he asked.

'*You may use them to trade with the Strategos for undiscovered or unplaced remnants. It is how the previous contenders brought Quintus and his legion here.*'

His eyes widened. This game was more complicated than he had thought. He would have to explore that later, but for now they had nothing to trade, unless the few coins Yoshi had found in the baths were worth something.

'If that's true,' Amber said. 'It's unlikely the Roman explorers would leave it behind. Jewels and gold for a crown can't be too heavy.'

Cade cursed under his breath. She was right – they might travel all the way to that remnant, only to find the looted body and nothing else.

Still, it seemed treasure *was* an option. Perhaps they could buy some armour, if they happened to come across some.

'Continue,' Cade said.

'*Alexandrine Tinné, a Dutch explorer and richest woman in the Netherlands, left for dead in the Saharan desert in 1869.*'

'Badass,' Amber whispered. 'She might have some survival gear.'

She caught Cade's gaze.

'Not worth it though,' she said. 'No armour. Next.'

'*Scottish botanist John Jeffrey, disappeared in the Colorado desert in 1854.*'

'Looks like Abaddon likes taking people from deserts,' Scott said glumly.

Silence.

'OK,' Cade said. 'Now run us through the rest of them.'

'*Remnant is Dr Benjamin Church, a spy for the British captured by Washington in the Revolutionary War. He disappeared along with his prison transport ship to the West Indies in 1778.*'

The Codex paused, as if waiting for his reaction. Cade ruminated on this for a moment, then shook his head. They fought in cloth uniforms, not armour, during that time period.

'*King Władysław of Poland was beheaded in a battle during*

39

a crusade against the Ottomans in 1444. Neither the king's body nor his armour were ever found.'

'Now we're talking!' Scott said, slamming his fist into the table.

Amber grinned. 'It's like Abaddon put him there *for* us.'

Cade was suspicious. It was almost *too* perfect. Still, hope fluttered in his chest.

'Anything else?'

'An A-4E Skyhawk attack aircraft loaded with a B43 nuclear weapon fell from the deck of the USS Ticonderoga *in 1965. Pilot, plane and weapon were never found.'*

Shocked silence followed.

'A goddamn nuclear bomb?' Grace whispered. 'How many of those can go missing?'

'There are a total of four remnants containing nuclear weapons,' the Codex intoned. *'Though only one has been scanned.'*

Cade let that sink in. Four. How had humanity lost *four* nuclear bombs? It boggled the mind.

'Overkill much?' Yoshi asked.

Cade couldn't decide if it was good or bad. Explosives weren't allowed in the duel, but this was something else. Perhaps useful later, but for now . . . unthinkable.

'Yeah . . . we aren't touching that,' Cade muttered.

The others nodded in agreement.

'Next,' Cade said.

EIGHT

The Codex ran through a half-dozen more remnants. A lost railway engine called Dolly, missing in 1945. The ruins of the Viking settlement of Leifsbudir, the first European colony in North America, long abandoned to the mists of time.

Lost ships from time periods too late for armour, but too early for engines, seemingly planted in the middle of the jungle. Planes they had no hope of flying. Explorers from all over the world: Roald Amundsen, Andrew Irvine, James Harrod, Ludwig Leichhardt.

No remnant seemed as useful as the Polish king's armour. Plate armour, if Cade was lucky.

So, they made their decision. It was this king's body that they would seek out, rusted and rotted though their prize may be. There was good news though. According to the Codex, it had been scanned three years earlier. There was a chance that the armour would still be serviceable, if Abaddon had left it somewhere sheltered from the wind and rain – quite likely, since he liked his contenders to use the remnants he provided.

41

And the Romans who had found it might have left it sheltered too, if they ever planned to return to get it.

'There's something else,' Amber said, even as the Codex ended its run-through of the remnants.

'Oh?' Scott asked.

Amber hesitated.

'The men who captured us . . . put us in that cage. They all wore good armour, and if it's anything like my axe, it was made right here, on Acies. No chance of rust. No missing pieces.'

Cade stared at her. It was an interesting idea. He just wasn't sure how he felt about it.

'What are you suggesting?' Trix asked, her eyes wide.

Despite all they had gone through, the memory of their captivity was not forgotten. Even Cade woke up in cold sweats, thinking of what might have happened if Amber hadn't orchestrated a break-out. Where they might have been, at this very moment. What might have happened to Earth, had they not escaped.

'We repay them the favour,' Amber said, jarring Cade from his thoughts. 'Abduct one of *them*. Take their armour, release them back into the jungle.'

Scott laughed.

'You're twisted, girl.'

Amber shrugged.

'I'm just being realistic. We need armour, they have it. And it's not like they're good people.'

Cade was warming to her idea, but Grace didn't look convinced.

'The problem is that they *have* armour,' the tall girl said. 'You want to capture one alive? It's not like we can bop one over the head with a tree branch – they wear helmets.'

Amber bit her lip, and nodded.

'So let's say we kill them instead,' Grace continued. 'Who's to say we even catch one of them alone? They travel in groups from what we've seen.'

Cade saw her point.

'And we won't get the drop on them either,' Grace said. 'They've clearly been hunting in the jungle for a long time, and they never took their armour off, even in their camp. Even if we do surprise them, it'll be us attacking a group of armoured, armed, experienced men and hoping we somehow defeat them all.'

'OK, OK,' Amber said, holding her hands up in defeat. 'It was just an idea.'

'But she does raise a good point,' Cade said. 'It's not just the animals we have to fear out there. We should be careful with campfires at night, and keep quiet when hiking.'

'Great,' Scott muttered.

There was a moment's silence. Their plan was seeming riskier by the second.

'Before we decide anything,' Amber said, 'we need to leave pride at the door. The group that leaves the Keep will only be as fast as their slowest member. So . . . who thinks they can't make a week in the jungle?'

She looked pointedly at Bea and Trix, who lowered their eyes and raised their hands. Cade could not help but feel relieved. The pair were in no condition to travel, but he

43

hadn't wanted to be the one to say it out loud. At the same time, he could not imagine leaving the two sickly teens to fend for themselves here. And they needed another strong fighter to stay, should Cade's group . . . not make it. Grace perhaps.

As if he could read Cade's mind, Yoshi lifted his hand too.

'I'm not good at hiking,' Yoshi said. 'I have mild asthma, and it gets worse when the air is humid. I'd only slow you down.'

Bea and Trix smiled with relief, if only because they would have some company. And perhaps because their cook was staying behind.

Cade looked to Amber, Scott, Grace and Quintus. They met his gaze. Except for Quintus. He smiled and picked his nose instead.

'Right,' Cade said, stifling a grin and going to stand by the map.

Now for the hard part. Together, they examined the single, glowing point that delineated Władysław's body's location. The Codex had told them it was seventeen miles into the jungle. Sadly, not so close to Hueitapalan that it made sense to take the river all the way to the rapids. This was unfamiliar territory.

'So, we build a raft and float it down here.' Cade traced the thin lacing of the map's blue river, splitting and merging through the jungle, and eventually leading to the large sea at its centre. A thin tributary, almost too small to see, ended close to the armour. That was where they would go.

'We continue on through the swamp,' Cade said, moving

his finger further. 'Seven miles from where we leave the raft. Collect the armour and hike seventeen miles as the crow flies, back to the Keep. Easy enough, right?'

He forced a smile, and Amber returned it.

'Piece of cake,' Amber said. 'I could use the exercise.'

'Should you even go, Cade?' Grace asked. 'Shouldn't you stay here and . . . train? Save your strength?'

'Train with what?' Cade asked. 'Fence with Yoshi using some practice sticks? My opponent has *claws* and is twice my size. There's no way to prepare for this fight . . . and there will be enough time for me to do all that when I get back anyway.'

Grace shrugged, but Amber raised an eyebrow at Cade. Clearly, she agreed with Grace.

'I've spent more time in the jungle than anyone, bar Quintus,' Cade said, trying to sound convincing. 'And I speak the best Latin of all of us if he needs to tell us something, or we run into other Romans.'

Amber's expression remained unchanged, and he crossed his arms.

'Look,' his tone softened. 'I don't like leaving my fate in the hands of others. And I'm sure if I die, Abaddon will choose a new fighter.'

'You mean you're a control freak who doesn't trust us to get the armour for you,' Amber said flatly.

'Look at it this way,' Cade said. 'Armour is heavy, and we'll be carrying it a long way. Would you rather share the weight with three others, or four?'

'Fine,' Amber relented, slumping back.

45

The tension remained, though Cade wasn't sure why Amber cared so much.

Scott broke the silence.

'Anyone ever made a raft before? You know, one sturdy enough to carry five people and a week of supplies?'

There was some shuffling of feet, and all eyes suddenly seemed interested in the ceiling.

'Oh, that's OK,' Scott said. 'It's not like there are river monsters and giant fish that'll eat us if we fall in.'

Amber snorted, and any animosity was gone.

'I've still got my axe,' she said. 'We'll cut down some saplings.'

'And we can use all that old twine from the orchards to tie them together,' Bea offered. 'There's plenty of it.'

Cade wasn't so sure about that – it was mostly frayed old ropes the previous occupants had corded from stripped bark, left in pieces here and there and exposed to the elements for years. Beggars couldn't be choosers though.

He knew the raft would be flimsy, even if they spent several days making it, but the river saved them time, and was far safer than hiking the jungle, if their time on the *Witchcraft* had been any indication.

It was worth the risk.

NINE

Building a raft took them most of the day. It was not so much the construction itself, it was finding long, straight logs that didn't taper. The trees that grew along the edge of the jungle were sequoia-like – tall and straight with few branches – and so thick it might take all year for someone to cut one down with an axe. Fallen branches from their tops were all rotted or brittle and dry. Good enough for the stakes they had used in the battle months earlier, but not much else.

Once again, Cade cursed Finch's betrayal. The boy's theft of the *Witchcraft* had cost them dearly. So, lacking raw materials, the group was forced to dismantle the bunk beds from the ground floor, yielding them thin planks and even some rusted nails. With these, they were able to build something sturdy, if a little heavy-looking, beside the plunge pool of the waterfall.

Ten feet wide, it was knotted with twine and nailed at the weakest points, making for a raised, square platform of interlocking planks, with a flat surface covered in a layer of sacking for comfort. The oars, however, were a trickier problem. These they made from the few good branches they did find, nailing flat rectangular boards to their bottoms.

More preparations were made in the night, by the light of their campfire. Sackcloth was stitched together and used to make a tent of sorts, one that would shelter them from the wind and rain at night. Sacks of fruit were set aside for their supplies, and two amphorae of well-water were added too – though they would be left with river water soon enough. Cade knew the river water was likely teeming with bacteria, but it could be boiled when the need arose.

Swords were sharpened. Fur blankets were retrieved from the officers' quarters. Hair was trimmed, and grazes were cleaned. Prayers were said, and tears were shed. It was only when the light of the sun began to blush the sky that they went to bed, snatching an hour's sleep before it was time to leave.

Now, they trooped out, exhausted and anxious, to the waterfall's edge.

'We should give her a name,' Scott said, as they stood beside the pool. 'It's bad luck to get on a ship without a name.'

The raft lay on the shore, waiting to be shoved into the water. In truth, Cade was not even sure it would float.

'You want to smash a bottle of champagne on it too?' Amber teased.

Scott grinned.

'What a waste,' he said. 'Maybe after I've drunk what's inside.'

Amber laughed.

'Well, what do you want to call it?'

Quintus stepped forward, his face unusually solemn.

'Claudia,' he said.

Grace lifted an eyebrow at him.

'My . . . she was like a mother,' Quintus said, and Cade saw a hint of sadness in the boy's eyes.

Cade and the others fought for their friends, their families, and a world they knew well.

But for Quintus . . . everyone he once knew was dead. The Earth he now fought for was as alien to him as this one, more so even. Yet here he was, risking his life for it. Once again, Cade could not help but admire and respect the young Roman.

'Claudia it is,' Cade said, clapping Quintus on the shoulder.

The boy grinned, and patted the boat as if it were a friendly dog.

'Right,' Cade said, stifling a yawn. 'Let's get this show on the road, shall we?'

He placed his hands beneath the raft, and together, the eight of them lifted, scraped and shoved the heavy wooden structure into the water. For a panicked moment, Cade saw water slop over the top of it. But it was only the angle of entry, and the momentum of its fall. To his relief, the raft settled on the surface, bobbing ever so slightly.

'Think it'll manage all five of you?' Yoshi asked.

'One way to find out,' Grace said.

She backed up, then launched herself from the bank, her long, dark legs flashing over the water. The raft rocked as she landed on its edge, but there was as much as a foot of space between its top and the water even then. Grace stomped around its edges, jumping once or twice for good measure, making Cade wince.

'Looks good,' she said, stretching out her hand at Amber. 'Come on.'

Amber followed, and soon all five of the explorers were sitting on its surface, gripping their oars. Their supplies were piled up in the centre, with one of them at each corner, and Quintus squatting at its head, facing where the pool ended and the river began. The Codex, seemingly still attached to Cade, floated above his head.

Cade turned to the bank, and saw Yoshi, Trix and Bea looking forlornly back at them. Cade wasn't sure what would be worse – being out there in the jungle, or waiting in the empty Keep, not knowing where the others were. Somehow, the former seemed better in this moment.

'Bring some fish back for us,' Yoshi said, giving them a forced smile.

'Anything else?' Grace asked. 'A packet of crisps maybe?'

'A triple venti soy latte, hold the foam,' Yoshi said.

Grace stared at him, clearly having no idea what most of those words meant. Cade supposed Starbucks wasn't really a *thing* in the 1980s, especially in rural England.

Yoshi laughed and shook his head.

'Just come back in one piece,' he said.

He paused, then added:

'And the armour would be nice.'

By now, the river's current had drifted the raft further from the shore, and was picking up speed.

'Look after yourselves,' Amber called out. 'Eat well and stay warm!'

'Thanks, Mum!' Trix teased back.

The trio waved to them from the shore, fading smaller and smaller as the raft went from the pool's calm waters to its sluggish eddies. Soon enough, they were in the river's broad centre, and Cade felt a deep sense of *déjà vu*.

Had it really been three months since he had made this very same journey, ignorant of where they were and what the jungle contained? It felt like half a lifetime ago.

Now they entered with purpose. And Cade would not be separated from his friends again, nor would he be a defenceless lost lamb, ripe for the hunting.

He was going to kick this jungle's *ass*.

TEN

The *Claudia* did not like to stay facing one direction, spinning lazily in tandem with the current. The crew dipped their oars into the water, in an attempt to stay facing one way. It gave them some semblance of control, though in reality they were at the mercy of the river's flow.

With the churning water dappled by canopy-filtered sunlight, Cade did not allow himself to relax. One fall into the rapids had been enough for him, and he had an idea of what lurked beneath the surface.

'Codex, show me the map again,' Cade said.

The map appeared, and Cade pinched it to see their route. If they followed the river along its main course, they would wind up back at the wreck of the *Sea Dragon*, where they had beached the *Witchcraft* the last time. But that was not where the armour lay.

Instead, they would need to take a right where the river forked, forcing the raft along a narrower tributary. This would mean paddling, and Cade realised it would be a bad idea to attempt it without a practice run first.

'Let's head for the river's right side,' Cade said. 'It'll be easier for us to go down the correct path.'

'Good idea,' Amber said.

Cade, sitting at the front-left corner, dipped his oar into the water and paddled forward. And yet, even as he did so, the raft began to spin.

He let it revolve once, then turned to see that Amber, on his right, was paddling backwards to change the raft's angle, while Grace was paddling forward behind him. Scott was splashing aimlessly, in no discernible direction.

'Stop,' Cade called.

They stopped, and the raft was no closer to their right-hand shore than before.

'OK,' Cade said. 'Let's figure this out.'

Only, they didn't have much time. The fork was approaching, and would likely come into view soon. Then Cade realised something. They didn't *need* to turn the raft's direction – it was square.

'Everyone face the shore,' Cade said, swivelling on his bottom.

'Aye, Captain,' Scott joked.

They did as he said, and now Cade was at the *back*-left corner of the raft, with what was now their 'front' facing the shore.

'Paddle straight,' Cade ordered.

This time, it worked. Slowly, the raft edged away from the river's centre, just as the fork ahead appeared. It was a sharp one, more than it had looked on the map or he remembered from before. The spit of land where the river split in two was a craggy, overgrown bluff that would smash their raft to pieces.

'Row!' Cade yelled, realising the danger.

He did not need to say it twice, and Amber's oar splashed water over him in her frantic efforts to move them. Even Quintus dipped in an oar, paddling awkwardly from the front. It was slow going, so much that Cade imagined they were hardly moving at all. But as the bluff loomed closer, the raft edged further and further to the right.

For one heart-stopping breath, the vessel scraped along the rock's edge, and Cade's shoulder brushed mossy stone. Then the raft shuddered and scraped free. A loose spar snapped from beneath, but moments later they were spinning along the channel's edge, and the current naturally pulled them back to the new river's centre.

'Bloody hell,' Amber groaned, massaging her hands. 'That was close.'

Cade shuddered, imagining the disaster that would have been. How closely the Earth and their own fates had come to ending. This was no game. Or at least, it wasn't for him.

'How many more turns?' Quintus asked.

Cade examined the map and grimaced.

'Three,' he said. 'But that was the worst of them.'

Quintus grunted and settled back in the centre of the raft, where he made sure none of their supplies had fallen out in their mad panic. Cade watched him until the boy nodded approvingly, then turned back to their surroundings.

They were in new territory now. There could be remnants, like the Olmec head and the *Sea Dragon*, along the river's shore. It seemed likely that the Roman explorers had come this way before though, and anything of use might have already been scanned. But it was worth keeping an eye out.

This river was shallower, slower and narrower than the main course, with the sandy bottom clearly visible. In fact, even when in the channel's centre, they were still barely a few car lengths away from the shore. That fact did not put Cade's nerves at ease. A large predator could splash towards them with its head above water, and pluck them from the raft like canapés on a platter.

He distracted himself by looking at the map once more. They had made good progress, around half a day's walking in an hour or so. Yet the distance to the Polish king's armour still seemed so great, and that mottled green swathe of jungle and swamp beyond where they would have to leave their raft worried him.

What had brought the Roman explorers there, to so inhospitable a place? Surely they would have chosen easier ground when they saw the swamps? This mystery had been nagging at the back of his mind all the previous evening, but he had not quite realised its importance until now.

It was then that he saw it, through half-glazed eyes, his mind elsewhere but yanked swiftly back. A shadow, following beneath them. At first, he thought it was the raft's own, but the dark blob was twice as long as the raft, and half as wide, shaped like a tapered cigar.

He edged closer to the raft's centre, beckoning the others to do the same. Then, he peered out over the edge, watching below.

'What is it?' Cade whispered, flicking his eyes to the Codex.

'*Rhizodus, named for the Latin, "root tooth", lived approximately 300 million years ago. It preyed on both water-bound prey and terrestrial, shore-bound prey, as does a modern-day crocodile. Weighing as heavy as 3 tons, the—*'

'Quiet,' Cade hissed.

Beneath, the dark shadow pulsed its tail, emerging from the raft's shadow and drifting closer to the surface. Now, Cade could see the beast in its entirety. But this was no crocodile.

It was a fish. Or something close to it. Covered in thick scales, it bore a long finned tail and a mouth that reminded him of a fanged eel. At the same time, he could see appendages along its body, including two large fins that extended out of its upper torso, long enough that they might prop it up on land.

Cade reached back and tugged at his blade, wincing at the scrape of metal until he held it poised above the water. He wasn't even sure if he could penetrate the scaled hide, but he knew that if it lunged for them, it could shatter the raft into kindling and then eat them at its leisure.

A gasp from one of the others was all that broke the sudden silence. But Cade did not look back to see who it was.

Slowly, ever so slowly, the creature ascended, until Cade could see its bulging eyes staring up at them. It was within reach. Should he strike? Or hope that it tired of them and moved on to more palatable prey?

His decision was made for him as the tail flapped once more, sending the fish beyond the raft. He watched it fade out of view, until the only sign of its passing was the sweat that coated him.

'Anyone want to go for a swim?' Scott quipped.

Cade let out a long breath and sheathed his blade.

'Shut up, Scott.'

ELEVEN

There were no more incidents over the next hour. Only the sounds of the jungle, made up of a chorus of buzzing insects, chirping birds and the occasional deep cough or howl of some unknown beast.

By all rights it should have been peaceful, but Cade could hardly hold the oar, his palms were so sweaty from nerves. His appetite was gone, even when Scott revealed a stash of tomatoes Yoshi had donated from their sparse larder.

Still, he forced himself to eat. He needed his strength, now more than ever.

Now that they had a plan, and the raft was built, Cade found he had more time to dwell on the monstrosity he would be fighting in a little over a month. Even with armour, could he truly win such a fight? After all, the beast had shell-like armour of its own, and could match his single blade with the six claws of its forearms and the pair of deadly raptor talons on its feet.

His thoughts were riddled with an imagined battleground,

where a juggernaut of tentacles, flesh and bones hurtled towards him. And him standing there, sword extended like an old man's cane, waiting for the impact.

In their haste to find the armour, he had forgotten his need for a projectile weapon. If he could find a bow and arrow, perhaps he could kill the monster before it reached him, or at least injure it enough to give him a fighting chance.

With that thought in mind, he looked for blue dots closer to Władysław's armour, one that might yield a bow or javelin. But there were none. It was as if the Romans had gone well out of their way to reach this remnant, away from the clusters of blue dots that indicated their route. Why?

He traced the blue dots with a finger, and realised there was a pattern there, beyond those in the immediate vicinity of the Keep. There appeared to be two lines of sorts leading out into the caldera. One that had gone towards Hueitapalan, following the river and then returning, via a somewhat circuitous route, on land.

He asked the Codex to tell him time stamps of each scan, and found them to have all taken place in the same two-week period, following the route Cade guessed the Romans had taken.

'Hey, that's pretty smart,' Scott said, listening to what Cade was doing. 'So they found all those remnants near Hueitapalan in just one trip?'

'Looks that way,' Cade said, looking to the next pattern of blue dots.

This second line was different – seemingly beginning a few months after the first. This second expedition had been on foot, and appeared to have gone far deeper into the jungle than the previous one, as well as taking far longer. In fact, this second Roman expedition had spent almost half a year in the jungle, ranging back and forth within the depths of the caldera.

It was a good sign – Cade thought it unlikely that they would have been able to bring back *everything* they had found out there. And it gave him confidence that they would survive the next week of travel; perhaps the jungle was not so dangerous, after all.

But there was a point where the line went cold, as the Romans were returning for the Keep, following the shoreline of the same river Cade and his friends were on now. And then, some way off deep in the swamps was Władysław's remnant, scanned two days after the last one. The Polish king's body looked as if it was their last scan.

Cade knew this was the group who had not returned, the ones that Quintus had mentioned.

It was as if they had been chased from their path . . . or been forced to change it. That was the only explanation Cade could come up with, since they couldn't have become lost with the Codex's map guiding them, and the river led directly back to the Keep. The question was . . . what had chased them, and for so far?

Cade imagined a pack of raptors, hunting Romans through the jungle. But would the raptors track them for days? Had they chased the Romans into the swamps, or had the Romans headed there to hide? It was possible; he himself had experienced raptors tracking him for a while.

Still. It felt off.

Regardless of the cause for their change in course, the discovery gave Cade *some* hope. Explorers on the run were unlikely to try and carry off heavy armour – they had likely left it where they had found it.

And, he reasoned, whatever creature had chased them was unlikely to still be hanging around, three years later. Not unless it was territorial.

'It is almost night,' Quintus said, pulling Cade's thoughts back to the present.

Cade scratched his chin, and saw Quintus was right. The sun was beginning to dip, and the red moon was already visible in the sky.

'We should camp soon,' Grace agreed, 'or we'll be doing it in the dark.'

'Good idea,' Cade said, rubbing his eyes. 'Should we stop here?'

Quintus bit his lip, looking at the shoreline on either side. It was thick with bushes, their green branches trailing fronds along the water's surface. He shook his head.

'He's right, maybe a bit longer,' Grace said. 'By the time we've hacked through that, we might have found somewhere clearer upriver.'

'We're only throwing up our tent and maybe making a fire,' Amber added. 'Shouldn't take us too long. Let's find a better site.'

They waited, nervous, watching the setting sun and keeping the raft straight with the occasional dip of their oars. Now the insects were descending from the trees, flitting above the water. Up and down the river, they could hear the plop of fish and other creatures surfacing, splashing as they leaped for mouthfuls of insects.

The noises put the others on edge, but it made Cade want to fish. He couldn't of course, they had left their lone hook with Yoshi. It would be more fruit with a small side of vegetables tonight.

Still they waited, and now Cade was beginning to worry too. Darkness was descending fast, yet the bushes on either side showed no sign of clearing. They would have to hack through it in the dark.

Worse still, the river was widening and speeding up as tributaries rejoined it. And they would need to paddle their way down another split soon.

It wasn't something he wanted to do in the dark. In fact, their only source of real light was now the Codex's map and timer.

35:22:03:36
35:22:03:35
35:22:03:34

But this came with its own problems. The light was attracting insects now, and fish with them. Already the others were slapping at their faces and necks as the stinging began, and in the water surrounding them he could see the dark forms of river-creatures circling.

'Maybe we should stop now,' Amber said.

'Or make camp on the raft?' Scott suggested. 'Tie it up

against the bank?'

'And leave ourselves open to that . . . *fish* thing?' Grace asked.

'There's worse out there,' Scott replied, pointing into the jungle.

Cade thought on it a moment longer. They were both right. Setting up camp on either land *or* water still left them vulnerable to passing predators, wrapped up in their tent like a breakfast burrito.

But the giant fish had ignored them before, so water seemed the lesser of two evils. He was about to agree with Scott when he saw it. A dark form ahead of them, right in the middle of the river.

'Shit,' he hissed, squinting as it loomed closer. 'Is that the split? Codex, scan that.'

He pointed, hoping that in the brief flare of the Codex's scan, he would see ahead more clearly. And as the blue light flashed . . . he did.

At first, he thought it was an island, but then he caught a glimpse of a humped structure, surrounded by a palisade. The Codex zoomed back.

'*Remnant is an unnamed crannog that was rumoured to have existed on Loch Lubhair, Scotland. No evidence of such a structure has ever been found on Earth.*'

'I don't know what half of those words mean,' Scott muttered. 'But sounds promising.'

Cade was of the same mind, but a palisade meant shelter, and likely a flat surface beneath. Problem was . . . they were heading straight for it. Fast.

'Back paddle,' Cade hissed. 'Hard.'

They didn't need to be told twice. Half-blinded by the night, and with only the Codex's glowing projections to guide them, they drove their aching bodies to one final effort. It seemed they barely slowed at all, and now Cade could see what looked like a forest of wooden poles and logs ahead of them.

'Brace yourselves,' Amber yelled.

Cade snatched a handful of sack-cloth from their raft-top – there was little else to hold onto. His eyes widened, as the structure rushed to meet them with sickening speed.

There was a splintering crash, and Cade was hurled forward, his face flaring with pain as he slammed into rough-hewn wood.

Wincing, he listened for a splash, but there was nothing but groans. All had managed to stay aboard, still grasping their oars.

Scott moaned in the gloom, clutching his forehead.

'What the *hell* is this thing?'

TWELVE

Whatever the 'crannog' was, it was held up from the riverbed by hundreds of long wooden stakes, driven into the mud beneath. Some strange combination of clay, tangled wood and sacking made up the floor of the structure above them, but from their vantage point, Cade could see little else.

It was clear that there was no easy way up – not unless they manhandled the raft around it in the hopes that a convenient ladder had been placed at the structure's side.

'Someone needs to climb up there,' Cade said.

'Thanks, Cade,' Scott said, patting him on the back. 'Appreciate it.'

Cade groaned. It was like when they had arrived at the Keep all over again. Forever the guinea pig. At least this time it was good-natured.

'Right,' he said.

He went to grasp the nearest pole, but Quintus pressed him back down, laying a hand on his shoulder.

'If you are hurt . . .' Quintus said.

He was right. If Cade died out here, he was sure Abaddon would pick another champion. But an injury? He might still make Cade fight.

Cade nodded, and watched as the boy scrambled up the structure's side, gripping the wooden poles and pulling himself up with wiry strength. There was a ring of tight wooden fencing around the structure; Quintus grasped that and hauled himself over the top.

They heard the pat of footsteps – muffled ones, as if he were walking on soil rather than the wooden boards that Cade had expected.

'What do you think is up there?' Amber whispered.

'No idea,' Cade whispered back.

Scott leaned in.

'Why are we whispering?'

Quintus's face suddenly appeared over the parapet, and a knotted rope flopped down to them. Cade caught Scott's expression at the sight of it.

'Better than nothing,' Cade said, patting Scott on the back.

It was a struggle to climb the rope, not least because it was slimy with algae – it must have been hanging in the water from another part of the structure. So, it was some relief when Cade surmounted the fencing and fell flat on his face.

Lucky for him, it was a soft landing. Grass. He hadn't expected grass. Now at the top, and accompanied by the Codex's light, Cade was able to take in the view.

It was a manmade island. As if someone had placed a raised platform atop a reinforced jetty, covered it in peat and soil, and ringed its edges with a fence. But more fascinating still was the single hovel at its centre. A large hut, made of logs and a thatched roof.

'Codex,' Cade asked, keeping his voice low. 'What is a crannog?'

'*A crannog is an ancient form of artificial island and defensive dwelling, constructed by Gaelic societies upon bodies of water.*'

Defensive. Cade liked the sound of that. In fact, as he turned to see Amber flopping over the palisade beside him, he realised that they had lucked out. This place was out of reach of any river monsters, or land monsters for that matter. Here, they would be safe for the night.

'What luck,' Amber said, staring around them. Behind her, Grace's cornrows appeared as the tall girl struggled to climb over the fence.

'Not luck,' Quintus said, quietly.

Cade furrowed his brows. 'What do you mean, Quintus?'

Quintus shrugged, then pointed to the Codex.

'Abaddon put this here,' he said. 'Nothing here is . . .'

He paused, searching for the words.

'. . . accident.'

Cade nodded slowly. Quintus was right. They were almost exactly a day's boat journey from the Keep. Abaddon must have expected contenders to come this way, and put the crannog here as a resting place. Hell, he might have even put it there just before they got here – it had never been scanned before, so it was impossible to say.

Grace collapsed onto the grass, finally over the wall.

'Heads up!' Scott shouted.

A sack of fruit soared over the fence, hitting Grace's belly.

She groaned and rolled over as more sacking and supplies followed. She lay there, gazing at the sky in mild annoyance, until Scott landed beside her. She prodded at him with her foot, but he dodged it easily enough.

'You're a pain in the—'

'Stomach?' Scott grinned, helping her to her feet.

She shook her head, allowing him a rueful smile. He stretched and took a few steps, examining their surroundings.

'Nice digs,' he said. 'Better than being out there.'

He sniffed and looked up at the sky. Cade followed his gaze, and saw that clouds were beginning to gather.

'Good thing too,' Scott said. 'Looks like it's going to rain.'

He bowed to the Codex, sweeping the ground.

'Thank you, oh great one, for your generosity,' he said in an exaggerated, worshipful voice. 'This rotting shack is more than we deserve.'

Grace chuckled, but not before she pressed her boot against his butt and pushed him sprawling onto the ground. Scott turned, spat out a mouthful of mud, then broke out into laughter as well.

Soon they were all laughing, the tension and anxiety of the day dissipating like a bad stink that had lingered too long.

'Shall we investigate our humble abode?' Grace asked, leading the way.

They followed her through the open doorway. For a moment they peered into the darkness, unable to see much at all. Then Cade heard the *chink* of a flint being struck, and Scott strode forward, holding a sputtering torch.

It was clear that the place had been abandoned for some

time. There was a hearth in the chamber's centre, and an opening in the thatched roof above for smoke. It was large – enough for five people to stretch out comfortably with room to spare, and the ground was lined with mildewy straw.

A stack of old firewood sat in the corner, untouched by whatever people had lived here before the crannog had been unceremoniously transported to this spot. It was dry, for the most part, but cooler than Cade would have liked. It sheltered them from wind and rain, nothing more. Well, that and the animals outside.

'Not bad,' Amber said. 'I imagine we would have ended up in a place like this, had we chosen not to become contenders.'

'Regretting it already?' Scott asked.

Amber smiled and shook her head.

'Not a bit. But hey, this is a good outpost for us, should we ever want to make another expedition.'

'Oh yeah,' Scott said, only a little sarcastically. 'I mean, the Roman explorers made it back half the time. I like those odds.'

Amber rolled her eyes at him.

Cade kicked some of the straw surrounding the hearth into the firepit, as Quintus brought some of the firewood over, seemingly oblivious to the shower of woodlice that crawled over his forearms.

Together, they built up a pyramid of logs, with the straw and smaller wooden pieces beneath.

'You OK, Quintus?' Cade asked, shaking a centipede from his fingers. 'You're quiet today.'

The boy paused and looked up, his mismatched eyes flashing.

'I am thinking about the men who took you,' he said, then stopped and closed his eyes, searching for a word. 'The . . . slavers.'

After the battle, Quintus had told them what little he knew about the slavers. That the Romans knew of them, though they never seemed to venture close to the Keep. They tended to avoid the contenders, from what Quintus had gathered, mostly seeking groups abandoned deeper in the caldera.

'We'll cross that bridge when we come to it,' Cade said, after a moment's thought.

Quintus furrowed his brows, confused at his phrasing.

'I mean, there is nothing we can do about them now.'

That, Quintus seemed to understand.

'If we see slavers, we run, yes?' he asked.

Cade gave a reluctant nod, though he could not help but think of the shiny armour the men had worn.

A prod from Scott's torch later and the fire was blazing merrily, though the musty smoke and crackle and pop of burrowed insects marred the cheery scene somewhat.

Together, the contenders huddled by the fire, holding their hands and feet up to it for warmth. The sack-cloth tent was folded over to be used as both seat and blanket, and though it was scratchy, it warmed them more than Cade had expected.

'So,' Amber said, breaking their contemplative silence. 'Not bad for our first day.'

'Yeah, and we got to see the local wildlife too,' Scott said. 'Like whale watching, only the whale might eat you.'

'Don't you take anything seriously?' Grace asked, punching Scott's shoulder lightly.

He winced and rubbed it in mock agony.

'I use humour to distract myself from all the beatings you give me.'

Now it was Grace's turn to roll her eyes.

'What I mean,' Amber said, a little more loudly, 'is that we got here in one piece. We're warm . . . ish. We're safe from predators and exposure. We know where we are. I'm saying we might pull this thing off.'

Cade shot her a smile and patted her hand. It was ice-cold, and for a moment he absently warmed it with his own. He caught himself a few seconds later, and pulled away, though Amber seemed not to notice. Flustered, he gabbled the first thought in his head.

'We can't forget, Abaddon is technically on *our* side. I mean, he still enjoys tormenting us. But he also kind of wants us to win. Even if that means about as much to him as a game of cards with his buddies.'

Quintus grunted in agreement.

'Abaddon is not . . . competitive,' he said. 'So we must be, instead.'

That put a damper on the mood. Cade realised he was right. Abaddon was far more focused on entertainment value than keeping them alive.

'We should get some rest,' Cade said. 'I know it's only just gone dark, but we'll be up at the crack of dawn tomorrow.'

71

'Agreed,' Amber said.

'No dinner?' Scott asked, lifting a sack.

'Be my guest,' Cade said. 'But I'm too tired to cook.'

'That's OK,' Scott said brightly. 'Who's up for some figs?'

They groaned.

THIRTEEN

It was hard to leave the crannog. It had felt so safe, held up there by the stilts, away from the nocturnal predators of the jungle and the ravenous fish beneath.

Still, they returned to the raft as the day's first sunlight drifted down, having woken an hour earlier to the morning chorus of singing birds.

The only reason they had not cast off immediately was to replenish their water reserves, drinking the remainder of their fresh water and taking advantage of the fire to boil up some more. The boiled river-water was a little brackish, but Scott's taste test had confirmed it was drinkable.

The morning was a chilly one. A light mist had settled over the jungle, coating their skin enough to make the morning wind bite. Cade was thankful for it nonetheless; it might help hide them from any slavers hunting for them.

With the crannog fading into the distance behind them, Cade looked to the map once more. They were more than a third of the way, and there was only one more turn to make.

Once on this new tributary, it would lead them to the swamps, and soon after, the Polish king's armour.

Cade did not want to think of what they might do if they arrived and the remnant was gone, or unusable. There were no other remnants nearby, and getting the raft back up the channel would be impossible.

They would instead be forced to hike through unexplored territory, and search for new remnants themselves. And a swamp was not the best place to start from.

Still, there were no more giant fish to terrify them, nor did he see any carnosaurs or raptors on the banks of the river. But every so often a fascinating creature crossed their path.

His favourites were the pterosaurs that flitted by, seemingly unafraid of Cade and the others. They settled on the raft if the group sat still enough, with a few even attempting to gnaw through their food sacks.

They were tiny little things, barely larger than hummingbirds with bat-like wings. Some had bony beaks, others toothed ones, and there were even a few with snouts. Most circled above them in a kaleidoscopic display of colour, curious at their presence. Those that settled seemed to appreciate the free transportation. They preened in the sunlight and nuzzled at the fuzzy protofeathers that coated them, seeking lice and fleas.

Cade spent much of the day trying to tempt one onto his hand, using a morsel of fig. Only one was brave enough to do so – a somewhat bedraggled specimen who was clearly desperate enough to risk being eaten for the glistening red flesh.

Its fur was striped black and white, and the claws of its wingtips tickled as it settled in his palm. The head was unusual, sort of like a cute, furry frog's but with teeth. Cade saw the little thing was injured.

Some predator had clawed its wings ragged; he was surprised it had managed to reach the raft at all. As it was, the creature did not leave his hand even when the food was gone, instead crouching down against his skin for warmth.

'Neat trick,' Scott mumbled, spitting a mouthful of fig onto his own hand. He extended it up to the circling creatures, waggling his arm to tempt them. There were no takers.

'Not like that,' Cade said. 'You should probably—'

'Oh my god!'

It was Amber, and Cade looked her way. But it was not Amber that his eyes fell on, but beyond her. Up the river, he saw something that made his blood chill. A ship, its form just visible in the morning mist.

'Row for shore,' Cade ordered, shaking the pitiful creature from his hand. 'Everyone, now!'

There was a mad clattering of oars, and in the confusion they rowed in opposite directions.

'Right,' Grace hissed. 'To the right!'

Only then did they begin to inch to the riverbank. Slowly. Too slowly.

Cade could see the other ship's oars rising and falling in tandem on either side, like some great bird flapping its way up the river. The pace was fast, as if the ship were racing towards something. Had it seen them?

Still he rowed, the skin of his fingers rubbing raw with

each dip of his makeshift paddle. He cursed the oar under his breath, cursed its poor, rushed design and the unwieldiness of the raft it propelled. It did not help.

Now the ship was but a stone's throw away, and he could see the tall man standing at its prow, swarthy and black bearded. A smile, broad across his face, gave Cade a moment's hope.

Then he heard the whip-crack. The scream of pain that followed, and the clink of chains that rattled in tandem with the ship's oars. And the drums, at first soft, but growing louder and more frantic, pounding out the rowers' pace in a staccato *boom boom boom*.

'Slavers,' Quintus moaned. 'Fast, fast!'

By some Herculean effort, they finally reached the riverbank, but now they were faced with that same entangled shoreline that had stopped them from camping before. Despite it all, Grace leaped into the shallows, up to her waist in water. She unsheathed the long sword she had taken from Eric's body and swung it once, twice.

Still the ship came, drawing alongside them, the drums pounding in tandem with the beating of Cade's heart. Grace screamed with frustration, chopping again and again at the tangled web of reeds, bushes and branches. It was useless. Although she had cut a ragged gap, there was only more vegetation beyond.

Behind them, the drums stopped. The silence was deafening. Then:

'*Sagittarii!*' yelled a deep voice.

Cade turned, his hand straying to the sword slung across

his back. Then he saw it . . . and his hand stopped.

All along the boat's gunwale, a half-dozen men stood with bows drawn, the arrows pointed directly at Cade and the others. Still standing at the prow, the bearded man's grin widened, and he swept his arms apart.

Sagittarii. That was a Latin word, meaning 'archers'. Cade went to speak, but Quintus got there first, shouting in his own tongue. The man only smiled.

Grace collapsed to her knees, leaning on her sword in the shallows. They were well and truly caught.

FOURTEEN

It was, all in all, a polite affair. As polite as being made captive could be, anyway. Only Quintus caught any flack, his shouting cut short by a barked order from the man on the prow, and a tightening of the bowstrings above.

'Don't. Say. A word,' Amber hissed through gritted teeth.

As the bows were lowered and the sailors began to laugh and chatter among themselves, she whispered again.

'Say nothing until we're alone. The less they know about us the better.'

Even as she spoke, a rope ladder was lowered from the deck, and the sailors beckoned them aboard. Now Cade could catch the snatches of Latin in their speech. Could these be Romans too?

Left with no choice, and more impatient shouts from the man who Cade had decided was the captain, the five of them waded through the water, taking what they could carry with them. Cade was the first to reach the ladder, and clambered up with a sack of fruit between his teeth.

It felt a little pointless when he reached its top, for he was immediately dragged onto the deck, the bag, his sword and even his shoes torn from him in a flurry of practised hands and bearded faces. A knee pressed into his back as his pockets were turned out and his body patted for hidden weapons.

One by one, the five of them were laid out on the ship's boards like a catch of fish, and exposed to the same treatment. Cade craned his neck to see the captain approach.

There was something of a piratical air to him, though he wore clothes that made Cade think of the Middle East, complete with bejewelled fingers and gold threading to his clothing. This was in sharp contrast to the men on board, who wore nondescript clothing that could have come from any era.

Still, Cade stared at the captain until the man met his eyes, a gaze returned with a calculating intensity that made Cade look away. One thing was certain – this man held their fate in his hands.

Sure enough, the captain called for silence as soon as they were all aboard. Then he crouched before them, a friendly, if entirely unconvincing smile upon his face.

He motioned with his hand at them, pointing at his own mouth as if telling them to speak. Together, the five of them remained resolutely silent.

The man sighed.

'Doctor?' he said, clicking his fingers.

He glared at Quintus, then repeated the word. Quintus stared back, blankly.

Doctor? Is someone sick on board?

'*Nagid?*' the captain tried again, looking searchingly at the others.

That word didn't sound like Latin.

'*Anax?*'

Nothing. Still the man spoke. Rattling off word after word, each stranger than the next. Some sounded Asian, others African. Then, finally, in among them all, he heard it.

'Leader?'

It clicked, in Cade's head. Not Doctor. *Ductor*. The word for 'leader' in Latin. The man wanted to speak to their leader.

Now the captain was growing impatient, and nodded to a nearby bowman. Scott cried out in pain as the man kicked him. Still the captain jumped from language to language, but Cade managed to raise his hand before the sailor's foot lashed forward again.

The captain arched an eyebrow at Cade, and repeated the last word he had said. Cade nodded vehemently, if only to stop the beating from continuing.

The foot withdrew, and Cade cursed his luck. He didn't *want* to be in charge. Being the contenders' 'champion' was burden enough.

Grinning, the captain motioned at the men around Cade to lift him to his feet, and Cade was manhandled away from the others. He hardly had time to take in their surroundings, catching a brief glimpse of sails, rigging and barrels, before he was shoved through a narrow doorway built into a raised deck at the back of the ship.

Blinded in the new darkness, he was pushed down a short, narrow wooden corridor, ducking so his head would not scrape along the ceiling, before being pushed unceremoniously through another door.

He groaned as he skinned his knees on the floor. Rough hands dragged him back to his feet, and he found two burly sailors on either side of him. The captain strode into view behind, his hands clutched behind his back as he examined Cade, taking in his clothing.

Cade ignored him, searching for his own clues. The room was plush, and clearly the captain's quarters, if the lavish furnishings were anything to go by. In the corner, fat, garishly coloured cushions and furs lay piled on top of bedding, while opposite, incense smoke curled from a pot on a broad, low desk, complete with quills and jars of ink.

The captain leaned closer, and tugged on Cade's lower lip. Cade yelped in surprise, earning himself a slap to the back of the head from one of his guards, and a short, sharp tug of the hair by the other.

This time, he held still as the man grasped Cade's lip again to inspect Cade's teeth, pushing back his forehead to examine deeper. Next, he fingered Cade's clothes, rubbing the material between his fingers, before leaning over Cade's shoulder and examining the inside of the back of his top.

Now the man grinned, and nodded with approval. Then, to Cade's surprise, he ordered the guards away with a shooing motion and a sharp word that Cade did not understand.

He proceeded to his desk and settled cross-legged upon the cushion behind it, then beckoned Cade to take a seat opposite.

Why the sudden change in demeanour?

Cade took his seat, and for a moment the two stared at each other, the incense smoke drifting between them and leaving its cloying scent in the air. The man drummed his fingers upon the desk, then plucked a quill from its holder and opened a thick ledger to his right with a dusty thud.

He jotted some quick notes down, blotting ink on a pad, and Cade craned his neck, but could not make out the slanted scrawl from upside-down. What he did see was five rows of words. Likely one for each of him and his friends.

As the man wrote, Cade looked for the Codex. He saw the faintest shimmer in the corner of the room, the Codex having concealed itself just as it had done all that time ago when Cade had been captured by other slavers.

The ledger was closed, the desk cleared of its various maps and instruments with meticulous care, and then the captain leaned forward, examining Cade with a gleam in his eye.

He pursed his lips. Sniffed. Then spoke.

'Let's dispense with the charade, shall we?' he said.

In perfect English.

FIFTEEN

Cade blinked, trying desperately to hide his surprise. He failed utterly. The man clapped his hands in triumph, then delved beneath his desk and withdrew a flask and two glasses. He popped the cork and poured some unspecified foul-smelling liquid into both.

'Forgive me, it is a hobby of mine,' the captain said. 'And you . . .'

He shook his head, as if what had just transpired had been particularly interesting.

'What hobby?' Cade said dully, giving up his silence.

It seemed pointless now.

'The guessing, of course,' the captain said, waving his hands. 'Of who you are.'

His accent was thick, but not one Cade could place. He chuckled again, pushing forward a glass and looking at Cade expectantly.

'And who am I, then?' Cade asked, ignoring the glass of clear brown liquid. It was alcoholic, certainly, and he wanted to keep his wits about him. His stomach lurched at both its stench and a rocking as the ship moved in the water. Outside, he could hear the yells of the sailors. The ship seemed to be underway once more.

'Ah!' the man said, lifting a finger. 'That is the fun of it. First, your features, skin tone. The Indus, or perhaps the lands of Araby and Persia. But then I see your companions. One from the Orient, or partly so, another from Africa. Strange, to see such a grouping together, though perhaps you had met in the jungle.'

He tapped his chin.

'The clothing of the girls was strange to me. European, most likely, but then the courts of Europe have had such a variety of fashions over the centuries that what I saw could fall anywhere among them, and who was to say if their clothing was not taken from the bodies of others, out there.'

The captain motioned through the porthole windows surrounding them, the only sources of light in the dark chamber.

'And then your friend, who spoke in Latin, I think. But hard to understand, no? Had he learned it elsewhere?'

He looked at Cade as if seeking an answer, but he received none.

'But you . . . well. Your teeth first. Clean, healthy and white, a sign of the nineteenth century or beyond. The fillings in your molars confirmed it.'

He shook his head, proud of his own genius.

'Modern dentistry. A marvel, to be sure. And your clothing . . . what is it you call it? Nylon?'

Cade stared blankly, unwilling to give the man any more satisfaction than he already had.

'Of course, when I read the tag at the back of your shirt, the game ended. Modern English. Then, I knew I had you.'

He paused, then looked at the glass pointedly. Sighing at Cade's hesitation, he took a pointed gulp of his own, then smacked his lips with satisfaction.

Knowing he had to curry favour with this man, Cade took a polite sip, wincing as the foul taste washed the inside of his mouth.

'Good, eh?' The man winked. 'I save it only for special occasions. And you . . . well, you are a most *special* specimen. American?'

Cade gave a hesitant nod. No use hiding it now. 'Can I ask who you are? I don't have your . . . talent,' Cade said, dropping in the compliment with as much tact as he could.

The man beamed at him. 'You may call me Ishak. But as for my origins,' he gestured at himself, 'I was born here, in this world. As almost all my men were. But our forefathers were not.'

Cade felt a sense of internal satisfaction, even in this moment of despair. He had been right. The slavers were the descendants of those Abaddon had left in the caldera, long ago. Somewhere out here, a civilisation had sprung up.

'And who were *your* forefathers?' Cade asked, gesturing at their plush surroundings. 'Did they build this ship?'

Ishak smiled again.

'Indeed. My forefathers were the Barbarossas, or so my mother told me. Corsairs of Barbary. Pirates, if you will. And

I have carried on the family tradition.'

Cade's stomach twisted. He had read about the Barbary pirates. Ships of raiders from the east who had taken as many as a million Europeans as slaves over the centuries.

Suddenly, his surroundings made sense.

'Are there others like you?' Cade asked, as Ishak took another sip and stared at him over the glass. 'Pirates, I mean?'

'Oh yes,' Ishak said. 'Though few have my heritage. All sorts of men try their hand at finding remnants out here. It is a lucrative trade, but a dangerous one.'

He wagged his finger and gestured out into the jungle once more.

'More often than not, my sailors must venture into the jungle to find those such as you, and I may lose more men than captives we come back with. Sometimes it is easier to light a beacon and see who comes running, desperate for civilisation. You'd be surprised, but some are quite relieved, even after we capture them. Those creatures out there . . .'

He trailed off and shook his head. Cade tried not to let the hate he had for this man show, though it burned in his chest like fire.

'We were very pleased to find you on the river itself, waiting to be snatched up like a pheasant for the plucking!'

He let out a belly laugh, and Cade resisted the urge to throw his drink in the man's face.

'You speak English well,' Cade said. 'How?'

Ishak revealed a sly smile. 'I speak many languages, for the people I capture come from many times and places. But the gods saw fit to send us many Englishmen over the past years.

The Great War, you call it, yes? Trenches, poison gas, machine guns.'

Cade stared. Soldiers from the First World War. How many had ended up in this jungle, snatched from no man's land and forgotten, said to be buried somewhere in an unmarked grave?

'I kept one such man, for a while. He was a learned man, a doctor. It was he who I spoke with the most, and he taught me many things about the world.'

He tapped his chin.

'Of course, our laws forbid such conversations, so I did not keep him for too long. Any captive discovered to have lived beyond the year 1750 is to be put to death. I kept him as long as I dared, but alas, my hands were tied.'

He said it so casually. Like it didn't matter that he planned to end Cade's life. Cade had barely a moment to think of a reply, and the words left his mouth unbidden.

'Why?' Cade asked, almost pleaded. 'What does it matter?'

'Because your ideas are dangerous,' Ishak shrugged. 'Our emperor does not wish our people to know of your bright future, of telephones, radios, printing presses and human rights. Or at least, that is my guess. He does not have to justify his decrees.'

'Can't you just let us go free?' Cade begged, desperate. 'We can bring you things. We can find them!'

Ishak grinned, and shook his head.

'You are still of value to me, even condemned. More so, in fact. And as for treasures the gods left out there, most have already been found.'

87

Cade felt his eyes flitting about the room, as if seeking inspiration for something he could bargain with. But there was nothing. The slavers had already taken their weapons, their food. And the Keep held no treasures beyond a handful of Roman coins.

But it seemed that Ishak would provide his answer for him.

'Tell me, boy. Where and when are you from?'

He pitched the question with such innocence that Cade took note, seeing the desires behind the man's eyes. This question. That was what he wanted from Cade. And for now, the answer was all Cade had to barter with.

'Why should I tell you?' Cade asked. 'If you're going to kill me anyway?'

'Perhaps I will keep you,' Ishak said. 'Should you prove useful enough to me. Pretend you are not a *modern*. Let you live as my servant.'

'All of us?' Cade asked, his mind racing.

'No,' Ishak said, steepling his fingers. 'The risk is too great. The punishment for keeping one such as you is death. Any more would be too risky. Too many wagging tongues.'

Cade's heart fell. Even that deeply unsavoury alternative was off the table. But an idea struck him.

'The others don't speak English,' Cade said. 'Or Latin for that matter, other than one, who is a Roman, and deaf.'

'Oh?' Ishak asked. 'But they are moderns, obviously. Of that I am convinced.'

Cade thought quickly. What language might Ishak not know? One so rare that perhaps he would allow them to live as servants too, as he had offered Cade, given their inability to communicate.

'They speak Afrikaans,' he said.

It was the most recent language he could think of, and the most unusual, given its mix of Dutch and African origins. Ishak shook his head and raised his eyebrows questioningly.

'A language of South Africa. They are a major power in my time.'

Ishak's eyes lit up.

'So you *are* from later than the Great War?' he asked.

Cade nodded.

Ishak considered him for a moment, then shook his head.

'They will learn Latin eventually, which is the language most of us speak. And then . . . I cannot trust them.'

Cade clenched his fists, resisting the urge to scream. He was bargaining for the lives of his friends, and he was failing.

'Now, tell me where and when you are from, and I shall consider if you are worth my breaking the law. You *alone*.'

Cade pursed his lips, shook his head. Ishak sighed, then lifted a small bell from his desk and let it jingle.

'Perhaps some time in the brig will give you time to consider. Know that you do not have much left.'

As the bell went on tinkling, the two burly sailors from before burst in and wrenched Cade to his feet. In his desperation, the seed of an idea entered Cade's mind.

'We're contenders,' he cried as he was dragged away. 'If you don't let us go, the world will end!'

Ishak held up a hand, and the sailors stopped. The captain stood laboriously and stepped closer to examine Cade through

89

narrowed eyes. Surprise and suspicion were stamped across his face.

'The contenders are Romans, and have been for a long time,' he said. 'How do you know about them?'

'They were wiped out,' Cade said quickly. 'We're their replacements. We're all that's left.'

Ishak considered him for a moment.

'We know of the contenders. But our emperor has declared them fair game, as was decided several years ago when I caught a group of them myself.'

And with that, the answer to the mystery of the second Roman expedition was answered. Ishak had chased them into the swamps and enslaved them.

'You know how important we are?' Cade asked, the faintest glimmer of hope appearing. 'And what happens if we lose?'

Ishak nodded gravely.

'We know. Many of our ancestors were contenders themselves, at one time or another. But I think you heard of the contenders from your Roman friend. You are not warriors, and are far from the Keep where the contenders live. We are forbidden to go there, but I know where it is.'

Cade went to call for the Codex to reveal itself, but Ishak spoke again before the words had left Cade's mouth.

'Even if you *are* contenders, and what you say is true, it matters not to me if you succeed or fail. It is the old world that will be destroyed. And I live on this one.'

He nodded to the sailors, and Cade was dragged away, back through the dank corridor.

'You can't do this!' Cade screamed. 'Billions of liv—'

A rough hand was clamped over his mouth, and a knee to his testicles left him gagging with pain. Cade was jostled through more darkness, then the glaring light of day, and thrown through a trapdoor.

He lay on the boards below, gasping like a beached fish.

'So I guess negotiations didn't go so well then,' Scott's voice came from the shadows.

Cade cursed through a hissed breath, his hands pressed between his legs.

No. They had not.

SIXTEEN

'Codex,' Cade said, as the others gathered around him. 'Are you there?'

'*Yes, Cade,*' came the calm voice, close to his ear. '*I am.*'

Cade grunted with relief and rolled onto his back. Above, light filtered through the trapdoor's grating, where a canopy could be seen, shifting as the ship moved.

'Are you OK?' Amber's voice filtered through the shadows, and he answered it with a forced smile.

'I'm OK,' he said. 'But our situation is worse than I thought.'

He looked around, to see they were in a small wood-panelled chamber. There were chains and manacles embedded in the walls, but he saw none of the others had been shackled, and that beyond his friends, there were no other occupants of the room.

It felt like a temporary holding cell, and he suspected the usual captive quarters were somewhere below. Who knew how much time they had before they were transported down there, perhaps even separated.

He wondered if the rowers were slaves. Especially given the sound of the whip crack, and the drumming he had heard before. Only, now there was no such drumming, or whips cracking. Which meant the ship had likely turned downriver and was following the current. The rowers were no longer needed.

The slavers were heading back to whatever place they called home.

'Cade,' Grace said, clicking her fingers in front of Cade's dazed face to get his attention. 'What's worse than you thought?'

Cade spoke as quickly as he could, holding up his hands to their questions as he ran through everything he had seen and heard in Ishak's cabin, only pausing when Quintus needed him to repeat or explain a word. In that time, he could only watch as their faces grew grim with worry, and saw the horror there as he told them of the emperor's rule, and their eventual fate.

'So the second expedition of Romans was taken by this guy?' Scott asked.

'Looks that way,' Cade replied.

'And we are all to die?' Quintus asked.

'Not you,' Cade said. 'You are from before 1750.'

Quintus shook his head. 'I am with you.'

Cade smiled at the show of friendship.

'Maybe you will know others in the city, legionaries like you who abandoned the Keep as you did. Being a Roman might help you, and that will make it easier for you to help us.'

93

Quintus hesitated, then nodded reluctantly.

'Why 1750?' Amber asked. 'It's so . . . arbitrary.'

Cade shrugged. 'Maybe because of the Declaration of Independence – it wasn't too long after that, right? It seems this emperor that Ishak spoke of doesn't want any ideas among his subjects that might loosen his grip on power.'

'Yeah, like *that* was when America got the bright idea that slavery was wrong,' Grace snapped. 'He's more than 150 years too early.'

'I'm sorry,' Cade whispered. He had been insensitive.

'It doesn't matter anyway,' Grace said dully. 'We're not even close to that date. We're about as free as anyone's ever been in history, and the emperor won't want us spreading those ideas among the other slaves.'

Cade sat straighter in realisation. 'Maybe that's why they're keeping us separate – if they have other slaves captive below. Maybe they are rowing the ship.'

'Thank heavens,' Amber whispered. 'I would not like to be them.'

Cade sighed.

'I shouldn't have said anything,' he said.

'You'd rather be chained to an oar down there?' Scott asked.

'I'd rather be chained to an oar until we get there and live than sit in here with some fresh air and then die.'

Cade turned to Amber. 'I'm sorry. You said not to say anything.'

She forced a smile. 'You couldn't have known. Plus, he knew you were a modern teenager before you even sat down.

At least by talking to him, we know how much trouble we're in. Escape or die.'

'You think we can escape?' Scott asked, his usually cheerful voice now full of misery.

'Nothing is impossible,' Amber said firmly.

But Cade was not so sure. They were in the very centre of the ship. If they were to burrow through the walls on either side of them, they would enter the living quarters of the sailors, and below, likely the slave holds, which would be even less escapable than this place.

The grating above was their best bet, once through they could be over the side and swimming for shore in a few quick steps. Yet it wasn't much of an option – the thing was made of solid metal and held in place by a large padlock. Cade had no idea who held the key either.

They did have one thing going for them: Ishak's curiosity. He wanted Cade to speak. To tell him of the future.

'Listen,' Cade said. 'He may bring you in for questioning too. Whatever you do, act as if you can't understand him. Remember, I told him you all can't speak English. And he's got to believe I'm telling him the truth when I negotiate with him again next.'

Quintus cracked a rare smile. 'That will not be so hard for me,' he said.

Cade patted Quintus's knee. 'Maybe *we* should have been practising our Latin, rather than you learning English,' Cade said. 'Ishak said it's the common language of the Empire.'

Amber groaned and closed her eyes.

'Bloody hell, I guess I know what we're going to spend the next few days doing.'

'Oh yeah, well at least you girls and Cade learned it in school,' Scott wailed. 'I'm so far behind.'

But Cade had stopped listening. Because there was an uncomfortable lump, scratching beneath his pant leg. He had been dimly aware of it as the events of the past half hour had transpired, but now . . . it seemed to be *moving*.

He cried out and stood, swaying in tandem with the ship's movement on the water and nearly falling over as he shook out his pants, hopping on one foot.

The others stared at him as if he were a mad man, until the offending object fell from the dark folds of his old uniform.

It tumbled across the floorboards, like a small, furry pool ball. A tiny pterosaur, that same bedraggled specimen that had eaten the fig from Cade's hand. It looked up at him with its large, plaintive eyes, and the others burst out laughing, as if releasing all that pent-up tension in a single moment.

'What . . . is . . . that thing?' Scott said, squeezing out the question through wheezing laughter.

'*Anurognathus is a genus of small pterosaur that lived during the Jurassic Period, approximately 150 million years ago,*' the Codex dutifully intoned.

As always, it took everything literally.

Cade plucked the tiny fuzzball from the ground and held it in his hands. It nuzzled his palm, seeking more food, its tiny whiskers tickling his skin. Cade dug into his pocket and found the squashed remains of another fig he had been saving for later. He stuffed it into his mouth, not knowing where his next meal would come from, then transferred the creature to the juice-stained hand, letting it lap at the remainder.

'Here, little guy,' Cade said to the mini beast. 'We'd both better keep our strength up.'

SEVENTEEN

In the hours that followed, conversation was brought to a halt by Amber's realisation that the men above might hear snatches of English in their talking. So instead they huddled and whispered in the corner if something needed to be said, and in the end, little did.

There *were* some outlandish ideas from Scott, one of which involved training Cade's new pet to retrieve the key from whoever held it, but beyond that, they could not think of another way to escape their predicament.

They had also explored the brig thoroughly for tools, or weapons, but beyond the chains and shackles firmly embedded in the walls, and a tin bucket in the corner with the name *Charles Ashmore* engraved on the side, there was little more than graffiti to examine.

Cade saw dozens of English names scratched out there. Ishak had not been lying when he had said that many of his captives had come from the First World War, in particular what appeared to be Irishmen from the 1st and 2nd Battalion

Connaught Rangers, Englishmen from the 5th Battalion of the Norfolk Regiment, and even some Americans from the 77th Infantry Division.

It made Cade wonder what these men must have suffered. In what manner had they eventually died? Would Cade and his friends suffer the same fate?

Executed in public, for all to see? Or privately killed as soon as they reached the shore, perhaps after an interrogation . . . or even torture.

From the silent tears and dull, thousand-yard stares of the others, Cade imagined they were thinking the same. If some opportunity to escape was to come, it would only come when they were moved out from their cell.

And then, the rocking started, accompanied by the beat of a drum. This was not the gentle tilting of the ship as before, but a full left-to-right, back-and-forth sway that churned their stomachs and left more than one spewing their guts into the bucket, Cade among them.

The little pterosaur, which Cade had named Zeeb after its black-and-white-striped fuzz, took great relish in lapping up these regurgitated offerings, as perhaps it had once done from its mother in a nest. Once other substances were added to the bucket though, as bladders became full and turns were taken to use it, Zeeb's interest took a sudden turn.

So, as a worse and worse stench filled their small space, it was some relief when the sailors threw open the hatch and barked Latin orders for Cade to climb up the rope ladder that followed. Cade did so, leaving Zeeb below with the others.

There was no tree canopy above them. No animal calls.

They were no longer in the jungle. A lake, then?

Emerging from the gloom, Cade had a moment to look around him, as he blinked in the new light. His guess had been close.

It was a sea. There could be no other word for it, the waves rolling gently on either side, and a wide expanse of blue sky above bereft of cloud, tree or mountain.

Of course, he had seen the large sea at the centre of the caldera on the map, though he had not looked closely at it; no remnants were highlighted there. He had not imagined that this so-called empire would be somewhere within it.

Any hopes of escaping over the side were dashed. Even if they made it over, what direction would they swim in? And what beasts would be waiting to snatch them beneath the surface, even if they knew?

Only a full takeover of the ship would allow them to escape. How they would do that . . . Cade had no idea.

'Impressive, is it not?' called a familiar voice.

Cade turned to see Ishak striding towards him, beaming.

'The ship, I mean,' he went on, gesturing above him at the white sails, billowing. 'This beauty once belonged to the Vivaldi brothers, would you believe? Great explorers in their time, and predecessors of Columbus. Perhaps they would have first discovered the Americas, if they had not been taken by the gods and left in our seas.'

He chuckled, as if he had made a joke.

It was indeed an impressive ship, now that Cade had more than a moment to look at it. A single mast and sail sat at its centre, and over its side, Cade could see a long line of oars rising and falling in tandem with the drum's beat, like the pulsing of a feverish heart. Somewhere below, as many as a hundred men must be sweating in a stink-filled gloom, chained to an oar they may not have left for years.

Would he prefer such a fate to the death Ishak promised him? As if reading his thoughts, Ishak clicked his fingers and led Cade, along with the pair of burly bodyguards, down a set of steep steps built into the deck of the ship.

Ishak wrinkled his nose as the first hints of a foul stench reached their nostrils. Cade could only imagine where it came from.

'I do not often come down here,' the captain said, 'but I think it will help . . . convince you.'

He nodded to the two guards, and they were led further down a corridor, where on either side, Cade could see the hammocks of the crew.

At the very end, a second trap-door lay, but this one had no grating as theirs did. Instead, it was a solid square of metal nailed in strips over wood. A padlock, a twin of the one that held their own grate where it was, kept the trapdoor in place.

Ishak barked an order, pre-emptively lifting a sleeve to his nose with one arm. With the other, he tugged a key from his pocket, and proffered it to the bodyguards.

There was a flurry of activity as the padlock was clacked open, and then the door was lifted with a heave from the two sailors. It slammed to the side, and Cade reeled back as if hit by a physical blow.

The *stench*. He had never imagined such a smell. Like rancid meat, sewage and body odour, coalescing into a miasma that almost coated the skin.

A shove propelled him down more steps, and there, he saw it.

Human forms, pale as wraiths and less substantive still, made up of skin and bone. Beards and long hair framed sunken eyes and toothless mouths, and the slop of unspeakable liquids washed back and forth in the bilge.

Manacles, rusted shut, kept hands to oars at all times, while at the very end of the ship, a large man beat out an endless dirge on a broad drum, with what looked like a First World War gas mask upon his face. Others, wearing similar masks, strode among the slaves, whips slashing down at the barest hint of slacking, wearing high boots to avoid touching the putrid effluent that swashed along the floors. No men cried out where the lashes struck, years of endurance accustoming them to the pain.

All faced away from them, but Cade caught the sidelong glances of the men in the closest rows, their faces haggard and drawn. Then one of the prowling whip-holders barked, and their gazes darted forward once more.

Cade stood on the lowest step tentatively, as if to place his feet at the bottom level might condemn him to remain there. He felt Ishak's hand on his shoulder, and shuddered at the man's touch.

'Such is the fate of criminals and vagrants in our empire, scraped from the streets and prisons and sold directly to men like me for a fraction of their worth.'

Now Cade knew for sure what kind of place they were heading for. This empire was no utopia, but a despotic civilisation. At least he knew that these men were not captured remnants – but rather criminals from Ishak's homeland. Small comfort though that was for his own fate.

Ishak snatched up a handful of Cade's hair and forced Cade's head to turn. Now, looking beyond the steps, Cade saw past more dead-eyed rowers. There stood a cage, placed at the very end of the ship. Within were more people. Tan-skinned men and women, wearing simple tunics, chitons and sandals.

'Our latest catch,' Ishak said. 'Before we came across you. Not moderns, but Sumerians. Valuable as labourers. Perhaps one or two might serve as scribes, or some other such role. That will be determined by the assessors at the slave markets.'

Cade saw the fear in the Sumerians' eyes, as they huddled together at the back of the cage. To be abandoned in a jungle of monsters, and then thrown into this cage soon after. What did they make of this place? Where did they think they had gone?

'A better fate than these rowers, certainly,' Ishak went on. 'And a far better one than yours, if you defy me.'

He released Cade's hair, and Cade faced forward once more.

'Should you refuse me,' Ishak said, pulling him close, 'I shall put out your eyes, prick your ears and cut out your tongue, so that none will know of your origins. You shall be left here among this human filth, your world reduced to the pull of an oar and the slops forced down your throat to keep you alive through it all. And when you are dead, I shall toss you over the side for the sea-monsters, should they care to swallow the wretched remains that are left of you.'

Cade gagged, his empty stomach constricting in the horror of it all.

'Do not think I will not do it,' Ishak whispered, leaning even closer so Cade could feel the man's cloying breath in his ear. 'Look.'

He pointed a thick, bejewelled finger at a man close by, a man with sightless holes for eyes. There, Cade saw the unmistakable British Royal Air Force symbol – a red, blue and white target – tattooed upon his shoulder.

'Such is the punishment for those who defy me,' the captain hissed. 'As this man did, to his great misfortune.'

Cade stared in horror.

'Now, shall we take this conversation upstairs?' Ishak asked.

Cade nodded wordlessly, as his stomach heaved once more. Hell. There was no other word for this place. He would rather die than live this way.

'Good.'

EIGHTEEN

They sat there among the finery of Ishak's cabin, but Cade could still feel the stench of that place, like an oily layer upon his skin. His mind could not shake the terrible image of what lay just a few storeys below, even as his eyes took in embroidered cushions and gilded wood panelling.

Ishak leaned closer, as if to gauge the impact of their recent trip. Cade could hardly meet his eyes. To be a slaver such as Ishak, one had to be a monster. But to know the man was capable of sinking to such depravity, to reduce men to the machinery of flesh and bone, pitiless to the minds that lay behind them . . . only a psychopath could do such a thing.

'Speak,' Ishak commanded, flapping a hand at Cade.

Cade jumped at the movement, and Ishak allowed himself a broad smile.

But Cade waited. This shock tactic had been intentional, but he could not give away the only card he held just yet. His knowledge of the future was valuable, and though Ishak could punish him terribly if he refused, that did not mean he should give it away.

Still, he could not barter without Ishak knowing what Cade was selling. He had to give him something.

'I said speak!' Ishak snapped, slamming a fist down on the table.

Cade held up a hand. 'Before I begin . . . answer me this. What is the most *modern* man that you have captured before us?'

Ishak scratched his beard.

'The doctor from 1918,' he said, with just a touch of pride to his voice. 'Or perhaps the man who refused to speak to me – the one you met down below, he might have come from later. A fool, who was silent till the last, though my grasp of English was not so good back then, so he could hardly understand what I was asking him. Perhaps the fact that we killed his friend had something to do with his silence.'

He shook his head, as if amazed that someone might be so stubborn. Yet Cade could only admire the man. Such courage . . . in the face of such threats.

'We slavers,' Ishak interrupted Cade's thoughts, 'we compete for the most modern specimens – but they are few and far between.'

He sighed, as if disappointed in that fact. 'I have heard from my competitors that men harking from the year 1950 have been captured before, and they also shared rumours of another war, even more terrible than that of the Great War. I only know of the year of origin, which we are allowed to ascertain. Further conversation with our captives is illegal, so we play our cards close to our chests.'

Cade took all this in with as much of a poker face as he could muster. His capture would be a triumph for Ishak. And the knowledge he possessed, invaluable.

'I am from the twenty-*first* century,' Cade said. 'More than a century later than when your doctor lived.'

Now it was his turn to examine Ishak's face. And what he hoped to see was there in an instant. A look of delight. Of *desire*.

'This world that these men of the Great War, or World War One, as we call it now, lived in a far, far more primitive place than I did. *Radio* you said earlier?' He laughed. 'Nobody uses that any more. Maybe in their cars.'

Ishak leaned closer.

'So there was a World War Two?' he asked. 'A second Great War?'

Cade nodded. 'A war with weapons that could level entire cities in a flash of light. And in my time, these weapons can destroy entire countries. In fact, wars have been declared on the suspicion that another country might even *have* such a weapon.'

Ishak's eyes glowed with fascination, and he drew the bottle and glasses from beneath his desk once more. As he placed them on the table, Cade swiftly took the bottle and filled both glasses, giving Ishak a far more liberal measure. Ishak threw back the drink, and Cade dutifully refilled it, before taking a small mouthful of his own.

It would be a difficult balancing act – he had never touched more than a light beer before. He had not particularly enjoyed it either, sipping it while watching the last Super Bowl with his father. Meanwhile, Ishak would be an experienced drinker. The trick would be to get Ishak drunker than himself, while still maintaining the pretext of drinking together.

He placed the glass back on the table and forced down a gulp of the foul liquid. It was time to put on an act. To be an intellectual. And a charming one at that.

'You are lucky that I, though I may not look it, am a historical scholar. Now, my knowledge is more focused on that of the Romans and the other ancients – you may test me on such things if you doubt me. But it puts me in a good position to fill the gaps in your understanding of what has transpired since what the First World War doctor told you.'

Ishak slapped his knee, satisfaction stamped across his features.

'I knew it,' the man chuckled. 'Knew it as soon as looking at you. A valuable catch, to be sure. Drink!'

It was more a question than a command, and Cade dutifully sipped as Ishak threw back another draught of the beverage. Cade swiftly refilled it once more.

'Go on,' Ishak said, impatient. 'Tell me more of this war, and why radios are no longer used.'

Cade paused. Was now the time to barter? Ishak was on the hook. But Ishak was a shark, and Cade a boy standing in the shallows with a reed rod.

He would have to reel him in carefully.

'Are you familiar with the phrase, the carrot and the stick?' Cade asked.

Ishak nodded, though his brow creased. 'To make a donkey walk faster, you threaten it with a stick, or offer it a carrot. What does this have to do with the radio?'

Cade held his breath. 'You've shown me a big stick today. But I need a carrot. Quite literally. Maybe some food? And for my friends as well?'

Ishak rang his bell forcefully before Cade had even finished speaking, and barked orders at the two bodyguards who burst in immediately.

Cade understood the Latin, accented and swiftly spoken though it was. Food and drink was to be brought in, and more of it – the stuff the sailors lived on – would go to modern captives.

'Happy?' Ishak asked, as the sound of their hurried footsteps receded.

Cade nodded slowly. But a meal was not what he was here to negotiate for.

'I also wish to exchange knowledge for knowledge. To know what awaits my friends, should I become your servant. What manner of death will they endure? And is there anything I can do to save their lives?'

Ishak glared at Cade.

'Ungrateful little swine,' he snarled. 'You are not in the position to be asking questions. You are lucky to be fed at all.'

The bodyguards returned, laying food out on the table. Fruit, bread, olive oil and slices of salted beef. Cade's belly gurgled at the sight of it. Figs, this was not.

Still looking at Cade through narrowed eyes, Ishak tore off a hunk of bread and dipped it in the olive oil, then stuffed it into his mouth.

'Understand, this is the only time I will humour you,' he

said, waving the bread loaf in the air as he spoke. 'After that, the subject shall not be raised again. Do so, and you will be whipped.'

Cade nodded, and Ishak grunted in satisfaction. He swallowed, and chased the food with another gulp of booze. Cade was swift to refill his glass. Yet, somehow, the man's words did not slur. He seemed as sober as ever.

'When I said that moderns were to be put to death, that was not entirely true,' Ishak said, and smiled as he saw the flash of hope in Cade's eyes. 'Or at least, there is more to it than that.'

He pushed more food into his mouth, and Cade waited with bated breath. Ishak seemed to savour Cade's anxious look, and even took the opportunity to quaff another glass of liquor.

'The Colosseum,' Ishak said, throwing his hands out theatrically. Crumbs dashed across the room, the first sign of the alcohol taking effect. 'Our first and last form of entertainment. Only moderns may fight in it, as decreed by the gods, and the emperor, who the gods commune with. And we are ever in need of new fighters. The attrition rate is . . . *high*. That is why you are more valuable to me alive.'

'We fight each other?' Cade asked.

Ishak shook his head and wagged a finger.

'That is *all* the information you get,' Ishak said. 'The rest, you shall learn for yourself later. Now, speak further of this second war. I have yet to decide if I shall keep you as a manservant, or sell you with the rest of your friends.'

NINETEEN

They talked into the night. Or rather, Cade did. Ishak seemed more than happy to let Cade summarise the last hundred years however he liked – though he adapted his storytelling to match Ishak's interests, given the questions the slaver kept asking.

Warfare, it seemed, was the most fascinating to Ishak, and they spent much time speaking of World War Two. Of submarines, tanks, helicopters, fighter jets and bombers. And of the nuclear bombs that had ended the war, and the consequences of their invention.

Once Cade had exhausted those topics, they covered more general things. Smartphones, the internet, the moon landing, and Martian exploration. Skyscrapers and commercial jets. Sports cars and flatscreen TVs.

And with each word, the decanter of liquor became ever more empty, and Ishak's eyelids heavier with the dimming of the porthole's light. Twice, his bearded chin nodded forward to rest on his chest, but it would bob up seconds later, and the slaver would grunt out another question.

Eventually, it happened. That final drop of Ishak's head. And, as Cade held his breath . . . a snore. Then another, longer this time. Somehow, the man remained upright, cross-legged on his velvet cushion.

It was what Cade had been waiting for. But *what* was he supposed to do here? He'd had ample time to examine the room, and there were no weapons on display. If he was going to take Ishak hostage, he would need to hold a knife to his throat. But there wasn't even a letter opener there.

Still, Cade took the risk of standing, resisting the urge to groan as his legs prickled with pins and needles. He crept about the chamber, opening and closing the trunks and cabinets in the walls, but each was filled only with fine clothing, hookah pipes and jewellery.

An examination of Ishak's sleeping form also showed no blades, not even a small personal dagger. So, no hostage taking then. Outside, he knew were the two bodyguards – and the portholes were too small to crawl through. He only had access to this room.

So, that left him one option: the key around Ishak's neck. With any luck, it would open the padlocked grate that kept them trapped. With another generous lashing of good fortune, they might find their weapons, and fight their way past Ishak's two bodyguards to take him hostage.

They could then negotiate for the ship to be turned around, and . . . well they'd make up the rest along the way. One step at a time.

Cade slunk to Ishak's side and crouched, wincing as the

floorboards creaked. The necklace was buried beneath the folds of the man's collar, and had Cade not seen him take the chain from around his neck earlier, he would not have known it was there. As it was, Cade hardly knew where to start.

The longer he took, the more likely Ishak was to wake. But too quickly, and he would disturb the sleeping monster-in-human-form.

Carefully, ever so carefully, Cade tugged back the cloth of Ishak's robe, and found the glint of chain there. Gripping a single link between thumb and forefinger, he pulled with as much force as he dared, lifting it an inch from the neckline and allowing the robe to fall back in place.

Ishak grunted. The snoring, once constant, stopped. Then, like an engine on its last legs, he snorted and sputtered back into the gentle rumble of before.

Now for the tricky part.

Cade pulled the chain higher, then reached beneath the man's chin to pull the dangling key free. Then he lowered the chain so that the key sank back down, settling upon the fabric at the centre of Ishak's upper chest, beneath Ishak's beard. With the concentration of a surgeon, Cade drew the chain loop forward, over and around Ishak's ears, and withdrew, dipping the chain beneath the long, luxurious beard and holding it aloft.

Cade wrapped the key in the chain as tightly as he dared, so that it would not clink, then stuffed it into the pocket of his uniform. That done, he contemplated whether to wake Ishak, and continue their conversation until he was dismissed. But with that came the risk of Ishak noticing the chain was missing, the familiar weight of the ornament gone from his neck.

So instead, Cade crept to the door, and opened it a crack. There stood two bodyguards, still as statues, their eyes turned to new light from the doorway. Their hands went to the machete-like blades at their waists.

Forcing a smile and lifting a finger to his lips, Cade opened the door a little further, motioning behind him to Ishak's snoring figure.

He shrugged, as if to say he did not want to wake him, then motioned questioningly in the direction of the brig. For a long second, the two men's eyes remained on Cade, then they turned to each other as some unspoken decision passed between them.

To Cade's relief, he was pulled into the corridor, and the door closed behind him. They marched him, more gently this time, to the brig, and unlocked the grating using a key of their own.

They allowed Cade to jump down into the low-ceilinged brig himself, encouraging him with a shove when he hesitated, before slamming the grate down behind him and locking it shut once more with a clack.

In the dim light of the brig, lit only by the red-white light of the twin moons above, the others stirred from their respective sleeping spots.

'You OK?' Scott asked.

'Yeah,' Cade replied, rubbing his ankles.

It wasn't a long way to drop, but it still hurt.

'What time is it?' Grace's sleepy voice asked.

'Like we ever know the answer to that,' Amber replied. 'It's late.'

For a moment Cade crouched there, gathering his thoughts, as the others waited for him to speak.

'I have a plan,' Cade finally said.

'Does it involve teaching Zeeb to steal that key?' Scott asked, only half-jokingly. 'I saved some food to start training him.'

Cade grinned, for what felt like the first time in a while. He drew Ishak's chain from his pocket and let it dangle, glinting in the moonlight.

'Way ahead of you, buddy.'

TWENTY

Cade sat on Grace's shoulders, swaying in time with the waves that buffeted the ship. She was the tallest, and his head the smallest, so it had fallen to him to push between the grates of their trapdoor to see what guards had been left on deck.

He did so with trepidation, but was heartened by the distinct lack of light in their immediate surroundings. In fact, as Grace slowly turned beneath him, guided by nudges from his ankles, he saw only one light, at the very prow of the ship. And there . . . an ill-lit figure, standing by a lantern. A pilot light – one to stop ships from running into each other in the dark, and to illuminate the way in case of debris or obstructions ahead. And as few people as he could have hoped for.

Ishak's cabin, and the corridor that led there, was just a stone's throw away. Behind it, he could hear the gentle murmur of conversation. The bodyguards who had thrown him in there were still awake.

And, as he looked beyond to the horizon, he could see the

116

first hints of dawn colouring its edges. He had been talking to Ishak longer than he thought. Their time was running out.

'Down,' he hissed, and he was awkwardly lowered to his feet.

'What's the verdict?' Scott asked.

'One guy, at the head of the ship, and Ishak's bodyguards are awake in the corridor. Nobody else – looks like they're more concerned with the galley slaves than us.'

'Great,' Amber said, rubbing her hands together. 'What's next?'

'We have some decisions to make,' Cade said. 'Ishak's guards are armed, and we're not. So . . . that's out, unless we can get our swords back and fight our way through them.'

It didn't seem a pleasant proposition.

'I doubt they keep weapons on the deck, which means we're going to have to sneak below,' Cade said. 'Steal some from the sailors.'

'And then fight those two brutes to take Ishak hostage?' Grace asked. Her eyes were wide with fear, and Cade felt the same way she did.

He nodded grimly. 'We can't wait for them to go to sleep, if they plan to at all. It's almost morning, and by then Ishak will know his key is missing, and the crew will be awake.'

Even as he spoke, he glanced upwards, as if the slowly lightening sky was a timer, ticking down.

'Let's do it then,' Amber urged.

'There's an alternative,' Cade said, the idea forming in his mind, more out of fear of the bodyguards than logic alone. 'Our other option after finding weapons is to go down to where the rowers are kept. Arm and free as many of them as we can, and lead a coup of the ship from below. There's at least a hundred of them down there. Can't be more than fifty sailors. If we can get the drop on the sleeping sailors, we might take the ship before Ishak and his bodyguards are any the wiser in his cabin up top.'

'Too risky,' Amber said. 'What if they make a noise? What if they won't fight? And how long will it take us to arm and free enough of them? And who is to say they won't ignore us and start attacking sailors before we can organise them? There's no way this doesn't end with a bloodbath, we'd just be hoping we're on the winning side of it.'

Cade nodded. She was right. Fighting was inevitable. Foisting the job on those tortured souls below was the coward's way out.

'Maybe only one of us should go looking for the weapons,' Scott said. 'More people means more noise, more of us to be seen. We only need one person to carry a handful of weapons upstairs.'

'Right,' Quintus said. 'One. Who knows ship best.'

Cade felt their eyes turn to him expectantly. Of course. He knew the layout, more or less. It had to be him. When was he going to catch a break?

'OK,' Cade said, rubbing his eyes. 'I'll go.'

'Are you sure?' Amber asked.

Cade nodded. 'It's the best play.'

'Then let's get you up there,' Grace said, crouching down and patting her back. 'Hop on.'

Cade did so, and moments later he had the padlock

unlocked, the mechanism opening with a smooth click. Grace held up the grate as he scrambled through, then lowered it with a soft rap behind him.

He was on deck. The sea breeze chilled his skin, and he could remain on his hands and knees as he crawled across the ship's boards to the hatch that led below.

Beneath, the square entrance yawned open like a pit, so dark he could not see its bottom. He pushed aside his fears, focusing on the knowledge that the alternative to not going down there was certain death.

Glad of his missing boots, Cade slipped down upon bare feet, letting his toes feel their way down each step. Now, in the dark gloom of the ship's tight corridors, he allowed his eyes a moment to accustom to the new darkness. On either side were the doorways he had seen before – with the ones on his right open, leaving visible the berth where sailors slept in hammocks. A single candle glowed there, but Cade kept his eyes away from it, not wanting to lose his night vision.

He crept down the corridor, ignoring the snores and creaks that echoed about his head, his palms pressed against the walls to steady him against the pitch and roll of the ship.

The first door to his left was closest, sealed with a metal latch – more to stop it from slamming open and closed with the ship's swaying than to secure it. Within, Cade found only sacks of grain and barrels of water. He could only peer in – going any deeper would mean releasing the door and letting it swing free, since it only latched closed from the outside.

So, he moved on to the next door – the twin of its

neighbour, but further down. But this one contained only sailcloth, spare oars and other such items. A wooden hammer, rough-carved and heavy, was the only weapon there. Cade took it regardless, tucking it into his uniform's front pocket.

The third door was the last built into that corridor, with only another door directly opposite, built beneath Ishak's private quarters. And yet, even as he went to open it, he heard footsteps approaching. The next door was secured with a padlock, and Cade cursed internally, knowing that it must be where the weapons were kept.

But there was no time to open it, and flickering candlelight began to bathe the walls behind him. So, he moved past it, pacing over the hatch that held the galley slaves to the small door at the end of the corridor. He ducked behind it, and was glad to see this door *did* have a latch on the inside, which he slid across swiftly. Then he was met with a foul stench.

He turned to see the wooden bench and hole in the floor that told him this was the galley toilet. And that was when he realised his mistake. There could only be one place where that sailor could be heading. Here.

Cade tugged the hammer free of his pocket, holding it high. The door rattled, then he heard a sigh, and a knock. This was followed by a soft-spoken word, Latin, though he could not hear it well through the door above the creaking of the ship and his own, pounding heart. Mind racing, Cade simply coughed loudly in response.

Another muffled word from outside, then silence. Cade waited, but there were no footsteps of the person leaving, and he could see a light, flickering through the cracks in the door. He stood, and so did his enemy, separated by a thin layer of wood.

It was almost comical. This man, waiting for Cade to finish his business. Completely unaware of the knife's edge that both his and Cade's life lay on . . . and no room now for both of them to remain there. Cade had no choice. He was going to have to come out swinging.

Cade wiped his slippery palms on his pants, then redoubled his grip on the hammer. Slowly, he tugged across the latch. He took a deep breath, and barged the door open, sweeping the hammer up, ready to strike.

Beneath him, the pale face of a small boy flashed up, fear stamped across his candle-lit features. The sight froze Cade, the weapon nearly tumbling from his hands as the horror at what he had almost done chilled his blood.

For a single, heart-stopping moment, the two stared at each other. Cade, his hammer a few inches above the boy's head, the boy, no more than a child, staring wide-eyed at the figure in front of him, a slow stain spreading across the front his breeches.

An intake of breath.

'No,' Cade hissed, lowering a hand to cover the boy's mouth.

But it was too late. The boy screamed.

TWENTY-ONE

The sailors had come in a tumbling, sleepy wave of men, pouring into the corridor and towards him with bleary eyes. None held weapons, but Cade knew it was useless to resist. He tossed the hammer into the toilet behind him, as if hiding the weapon would somehow absolve him of his escape attempt.

Then his world devolved into one of pounding fists and flying feet as the sailors beat him to the ground, until Cade hardly knew where he was. He remembered the ropes encircling his hands and feet. The rough hands lifting him, the sea wind against his skin as he was carried back onto the deck.

The shouts of anger, and triumph. And Ishak, stumbling out of his quarters in a hungover daze, flanked by his two guards. He remembered being lifted to his feet, Ishak's liquor-tinged breath in his ear, as threats were hissed and fingers encircled his throat.

What he didn't remember was the blow that knocked him out.

He woke to the sounds of birds. The wet spray of sea on his bare feet, and the pain, blossoming up and down his body in waves that seemed to match the cadence of the rise and fall of the ship.

His eyes cracked open, though he found it hard to see through the swelling of his black eyes. Water, beneath him. Sky, above him. Salt on his lips.

And twin circles of pain around his wrists, where his weight hung like a sack of potatoes. He swung back and forth, the spray of waves splashing the ship's front leaving him cold beneath the morning sun.

Cade was dangling from the prow of the ship.

As he looked up Cade saw he had been hung from between the jaws of the ship's figurehead – a shark's skull, a real one. A *Megalodon*, if Cade was to guess. That ancient, giant shark that had once filled Earth's primordial seas.

Disjointed thoughts shot through Cade's head. His guts turned to water, and made him wish for the oblivion of fainting once more. A scream boiled from his throat, yet came out in little more than a dry gasp. But the internal scream in his mind was never-ending.

He could hear the cries of sea birds, and knew that their presence meant land. Meant that soon, they would be arriving in the godforsaken harbour that was part of this empire. Soon, he and his friends would be killed in whatever fashion the so-called emperor had decreed.

The birds circled above, too distant for his sun-blind eyes to see. But the creatures that leaped in the waves beneath him – those he *could* see.

At first, Cade thought they were dolphins, bursting from the water and splashing down, dorsal fins slicing the water, powered by fluked tails. They bore the same shape, moved in the same way. But their eyes were too large, and gills adorned their sides. These were no dolphins.

Did this world contain *any* modern creatures?

'Codex,' Cade whispered, his voice coming in barely a croak. 'Codex, are you there?'

'*Yes, Cade,*' the invisible drone said, its voice coming from directly above him. '*I am.*'

Cade breathed a sigh of relief. He'd always assumed it was there, invisible and watching in the background – Abaddon clearly did not want it to be seen. But it was one of the few tools left to him.

'What are those things?' Cade asked. 'Will they try to . . . get at me?'

A brief flash of blue, barely visible in the morning light, told Cade the Codex had scanned the water.

'*Ichthyosaurs are a classic example of convergent evolution, demonstrating how similar environments and ecological niches can create creatures with near identical traits and appearances, despite sharing no relation.*'

Cade was almost beginning to regret his request.

'*Thus, the Ichthyosaur, a reptile, and the dolphin, a mammal, become near identical – sharing a shape, flippers, dorsal crest, even blubber. Though some species of Ichthyosaurs evolved to be as large as blue whales, those I have scanned are smaller, and would present as much a threat as a dolphin would, their modern equivalent.*'

Cade took a moment to take in its words, sorting through them in his head. So, as dangerous as dolphins. Fine.

'However, if your query of "things" includes the creature beneath the Ichthyosaurs, I should advise you that that specimen might certainly try to "get at" you.'

'What creature?' Cade rasped.

He stared beneath him, the rushing azure water clear, but disturbed by the leaping of the Ichthyosaurs. And then, as if they had become aware of his scrutiny, the beasts scattered, there one second, gone the next.

The water, now broken only by the waves, cleared. For a moment, Cade saw nothing. Only that the water beneath the ship was darker than the rest. A trick of the light? The ship's shadow?

The shadow shifted. Moved, ahead of the ship, in a sudden movement that spoke of life. He watched, transfixed, as that great dark form rose from the deep. At first, he could not see its shape, only its outline, the monster's visage blocked by the dappled sunlight on the sea's surface.

Then a fin-tip broke the water. A shark's fin. But it kept rising. Rising and rising and rising, until it was like a black windsurfer's sail, slicing the water ahead of the ship.

There was a cry from above him.

'Pistris!'

Sea-monster.

Cade could almost feel the thunder of feet as sailors crowded the prow above him, and as he twisted his head to look, there was Ishak, looking down at Cade with an expression of both anger and satisfaction.

'Our pet,' Ishak called, slapping the great pointed snout of their ship's figurehead, from which Cade hung. 'Come to be fed. Right on time.'

Cade's eyes turned, as if of their own accord, taking in the full sixty feet of the leviathan in front of him. *Megalodon*. The subject of a dozen cheesy movies . . . but this was a monster in the flesh.

Like a great white shark, scaled up to monstrous proportions. As he watched, the beast turned with a single beat of its tail, its blunt head rising above the surface, and the dark orb of its eye glaring where he dangled.

'Shall we feed our little friend?' Ishak called.

'No!' The word rasped from Cade's throat unbidden, practically a scream.

Ishak repeated his question, louder and in Latin. A cheer came from the sailors, and Cade knew it then. Knew that he was to die. Panic overwhelmed him. Terror. Mindless, and all encompassing.

But his eyes could not stop watching. Not even as the beast sank beneath the waves once more, its form spiralling deeper, shrinking, then growing larger as it rose, almost lazily from the deep.

The dark, expanding form turned pink, a sudden flash as the dark mouth opened to reveal the fleshy maw, ringed by row upon row of jagged teeth. It waited just beneath the surface, like a baby bird waiting to be fed.

Cade hung, suspended between life and death. It was the fear at the crest of a rollercoaster, multiplied a thousand times over. Waiting for the drop.

Something tumbled past him, jarring his shoulder and sending him into a stomach-lurching swing. He saw it splash into the water. Caught a glimpse of a haggard, sightless face, eyes open, even in death. The tangled beard and hair. The filthy rags.

Then the monster's mouth closed, the corpse disappearing utterly. Another rower's body whirled past, half-sinking as the shark swam in a slow circle. It took the next offering almost gently, then that body too was gone.

They were feeding it their dead. The rowers who had not survived the journey to and from the jungle. But were they the appetiser, and Cade the main course?

Cade hunted desperately for some path back onto the ship, should the rope be cut. Some handhold he could cling to. But only the sharp barnacles and sea slime made any impression on the sides of the vessel. Once he was in . . . there was no coming back.

Yet, as the ship ploughed its way on through the sea, Cade saw the water lightening, turning from azure to turquoise. The cries of the sea birds grew louder, and the dim outline of what must have been land was emerging from the corner of his vision. But he dared not turn his eyes away. Still, the beast circled. How many times had it swum by here, waiting for Ishak's ship?

A jerk on his lifeline made Cade scream, his eyes closing instinctively. But instead of the drop, he felt himself yanked upwards. Then again, and above, he heard the grunts of men straining.

He passed by the figurehead, the weathered skull a weak

parody of the monster below. Seconds later, rough hands seized his uniform and hair, tugging him roughshod over the ship's rail and onto the floorboards.

A dagger pressed against the soft underside of his chin, and Cade stared up into Ishak's dark eyes.

'A lesson,' Ishak said. 'A poor substitute for the punishment I would have preferred for you. Sadly, you are too valuable to be killed.'

He brought his face close and whispered softly in Cade's ear.

'But I cannot have a disobedient manservant. You can die with your friends instead.'

TWENTY-TWO

He was not thrown in the brig with his friends, but rather left forgotten on the deck, trussed up like a turkey. Unable to move, and still aching from his beating, Cade could only watch through the ship's railings as the sailors went about their business, turning the ship towards the shore.

For that was where they had arrived. An island, if Cade had to guess.

'Codex,' Cade whispered. 'Where are we?'

It was a vague question, and in truth, he did not expect an answer – he just wanted to know the drone was there.

'*Remnant identified as Bermeja Island. First discovered by explorer Alonso de Santa Cruz in 1539 as an island of 80 square kilometres in the Gulf of Mexico, its existence was later confirmed by multiple cartographers in the years to follow. The island was included in maps of the area for centuries after. It later vanished from the geographical record in 1775, when the area was mapped again. The time and circumstance of the island's disappearance are unknown.*'

Abaddon had upped and taken an entire landmass. Cade stared at the red-yellow shoreline, straining his eyes to catch the details there. If what the Codex was telling him was true, the island had been moved to the caldera centuries ago.

Which meant the Empire would be centuries old. Even now, Cade could see structures built there: towers, stretching high, and pillared state houses at the centre of a sprawling city, all of white stone. Encircling that pale centre, the ramshackle of slums spread far, its black smoke of cooking fires drifting into the sky.

But a single building dominated everything. A green-domed superstructure, as large as any cathedral he had seen before. It had many levels and offshoot minarets, but a great staircase led up its middle. This, undoubtably, was the emperor's palace.

As they neared the port at the city's shoreline, Cade's view of the palace and grand buildings was obscured by the warehouses at the harbour. A lengthy jetty was filled with dozens of ships, though fewer than Cade would have expected. He supposed fishing in waters populated by monstrosities as large as the *Megalodon* was rare, especially in a small boat. Still, there *were* other, larger ships, and these were made up of myriad types and styles. Some were galleys, not unlike Ishak's, but still more spoke of vastly different origins.

Ships of war that would belong in the Napoleonic wars were perhaps the most common, cannons rusting in their berths, but others were the triremes he knew from the time of the Romans and Byzantines. Chinese junks, Viking longships, and still more he hardly recognised were peppered among them.

How many of these vessels had found themselves plucked from the water and dropped in an alien sea? What had those men thought, when they first looked upon the fraternal moons of Acies? And what fate had awaited them when they berthed themselves at the port of this emerging civilisation?

The ship slowed to a halt and tied off at the harbour. Within seconds, Cade was seized by his shoulders and lifted to his feet by Ishak's two guards. He craned his neck to look behind, and saw the Sumerian captives brought on deck, blinking in the morning light.

Cade hardly caught a glimpse of the brig's trapdoor being thrown open and tried to spot his friends.

But something distracted him. He found himself faced with a thin bespectacled man, who had stalked onto the ship via the gangplank lowered to the jetty. The man wore fine clothing, even finer than Ishak's, a strange mishmash of layered toga and Middle Eastern robe.

He was followed by two men, clad in loincloths and nothing else, who carried a heavy wooden desk between them. Iron collars were locked about their necks, and their skin shone with sweat as they set the desk down.

A third collared slave hurried after them, placing a cushioned chair behind the desk, and an enormous ledger upon it. Finally, a group of four armoured soldiers marched aboard, standing at each corner of the desk. They wore mail, with helmets, shields and spears.

Each shield had the symbol of an Ancient Egyptian

hieroglyphic ankh: a 'T' topped with an upside-down tear drop, wreathed by laurel leaves like those worn by the emperors of Rome. What could that mean?

Finally, the man sat, ignoring the three slaves as they stepped back and knelt on the boards of the ship.

Ishak, for once deferential, hurried from his quarters, his own ledger in his hands. This he lay beside the larger ledger, then stepped back and bowed.

The bespectacled man ignored Ishak, instead clicking his fingers, prompting one of the kneeling slaves to open both ledgers to their most recent pages. Only then did the man deign to look up, drawing a magnifying glass from his pocket and running a thin finger down the spider-scratched writing.

With each line of the ledger, he examined the Sumerians, shoved to the fore by the sailors in a shaking huddle. His eyes swept their clothing, and he seemed to listen to the muffled wails and conversations. It seemed enough, and he made a few notes in his own ledger, mirroring Ishak's own.

Then, as he came to the section where the names of Cade and his friends had been added, his eyes widened. He looked to Ishak sharply, and the slaver nodded, a grin plastered across his face.

And then, the man spoke.

'American?' he asked, his eyes snapping to Cade.

His accent was strange. Familiar, almost European, but Cade could not quite place it.

Still, it was no use lying. Cade nodded, and the man's eyes gleamed with what looked like greed.

'Twenty-*first* century?' he asked, tapping the page.

Cade nodded again.

'Has this man asked you to lie to me?' the man demanded. 'Are you a simple soldier from the Great War, pretending to be something you are not?'

The man turned to Ishak before Cade could answer, speaking in English, perhaps for Cade's benefit.

'If I later learn that this is some trick to extract a higher price, you will be stripped of your ship. This boy shall be tortured to death for all to see, and you shall be made a slave. This is your last chance to make the truth known.'

Ishak stepped forward, his face grave.

'I swear by all the gods, and let them strike me down should I lie,' Ishak said. 'I am no great *assessor* like you, but this is what the boy told me. If it is a lie, the lie is his and not mine. See, my report on his teeth, his clothing. He is a modern, no doubt.'

The assessor glared at Ishak, then looked behind Cade. Cade followed his gaze, and saw his friends, their hands tied together in a line. Then his head was turned forward by a bodyguard's rough fingers.

'If this is true, these are the most modern captures yet,' the assessor said. 'The emperor shall reward you handsomely. As for the Sumerians, my lessers shall interview them for appropriate skills, and you shall be paid accordingly. These others, I shall deliver to the emperor myself. Personally.'

TWENTY-THREE

The soldiers marched Cade and his friends down the gangplank with spears lowered, but Cade's greatest relief was that Quintus was among them. Perhaps it was some oversight, but for now the legionary was with them.

'What happened?' Amber whispered.

'Silence!' barked the closest guard.

His spear jabbed forward, slicing open her shoulder.

Amber cried out and clutched her palm to the wound, but their herding down the jetty hardly slowed. The message was clear enough. Moderns were banned from speaking.

Biting his tongue, Cade could only walk on, watching as another assessor strode by, stopping to take charge of the Sumerians that followed behind Cade. These men and women, ancient people from the earliest of civilisations, were left there, broken, terrified and confused.

On they marched into a cobblestone square thronging with people, though the crowds gave the soldiers a wide berth. Men and women glanced at them with only the mildest of curiosity, as if their presence was not so uncommon a scene.

It was when they were almost across the square that Cade had a moment of recognition. His eyes turned to a group of men. Standing in their armour, watching the progress of the soldiers impassively.

It was the boy he recognised. That same boy whom Amber had once threatened with an axe blade. The armoured men who had captured him and the girls, all those months ago.

If there had been any doubt before, now there was none. Those men were just like Ishak. And this was the fate that would have awaited them, had they not escaped.

Then the men were blocked from his view, and Cade was shuffled on down a broad paved causeway, faster now, and ahead, the wide steps of the palace came into view. On either side, great statues gazed down, soldiers frozen in acts of valour. Each had been vibrantly coloured, almost garishly so, with cloaks cherry red, shields painted a blazing bronze, even their skin lavishly coated in tan paint.

Another clue for Cade, as to where this civilisation had come from. The ancient Romans, and the Greeks for that matter, had all painted their statues. The alabaster white pieces that were kept in museums had not just lost limbs and noses to erosion over time, but the very colouring that had once coated them.

If this place was an amalgam of history's cultures, the ancient Mediterranean element was particularly strong. Compounded with Ishak's mention of a colosseum, Cade now knew this place was, at least in some ways, Roman.

With these thoughts swirling in his head, he and the

others finally arrived at the base of the great staircase. Despite their situation, Cade could only marvel at the size of the building.

It was massive in its scope and scale. And bordering those hundred stairs stood an army of soldiers, two to a step, facing one another in stoic silence across the broad divide.

They were sweating when they completed their ascent, standing among the huge pillars. The floors, marbled where they were visible, had been covered by enormous plush rugs, woven in intricate patterning that spoke of decades of work, had they been handmade – which Cade knew they must have been, in this world.

'You, boy!' Cade turned, to see the assessor had followed them up the steps, his bald head spotted with perspiration, spectacles slipped down his aquiline nose.

'Ishak's notes said that you are the only one to speak English. That the others speak . . . something else.' He waved his hand irritably.

Cade hesitated, then chose to remain silent.

'Come,' the assessor said, sweeping ahead and motioning at the guards to let Cade through. 'The rest shall remain here, until the emperor is done with you.'

Ahead, Cade caught glimpses of an enormous throne room, and there, dozens of well-dressed men, seated on small portable stools, being fanned by personal slaves. Queuing for an audience with the emperor, most likely. And here was Cade, jumping line.

All he could do was follow. Into a side chamber, up more steps, past more guards, now spiralling skyward to the dome of the building itself. On, down corridors with hurrying servants, their hands clutching piles of paper or platters of food.

In places, they were stopped, but the assessor only had to flash a golden amulet, one bearing the same symbol that the guards bore on their shields, to be let through. It seemed perfunctory, some even nodding in recognition of the assessor as they passed.

And finally, he arrived at a set of double doors. Here, there were over a dozen heavily armoured guards waiting on either side, yet not one moved to stop the assessor from stepping between their ordered ranks and pushing the doors open.

The assessor paused at the threshold, peering through. Light from small windows streamed in from the concave ceiling, and Cade realised they were at the very top of the dome.

'In,' the assessor muttered, propelling Cade through. 'I sent word ahead of us. He will be expecting you.'

And with that, the doors slammed shut.

TWENTY-FOUR

It was a massive space. Such that Cade's footsteps echoed as he took a few, tentative steps into the chamber, and examined his surroundings.

The furnishings were plush, the marble floor layered with more expensive rugs, cushioned alcoves and polished furniture. Upon a raised platform at the very end of the room, a broad bed – wider than three king-sized ones pushed together – was covered in luxurious, gold-laced bedding.

Yet what took up the most space were the glass cabinets, filling the entire left side of the room, scores and scores of them. On the right side, ancient books lined row upon row of wooden shelves, a library filled with leather-bound tomes.

As Cade's heart pounded, he let his eyes stray across the items protected behind the glass, each one laid out on a velvet cushion. They were mainly weapons, but there were also some statues and paintings.

The nearest cabinet drew him closer. A frayed piece of cloth, its very drabness out of place, yet its cabinet larger than the others to contain its considerable length. It was longer than he was tall, and the stitching depicted various men in battle with sword and shield, while further along, a king was being coronated on a throne. There was a plaque at the cabinet's base that read: *1072 – panels from the Bayeux Tapestry.*

And instantly, Cade knew what this place was. A collection. One of hundreds of remnants, taken from the jungle by the emperor's slavers.

'Impressed?'

The voice made Cade jump, and he spun in surprise. In front of him stood a young man. Older than Cade certainly, but not by much. He bore a prominent aquiline nose, with wavy brown hair and grey eyes that had been enhanced with what looked like eyeliner.

He wore a gold-and-purple toga, and was bedecked with enough jewellery that it almost looked uncomfortable to wear it all. Upon his head was a laurel wreath.

Behind him, an enormous man stood with hand on hilt, his face and body obscured by armour, but eyes fixed upon Cade, as if daring him to make a sudden move.

'I asked you a question.'

Cade managed a nod.

'Good,' the emperor said, clapping his hands. 'An American, yes?'

Cade nodded a second time, and the emperor smiled.

'I was tutored by an American. Well, my latest tutor. The first one tried to kill me.'

The emperor allowed himself a broad smile, then motioned

for Cade to follow.

Cade did so, almost meekly. The emperor's accent was a strange one, but he spoke English well, which was a surprise. But why bother to learn it?

'Of course,' the emperor went on. 'I hardly can take credit for the collection. It was mostly my predecessors who brought it all here. I am more interested in *people*.'

The emperor strode faster, and Cade was shepherded behind him by the enormous bodyguard, the trio weaving among the glass cabinets and heading for the curved wall at its end.

Cade could not help but glance at the objects on either side. A letter purported to have been written by Jack the Ripper, titled 'From Hell'. A half dozen Fabergé eggs, piled atop one another like the contents of an Easter basket.

It was a treasure trove of artefacts from history. Indeed, there were actual treasures scattered among them, too – crown jewels supposedly belonging to King John of England lay within a muddied chest that was filled with gold coins.

They came to a stop at the end wall, and there, dozens of stone busts formed a neat row. Heads: bald, bearded, clean-shaven, crowned, wreathed. All men, but none looked particularly alike.

'Abaddon *does* have good taste in rulers,' the emperor said, gesturing at the long line of faces.

He turned, fast enough to catch the look of surprise on Cade's face.

'So it's true. You know his name. A *contender* in our midst.'

Cade felt his heart quicken.

'You know Abaddon?' he asked.

The emperor shrugged. 'Who can truly *know* a god. I receive instructions, from time to time. A voice in my head. I would think myself quite mad, if all my predecessors had not experienced the exact same thing.'

He stopped, and pointed at the very first bust. 'Do you know why we call this place New Rome?'

Cade stared at the emperor, lost for words.

New Rome?

'You disappoint me. Abaddon said you were a historian.'

Abaddon told the emperor about me.

'That is Romulus. The founder of Rome. A twin, raised by wolves, who murdered his brother Remus and founded the greatest empire on Earth. He disappeared in a cloud of smoke at the end of his reign in 714 BC, or so the legends say. What they don't say is he was brought here.'

He smiled. 'It was a brief reign – he was an old man, after all. But then, his successor.'

He pointed at a chubby-faced man's effigy, the next in line.

'Emperor Gordian the second. He ruled Rome for but twenty-one days on Earth, before supposedly dying in the Battle of Carthage in the year 238. His body was never recovered. Because he was brought here. And ruled New Rome for as many years as he did days in old Rome.'

The emperor's bejewelled finger switched to the next bust.

'Emperor Valens, said to have fallen in the battle of Adrianople in 378, again with no body to speak of. They

141

were wrong – he was the next emperor of New Rome, in this world.'

Cade swallowed. He recognised these names. And it was all true.

'Abaddon ran out of Roman emperors eventually, so he moved on to Roman client kings.'

The emperor strode on.

'Emperor Vaballathus, of the Roman off-shoot, the Palmyrene Empire, disappeared in 273. Then Constantine the eleventh, last emperor of Byzantium – Rome's successor – lost in battle in 1453.'

The emperor grinned.

'Of course, Abaddon did not just choose Romans, he scattered in some other nobles and kings. He will have his fun, after all.'

Now the finger danced from bust to bust as the emperor strode up the line.

'Hereward the Wake of Wales. Young Arthur the first of Brittany. Olaf, the Viking king of Norway. King Sebastian the first of Portugal. King Sargon the second of Assyria, King Damasithymus of Calyndos. All ruled before me.'

Finally, the emperor stopped at the very end of the line. A bust of his own face was already there, his likeness captured perfectly.

'And finally, the greatest of them all. Me. The most worthy ruler based on my pedigree, and New Rome has enjoyed my reign for three years. Can you guess, who I am, Cade?'

But Cade could not. His mind was still reeling from the revelation that so many of the most famed leaders in history had been brought here. Scavenged from sinking ships and chaotic battlefields alike. Who could this youth, hardly older than twenty, be?

The emperor tutted.

'Come now, I thought you were a scholar. But I suppose I should not be surprised. History has forgotten me. A clue then? If you can guess it, I shall grant you a favour. How does that sound?'

'Yes,' Cade said, uttering the first word he had in the emperor's presence.

A chance. A chance for freedom.

'He speaks at last. I should hope the next word I hear is my *name*.'

The emperor cocked his head and narrowed his eyes.

'My father was Julius Caesar himself. My mother was Cleopatra, and my stepfather was Mark Antony. My adopted brother was Octavian, later emperor Augustus, and the cause of my mother and stepfather's death . . . and supposedly my own. Who am I?'

Cade stared. It was impossible. This man was a footnote in history.

Julius Caesar had only ever had one son who might one day have been Rome's first real emperor, had Caesar not been stabbed to death by his own senators. Caesar's posthumously adopted nephew, Octavian, took power instead, and the rest . . . was history.

Octavian had quietly ordered Caesar's son's assassination after defeating Antony and Cleopatra in a civil war made famous by Shakespeare, and several Hollywood movies.

Supposedly, the teenage boy had been strangled by his own tutor, though rumours of an escape to India had long abounded afterwards.

A union of Egyptian and Roman nobility. Hence the ankh and the laurel wreath.

'My name, boy,' the emperor said, clicking his fingers.

Cade swallowed. Then he uttered a single word.

'Caesarion.'

TWENTY-FIVE

Caesarion clapped in delight, his rings jingling with each slap of his hands.

'A historian *indeed*. Well done. Come, follow me.'

Again, Cade found himself herded forward by the enormous bodyguard, and this time they went to a balcony behind the emperor's bed.

Stepping into the light, Cade was once again confronted with a view of the city, this time seeing the rear of the palace. And what was waiting there astounded him.

An amphitheatre.

It put him in mind of Rome's own ruined Colosseum, that huge historical stadium, where tens of thousands of spectators had watched gladiators fight, prisoners executed, animals hunted and theatrical battles re-enacted.

But this was larger. As large as any football stadium. It seemed to Cade the entire population of the city, as well as its satellite towns, could fit inside this one place.

And there, at its base, was a colossus, just like Rome's had once had. No wonder Ishak had called it a colosseum.

Caesarion sighed wistfully.

'I am told the very first bout featured Spartacus himself, a gift from Abaddon. What a sight that must have been. I only wish I had been there to see it.'

The emperor stared down at the structure, lost in thought.

Spartacus . . . the most famed gladiator to have ever lived. For a brief moment Cade fantasised about leading a slave rebellion, as Spartacus had done long ago. A gladiator that had escaped his own *ludus* – gladiator training school – and gathered an army of slaves. A master tactician, he had slaughtered legion after legion until his eventual defeat. The man's body had never been found.

Having the great man die in the Colosseum's first bout was an obvious message to all those who watched. Such was the fate of rebels.

'It took generations to build,' Caesarion gestured at the structure. 'The Colosseum, I mean. For the colossus, we have Abaddon to thank.'

He pointed at the giant statue, one that Cade estimated almost as large as the Statue of Liberty.

'Remade from the brass pieces of the Colossus of Rhodes. Or so the writings of my predecessors claim.'

Cade hardly heard him, still in awe. Although now that he saw the building with his own eyes . . . it reminded him of what he was doing here. He needed to save his friends.

'So,' Caesarion said, after allowing Cade to gaze a few moments longer. 'I am still remembered on Earth. That is good.'

Cade took a deep breath, as the warm breeze buffeted him.

'If you care about Earth, you'll let my friends go. In fact, you'd send some men with me, to help us. We're the last of the contenders. Without us . . . Earth is doomed.'

Caesarion glanced over Cade, then shrugged, the mess of necklaces on his neck clinking with the movement.

'That is for Abaddon to decide, and Abaddon has made his rules very clear. Contenders are fair game. And *all* moderns are to fight in the arena. No exceptions.'

Cade gritted his teeth. Ishak's apathy he understood – the man had been born here. But Caesarion was from Earth.

Still, he had to bite his tongue. This man was his only ticket to freedom.

'Why?' he asked. 'Why must moderns fight?'

Caesarion turned to him and looked Cade over with a careful eye.

'Abaddon loved Rome. The political intrigue, the civil wars, the invasions. But most of all, the gladiatorial bouts. So, when he helped create New Rome, he had two desires. One, that the culture here would not be sullied by modern ideals and technologies. And two, that the gladiatorial bouts would live on. Having moderns such as you fight helps cement those two ideals.'

The emperor grinned and gestured to the city below him.

'That the system also helps keep me in power is but a bonus. Human rights, freedom of press? None of my subjects will ever hear of it. And watching the gladiators fight is our empire's greatest pastime. It keeps the citizens happy, and the slaves sleep better knowing that there are others less

147

fortunate than they.'

Caesarion sighed.

'Although, that being said, Abaddon does *love* conflict. Should there ever be an uprising, he won't intervene. That is why I must be ever vigilant.'

Cade took the information in, trying to figure a way out of this mess.

'Why should I fight at all?' Cade asked. 'Why should we put on a show for you? I might as well jump off this balcony right now.'

Caesarion shook his head and smiled, as if he had heard it all before.

'Because it allows you to live another day, if you win. Only until the next bout, of course, but still . . . the survival instinct is a strong one.'

Cade knew it to be true. There was no way out of this. But then, there was no way out of Abaddon's game. And wasn't all this much the same, but on a smaller scale?

Only . . . there *was* a way out of Abaddon's game. He had almost forgotten, since it had felt like such a long shot. The game's rules stated that they could be returned home if they topped the leaderboard. That's what they needed now. A chance.

'You'll fight when the time comes,' Caesarion said, turning away from Cade and staring out at his empire once more. 'And I look forward to watching it.'

But Cade hardly heard him, his mind racing.

His mind flashed to a film he had watched with his father almost a dozen times. *Gladiator*. And the seeds of an idea formed.

'Survival is one thing,' Cade said, weighing each word with care. 'But the promise of freedom is a much greater motivator.'

Caesarion's eyebrows lifted.

'Oh?' he asked, turning his attention to Cade once more.

'The Romans knew this. They would grant freedom to gladiators that fought well.'

'Get to your point.'

'Why not make that a rule. An elimination tournament, with teams, so the crowd have someone to root for. Modern against modern, from different eras. The winners are granted their freedom . . .'

Cade stumbled, his mouth catching up with his train of thought.

'. . . And a ship. Let them sail back to where you found them. They'll die out there soon enough anyway, or be recaptured. Either way, they won't taint New Rome. Everyone will fight all the harder for it.'

Caesarion looked at Cade with clear interest.

'It is true that the games have been growing . . . stagnant,' the emperor said. 'I had been planning a grand spectacle to celebrate my third year of reign.'

He pondered Cade a moment longer, then clapped his hands again.

'I'm not sure if Abaddon would allow such a thing, but I shall think on it! For now, you must update me on the world. If you're from the twenty-first century, there is *much* to discuss.'

TWENTY-SIX

As it turned out, Caesarion already knew plenty about the modern world, not to mention world history. This was, in part, due to his tutor, an American from World War Two who had spent the past three years teaching Caesarion English. The man had been put to death in the arena, once Caesarion had bored of him.

That, however, was not the only reason the emperor was so knowledgable. The library that took up most of the chamber's space had begun with the so-called 'Lost Library of Ivan the Terrible', containing rare books salvaged from the burning libraries of Alexandria and Constantinople.

It had been a gift from Abaddon to New Rome's emperors, and one supplemented with more books as new captives were brought back by the slavers. Cade had been taken aback to find half a dozen *Harry Potter* books neatly slotted in beside a script for a Shakespeare play he had never heard of: *Cardenio*. Cade also had to stifle a chuckle when he spotted the well-thumbed copy of *Fifty Shades of Grey* by the emperor's bedside.

It was hard for Cade to conflate the eager, excitable young man with an iron-fisted emperor who would condemn him and his friends to death.

Caesarion wanted to know what it *felt* like to be a modern person. Unlike Ishak, he wasn't interrogating Cade for the broad strokes of what the modern world was, or potentially useful technologies or weapons.

Instead, Cade found himself trying to explain internet memes and Twitter . . . to the son of Julius Caesar. It was, in a word, madness. Cade wanted to burst out laughing and scream at the same time. And all the while, at the back of his mind, he waited for Caesarion's decision.

Whether they would be given a chance to survive.

It happened when Cade was halfway through explaining smartphones. Caesarion's head twitched, and a finger was held up to silence Cade.

Caesarion cocked his ear, listening to something only he could hear. Cade stood there, his throat dry from talking, exhausted from the frantic beat of his heart, and the buzz of anxiety that had not left him since Abaddon had broken his silence.

Abaddon.

Then Cade knew. Caesarion had not lost his mind. Abaddon was speaking to him. Cade would not be surprised if an invisible Codex was hovering beside the emperor's ear at that very moment.

Cade waited in the dim light of the late afternoon sun, and watched as the first, loincloth-clad servants pattered about the chamber's edges, lighting candles in embrasures.

It felt like a long time. So long that the emperor walked away from him, to sit at the edge of his bed. Cade swayed in the shadows, trying to listen in. But he only managed to overhear one phrase.

'*Sic domine.*'

Yes, master.

Whatever their fate would be, Abaddon would have a hand in it.

'Cade.'

Caesarion's voice brought him stumbling closer.

'I will grant your request,' the emperor said, a smile upon his face. 'Teams of five, to accommodate your friends, and I'll have the deaf legionary reclassified as a modern. The winners shall be returned to the jungle. Now, your favour?'

Cade stared. He'd thought that giving them a chance at freedom would be the favour.

'Some kind of advantage in the tournament . . . perhaps better weapons?'

Caesarion shook his head.

'Abaddon won't allow it – from this point forward, I must remain impartial in the tournament itself. In fact, he has asked I do not speak to you after today. Something else.'

Cade racked his brain. If he could not help their chances of winning Caesarion's game . . . perhaps he could better their chances of winning Abaddon's.

He had no doubt that upon their return to the jungle, it would be hard enough to get back to the Keep unscathed, let alone find the Polish king's armour. Even if their chances of surviving the Colosseum were slim . . . he had to think of the bigger picture.

'We get to choose ten remnants from this room to take with us,' Cade said, eyeing the cabinets. 'And the weapons Ishak took from us. Money to buy items for our return journey. And to be returned to our Keep, not just abandoned on the shore somewhere.'

Caesarion considered this for a moment.

'*One* remnant,' he said. 'And I'll return your weapons too. But supplies will be provided for you; I won't have you shopping our streets, flaunting your freedom. As for your delivery to your Keep . . .'

He tapped his chin, musing on it.

'Done.'

Caesarion extended a hand, and Cade shook it. It was a strange formality, considering the man had practically signed Cade's death warrant.

Then, as if Cade had ceased to exist, Caesarion turned his back on him. A heavy hand grasped Cade's shoulder, and he was escorted back towards the double doors by the bodyguard.

As the doors slammed behind him, the assessor stood up from a nearby chair.

'Finally,' he sighed, waving the guards aside. 'Come along. Your buyer is waiting.'

TWENTY-SEVEN

Cade hadn't been sure what to expect as they descended the steps. His friends were gone, and the assessor led him to the great causeway in front of the palace, flanked by the same guards who had accompanied them there.

A carriage awaited him, and Cade was surprised to see horses at the front. They were the first *normal* animals he had seen, and it was almost comforting. He was ordered into a cage in the back, where he found himself alone in a cramped windowless space.

'Ishak will be pleased,' the assessor said through the bars. 'You commanded a high price, what with the grand games the emperor has been planning, and your *modernity*.'

'Where are my friends?' Cade asked, as politely as he could force himself to be.

'You'll see them soon enough.' The assessor went to close the door, then stopped and returned his gaze to Cade. 'A word of advice,' he said. 'I'm feeling in a generous mood, since I didn't have to drag you kicking and screaming through the palace today, and my cut of your sale was a good one.'

Cade attempted an encouraging smile, which was not returned.

'You are going to a *ludus*. There's only one trainer there worth their salt. Choose Tsuru, if you are given a choice at all.'

'Thank you,' Cade said.

The assessor shrugged.

'I'll put a few coins on you winning your bouts. Try not to die.'

And with that, the door was slammed shut.

The carriage jerked as the driver cracked his whip, leaving Cade alone with his thoughts. It was perhaps the first time in a while that Cade had any respite, and he felt like sleeping, stained and dirty though the splintered boards of the carriage floor were. But first, he had to try something.

'Codex?' Cade asked.

'*Yes, Cade.*'

The drone materialised a few inches from his face, and Cade nearly jumped out of his skin.

33:22:27:04
33:22:27:03
33:22:27:02

'Don't do that!' he hissed.

'*Do what?*' the Codex asked in its bored voice.

'Never mind,' Cade sighed, rubbing his eyes. 'I want to speak to Abaddon.'

Silence. Then:

'*Abaddon will not speak to you.*'

Cade groaned aloud. 'So he'll speak to the emperor, but not me?'

'*Yes.*'

'Does he not realise he might never get to watch me fight that . . . monster if we don't win this tournament? That won't be much fun for him.'

'*Should the five of you die here, Abaddon will choose a new champion from the three contenders remaining at the Keep. That will be entertainment enough. Do not think yourself special.*'

Cade hissed between his teeth, the image of one of the twins or Yoshi being attacked by that alien monster filling him with rage.

But he supposed this was all part of the wider game that Abaddon had designed. The prehistoric animals, New Rome, the remnants. He couldn't expect Abaddon to bail him out just because he was losing.

Still. They had a chance now, however slim. The carriage juddered to a halt, and he heard shouting outside. The back doors of the carriage opened, and the cage's gate was unlocked by the sour-faced driver. He motioned for Cade to come out, and Cade did so, stumbling onto the ground on aching legs.

He was in a courtyard of sorts, with the gate they had come through behind him, and high walls studded with barred doors surrounding the rest. The balconies of two-storeyed buildings beyond the walls seemed to extend over the barrier, as if the residents would come out to get some fresh air above the barren sandpit.

It seemed a plain place for the balconies to look down upon, until he saw the flecks of blood staining the ground, and the wooden training dummies leaning against the walls.

He turned as the gates were slammed shut by a slave – that was obvious from the loincloth he wore, and the iron collar about his neck. He was hunched over, his back as crooked as any Cade had seen.

'Hello,' Cade said. 'Do you know where my friends are?'

The old man simply shook his head, clearly not understanding, and motioned for Cade to follow. Cade was surprised to find the slave had his own key, one that he used to open one of the myriad barred doors in the training ground's walls and beckoned Cade through.

By now, the sun had almost set, but there were no candles lit. Cade stumbled through a darkened corridor until he turned into a low-ceilinged room, where a bearded man wearing a leather apron stood, and another sat behind him. The room was dominated by a single wooden table, one with leather cuffs at the four corners where a person's limbs might be secured.

Cade's eyes widened with fear as he saw metal tools, blades and saws arrayed on a cloth at the table's head.

The leather-aproned man raised his hands with a friendly smile when Cade backed away, even as the door was closed behind him and Cade's shoulders stopped against solid wood.

The man pointed to himself. '*Medicus*,' he said in Latin. Doctor.

Cade relaxed at the word. He had let his paranoia get the better of him.

157

Cade perched on the edge of the table, trying to ignore the crusted blood on the medical tools and the table itself. He only hoped that the people treated here had been injured from the Colosseum bouts, and not from the training school.

For the second time, Cade found his mouth opened and examined, and now his limbs lifted, squeezed and measured. Lacking much else to do, Cade allowed his eyes to stray to the onlooker.

A muscled man with olive skin and enough scars to rival Frankenstein was watching him with an incisive gaze, and Cade felt as if his very soul was on display. The man bore the same iron collar that the other slaves of this world did.

As Cade caught his eye, the man stood, spat on the sawdust-covered ground, and walked on. Clearly, Cade had not impressed him . . . though given his half-starved state, Cade wasn't surprised. The door slammed shut behind him as he left, and the doctor gave Cade a sympathetic grimace.

'*Doctor*,' he said, rolling his eyes in the man's direction.

For a moment Cade was confused, thinking the word meant that the man was another doctor. But then he remembered that the word in fact meant 'instructor', or 'trainer'. Quintus had used it to describe himself, when they had continued their slingshot training back at the Keep.

A slap to his shoulder told Cade it was time to move on, and he was pointed to the door, where the old man waited for him. He was led through the dark corridors by the light of a single candle. Frescoes of battles fought upon the bloodied sands of the Colosseum flashed by, but the man moved deceptively fast, too fast for Cade to catch more than glimpses of the scenes depicted there.

To his surprise, it was not just people fighting, but creatures as well. Teeth, claws, scales, feathers.

Cade knew now that these games would not be as straightforward as they seemed. In some ways, it made him feel relieved; he might not have to kill another human being to progress in the game.

They stopped abruptly, where the metal lattice of prison bars lay on the left and right side of a long corridor. Even by the light of the candle, he could see the long-haired women on the left side, and the bearded faces of men on the right. All seemed to be sleeping or talking quietly among themselves, and none reacted to his arrival.

There couldn't have been more than twenty people here, and he could see Amber and Grace curled up together on a straw mattress nearest to the door, asleep. Relief at the sight of them almost brought him to his knees. He hadn't been sure if the assessor had been lying about seeing them soon.

Two guards patrolled the centre aisle, both wearing simple chitons and armed with little more than clubs. Both bore the iron collars of slaves.

Cade was ushered through the barred door in the men's section, and was relieved to see Quintus and Scott too, the pair sleeping on a straw mattress of their own.

Other people were there, but Cade did not have the energy to go snooping through the gloom to find out more about them. Instead, he headed for the nearest free space on the mattress-strewn floor.

Another occupant shared the bedding, but Cade found

room enough to curl up atop it. He caught a glimpse of the sleeping form opposite him as he closed his eyes.

They flew open again, Cade's heart pounding with shock as he recognised the uniform the figure wore.

It was the same as his own.

He took in the boy who shared his bed. His hair was now long and lank, and patchy fuzz sprouted on his face. But his bedfellow's identity was unmistakable.

There, sleeping but a few inches away from him . . . was Finch.

TWENTY-EIGHT

Cade woke to the sound of birdsong. Or pterosaur-song anyway. The little furball that was Zeeb had curled up against his chest in the night, perhaps crawling from Scott's pocket, and now the tiny beast chirped plaintively as if to ask Cade for a morsel of fig.

'Awake then, I see.' Finch's voice drifted from the shadows, and Cade sat up to see the boy propped against the wall, watching him.

The others were still asleep, and the sound of snores permeated the room. There was no way of telling what time it was, though some light filtered through the doors at the end of the central corridor.

Cade wanted little more than to go back to sleep, but the sound of that coward's voice replaced his exhaustion with a dull anger.

'Wondered what happened to you,' Cade muttered. 'Shame. Thought you'd be dead by now.'

Finch shrugged and looked at his fingernails.

'Will be soon enough,' he said. 'Only reason I'm not is they're saving me for the big games coming up. These guys too.'

He motioned at the sleeping forms behind him. Now that Cade's eyes had adjusted to the gloom, he could make out more captives.

'Are they . . . modern?' Cade asked, curiosity getting the better of him.

'If you can call the 1920s modern,' Finch replied.

Cade eyed the sailor-style uniforms the boys wore. There were roughly a dozen of them all around his age.

'Codex?' Cade muttered. 'Who are they?'

The Codex's voice was quiet, barely a whisper in his ear.

'*The* København *was a Danish trading ship that disappeared on December 22nd, 1928, along with its twenty-six crew and forty-five cadets.*'

'There were maybe seventy of 'em when I got here,' Finch said, his eyes glazing over in what looked like fear. 'That's all that's left. The adults volunteered to fight first.'

'They die in the Colosseum?' Cade asked.

Finch nodded.

'Don't know how. They just never came back.'

Cade had no response to that.

'So you left the Keep too, then?' Finch asked. 'Decided not to play their game?'

'We fought,' Cade snapped. 'And won. No thanks to you. People died, because we didn't have the fuel from that boat. We could have lit the vipers on fire with that diesel. Gobbler. Jim. Spex. Eric.'

Finch shrugged again.

'Guess I made the right call. You guys still ended up here and the world's still doomed.'

Cade resisted the urge to shout, forcing his anger down in a tight ball at the pit of his stomach.

'My conscience is clean,' he replied instead, through gritted teeth. 'I can't say the same for you.'

Cade turned away and looked at Zeeb perched in the hollow of his palms. The little creature stretched and yawned, before digging its claws into the crevice of Cade's fingers, like a squirrel searching for grubs among the bark.

It was strange, but watching the little creature go about its business, oblivious to the new environment it had been transported to, relaxed Cade. He only wished he could live in the same blissful ignorance.

The sound of footsteps echoed, disturbing Cade from his thoughts. One of their enslaved guards had arrived on the scene, and now he ran his cudgel along the prison bars, the clanging waking the others.

'Come!' the man bellowed, as the door rattled open. The guard entered the space, raising his weapon at any who didn't move fast enough. Cade stowed Zeeb in the corner of the cell before leaving, hoping the little creature would stay put.

Cade was trooped down the corridor with the rest of the bleary-eyed captives, stumbling past Amber and Grace but unable to greet them as he was forced to run on by more shouting guards.

Within minutes, he was out in the morning sun, and shunted into a rough line along with the others. The guards shoved them into groups of five, with Cade, Grace, Amber, Quintus and Scott together.

Blinking in the new light, Cade found himself faced with a row of those same guards, and behind them, a woman stood on the balcony overhanging the wall, looking down upon them.

She was middle-aged and dressed in fine clothing. Though she was beautiful, with raven hair and delicate features, there was a cold superiority to her gaze that made Cade uneasy.

A slave girl appeared beside her, crouched in deference as she offered a jug of wine. The woman waved her away, barely giving the girl a second glance.

The courtyard was silent but for the breathing of those around him. After a few moments, four more people joined the woman on the balcony, pushing their way through the beaded curtains behind her. All were slaves, as indicated by the collars around their necks.

Cade recognised the scarred man among the new arrivals. Another, an Asian lady who seemed so old, Cade could hardly believe she was standing unaided. The remaining two were blonde, muscled men, whose long beards and hair made them hard to tell apart. One of them stepped forward.

'Bow to your *domina*,' he bellowed.

As one, the Danes and Finch bowed, and Cade followed their example.

'This morning, the emperor sent instructions to all the *ludi* in New Rome. The grand games we have been waiting for will happen less than a month from now. They will be in the form of a tournament, where teams of five will be pitted

164

against each other in three bouts over three days. And in his generosity, he will grant the ultimate victors their freedom.'

A month.

Even if they survived the Tournament, that gave them less than a week to return to the Keep. Cade only hoped it would be enough.

The man let his finger sweep from group to group.

'Your teams have been selected according to your time and place of origin, with some allowances for the sake of simplicity. Those who you have been grouped with *shall* be your partners for the remainder of the tournament.'

He motioned at the men and women on either side of him.

'The rules of the tournament are to be kept secret from us, but we do know each bout will be different. It leaves us little time to prepare you, but *domina* Julia has graciously hired new *doctores* to train you.'

Domina. Mistress.

So, this well-dressed woman, the *domina*, was their owner too. As he considered that, the trainer pointed towards one of the groups arrayed in the courtyard.

'You. I shall train you.'

Cade turned slowly and noted the strength of their competition. The other three groups were mostly made up of the Danes of the *København* – strapping sailors used to the rigours of the sea, much like their Viking ancestors would have been. A few girls were scattered among them, European in appearance, but wearing clothing made of sack-cloth that revealed nothing of their origins.

Compared to Cade and the others, skinny from weeks of malnutrition and clad in their dirty, ragged clothing, the other groups seemed a far better option. Much like a high-school football game, Cade and his friends were going to be picked last.

Tsuru could be any one of the trainers. The name sounded vaguely Asiatic, but surely the old woman he had seen up there could not be a trainer?

Yet, as the man stepped back, the wizened lady came forward, her walking stick clicking on the boards. Had it been some kind of trick? Did the assessor want them to lose? Perhaps he would bet *against* them.

The woman's eyes roved across the groups, and Cade saw those around him looking at their feet, as if wishing not to be picked. Cade saw his chance then.

He stepped forward, earning a snarl of anger from the nearest guard. As a truncheon slammed into his stomach, Cade managed to shout a single word.

'Tsuru!'

He choked as the wind gusted out of him, falling to his knees. Above, the old woman glanced at him with a measured look, and Cade met her gaze with his own, as the truncheon fell a second time, thudding into the meat of his back.

Still, he held her gaze. A twitch from the woman's hand stopped the guard from hitting him again, and she watched a moment longer as Cade wheezed.

Then, with a simple nod and a flicked finger, her selection was made. The scarred man stepped forward, grinning as he selected the group Finch was in.

Cade shuffled back, still on his knees, and Quintus lifted him to his feet.

It was done. The die was cast, in the words of Caesarion's father. For better or worse . . . Tsuru would be their trainer.

TWENTY-NINE

The main courtyard was one of several in the complex that made up the training school. It seemed that the place must have been teeming with gladiators once, as Cade and the others were led past empty cells and into a smaller sandpit adjacent to their own.

Here, the five friends were watched by the guard who had accompanied them. Cade, still clutching his belly from the earlier blow, decided to risk a word.

'I thought I'd lost you guys,' he said in a low voice.

The guard seemed not to react.

'*You* thought you'd lost *us*?' Scott said, giving him a swift hug. 'You're the one who keeps disappearing.'

The boy suddenly stepped back, as if he had remembered something.

'Why did you do that?' he demanded. 'Pick the old lady? The other guys looked way better.'

'The assessor told me she was the best,' Cade said.

'And you trusted him?' Grace snapped. 'You think that

168

evil git has our best interests in mind?'

'He said he'd place a bet on us . . .' Cade muttered, suddenly unsure of himself.

'What's to say he's not betting against us, setting us up to lose?' Amber asked, a little more gently than the others. But only a little.

Cade stuttered. The thought had not occurred to him.

'You made this decision without us, Cade,' Amber said. 'We're here too.'

'I'm sorry,' Cade said. 'It all happened so fast. I didn't ask to be the one that makes decisions. Trust me.'

Amber's look softened.

'It's done now,' she said. 'Just . . . try to keep us in mind next time.'

But he *had*. Every choice he made weighed heavy on his soul. But he didn't begrudge their frustration. He knew what it felt like to have his fate decided by others. Perhaps more than most.

'Well, even if that was a mistake, I *did* convince the emperor to give us a chance at freedom. This tournament and its reward . . . it was my idea. He'll even give us a remnant if we win.'

'You spoke to the emperor?' Scott asked, incredulous.

'It's a long story,' Cade sighed. 'I'll fill you in later.'

'You really think they'll let us go?' Amber asked.

'He said he would announce it to the people. He'd look bad if he went back on his word. But what about you? What did I miss?'

'Not much,' Amber snorted. 'The assessor went to talk to

that Julia lady, after he dropped you off with the emperor. She was queuing with those other rich nobs. Must have sold us to her then and there.'

She glared in the direction they'd come from, as if she could see their *domina* through the walls.

'They took us straight to the cells when we got here. You know the rest.'

Now Grace spoke. 'The other girls, they're called . . .' She furrowed her brow, trying to remember. 'Mary Seward and Eliza Carter were the ones still awake . . . the others didn't talk much. They all got taken in the late 1800s. They're a bit younger than us, and they're terrified.'

'What about Finch?' Cade asked.

'The bastard got caught almost as soon as he left us,' Scott answered, 'or so he says. That same group that caught you and the girls, by the sounds of it. They left the *Witchcraft* beached on the river near the rapids – seems modern technology is banned here too.'

Cade made a note of that information. It seemed a distant hope, but if they could recover the *Witchcraft*, their future hunts for remnants in Abaddon's game would be a lot easier. It would certainly allow them to outrun any slavers they came across in the jungle.

'Finch did say something interesting.' Scott continued. 'He overheard there's been a lot more captures in the jungle lately. Usually it's adults . . . warriors, you know? But more recently, it's been teenagers, and almost all of them after the 1750 threshold. It's true, right?'

He motioned at Grace and Amber. 'You lot. The Danes

are mostly teens. These Victorian-era girls. All dumped in the jungle this last month. Plus he saw lots of teenagers in the other training schools. Plenty of First World War soldiers – Brits, Americans, Germans. The ones who lied about their age to fight. Even some Civil War guys.'

Cade pondered this revelation, feeling a hint of regret. If they'd only gone out into the jungle earlier, instead of wasting away in the Keep, they might have found some of these people.

'It's Abaddon,' he said, forcing down his frustration. 'He's either been putting them in the jungle for *us* to find . . . or for Caesarion's games. Maybe both.'

'Teenagers?' Quintus asked, the word new to him.

'Young people,' Cade explained.

'Why young people?'

Cade thought on it. 'He probably didn't want experienced warriors fighting, either in Caesarion's grand games, or alongside us if we recruited them as contenders.'

'What do you mean?' Scott asked.

'These teenagers – even if they *were* soldiers, they'll not have seen much action yet. For some reason, he wants young amateurs to fight.'

'Seems to me we've seen more action than most of these guys,' Amber sniffed. 'We *did* fight off over a hundred vipers.'

Cade forced a smile.

'That's true,' he said. 'But we don't know what we'll face in the Colosseum. We have to be ready for anything.'

'That is correct,' an unfamiliar voice said from the darkness.

171

There was a tapping of wood on stone, and the hunched figure of Tsuru shuffled into view, her hands almost as gnarled as the walking stick she leaned upon.

Scott shot a look at Cade and shook his head.

A hissed order sent the guard away, and soon they were alone in the sand-strewn courtyard.

'You knew my name,' she demanded, and despite her seeming frailty, there was a command to her tone that brooked no nonsense. 'How?'

Cade lowered his head respectfully.

'One of the assessors said you were the best trainer that ever lived,' he said, embellishing the assessor's words to curry favour. 'We wanted to train under you.'

Tsuru stared at him for a moment, then let out a dry laugh.

'That may have been true, once,' she said, 'But I *am* the most experienced, of that you can be sure. I've trained more gladiators than I can remember . . . though that is not saying much these days.'

She laughed again, until her breathing became choked and it turned into a hacking cough.

Cade kept his head down, trying to avoid the glares from his friends.

'How long have you been here?' Amber asked, once the coughing fit had stopped. 'You don't look much like a fighter.'

Tsuru's eyes flicked to her, and Cade saw approval there at Amber's forthrightness.

'I arrived here at the age of eighteen, and they made me a serving girl to our *domina*'s mother.'

She motioned behind her with a wizened finger.

'I escaped, but this island is a prison in itself. I was caught within the week. And *domini* love to put their runaway slaves to death in the Colosseum, as punishment . . . and as a lesson to the others that serve them.'

Her eyes hardened at the memory.

'They underestimated me. A waif of a girl, to be slaughtered like a lamb by their trainee gladiators, for the spectacle of it. Two of them, moderns from your great war. Only, it was I who did the slaughtering that day.'

She shook her head. 'My *domina* took me back, impressed by my martial prowess. And I have been a trainer at this *ludus* ever since.'

Cade stared at her, surprised.

'But how?' he asked. 'It was two against one.'

Tsuru cracked a smile, her face creasing up.

'Appearances can be deceiving. As, it seems, are yours.' She pointed at Quintus, gesturing at his clothing. 'You, boy. Are you the deaf legionary who will take part in the bouts?'

Quintus nodded.

'I am,' he said in Latin.

'It is not unusual,' she said, speaking in English for everyone's benefit. 'Sometimes they dress up criminals and runaways to mix them in with the moderns, bolster the numbers for the grander bouts. The other *ludi* already know of you, unfortunately.'

Quintus shrugged. Tsuru rubbed her chin, where Cade could see a few white hairs sprouting. She seemed on the verge of an idea.

'As a non-modern, you'll be allowed to leave the *ludus*, do errands with me,' Tsuru said. 'And . . .'

She grimaced, then snapped her fingers.

'Which of you moderns speaks the best Latin here?'

The group exchanged glances, and Cade raised his hand.

'You,' she said, pointing at Cade. 'You will dress as the Roman, and our competitors will believe you deaf and unable to speak English when we visit them. They might speak with wagging tongues in your presence, thinking you cannot hear it. Quintus shall stay behind.'

'Isn't that illegal?' Amber asked.

Tsuru smiled.

'They have already done their worst,' she said. 'What is another crime when you're to be put to death anyway? And I don't have long left in this world. They can do what they want with me, if we're caught.'

She raised an eyebrow at Cade, waiting for his answer. He looked to Quintus, who inclined his head after a moment's thought. Cade nodded reluctantly, though he thought Quintus's lip-reading ability would be a better advantage. Not to mention the fact that Quintus's English was better than Cade's Latin.

But at the same time, the Codex followed Cade, and it could translate any language, as far as he knew. That alone made the switch worth the danger. They were playing for keeps now. He'd risk anything if it gave them a better chance of winning.

'Good,' Tsuru said.

Giving a deep sigh, she stepped forward.

'You have a great opportunity in front of you,' she said. 'One that I was never offered. If you put your trust in me, I promise I will do all I can to help you survive.'

There was a silence as Cade looked to his friends. But none returned his gaze. Finally, Amber spoke.

'We will,' she said.

Tsuru nodded. Then, she snapped her fingers at Cade and Quintus.

'Clothes off,' she said. 'The sooner you make the switch, the better.'

THIRTY

Training, as it turned out, could not begin until Tsuru had selected their weapons and food. Both of which required leaving the grounds to acquire them. Each trainer was provided with a stipend to rent weapons, armour and clothing, and buy the food for their charges.

Tsuru explained this to Cade while a metal collar was locked around his neck at the iron gates, affixed in place by the same slave who had greeted him last night. The old man's raised eyebrows told Cade he was well aware of their subterfuge, but fortunately he had the good sense to remain silent, even under the suspicious gaze of the nearby guards.

Now appropriately attired, and borrowing some sandals from a pile near the doorway, Cade followed Tsuru onto the cobbled streets of New Rome. Cade was amazed that he was allowed to walk so freely, but as the people who thronged the city came into view, he saw more iron collars as slaves scampered to and fro, or followed in the wake of their better-dressed owners.

The island was the prison, and one too small for a slave to scratch out an existence in the countryside if they *did* run away. It was no wonder that Caesarion was so paranoid about a rebellion – in a world where escape was impossible, overthrowing their masters was the only chance these slaves had at freedom.

Numerous guards patrolled the streets, marching in groups of six, their eyes scanning the crowds for suspicious behaviour. Tsuru grasped Cade's arm and pressed him onwards, into the broad paved rectangle of the city's forum.

Cade had not seen much of New Rome beyond the slave markets and palace, and now he caught his first glimpse of normal life in this strange city. What struck him first was the clothing.

Never had he seen such a mishmash of styles, colours and garments. From saris to gowns, tartans to animal furs, the range was astounding. The white lace neck-ruffs of Renaissance Europe seemed to be a current trend, and Cade even saw crotch-accentuating codpieces among the men.

In a world of haves and have-nots, it seemed fashion was the primary display of wealth here; a great many of the shops that bordered the square were focused on clothing, jewellery and perfumes. In sharp contrast, the lowliest of slaves wore loincloths, and the handservants wore tunics and other simple garb.

Few paid heed to the old lady at Cade's side, and he found himself stepping in front of her to allow them passage through the crowds. Thankfully, they soon passed through the forum and on to the food district.

Here, slaves made the morning rounds for their masters to restock their larders. Stalls lined the way, crammed among the cobbled streets. The food, as with the clothing, took Cade's breath away.

It was primitive – what fruit had once looked like. On Earth, selective cultivation had turned bananas seedless, made thin purple carrots thick and orange, and grown corn a thousand times larger.

So it was that Cade hardly recognised the specimens on display, and even those he did looked different. A watermelon, split in two to tempt passers-by, looked much the same in its exterior, but the inside was mostly white and full of large seeds, with only pockets of edible red flesh.

Tubers, roots and berries made up most of the display, a riot of colour and scents. But as they walked deeper, the sweet scent of fruit was replaced by the bloody odour of meat, and the stink of fish.

And what meats. He didn't know which beasts had once owned claw-tipped haunches that hung from the racks, but it seemed that the New Romans had their own form of prehistoric cattle here, only of the reptilian kind. These Tsuru ignored, and Cade wondered which stall she was headed for.

'Wonder what those were?' he whispered under his breath.

To his surprise, a quiet voice whispered a response in his ear.

'Tethyshadros, *a duck-billed Hadrosaur that lived eighty-five million years ago,*' the Codex said.

They continued to where the marine life of their new world was also up for grabs. Dominating the space was a sperm-whale-sized fish, hanging from a makeshift crane at an intersection. It looked for all the world like a tuna, but as he watched the sellers carving steaming hunks of flesh from its carcass, the Codex told him it was called *Leedsichthys*.

Further down, he saw a six-foot-long shrimp, *Aegirocassis*, laying alongside their smaller trilobite cousins that looked like enormous woodlice. Cade couldn't help but be thankful that Tsuru marched by these as well; despite his hunger, they looked as unappetising as anything he'd ever seen.

It was down a side street, where the stench was far worse and the old meat's edges greyed and curled that, to Cade's disappointment, Tsuru finally came to a stop. Here, the offal that nobody else wanted seemed to be the most common – giant gizzards, intestines and other unspeakable organs.

'Dominic!' Tsuru called out.

She released Cade's arm and embraced a man almost as old as she was.

They spoke in Latin. Too fast for him to understand more than a few words.

'Codex,' Cade muttered. 'Translate.'

Immediately, their conversation was relayed into Cade's ear in perfect, if monotone, English.

'. . . *come, you wily dog, won't you do a favour for an old friend?*' Tsuru said.

'*I couldn't possibly say,*' Dominic replied, though he smiled at her to show he was open for convincing. '*It's more than my life's worth.*'

Tsuru stepped closer and planted a kiss on the old man's cheek, and to Cade's surprise, Dominic blushed crimson.

'*For old time's sake?*' Tsuru asked, taking Dominic's hand and pressing a gold coin there. '*Your life is worth much to me, but I'm willing to pay the balance.*'

The old man stared at her, and Cade saw now that there was a history there. A romance, or something close to it. Dominic relented, and he pulled his hand away.

'*You take advantage of me, you sly creature,*' Dominic said. '*If you buy from me this month, I'll tell you.*'

'*I only ever buy from you, my dear,*' Tsuru purred. '*Why, your meats are the finest of the whole market.*'

Cade could hardly believe she kept a straight face, even as the flies buzzed about the dangling guts above them.

'*Fine, fine,*' Dominic said. '*But not a word to anyone.*'

Tsuru placed a finger to her lips and nodded.

'*The Colosseum has bought all of my meats and more besides,*' Dominic said. '*They're keeping something big in there; I've almost run dry. I know of at least a couple of – word unknown – likely for the first round as they're slowly starving those ones. There may be more I've not heard of.*'

Cade cursed under his breath. The unknown word must be a new term that had developed in New Rome, likely the one for prehistoric animals. Still, Tsuru seemed pleased enough, rattling off an order of meat to Dominic and then embracing him a second time.

'*Until next time, Dominic my dear,*' Tsuru called, as she took Cade's arm once more.

Then they were moving on, back through the markets.

'So?' Cade asked, once they were out of earshot.

Tsuru glanced up at him, deep in thought.

180

'Dominic buys up the meat from other vendors as it begins to rot, and sells it to the Colosseum,' Tsuru said. 'The animals will eat anything, and in large quantities. Even for a very low price, he still turns a small profit.'

She tugged Cade away from the food markets, and suddenly the streets were filled with soldiers. Far more than anywhere else, Cade noticed.

'The game masters at the Colosseum keep the specifics of the upcoming bouts a secret, especially the beasts they've captured for the gladiators to fight. But Dominic . . . well, he hears things when he delivers his meat.'

She grinned at Cade.

'He's an old flame. Isn't that what you say? So, he tells me what he hears, and I pay him for the privilege.'

Cade shook his head. She *was* smart. Experience certainly had its advantages. Tsuru knew all the tricks.

'How does it help us, to know the beasts we will fight?' Cade asked.

They turned another corner, and Cade's ears were filled with the clang of metal, and his nostrils the acrid stench of smoke. Now he knew why this place was so well guarded.

Here were blacksmiths, sweating over their forges in orange-lit rooms. Vendors hawked their wares, gesturing at racks of swords, shields and spears, burnished bright.

'Because now I know how to train you, and which weapons you shall use,' Tsuru said.

THIRTY-ONE

The shop Tsuru chose was dark and dusty. Cade had been a little disappointed when they'd walked past the racks of shining weapons outside, but these all bore the insignia of New Rome, perhaps reserved only for New Rome's imperial soldiers.

He imagined that there were only two other markets for weapons here: slavers . . . and gladiators. The armoured men who had captured him and the girls months before bore armour and weapons that had likely been sold in this very shop. He only hoped that gladiators were afforded the right to use weapons of similar quality.

It was no wonder there were scores of soldiers patrolling this single street. If the slaves were to revolt, this was where they would come first to arm themselves.

'Tsuru,' called a voice, distracting Cade from his thoughts.

A girl emerged from the shadows, and to Cade's surprise, she too had an iron collar around her neck.

'My *dominus* is away,' the girl said, Cade catching the

Latin before muttering for the Codex to translate once more. *'Can I help you with anything?'*

'Take my arm, Camila,' Tsuru replied, holding out her wrist. *'Help an old lady inspect your wares.'*

Cade handed her off to Camila, and the girl helped Tsuru walk down the racks of weapons on either side of the shop. They were depressingly empty.

'You did not need to walk all this way. Most of the trainers send a boy with their order,' Camila said.

'I like to see the weapons before I buy them,' Tsuru replied. *'I need to be sure there are no imperfections in the blades.'*

She paused at a rack of swords; they were gladiuses not unlike the rusted specimen that Quintus had once owned, before it was confiscated by Ishak.

'I'm afraid you are a little late,' Camila said, an apologetic expression on her face. *'Our stocks are low, most of the other trainers made their orders earlier this morning.'*

The girl pointed to a stack of papers on the counter at the shop's end. Tsuru simply sniffed in reply and motioned at a rack of spears further down.

'Show me those,' Tsuru said.

The girl dutifully led Tsuru down the shop, and Cade followed in their wake, mystified. Had Tsuru made a mistake, coming here in person? The other trainers had cleaned this place out while they were strolling through the food market. Why hadn't they come here first and gone to Dominic later?

If this was the only shop, they would have limited options to say the least. Still, Cade could only assume Tsuru had a reason for coming here last. Surely there was a method to her madness?

As Tsuru leaned closer, examining the weapons, she turned to Cade and spoke to him in perfect English.

'I need you to cause a distraction. Ten seconds at least.'

She accompanied her words with a shooing motion from her hands, as if Cade was walking too close behind them.

Cade stared, then backed away slowly. Camila smiled at him blankly, and Cade realised the girl couldn't understand. His heart pounded in his chest. Distract her? How? And more importantly, *why*?

It didn't matter. He had to trust Tsuru.

For a brief moment, he considered faking a heart attack, but it didn't seem enough. The girl would likely look around for help, or glance back at Tsuru to ask what was wrong with him.

No, he needed something . . . bigger. He needed props.

He spotted a suit of armour by the shop front. Still not sure what exactly he was going to do, he hurried closer as Camila hefted one of the spears and held it up for Tsuru's inspection.

Screw it. Here goes nothing.

He yelled, flailing his arms as if he were falling. Pinwheeling, he threw himself into the armour and sent it crashing to the floor. Sprawled among the fallen pieces, Cade snatched theatrically at the base of a weapons rack to haul himself up, yanking on it hard and sending the rack tumbling to the ground as well, its burden of shields with it.

A shriek was accompanied by a running Camila, who

looked down in horror at the splintered wood and scattered display, horror stamped across her features.

'*You no-good dungheap!*' The girl slapped at him with a fury Cade hadn't expected, and the Codex dutifully translated her curses in his ear. '*Clumsy blockhead! Lousy donkey! Scumbucket!*'

Cade covered his face at the onslaught, groaning more from the fall's impact on his cracked ribs and bruised limbs than the blows themselves.

Through his fingers, he watched Tsuru scamper over to the counter, walking stick abandoned. The wily old lady was as spry as a woman half her age!

She pored over the papers there with an intense look on her face.

But Camila was tiring, her hands hanging by her sides, and Cade saw Tsuru needed more time. So he did the only thing he could think of: he jibed Camila right back with the most ancient insult ever.

He held up a hand and extended his middle finger.

'Sorry,' he said, wincing at what he knew was to come.

A fresh scream of outrage elicited a pounding of fists and feet. This time, they actually did hurt, and Cade curled up in a ball as the blows rained down upon him.

'Sorry, sorry!' he groaned.

The blows only stopped when Tsuru called out to the girl.

'*Please, forgive the fool. The boy is a dunce, dropped on his head as a child, and deaf to boot. We will of course pay for the damages.*'

Camila gave Cade a final kick and trudged back to Tsuru.

'*He can clean up the mess too,*' Camila said.

Cade staggered to his feet, rubbing his head. He set about doing just that, tidying up as best he could.

'*Now,*' Tsuru said. '*About those weapons.*'

THIRTY-TWO

Tsuru spent what seemed an age testing the various weapons – checking their balance, their sharpness, their weight – and haggling for a lower price.

Even Cade, who had a vested interest in getting the very best weapons, grew impatient. Camila's master felt the same way when he returned to the store, and Tsuru started the whole process again.

Still, she seemed pleased enough, and Cade suspected the shop owner had given her a discount just to get her out of his store. However, as punishment for knocking over the armour, Cade had been sent outside, and missed most of the conversation.

Cade limped beside Tsuru as they returned to the *ludus*, refusing her proffered arm.

'You don't need my help,' Cade muttered. 'What was it you said? "Appearances can be deceiving"? You weren't joking.'

'Come now, don't mistreat an old lady,' Tsuru said. 'Did

I not just secure us a huge advantage?'

Cade relented and took her arm once more.

'Fine. But what exactly *did* you do?'

Tsuru chuckled to herself.

'Choosing your weapons is often a game of *mushi-ken*.'

Cade looked at her blankly.

'Frog, slug and snake?' Tsuru asked. 'Frog eats the slug, snake eats the frog, slug poisons the snake?'

'Oh,' Cade said. 'Like Rock, Paper, Scissors?'

Tsuru shrugged.

'By looking at what the other trainers have ordered at the other *ludi*, I can select the best counter to their choices – keeping in mind the beasts you will fight too.'

Understanding dawned on Cade.

'Right,' he said. 'But did they have what we needed? They said all the good stuff was gone.'

Tsuru grinned.

'They say that every time. It's a negotiation tactic. You think they don't collect the weapons from the dead after the bouts? Those chipped hand-me-downs are the ones they send first, they save the best weapons for their displays.'

Cade stared at her in amazement. Of course they kept back the best weapons. By showing up late, the store had saved her the trouble of sorting through all their stock herself.

'And what did you choose?' Cade asked, curiosity getting the better of him.

Tsuru smiled and gave a light shake of her head.

'You'll learn soon enough. For now, we have one last errand to run.'

Their walk through the city was faster this time, as Tsuru took him through the side-streets, where the shade was thickest and horse manure didn't cake the cobbles.

'Don't say a word from now on,' Tsuru said. 'And remember, *you don't speak English.*'

She said those final words in Latin, and Cade tore his gaze from the passers-by. They had stopped at a wrought iron gate, not unlike the one at Julia's *ludus*, with a similar sandy courtyard beyond. Within, Cade could see no gladiators. That made sense. Anyone could watch them training there, and report back to other *ludi*.

It was becoming more and more apparent that the game of gladiators was played a lot like poker, with cards hidden. And with more cheating, if Tsuru's behaviour was anything to go by.

'Why would they even let us in?' Cade asked.

'Because they invited me here,' Tsuru said. 'Julia's *ludus* is one of four, but this one is her main competitor – House Cornelius. Cornelius likes to invite her trainers down here, ply them with wine and food in case they let something slip, and Julia does the same to theirs. I usually don't bother attending. But this time, I thought I would try and turn their own tricks against them. Now, not another word.'

She rapped her knuckles on the gate, until a red-faced slave arrived. His eyebrows rose in surprise.

'*Tsuru,*' he said. '*I had not expected . . . let me fetch the trainers.*'

He hurried away, and Tsuru winked at Cade. They waited in silence a while longer, and within minutes a pair of trainers arrived on the scene, looking as flustered as the slave had been.

'*So, the great Tsuru finally graces us with her presence,*' said the first, a man built like a barrel, with a swarthy beard and bald head. '*I had thought you were too good to eat with us.*'

'*Come now, Atilius. Is that how you greet an honoured guest?*' Tsuru replied.

The man grunted and opened the gates, but not before he shot a long, pointed glance over his shoulder to make sure there were no clues for Tsuru to spot behind him.

'Will you take some wine with us?' the next asked, a woman with hair so pale it bordered on white.

'*Certainly, Lucretia,*' Tsuru said, as the woman barged Cade aside and took the old lady's arm.

At a loss, Cade trotted along behind them as Tsuru was led through some gates and into a parlour that was made up of four velvet benches, a skylight letting in the sunbeams from above. A pool filled with colourful fish lay off to the side, but Cade's eyes were instead drawn to the mosaics on the walls and floors.

They depicted gladiators in the arena, swords plunged into feathered, dinosaurian necks as claws disembowelled them. The blood, it seemed, was intended to add colour to the room as much as the fish did, but it only turned Cade's stomach.

Unsure where to stand, Cade leaned against the nearest wall as the three trainers settled onto their benches, and began digging into the fruit, bread, olive oil and salted meats that were arrayed on the table between them.

190

At the sight of it, Cade's stomach rumbled, and Lucretia turned to Cade with a cruel smile, before popping a grape into her mouth and chewing with exaggerated pleasure.

Cade did not like Lucretia.

THIRTY-THREE

Cade watched from his corner, contemplating asking for at least a glass of water to cool his parched throat. Surely they would not deny him that, being a fellow slave? But . . . he was supposed to be deaf, and his broken, accented Latin would give away that he was not a legionary.

So instead, he suffered in silence, listening to the invisible Codex as it translated in his ear.

'*We cannot stay for long,*' Atilius said. '*New recruits, you understand.*'

Tsuru groaned in sympathetic agreement.

'*I know what you mean,*' she said. '*I also have new recruits. And a sorry lot they are too.*'

Cade could not help but catch the glance between the other trainers, subtle though it was.

'*I have no hope of winning the tournament. My fighters are useless.*'

Tsuru waved at Cade dismissively.

'*Only that one has any experience – a legionary, though he's*

192

too young to have seen much action. Not to mention he's deaf as a post, and dumb to boot.'

'*Surely they cannot be* that *bad*,' Lucretia purred, pushing a chalice of wine closer to Tsuru.

The old lady took the drink and quaffed it with a nod of thanks.

'*I've given Julia's family my entire life*,' Tsuru said, her voice bitter. '*And this is how she repays me. The greatest tournament in the history of New Rome, and I'm given four weaklings, plus that dunce. All half-starved and sick from the jungle. And so modern that they've never known hardship. Soft as lambs, and as ready for slaughter.*'

The trio nodded sympathetically, taking in Cade's gaunt, filthy appearance at a glance. In truth, Cade was almost offended, her words hitting a little too close to home.

'*It's my age*,' Tsuru declared, waving a finger in the air. '*Julia thinks I've lost my touch.*'

She gulped down more wine.

'*I'm sure that's not true*,' Lucretia said. '*Perhaps the boy is more useful than you think? He will have some training.*'

Tsuru shook her head.

'*He can hardly understand my Latin, let alone the English I must teach these moderns in. How am I supposed to train them as a team if one can't even understand what I am saying?*'

She threw up her hands in disgust.

'*So I thought I'd come enjoy your food, since it doesn't matter anyway. I know you'll try to discover what I know in exchange, and that's your prerogative. I won't give away information about the other trainers at my* ludus. *But there you have it — I have four modern weaklings and a deaf, dumb idiot.'*

Tsuru sopped a hunk of bread in a bowl of yellow olive oil and stuffed it in her mouth. Cade's stomach rumbled again.

'How goes the training with you?' Tsuru asked, swallowing her mouthful after a moment's enraptured chewing.

'Well enough,' Atilius said. *'We must prepare them for any occasion, since the game masters are being so reticent.'*

He went silent, and Tsuru licked her lips before taking another sip of wine.

'And you, Lucretia?' she finally asked. *'Do you have any thoughts on what the game masters have in store?'*

Lucretia shook her head.

'Not an inkling,' she replied, with a sly smile.

Tsuru sighed.

'Well, I had thought you would be more open to conversation, now that my cards are on the table,' Tsuru said. *'But if you intend to be so guarded, I shall happily eat in silence.'*

'You know how it is, Tsuru,' Atilius said. *'You may have given up on your own fighters, but it might be that you are here to spy for the other trainers at your ludus.'*

Tsuru shrugged, and struggled to her feet.

'I have had my fill. That's all I wanted. Now, would you be a dear and point an old lady in the direction of the commode? My bladder is not what it once was.'

Lucretia snapped at Cade.

'Help your mistress to the toilet, fool boy.'

Cade could not help but blink at the woman's sudden outburst, and in that moment, he knew that Lucretia had seen through him.

'*No, no,*' Tsuru said, oblivious to Cade's failure. '*I'll do it myself. I'll not declare myself an invalid just yet.*'

'*It's that way,*' Lucretia said, keeping her eyes on Cade as she pointed.

Tsuru hobbled slowly from the room, and for a moment there was silence. Cade could feel the blood pumping through him, the pressure buzzing in his ears as Lucretia slipped from her bench and padded closer to him, stopping but a few inches from his face.

'Your belt is askew,' she whispered, in English this time.

Cade stared straight ahead, as he cursed inwardly in frustration. Tsuru's plan would never work now – they would not reveal a thing while he was in the room.

'Perhaps we should let the game masters know that this boy is lying?' she asked. 'Let them torture the truth out of him?'

She stared into Cade's eyes, and saw the fear there. Then she smiled and shrugged.

'But then, Tsuru might be given a new group entirely. And my spies . . . they tell me that she is telling the truth about how pathetic your team is.'

She chuckled and returned to her couch, a self-satisfied smile on her face.

'You'll die in the arena soon enough – I'll have my fighters target you first.'

Cade stilled an involuntary shudder and forced himself to maintain his absent stare.

'*Where is that damned crone?*' Atilius growled. '*I have things to do.*'

195

'*She's stalling, so that the boy can listen to us speak,*' Lucretia said. '*Enjoy the food. She will be a while.*'

So they did, munching on the food with gusto, until there was none left. Still, Tsuru did not come, and Lucretia let out a long sigh.

She glanced at Cade once more, then down the corridor before she spoke. Only this time, the Codex did not translate it. The language was different, and sounded vaguely Scandinavian. Certainly not English or Latin.

Cade muttered a single word under his breath.

'Translate.'

'*. . . if he understands?*' Atilius said, the Codex catching up mid-sentence.

'*Don't worry yourself. My spy tells me the boy is a modern American, I doubt he can understand Norse. Now, on the matter of spies, I have a trade of my own to propose.*'

'*I'm listening,*' Atilius said, raising a brow.

'*If you want access to my spy, and the information he will give me about the goings-on at Julia's* ludus, *you'll tell me exactly what* your *informant at the Colosseum has passed on.*'

Cade did his best to feign an expression of confusion. Atilius contemplated Lucretia for a moment longer. Finally, he relented.

'*The first bout will be a free-for-all. The twelve teams fighting at once. And they'll be releasing beasts into the arena at the same time. Once half of the teams are dead, the beasts will be withdrawn and the survivors shall proceed to the next round.*'

'*And what manner of beasts shall these be?*' Lucretia asked.

'*The larger kind,*' Atilius said, crossing his arms. '*That's all*

I'll say on the matter. Now tell me, what more has your spy learned at Julia's ludus?'

'*Fair enough,*' Lucretia said. '*As for Julia, beyond fielding a full third of the teams fighting in the tournament, she's—*'

But at that very moment, Tsuru chose to make her return, coughing hoarsely as she hobbled back down the passage. Cade resisted the urge to curse, clenching his fists instead. If only she'd waited a few seconds longer.

'*My apologies,*' Tsuru said, placing a hand on her belly with feigned embarrassment. '*All the rich food must not agree with me.*'

'*Not at all,*' Lucretia said, a fake smile plastered across her own face. '*Let us get you home, so that you can rest.*'

The two women's eyes met, veiled duplicity hidden just beneath the surface. Cade had no doubt of the animosity there. The young lioness, ready to take the place of the older matriarch.

And that rivalry would not play out here, but on the bloodied sands of the arena.

THIRTY-FOUR

Tsuru did not allow Cade to speak a single word until they were back at Julia's *ludus*, for fear of being followed by Lucretia's spies. But it *did* give Cade a chance to consider what to say.

The Codex needed to be kept secret. So instead, he suggested the trainers had become suspicious of him by the end of their conversation.

Now standing in the large courtyard, Tsuru groaned aloud when she learned that she had interrupted the two trainers from speaking further. But it was the knowledge that there was a spy at Julia's *ludus* that worried her the most.

'Think, boy,' Tsuru said. 'Did they give any clues as to who it is?'

Cade racked his brains. The spy had told them, specifically, that Cade was an American. Which meant that they knew he wasn't Quintus. Either they had guessed it from information given earlier, based on the colour of his skin or . . . it was someone who knew about the switch.

But only three people here beyond his friends and Tsuru had seen him leave in Quintus's clothing. Two of the guards at the entrance . . . and the old man.

'The old guy,' Cade jerked his head at the slave, who had just finished letting them in and removing Cade's iron collar. 'It had to be him, or one of the guards who let us out this morning.'

Tsuru bit her lip, and beckoned Cade closer.

'That's Strabo. The man has no tongue. *Domina* Julia had it cut it out a few years ago, when he made a comment about one of her daughters' dresses. It seems that rather than teach him a lesson in humility, it taught him one in disloyalty. He must be passing messages to Lucretia from the gate.'

Cade scoffed. 'Can you blame him? Are you loyal to Julia?'

Tsuru sniffed in response. 'There's no incentive to be disloyal. Disloyalty means death. And there's little reward in helping another *lanista*. But this man seeks revenge, which is reward enough in itself for him.'

Cade glanced at Strabo, who was ignoring them with such intensity that he was clearly paying them careful attention. Luckily, he was out of earshot.

To have your tongue cut out, for a few ill-advised words. Cade could understand the old man's actions. More than anything, he pitied Strabo.

'Do we *have* to tell Julia?' Cade asked. 'I can't exactly blame him.'

Tsuru gave him a weak smile. 'You've a more forgiving heart than most. But no, we will not tell Julia. Now, it is *our* advantage. Remember, though we train in Julia's *ludus*, the

199

other teams here are your competition too. Their weakness is our strength, and the more Lucretia knows about them, the more likely it is she leaves us alone and goes for them.'

Cade could see the logic in that.

'Moreover,' Tsuru continued, 'now that we know her source, we can poison that well. Feed her disinformation, should the need arise.'

It was a smart play, and Cade wished he had even a fraction of the strategic talent Tsuru had. Everything she had done today had increased their odds of survival, exponentially, and it wasn't even evening yet.

He felt relieved. Tsuru *was* the real deal. He hadn't let down his friends after all. The other trainers might have looked like veteran warriors, true. But if they weren't fighting alongside you on the battlefield, did that really matter? A smart strategist was far more valuable.

Tsuru's voice interrupted his thoughts. 'The weapons should have arrived by now, and the food for that matter. Let's go take a look at them.'

Tsuru took Cade's proffered arm and they returned to their smaller training ground, with Strabo following them as if intending to be of assistance. A hissed order from Tsuru sent him scurrying away.

Upon their arrival at the courtyard, the others leaped to their feet, embracing Cade with relief. Cade grinned back at them but ignored their questions, knowing there would be plenty of time to fill them in later.

Instead, his eyes settled on the boxes and sacks stacked behind them. To their credit, the others had not opened them

200

yet, and now Tsuru also sent away the guard who had been keeping watch over them.

Next, the old lady drew a handkerchief from her robes, and tore it in half with a strength that raised everyone's eyebrows. She handed a piece each to Grace and Scott, then pointed at the two doors that led into their small arena.

'Close those doors,' Tsuru ordered. 'And block the keyholes with these. Quickly now.'

Scott and Grace scurried to do her bidding.

'You and you,' she said, pointing at Quintus and Amber. 'Open those boxes and lay out the contents on the sand.'

Her voice cracked like a whip, and Cade sat on the ground, glad to finally rest.

'What are you doing, boy?' Tsuru asked. 'Lunch needs serving.'

She strode over to the sacks and examined each one.

'A handful of this, this and this in the bowls,' Tsuru snapped, prodding a sack in turn with her cane. 'Mix in some of the water too.'

Groaning, Cade got to his feet, earning a smack across his calves for the trouble.

'You think you've had a hard day?' she asked. 'It hasn't even started yet.'

Cade resisted the urge to mutter under his breath, and instead delved into each sack, helped along by his hunger and curiosity at what Tsuru would be feeding them.

To his surprise he found the first sack to contain oats. The second held what smelled and looked like dried seaweed, and the final one was filled to the brim with what looked like beef jerky . . . though he was pretty sure there wasn't a single cow on this island.

The meal, once mixed into a bowl, looked distinctly unappetising, especially when he added water to it. White mush, swimming in green flakes and rubbery nodules of brown meat. But he still spooned it into his mouth as soon as his task was done, swallowing it down if only to fill his achingly empty belly. He had not eaten since his meal with Ishak; thankfully water had been available in their cell the night before.

'This stuff is gross,' Cade muttered through a half-filled mouth.

'It is not the food of gladiators,' Tsuru allowed, though the hint of a smile edged her lips. 'But we are not the same gladiators as those of history.'

'What do you mean?' Amber asked over her shoulder, crouching over one of the weapon boxes.

'The gladiators of old were heavy men,' Tsuru said. 'Layered with fat, to protect their vitals, muscles and tendons.'

'That seems . . . weird,' Grace said, picking up one of the food bowls and giving it a tentative lick. 'A sword cuts through fat easily, doesn't it?'

Cade gulped down his final mouthful with a wince.

'Think modern-day wrestlers on TV,' he said, remembering his father's dinner-time stories. 'Gladiators were like that. Fake rivalries, choreographed fights. And superficial wounds, to make it look real. It was much easier to cut a fat belly without damaging the organs.'

'So gladiators didn't fight for real?' Amber asked.

'Oh they did,' Cade said. 'But the game masters wouldn't stop a fight until they'd seen some blood and one of the fighters yielded. It was less common for gladiators to kill one another, but they'd go up against criminals and animals too, and that was definitely real.'

Amber shrugged, winced at the pain in her shoulder, then hauled the last of the weapons from the box, scattering them on the sand.

'Well we don't need fat for fake wounds,' she said.

'Precisely,' Tsuru said. 'I want you to be lean, tireless hunting dogs by the time the month is out.'

Cade stared at the protein rich meal in front of them. There were more palatable ways of eating it, but the ingredients themselves wouldn't have been unusual to find in a bodybuilder's pantry.

'Now, fill it again,' Tsuru ordered, pointing at his empty bowl. 'Three helpings each now, and again before the night is done.'

Cade's stomach twisted, the gruel sitting in his stomach uncomfortably. Then he went back for more.

THIRTY-FIVE

Of all of them, Quintus seemed to enjoy the food the most. But then, he had spent much of the past year eating dinosaur jerky and little else. Quintus was skinniest, but his appetite more than made up for it.

With their bellies swollen, and Amber's face taking on a faint shade of green, they now stared at the weapons arrayed on the sand in front of them. Cade wasn't sure what he had been expecting, but it certainly wasn't this.

Tsuru stepped in front of the first pile, and hefted one, balancing it on the palm of her hand. Spears, and long ones at that, seven feet in length, by his estimation.

'They call this a bear spear,' Tsuru said. 'Used across the ages to hunt animals far larger than ourselves.'

She tapped the tip with her cane, where a leaf-shaped blade was affixed to the dark-wood pole.

'A wide blade to cut through the large organs and arteries,' she said, then rapped her cane against a sharp spike on the weapon's tail. 'And a point to brace the weapon against the ground when the beast charges.'

A third of the way down the shaft was an iron crosspiece, and Tsuru slid her fingers from the tip down to the point where the metal cross jutted out.

'The spear will impale up to this length, then the wings of the crosspiece will stop it penetrating further, and the beast getting close enough to maul you.'

She smiled and spun the weapon, hefting it overhand above her head.

'And, like the Spartans of old, you shall fight with spear and shield. A phalanx of five.'

Tsuru jabbed down, both to demonstrate the weapon's use, and to point at the shields she had selected, stacked like crockery in the sand.

These were the body length, concave rectangles favoured by the Roman legions, and now the soldiers of New Rome.

'Pick one up,' Tsuru commanded, and Cade did as she bade him, slotting his wrist through the leather strap of the topmost shield.

To his surprise, it was lighter than he expected, a touch heavier than a large bowling bowl, though still heavy enough that he couldn't imagine holding it off the ground for long.

'Why this kind of shield?' Cade asked.

'From what we know of the first battle, we must fight defensively, until the other teams have wiped each other out,' Tsuru said. 'This serves the benefit of protecting you from shoulder to ankle, and lets you rest its bottom against the ground in between the action.'

She pointed at Quintus. 'You, legionary. Demonstrate.'

Quintus must have been reading her lips or listening intently, for he snatched up a shield and crouched, his eyeline just above the shield's rim.

'A round shield requires long training in how to protect yourself, and the fellow to your left. We have no time for such things. This shall prove adequate, and Quintus shall help me train you. Right, Quintus?'

'Right,' Quintus replied.

'Cade, try to knock Quintus back with your shield,' Tsuru said.

'Seriously?' Cade asked.

Tsuru raised a brow, and Cade shook his head with a sigh.

'Sorry, Quintus,' Cade said, raising his shield.

Quintus grinned in response, and Cade took a tottering run towards him, his shield outstretched like a battering ram. The wood clattered, and their central iron bosses met with a clang. It was like running into a wall, and Cade's chin smacked the inside of his shield.

He shoved and sweated, but Quintus didn't budge an inch. Then, to Cade's shock, he was thrown back, landing hard enough to knock the wind from him.

He gasped, staring up at the blue sky, until Quintus's concerned face appeared there.

'Did I hurt you?' the legionary asked.

Cade wheezed for a moment longer, waving Quintus away. Gulping down a breath and struggling to his feet once more, he managed to squeeze out a few words.

'How did you do that?'

Quintus shrugged modestly, but Tsuru answered for him.

'Footwork,' she said. 'Bracing, timing, technique. A shield such as this is held on the arm, but the use of it is all in the legs.'

She tapped her cane against Quintus's skinny calves.

'You'll learn soon enough. Now, when they get too close, or your spear breaks, you must have a secondary weapon. We shall be using a gladius.'

She pointed at a forlorn pile of swords, these seeming of a far poorer quality than their spears and shields, the blades rusted and chipped. Catching Cade's expression, she shrugged.

'It is a cheap, light contingency weapon, and our funds were low as it was. The spear will be the key focus of our training.'

She turned to the largest pile, one that Cade had hardly looked at, so fascinated had he been by the weaponry.

'New garments and armour,' she said, giving Cade's old uniform, now worn by Quintus, a disdainful look. She snapped her fingers, and Quintus looked back at her in confusion.

'Strip,' she ordered, taking a bundle of cloth and equipment from the pile and placing it beside him.

Reddening, Quintus shrugged off his clothing, and swiftly tugged on the new outfit offered to him. It was not easily done, for there were many parts to it, and Tsuru helped him with each item . . . which only served to make Quintus's face redder, standing for the most part in his loincloth underwear.

Cade looked at the old uniform abandoned on the ground, noting the burns, the rips and the bloodstains there. That uniform appeared in many unpleasant memories. He would not miss it.

Quintus spun in a slow circle with his arms outstretched so that they could take in the full view of his new outfit. Cade, still feeling the breeze in his nether regions thanks to Quintus's skirt, was glad to see Quintus's legs were now clad in padded pants, along with a simple long-sleeved shirt of the same material.

'Quilted linen,' Tsuru said, plucking at the material on Quintus's upper arm. 'Light, durable, breathable. It will turn away a glancing blow, if you're lucky. Silk would be better but . . . we can't afford it.'

Next, she pointed at the curved metal plates tied to his shins and forearms, and the metal caps covering the shoulders, elbows and knees.

'Greaves, vambraces, spaulders, couters and poleyns,' she said, tapping each item respectively. 'The legs can be vulnerable when the shield is lifted, the shoulders are always exposed to overhand blows and the arms are vulnerable when extended in attack.'

'Why not more?' Amber asked. 'Why not a full suit of it?'

'Because, never mind the cost, bouts can last for hours. The sun will cook you like stew in a pot while you battle and run under all that weight. I've seen warriors collapse from heatstroke and be killed as they lie unconscious on the sands. This is the best balance I can strike.'

Amber chewed her lip, then nodded reluctantly. Tsuru pointed to the helmet on Quintus's head, the final item. It left the face exposed, though two cheek plates framed the sides, and there was a rim along the back to protect the neck.

A mohawk of red horsehair erupted from the top from forehead to nape.

'You're shorter than the Danes,' Tsuru said, running a finger along the bristles. 'So these will make you seem taller and more intimidating. The weakest are always targeted first in games such as these.'

She took a few steps back, admiring her living mannequin. Catching her look, Quintus took up his shield and spear, crouching low and holding the weapon aloft.

Cade was faced with a wall of wood, with an overlarge blade poised to plunge down above it, and a shining helm and red flare visible over the top. It was an intimidating sight, and he could imagine the five of them arrayed in a row, presenting an impregnable barrier that was tipped with stabbing blades. Tsuru was a genius.

'And the others?' Cade asked. 'What weapons do they use?'

Tsuru ran a hand across her face, and Cade saw the strains of that day were beginning to tire her.

'There are eleven other teams, but Lucretia and Atilius had not ordered their weapons yet – I can assume they will use spears, given they know about the beasts,' Tsuru said. 'But none of the others ordered spears, which gives us some advantage in reach against them. But we must make sure they do not get so close as to render our spears ineffective.'

'What about projectiles?' Scott asked.

Tsuru shook her head. 'Few and far between. A few javelins, nothing more. Your shields should serve as protection enough from those.'

Cade nodded at her words, still gazing at the formidable sight of Quintus. For a brief moment, he felt hope flare within him. They had the weapons, the equipment and a strategy.

Now all they needed to do was learn how to use them.

THIRTY-SIX

'Down!' Tsuru snapped.

Cade felt his stomach churn, but he squatted down until his buttocks sank beneath his knees.

'Up!'

Groaning, Cade strained upwards, and the rucksack full of rocks pressed uncomfortably against his spine. He just managed it, while Scott collapsed on his front, and Grace's legs locked halfway up, eliciting a string of hissed curses.

'Down!'

Cade's legs felt like dead meat, and the pain from his cracked ribs was beginning to take its toll. But Tsuru had said that this first training session was the most important, and so, he squatted again, even though he felt as if he were about to vomit.

'Up!'

Quintus straightened with a groan, but this time Cade collapsed on his backside, and Amber did the same. Grace toppled over with a final curse. Cade stared up at the night sky, the constellations and the sibling moons their only source of light.

It had been like this all afternoon and evening. Press ups, squats, running laps. All with the heavy weight of rocks on their shoulders, and wearing their new outfits to boot.

'Enough,' Tsuru said. 'To the baths with you.'

Cade felt pitifully grateful. His entire body ached, and whether the water was ice cold or hot, he knew it would ease the pain. But when she called the guards to escort them, Cade held back.

The one benefit of all the mind-numbing exercise was that it had given him time to think. Specifically, to think about what awaited him should they ever escape this place.

Getting a remnant from Caesarion was one thing, and training to fight was another. But he would not be facing the alpha with a spear. He needed training with a Japanese sword. And whether by some twist of fate, or Abaddon's dark influence, he had been presented with the perfect teacher.

'Tsuru,' Cade said. 'Can I ask you something?'

'Quickly,' Tsuru said. 'The guards do not like to be kept waiting.'

'I . . .' He hesitated. 'Do you know what contenders are?'

Tsuru nodded gravely.

'Most everyone does.'

'The five of us . . . we're almost all that's left of them. Even if we do win our freedom after all this, I will have another battle to face, one with a beast far stronger and bigger than me.'

Tsuru's gaze was unreadable, but the slightest nod told him to continue.

'You're training us to fight as a group, but I must fight alone, and with a Japanese sword. Can you train me?'

Tsuru remained silent.

Then the impatient hand of a guard pulled Cade away. He looked back over his shoulder as he was led down the darkened corridor with the others. Tsuru stood in the moonlight, staring back at him.

Cade was shoved unceremoniously into a stone room with Scott and Quintus, while Amber and Grace were split off to their own.

Cade allowed himself a smile as he took in the steaming interior, dominated by a wide, shallow pool that bubbled at its centre.

'There must be a hot spring below this place,' Cade said, stripping off as fast as he could. 'This is a genuine Roman bath.'

'I don't care if there's a dragon down there,' Scott muttered, already half-undressed. 'I've got three days of stank to boil off me.'

They eased themselves into the simmering pool, groaning like water buffalo as the heat soothed their aches and pains.

It had been a long time since Cade had experienced a hot bath, and he had never needed this more. His ribs were cracked, his muscles strained and his skin was bruised and broken. Blood from his nose still crusted his chin and neck, not to mention the sweat and grime that made him smell like a barnyard animal.

'You ever bathe in a place like this, Quintus?' Cade asked, waving for Quintus's attention after a few minutes

213

of blissful relaxation.

The legionary grinned.

'This place not best,' he said, looking around. 'But it has a *strigil*.'

Quintus waded to a low stone table on the far end of the pool, and Cade followed, curious. Upon it were two items – a strange, sickle-like tool and a jar of yellow liquid.

'Oil,' Quintus said.

He picked up the oil and offered it to Scott, miming the act of rubbing himself with it.

'Try,' he said.

'I just got clean, man,' Scott said. 'The last thing I wanna do is spend tonight all oily.'

'You scrape it off after,' Cade said.

'I'll stick to water,' Scott muttered.

Quintus grinned. 'Cade?'

'When in Rome,' Cade said, then chuckled. 'Or New Rome anyway,'

Quintus and Scott stared at him blankly.

'That joke would have killed at my house,' he grumbled, taking the oil and sitting down. He rubbed it liberally over his skin.

'Lie,' Quintus said, pointing at the stone table.

'Hang on guys,' Scott said. 'Can you hear that?'

The sound of raised voices and laughter was coming from outside. Moments later, Finch and a troop of three boys entered, the guards closing the doors behind them.

Cade took in Finch's three companions at a glance. All tall, all bearded, and most a year or two older than he was.

These were the Danish sailors, and he felt a pang of fear at the thought of facing them on the sands of the arena. Even so, this was not a time to show weakness.

The other team pointedly ignored them, stripping down from the simple tunics and skirts they wore before entering the water. They spoke in Danish, it seemed, but Finch didn't seem to mind being left out of the conversation, instead fixing his eyes on Cade.

'If the first round is a free-for-all . . . maybe we can make an alliance,' Scott whispered.

It wasn't a bad idea. As it stood, Finch would likely urge his team to take them out first, given the way he was looking at Cade in that moment.

'Yes,' Quintus said. 'They will not hurt their friends. If we are close in the arena, they will attack.'

Cade nodded slowly. He had not considered any of this. Every other team here was made up of the same crew of Danes, who would hesitate to attack one another. Their alliance was inevitable. Cade and his team needed to convince them to make it a *ludus*-wide alliance instead, focusing their energies on defeating the teams of the rival *ludi*.

Cade stood and waded to the centre of the pool, placing his hands on his hips. He was glad that the water came up to his belly and gave him some semblance of modesty.

At first, he thought of approaching Finch. But as he neared, he realised the Danes were the ones that needed convincing.

'Hello,' he said. 'I'm Cade.'

The boys looked at him, almost surprised that he would

greet them at all. He saw one turn his head and whisper to the other, eliciting a snigger. Despite the heat, it felt like the room had dropped in temperature by a few degrees.

'We'll all likely be in the arena at the same time,' Cade said, speaking with a confidence he did not feel. 'If that happens, I suggest we form an alliance against the teams at the other *ludi*. Our *ludus* has the most teams, after all.'

'You talk a lot,' said one of the boys, the Scandinavian accent thick on his tongue.

But the largest of them, a Dane with the tattoo of an anchor upon his chest, motioned at Finch to come closer.

A whispered conversation followed, with Cade standing awkwardly, waiting for the verdict. He swallowed, intensely aware of the hostility in the eyes of the others.

The discussion could not have taken more than a minute, but it felt like much longer. It was Finch who stepped away first, meeting Cade's gaze with a smirk. 'Bjorn here thinks your idea is a good one.'

The big Dane crossed his arms, revealing further tattoos of stars and swallows along his arms.

'But if we're gonna team up, you have to forgive me, Cade,' Finch said. 'Right here, right now. I can't trust you otherwise.'

Cade stared back with astonishment.

'You *abandoned* us,' he hissed. 'Stole from us. My friends died because of you!'

Finch shrugged. 'We can bury the hatchet, or you can fend for yourselves. We don't need you – there's two other teams of Danes.'

Cade clenched his fists. Why did Finch even care? Finch

would never trust them anyway, even if Cade forced out a few fake words of forgiveness.

'So, peace?' Finch asked.

He waded forward, his hand outstretched. Cade took a deep breath, looking down at it. The world was at stake. His friends were at stake. What was Cade's pride worth, against the balance of all that? Cade sighed and took Finch's hand.

'Fine, I—'

Finch heaved, jerking Cade closer. A fist glanced across his skull, and through the haze of steam and pain, Cade saw the Danes charging into the water.

Then an arm wrapped about his neck and he plunged beneath the surface. Cade collapsed to his knees, Finch dropping his full weight on Cade's back.

Cade's legs, still weak from exercise, scrabbled for purchase on the smooth floor. For a few horrifying seconds his world was one of pain and swirling bubbles, his fingers plucking at the forearm crushing his throat.

Finch was trying to kill him. The realisation was like a fire in his oxygen-deprived brain. Cade twisted his body, turning his head within the crook of Finch's elbow until his face was pressed against the meat of Finch's shoulder.

He bit down. *Hard.* Harder than he had ever bitten before, shaking his head like a rabid dog. His mouth filled with the taste of metal, red clouding the water. Finch's arm loosened for no more than a second, and Cade wriggled free with a strength borne of desperation.

Finch grappled at him, but Cade's oily skin was as slippery as an eel's. Gathering his legs beneath him, Cade sprang up,

217

seeing stars as his head connected with Finch's chin.

Through water-blurred eyes, Cade saw the boy fall away. He took in a great choking breath and threw himself back, just as a Dane lunged after him, nails scratching furrows in his chest.

Cade turned, and his eyes widened as the massive figure of Bjorn came into view. But the Dane only barged past, clutching at his face, blood springing between his fingers.

Quintus bellowed behind, swinging the *strigil* like a sword. Cade dived towards him, and Scott hurled the jar of oil over Cade's head. He heard it shatter, and the strangled yell of his pursuer.

Coughing water from his lungs, Cade stood shoulder-to-shoulder with his friends, facing their opponents together. Finch looked dazed, clutching a towel to his shoulder, while Bjorn cursed in a string of Danish expletives, nursing a bloodied slash running from temple to jaw. The third Dane moaned, pawing at the oil in his eyes, shards of glass embedded in his face like glitter.

'Come on!' Quintus yelled.

But the Danes had no intention of coming within range of the legionary's strigil. Instead, Bjorn hurled a curse across the water.

'Why?' Cade demanded, his voice croaking through his bruised throat. 'We could have helped each other!'

But Cade never got a response. The doors slammed open, and a dozen guards burst into the chamber, summoned by the commotion. The fight was over.

THIRTY-SEVEN

The Danes were taken to separate cells that night, but Cade could barely sleep. His skin was still coated in oil, but that was not the reason. It was the crack of the whip outside, coupled with the screams of the guard-slaves who had made the mistake of placing two teams in the baths at once.

Only later had Cade realised how naive he had been. Outnumbering them four to three, Finch had decided to take out Cade's group there and then. What punishment could Julia inflict upon Finch's team for doing so, without hurting their chances of winning in the arena? None that Cade could think of.

Moderns were expensive in this slave economy of this world. She could not afford to damage them. After all, her entire business was built around her gladiators and how successful they were in the tournaments.

In fact, there had been no consequences for the Danes beyond being moved to new cells, and he wasn't sure if that wouldn't have happened regardless. Given the number of different cells in the prisoner block, these sorts of attacks were probably normal.

They would need to watch themselves now. This was no summer camp. The game of life and death had started – just because they weren't yet in the arena did not mean they weren't already at war with the other teams. He should have realised that.

Cade took solace in the company of little Zeeb, the creature having taken up residence in the hollow of Cade's collar bone. The beast watched him with dark eyes, occasionally lapping a tiny pink tongue across his skin.

'You awake?' Cade asked aloud, not caring who responded.

'Yep,' Amber's voice drifted back.

Cade rolled closer to the bars, and found Amber's dark eyes. They were separated by only the iron rails of their cage, and the corridor between the male and female cells. The other teams had been moved to the floors above him, so there was no danger of being overheard. It was strangely eerie, just the five of them in the otherwise empty jail.

'You think the other teams will gang up on us in the first round?' Cade asked.

Amber pursed her lips.

'I don't know,' she said. 'I think Finch's team will be gunning for us after what Quintus did to Bjorn's face, but the other Danes will just be focused on surviving. They'll go for whichever non-Danish team is most vulnerable. We just need to make sure that's not us.'

Cade nodded.

'How are you?' Amber asked. 'You look like you've

been through hell.'

'Feels that way too,' Cade said. 'They *did* beat me senseless when they caught me on the ship.'

Amber grimaced in sympathy.

He hadn't looked at himself in a mirror lately, but now he touched his hand to his face, feeling the puffy skin around his eyes, and the cut on the bridge of his nose. His lips had scabbed where they had split, and he was lucky that cracked ribs healed quickly.

'I don't think I can stomach more of that oatmeal tomorrow,' Cade said, changing the subject. 'That stuff was gross.'

'I don't like porridge at the best of times,' Amber replied. 'What I wouldn't do for my mum's bao buns right now.'

Cade felt a pang of hunger, despite the six portions of turgid gruel congealing in his stomach.

'My mom cooked a mean pakora,' Cade said.

He lay back and pictured the sizzling minced balls of vegetables, crispy on the outside, and soft on the inside. To be home again. Back when things had been good. When he and his father would while away the evenings, watching documentaries and planning their summer vacation. But of course, that was all before the . . . arrest.

He tried not to think of his parents much. It was too painful. But at the same time, he worried he would forget their faces, their voices.

'When we win this thing and get sent back to Earth, our mums can have a cook off,' Amber joked.

Cade forced a smile, but Amber saw the hesitation there.

She closed her eyes.

'I know, Cade,' she said, as if reading his mind. 'My mom would be an old woman now, if she's alive at all. But at least I have a chance to see them again. That's more than Quintus can say about his family.'

Cade wasn't sure what to say. His mind had been so focused on keeping humanity from extinction that moving to the top of the leaderboard and being teleported home again felt like a pipe dream.

He had pushed his parents from his mind, ever since he'd been sent to the court-ordered boarding school. It had made things easier, even if they didn't deserve it. Here . . . well . . . he hardly thought about them at all.

But Amber . . . she clung to that hope of a reunion as her own reason to keep living. And Cade couldn't blame her for that. He envied her optimism.

'Let's focus on getting out of here alive first,' Cade said. 'Tsuru has given us a fighting chance.'

'Fighting's the right word,' Amber said, smiling. 'But maybe there's more we can do. Training hard is one thing. Playing smart is another.'

Cade thought on it. Tsuru knew how to play the game, but she hadn't considered making alliances for the free-for-all first round. There might be other strategies she had overlooked.

'You been talking to the other girls?' Cade asked. 'Maybe we can make an alliance through them – though there will probably be Danes on their team too.'

'One of the girls was in the baths with me and Grace, but

she didn't say much before the guards came to get us,' Amber said. 'I don't think we'll get a chance to talk again.'

Cade sighed. Perhaps it was for the best. Eventually, they would have to turn on each other. He didn't have the stomach for that.

'You know there's a chance we'll have to kill them, later,' Cade said. 'Do you think you could do that?'

Amber's face fell.

'They're nice,' she said, her voice quiet. 'Scared.'

'You've killed before,' Cade said.

'But never a person,' Amber snapped. 'Can you do it? Kill someone?'

Cade felt a pang of guilt, seeing the hurt in her eyes.

'I'm sorry,' Cade said. 'I don't think I'll know until the moment I have to.'

Amber rolled away, and Cade kicked himself. It was bad enough that they were forced to become killers. He didn't have to throw it in her face.

In that moment, he remembered the boy on the ship. He could have killed the kid in cold blood. Found the weapons, freed his friends, taken Ishak hostage. They wouldn't be here. The Earth would have been safer for it.

And yet . . . he'd stopped himself. He hadn't even considered it.

Amber spoke.

'I'll do it,' she said, her voice so quiet Cade almost thought he was imagining it. 'For my family. For all of us.'

THIRTY-EIGHT

They rose with aching muscles and bruised flesh, yet it seemed they had hardly opened their eyes before the guards were manhandling them through the *ludus*'s dingy corridors and out into the dawn light of their small training ground.

Food was already laid out in bowls – an array of strange fruits. Cade was overjoyed that seaweed gruel and jerky would not be all they were allowed to eat. Rather, now they stuffed themselves with the fruit.

One of the fruits looked like a red chilli pepper, and Cade baulked at eating it for fear of burning his mouth. But the Codex identified it as a red gherkin, noted for its unusually high protein content, and Cade found it had a mild, sweet taste. Some orange fruits, known as monkey oranges and egg fruit, reminded Cade of apricots and pumpkins.

A mix of mashed avocado and cornmeal lay at the bottom of their bowls, which tasted as gross as it looked. But then, these meals were not designed to be enjoyed, but rather to transform their skinny bodies into lean muscle. Or at least, that was what Tsuru told them.

As they ate, Cade filled Tsuru in on the events of the night before. She listened in silence, and gave no opinion. When Cade pressed her on the issues of alliances, she responded with only a single word:

'Patience.'

With the food finished – their bowls licked clean after a stern warning from Tsuru – their *doctrix* wasted no time in getting the armour onto their linen clothing, and the weapons in their hands. Cade was relieved that they would not be following the gruelling exercise regime of the prior afternoon, but the feeling was short-lived.

Now fully clad and armed, the five began their *real* training.

'Forget everything you know about the shield wall,' Tsuru said, as they stood in a row of five, shields raised in parallel.

'Should be easy enough,' Scott said.

'Not for me,' Quintus muttered.

'A straight wall of five is easily outflanked,' Tsuru went on, ignoring them. 'You shall restructure your formation as enemies approach from any side.'

She poked and prodded the edges of their wall, rearranging their formation into a shallow, concave crescent.

'This will be your standard formation when attacked from the front,' Tsuru said. 'But *this* is how you will position yourselves when they come from your left and right.'

She repositioned the curve to form a rough trapezoid, leaving a gap at the back.

'And now from all sides,' she said, closing the rear

end into a pentagon.

It was harder to coordinate than Cade had anticipated, especially as their backs pressed together and the upheld spears tangled behind their heads. But Tsuru did not stop there.

They had to learn to spin their formation to face one way or another, depending on if an attack came from the left, right, the back or all three.

It was complex and confusing, but Tsuru seemed to have thought things out. Each of them was given an angle to focus on, calling out the number and direction of incoming enemies. She would shout these directions and numbers for them, leaving them to change their formation accordingly while echoing her words.

In particular, they made sure to shout loud enough for Quintus, with the legionary positioned close to the centre for the best chance of hearing. When possible, Cade would repeat the shouts, yelling them into Quintus's ear. There would be no chance at lip reading once the fighting started.

By the time lunchtime rolled around, they were moving smoothly enough, with a few mistakes here and there. Cade knew that in the heat of battle it would not go so smoothly. But there was little they could do without more training partners.

'I'd say we're doing pretty well,' Scott said cheerfully, somehow still in a good mood despite their arms aching from the hours of holding their shields aloft.

'Try doing it for real,' Tsuru scoffed. 'You think they'll disengage and let you reposition yourselves when another group attacks you from behind?'

Cade shuddered at the thought. Well, it was either that or the taste of their seaweed gruel, which had made a reappearance for lunch.

They ate in ravenous if uncomfortable silence, sweat dripping from brows as they spooned two bowlfuls into their bellies. Once again, Tsuru looked on until the bowls were licked clean. Somehow, it was even harder to eat than the day before.

'We'll practise formations every day,' Tsuru said, motioning for them to get to their feet. 'But as you will also be facing beasts, there is another formation we must practise. Quintus, Amber and Cade, go to your usual places and crouch.'

The three shuffled into position with Cade in the centre, Amber on the left and Quintus on the right. Tsuru prodded Amber and Quintus back until their shields were angled back in the shape of a rough trapezium, the bottoms buried in the sand.

'Grace and Scott, you shall kneel close behind and lift your shields, covering the heads of the front row.'

The pair did so, and Cade's world darkened in the shade of Grace's shield.

'Spears angled up, bottoms braced in the sand, points through the gaps of your shields,' Tsuru instructed.

They clattered into position, and now, Cade could see what Tsuru's game was. He imagined a *T. rex* or some other large theropod towering over them. They were forming a barrier, unmoving and studded with sharp points. Any attempt to bite into them would result in its snout bashing into a shell of wood, unable to find purchase on the flat surface and pierced by the bristling array of spears. They would be protected like a mix between a tortoise and a hedgehog, and about as appetising as one.

'This position leaves you vulnerable from behind, but it is the best we can do,' Tsuru said. 'Let us hope the beasts give up and go in search of easier prey.'

Cade gulped. Hope was right; no amount of training could truly prepare them for the mess of battle.

'Now,' Tsuru said. 'You'll be happy to know that we will not be lifting rocks today, as your muscles need time to recover and grow. Instead, we will be performing mock battles. Stand and drop your spears.'

They did so, and Cade watched as Tsuru kicked open a long chest that lay among the pile of food sacks, clothing and weapons containers that had arrived yesterday.

'Come,' she ordered.

The five of them stumbled over, only to see five long poles, identical to their spears except for a stuffed leather sack in place of blades at each end.

'Are those what I think they are?' Grace asked.

'Practice spears,' Tsuru announced. 'It's time to get to work.'

THIRTY-NINE

Shields slammed against shields, feet slipped and struggled on the sand, and the blunted spears would dart overhead, thudding into faces, shoulders and chests.

At first, it was a messy affair of clattering wood as spears were knocked from hands and shields were pushed aside. Despite the padded spear-ends, each blow that landed was like being punched in the face, and Cade's split lip reopened, spotting the arena with his blood. Soon enough, a nose bleed for Amber added to the parody of modern art forming on the sand.

Thank goodness for Quintus.

The boy was a wealth of knowledge. He taught them to brace against attack, reposition their feet to make the best use of their weight, and hold the shield at their centre of gravity so both they and it would not be knocked aside.

He demonstrated how to jerk the shield up to block or deflect a blow, even bashing it forward to unbalance an opponent. Along with technique, timing was everything.

React to an incoming blow too soon and the opponent would change direction. Too late and the blow might still land, even if thrown off course.

Judging when to shield-bash was harder still; the defender had to somehow keep an eye on their opponent's weapon and their feet at the same time, waiting for a heel to lift, or the back foot to step forward. This was coupled with learning to launch their own attacks without becoming open to those same vulnerabilities.

These were not things that could be learned easily through teaching; they had to be on the receiving end of these techniques or have a go themselves.

With his helmet on, sweat dripping in his eyes, Cade could hardly focus on more than holding his shield straight.

Progress was slow. Cade told himself that Rome wasn't built in a day – another line that would have made his dad laugh. Then again, it wasn't built in a month either, and that was how long they had until the first bout.

They trained until the shadows grew long, and more gruel was served. But even then, Tsuru did not give them a break. Once Quintus had wolfed down his meal ahead of the others, she had him strip and stand in nothing but his loincloth. This time, he didn't seem quite as embarrassed.

Cade stared in confusion, especially when she used her cane to spread the legionary's legs wider. She chuckled at his expression and spoke.

'When *doctores* train moderns for the arena, rarely do they think there is something that they can learn from you,' she said. 'I, on the other hand, do. Modern man has little to add to the doctrine of martial combat, but in the world of medicine, your predecessors had much to offer.'

Amber raised a hand.

'Won't that only be useful *after* the fight?' she asked.

Tsuru grinned.

'Healers have sworn to do no harm for over a thousand years, but I have made no such oath,' she said.

Her cane rose again, sliding from Quintus's groin to his knee, making the boy jump and earning him a slap to the back of the head for moving.

'These are called the femoral arteries,' Tsuru said. 'A single cut can spray blood six feet and cause unconsciousness in thirty seconds, with death soon to follow. Who said that aiming for the legs was a fool's errand?'

Cade felt sick, his half-finished meal suddenly twice as unappetising. It was all so . . . clinical.

Tsuru's gnarled finger traced each side of Quintus's neck, then back up along the tops of his collar bone.

'The jugular and carotids. Your primary targets, given you will be striking overhand from above your shield. The eyes and face will likely be protected by a nose guard and helm. Small targets, and neither fatal. Go for these instead.'

She lifted Quintus's arm and jabbed her finger into his armpit. Quintus gave an involuntary shudder.

'The axillary arteries. Rarely protected by armour, but no less deadly. Drop to your knee and stab up and to the side for this one. More often than not, the opponent facing your neighbour is most vulnerable to this strike.'

Next she traced Quintus's chest, running her fingers along

his ribs like a piano. He was still so skinny; each bone was clearly visible.

'Slipping a blade between the ribcage is hard at the best of times, but a horizontally held blade might manage it. If not, go in beneath, and take out the heart, lungs and liver.'

She prodded Quintus's solar plexus, running her fingers along the bottom of his ribs.

'Yeah, I'm not finishing this,' Scott muttered, putting his bowl to one side.

Tsuru ignored him, instead slapping the back of Quintus's legs, making him fall to his knees.

'The popliteal artery,' she said, prodding the inside of his knee. 'Protected by the knee cap, but a worthy target if exposed, not to mention the hamstring.'

A gnarled hand gripped the back of Quintus's neck.

'Lastly, the spinal cord. Hard to sever between the vertebrae, but near instantaneous death if you do. Should an enemy turn their back on you, this will be your target.'

Cade could hardly imagine stabbing someone from behind. It felt cowardly. But he wouldn't put it past Finch and his friends.

'Tomorrow we shall practise targeting these vulnerabilities. After some vigorous exercise, of course.'

The others groaned, but somehow, Cade preferred the torturous weightlifting over the mock battles. The latter only served to remind him of what they would soon face.

'Now, finish up your food,' Tsuru said, ruffling Quintus's hair and pushing him back towards the others. 'We only have a month to put meat back on your bones.'

Cade lifted his spoon and let it fall back into the gruel with a splat. Tsuru crossed her arms, and Cade lifted the bowl to his lips, gulping it down with a grimace.

'Good boy,' Tsuru said.

She acted as if they were children half the time, and mere animals the rest. Decades of sending her charges to their deaths would surely have desensitised her to all this. Perhaps treating them that way helped her deal with the knowledge that they would likely meet their end in the arena. But that didn't make her condescension any more palatable.

Tsuru glanced down at him, and Cade realised he had been staring at her with annoyance in his eyes. He looked away, but it seemed the damage was done.

'Pack up these weapons and get some rest. Muscles are built while the body sleeps. Cade . . . you will wait behind.'

Cade sighed and helped the others put the weapons and food back in their chests. Tsuru locked each one to prevent sabotage or poisoning.

Then the others trooped away, with Amber casting him a worried glance. He flashed her a smile to put her at ease.

'Stand up, boy,' Tsuru said.

Cade set his jaw. He'd become used to getting shouted at by drill sergeants at boarding school. Somehow, he didn't think a tongue lashing from Tsuru would compare to one from a spitting, screaming, red-faced jarhead.

'So you want to learn how to fight with a Japanese sword?' she asked quietly.

Cade looked up, his eyes widening.

'Yes,' he blurted.

Tsuru gave him a hard stare. 'It cannot detract from your training. If I see you slacking once, my lessons stop.'

'Of course,' Cade said swiftly.

'Then look in there,' Tsuru said, pointing to a new box he had not noticed amongst the pile. 'And fetch what is within.'

He found a single wooden sword inside. It was made of bamboo, but the hollow interior had been weighted somehow.

'No sword for you?' Cade asked.

'Does the monster you will fight intend to fence with you?' Tsuru asked.

Cade inclined his head.

'I guess not,' he said.

He bounced the weapon in his hand.

'It is a shame we do not have the same sword to practise with,' Tsuru said. 'The weight, grip, length and balance will all be different. But this is what I was able to scrounge from our store rooms.'

Cade hardly cared at that point. Of all the people in the universe, he had somehow found someone who genuinely knew how to use a Japanese sword. And not only that, she would have some idea of how to use it against a larger creature. Of course, the creatures she was likely used to would be prehistoric animals rather than alien monstrosities. But beggars could not be choosers.

'Let's begin, shall we?' Tsuru said.

FORTY

'You took your time,' Scott said as Cade stumbled back into their cell.

'I was worried,' Quintus chimed in.

Cade collapsed onto his straw mattress, careful not to crush the waiting Zeeb. The little beast chirruped as he lay there, its wings seemingly healed enough to let it flutter up to perch on his head.

He didn't have the energy to shift Zeeb. Cade had thought his arms had already been pushed to their limit when the five of them had stopped for dinner. He'd been mistaken. Now, he could hardly lift a hand to itch his nose.

Tsuru's strategy for the alpha was a simple one, using a fighting style inspired by the martial art jujutsu. In principle, she intended to help him use his opponent's weight and size against them.

Much like their gladiatorial training, it seemed it was all about footwork. How to back away at an angle from a charging opponent, to allow more range to sidestep on contact. How to dodge one way or another without unbalancing himself, and how to position his blade to counter being side-swiped in the process.

For now, that was all she had time for, allowing Cade a brief minute to plunge into the baths before the next team arrived for their turn to wash. Combined with all they had learned in that day's session, Cade struggled to keep it straight in his head. More than anything, he wanted to sleep.

Cade felt the mattress sag as someone sat beside him.

'What she want?' Quintus asked.

Cade rolled over so his friend could watch his lips, and Zeeb complained at being unseated in a tirade of squeaks.

'Sword training,' he said, scooping the little beast up and quieting it with a belly rub. 'For the battle with the Hydra.'

Quintus nodded grimly.

'Can I help?' he asked.

Cade rubbed his chin, and felt the scratch of his fledgling beard there. It was strange, he had never grown more than a fuzzy fluff there before, which he had stripped with a razor once a week. He was becoming a man, it seemed. Though he had never felt less like one.

'I'll need someone to practise with,' Cade said. 'If you've strength to spare. You're working harder than any of us during the day.'

'Hey.' Scott sat up, an indignant look on his face. Cade raised an eyebrow at him.

'Yeah, fair enough,' Scott laughed, collapsing back onto the bed. 'I mean, it's not like Tsuru's making me strip down. I think she's got a crush on you, Quintus buddy.'

Quintus furrowed his brow.

'I do not think she is trying to crush me,' he said. 'She wanted me to help her.'

Scott opened his mouth, then closed it again.

'Forget it,' he chuckled.

Quintus turned back to Cade.

'I'll help you too,' he said. 'What is this all for, if you cannot beat the Hydra?'

'And me,' called Amber, from across the cells. 'We'll take it in turns.'

'Hard pass,' Scott said, prompting a bray of laughter from Grace.

'Yeah, I need my beauty sleep,' Grace added jokingly. 'Got my eye on that Dane, Bjorn – I like a man with tattoos.'

Cade laughed. 'Who am I to stand in the way of love? I reckon two of you is enough.'

He lay back on his bed and patted Quintus's shoulder.

'Thank you, guys. It means a lot.'

And it truly did. In all his years, he had always felt like a loner. Of course, he'd had friends . . . of a sort. People he'd hang out with after class, or go to the occasional party with. But nobody who would truly have his back.

Yet here, in the face of exhaustion, and with their very survival at risk, they were there for him. It brought a tear to his eye, but he didn't have the energy to wipe it away.

Something pricked his thigh, and Cade looked down to see Zeeb had escaped his hands and was crawling up his belly. He tickled Zeeb beneath its chin, and reached into his pocket. He'd stashed some jerky there, a small act of rebellion against

Tsuru's overzealous insistence that they eat up every morsel of her nasty concoctions.

Zeeb snapped it up in one bite, swallowing it like a frog. Cade marvelled at the beast's size – about half that of a dormouse – and placed it in its usual favourite spot the hollow of his neck. The little pterosaur nestled there, seeming to enjoy the warmth of his skin.

'We should get some rest,' Cade said. 'Tomorrow's gonna be a long day.'

A squawk jerked Cade from a deep sleep like a lasso around his consciousness. The sound grated through his ears a second time, and Cade opened his eyes.

A hazy figure came to a halt outside Cade's cell as he blinked sleep from his eyes.

Then Cade saw the raised hand.

He rolled on instinct; the hiss of a javelin spat between the bars and pin-cushioned the straw mattress beneath him.

An incoherent yell burst from his lips, but just as the others stirred, a bell began to ring outside, the clanging almost immediately echoed by others throughout the building.

The figure turned its back, sprinting down the corridor and out through the open doors there. Stumbling to his feet, Cade pressed his face against the bars to look beyond, only to see a moonlit doorway.

And there by the entrance, a motionless, blood-covered guard.

'What was that?' Scott yelled.

'Assassin,' Cade choked, the word unfamiliar in his mouth.

He put his hands to his chest, where a terrified Zeeb had crawled beneath the cloth. Had it not been for its crying . . . he could have died. Some protective instinct had made it call out. The tiny creature was smarter than he thought.

'Thank you,' he whispered, stroking its head. Zeeb preened, and a wet tongue slipped out to dab at his fingertips. Still, he stared through the bars, ready for the assassin to return. But the bells clamoured on, and he could hear the yells of approaching men above it.

'Cade?' Quintus called.

Cade turned, his eyes flicking between the two boys sitting up in the darkness and the javelin, sticking out from his mattress like the mast of a ship.

'Why would anyone want to kill you?' Grace called out.

'It could have been any of us,' Cade said. 'I was just the closest.'

'Maybe,' Amber said.

She didn't sound convinced.

Keeping one eye on the doorway, Cade tugged the javelin from its place and held it closer. It was a simple thing – tapered wood with a basic iron point. But it was balanced for throwing, and Cade swiftly stashed it beneath the bed as more yells emanated from outside.

'Lie down,' Cade hissed. 'Before they think we're the ones who killed the guard.'

The five of them swiftly collapsed onto their beds, their eyes wide and staring as a dozen guards clattered into the prison, weapons raised. Their eyes widened at the sight of their dead comrade. One dropped to his knees.

'*Quis hoc fecit?*' he bellowed, holding up bloodied hands where he had tried to stem the bleeding of his friend . . . too late. *Who did this?*

Outside, above the commotion, Cade heard a single, garbled scream. Then, one by one, the bells stopped ringing.

Silence.

FORTY-ONE

The five of them knelt on the marble, heads bowed. They were not permitted to raise their heads, or even their eyes, and Cade was intimately aware of the spearpoint resting against his spine.

They might have been there for almost an hour, dragged from their beds and into the *ludus* proper, where Julia and her servants lived. These were not the stone walls and rough paving of the lower levels, but white, polished marble, mosaics and fresh-cut flowers in vases.

Despite it all, this was being treated as a breakout attempt. Even though the perpetrator had been caught.

Which was why Cade didn't mind being unable to lift his head. If he could then he would be forced to see the face of the dead assassin and not just the pool of blood that had spread from the man's neck across the marble floor.

This was not the first time Cade had seen a dead body. Nor should he particularly care about a man who had tried to kill him. But neither fact seemed to shield Cade from the horror of those empty eyes, staring at him with faint accusation.

In the face of their impending battles, death had seemed abstract, a hypothetical concept. But here, with the blood drying and the flies settling on the corpse, the reality of what a violent death truly *was* filled Cade with a dread that tore at his very mind and left him clutching his arms about his skinny chest, feeling the oh-so vulnerable beat of his heart.

The double doors ahead of them slammed open. Cade started, wincing as the movement caused the spear to nick the skin of his neck. It was only when the sandalled feet appeared in front of him and the spear eased back a fraction that he allowed himself to look up. Julia looked down at him.

She wore a nightgown of silken white, edged with lace and embroidered pearls. Her hair fell in a sleek wave of black, and her eyes had been darkened with kohl on the edges. Their *domina* had taken the time to apply make-up. Or the servant girl crouched behind her had done it anyway.

'You are Cade.'

It was a statement, not a question; Cade nodded regardless. Julia's accent was thick, and her voice like velvet.

'Tsuru tells me you lead this team.'

She stepped aside, revealing Tsuru, standing with downcast eyes behind her. Again, Cade nodded.

'This man was here to kill my gladiators,' she said. 'He targeted your team. Why?'

Cade stared up at her, unsure of what to say. Julia sighed and clicked her fingers.

On Cade's left, two guards dragged a struggling figure

from an open doorway. A scrawny youth, no more than a child. A guard gave the boy an open-handed slap, yet he refused to be cowed, even as the red imprint of the man's hand blazed across his face.

'This child was found skulking within my *ludus*'s walls. I would have thought him a lookout for the killer, yet the guards say it was this boy who started the bells. Strange behaviour for a lookout, to be sure. But he won't say a word.'

Cade hardly heard her. He *recognised* the boy. The child's face had been etched into his memory, fixed there by that terrible moment when Cade had almost caved in his skull. It was the ship's boy.

Still, he kept his face impassive. The lay of the land was uncertain, and he did not know what any of this meant. In fact, there was only one thing he *did* know. This boy, whoever he was, had saved his life. The assassin might have made another attempt, had the bells not scared him away.

He owed the kid.

'Whatever the boy's motives, he trespassed.' She waved the guards away dismissively. '*Iugula*.'

Cade understood, even as the Codex whispered in his ear. *Kill him*.

'Wait,' Cade blurted, the word leaving his lips unbidden. He felt Amber's foot press against his, but he could not guess her meaning. A show of support? A warning?

Julia held up a hand.

'I recognise him,' Cade said.

'The boy?' Julia asked, her eyebrow raised.

'No . . .' Cade said. 'Him.'

He motioned at the dead assassin with his chin.

'Speak,' Julia snapped.

Cade's mind raced. He did not, in fact, recognise the assassin, but if the boy was there, it could mean only one thing. This was Ishak's doing, and the dead man was one of his sailors.

'Ishak,' he muttered. 'He's one of Ishak's men.'

'And the boy?' Julia asked.

'A street urchin, probably,' Cade said, shrugging. 'Probably sounded the alarm when he saw the assassin enter, thinking the man was a burglar. He was probably hoping for gratitude and a meal, not getting killed like a stray dog.'

'Watch your tone,' Julia said, lifting a finger. 'My mercy has its limits.'

She examined the boy. With his ragged clothing and scrawny frame, he certainly looked the part.

'*Tsuru can have him*,' Julia sighed in Latin, waving the guards away.

The boy stared at Cade with dark eyes as he was dragged from sight.

'*Take the others, leave this one*,' Julia ordered.

'Cade—' Amber started, but she yelped as the pressure of the spear point silenced any further words. Seconds later, his four friends were yanked away and down the stairs.

Then Cade was alone with Tsuru and Julia, save for the guard with blade poised above his spine, and the servant girl prostrated on the ground.

With the room now near empty, Julia tapped her chin pensively. She snapped her fingers and pointed, prompting her slave to drag forth a stool for her to sit on. Julia did so, kicking off her sandals. The girl took Julia's feet unprompted, kneading them with her hands.

Julia sighed with contentment, seemingly oblivious to the others around her. It was as if they were not even there. For a long moment, the room was silent. Cade wasn't sure why he had been kept back . . . but it could not be good news.

'Ishak took a big risk,' Julia finally said, boring of the massage and shoving the girl away with her foot. 'I own one of only four *ludi* he can sell his moderns to. Perhaps this was . . . personal.'

'I—' Cade began.

But Julia held up her hand. He had not been given permission to speak.

'*If I may, domina?*' Tsuru asked in a low voice.

Julia turned, and gave a curt nod.

'*I keep tabs on all the comings and goings of the slavers. Ishak purchased a large property on the outskirts of the city, and has borrowed a substantial amount of money.*'

Cade's eyes widened. Tsuru had not told him any of this.

'*If I had to guess, Ishak is leaving the slaving business. I believe he intends to set up his own* ludus *after this tournament ends and become a* lanista *himself.*'

'*But why attack my contestants?*' Julia asked. '*What benefit could it serve him?*'

'*Because Ishak cannot afford to set up his own* ludus, *even with the money he has borrowed. I also know he has placed a large bet. Now, I can guess that it was against House Julia.*'

Should our teams fail, he will get a large pay-out. Enough to bring his plans to fruition.'

Julia stared thoughtfully, then nodded.

'If he kills one of my teams, it betters his odds. Perhaps he chose yours because of your track record of winning.'

Tsuru inclined her head in modest acknowledgement.

'I had heard that the members of my team attempted an escape upon his ship. He likely held a grudge against them too.'

'Regardless, it was a big risk to take,' Julia said. *'Should he fail, he will become penniless. He will be desperate.'*

Tsuru bowed.

'I will double the guard in case there is a second attempt.'

Cade stared at the ground, hardly able to comprehend what he had just heard. Much of it had gone over his head. All he knew was that he had a new enemy to contend with.

But while he considered this, Julia turned back to Cade.

'So,' she said, 'you are the one who injured my Danes.'

Cade lowered his head. So *this* was what it was all really about.

'Only in self-defence,' Cade said, his voice low. 'And I was not alone in the fight.'

'So quiet, all of a sudden,' Julia said, her voice cruel and teasing. 'Where is the defiance I saw earlier?'

Cade avoided her gaze. What else could he say?

No, really . . . what *else*? A private audience with Julia was rare. Her intention was to chastise him, that much was clear. But perhaps he could turn this to his advantage.

'I had hoped to make a pact with the other teams of House Julia, to not attack one another in the first bout,' Cade blurted.

246

Julia blinked at him, surprised.

'All signs point to the opening bout being a free-for-all,' Tsuru said swiftly, the expression on her face unreadable. 'It is a sound strategy.'

Julia motioned for Cade to speak on.

'Even as we agreed it, they betrayed us,' Cade said. 'They tried to kill us.'

'Oh?' Julia said. 'Why?'

'The Danish teams had their own alliance already. We're on our own.'

Julia tapped her foot, then spoke as she inspected her long fingernails.

'Do you know how a *ludus* earns its money?' she asked.

Cade had an inkling, but instead shook his head.

'When my gladiators win a bout, I earn a portion of the money from the ticket sales at the Colosseum,' Julia said. 'That, and the prize purse for the winner. But when my gladiators lose, I get nothing. So, I do not care *which* of my teams win. Only that one does.'

She considered Cade for a moment longer.

'I will instruct the *doctores* to prioritise attacking the other teams over those of my own. Whether the Danes choose to honour that in the moment is beyond my control. That's all.'

She stood and strode back into the confines of her boudoir, her slave girl scurrying after her.

Tsuru looked at Cade, a half-smile on her face.

'Patience,' she said.

FORTY-TWO

They woke, ate, trained, ate and trained again. Sleep did little to alleviate their exhaustion. They drilled over and over, practising the same manoeuvres, yelling out the same orders. They charged and clashed across the sand, jabbing practice spears into each other's faces, necks and eyes.

On alternate days they exercised in the afternoons. Squats, sit-ups, push-ups, coupled with endless runs. All with the bags of rocks to weigh them down. It was monotonous agony. Repetitive torture that Cade thought would leave their bodies so broken that they'd hardly be able to stand by the time the first bout came around.

But, as time went by, Cade began to see a change. Where ribs had once been visible, now layers of muscle and even fat had returned. Shoulders broadened, limbs thickened. His chest, once flat as a pancake, jutted with thin pectoral slabs, and he could see the ridges of muscle along his arms as he flexed them.

Even Zeeb had been unseated from the hollow in Cade's

collar bone, now filled and padded with fat and muscle. Instead, the little beast nestled in the nascent fuzz of Cade's chest hair.

And it was not just their appearance that had changed.

What had once taken all their strength, could now be done with ease. Ten push-ups became twenty, became fifty. Ten laps of the arena had left them collapsed on the ground by the end – now they hardly broke a sweat.

Yes, they were still bruised and bloodied, and their bodies ached each time they lay their heads down to sleep. But they woke each day stronger than before.

Now, with one week until their first bout, the five of them were practising harder than ever. Though it didn't feel as if they were learning anything new, Cade could tell they were improving. Their movements, once stilted and awkward, now flowed with the grace of a single organism.

Cade had believed football players on TV were dumb jocks who mashed their bodies together until the ball popped out. But now he knew the truth of it – that there was a second type of genius, one embedded deep into muscle memory, instinct and subconscious.

It was something that could not be expressed, nor taught. To read his companions' movements from the corners of his eye. Hear the shuffle of feet in the sand, know the soft intake of breath before a blow, and its expulsion as it landed. That strange double-awareness, razor-focused on the opponent opposite, yet equally cognisant of his surroundings.

The pulse of battle was second nature now. The shove of shield against shield, the crack and clatter of weapons. His footing switched under its own volition, his body pulling taut as a bowstring before lunging like an arrow, his legs set like pillars against the push of his opponent.

Despite this, Tsuru was unrelenting. Every imperfection was called out now. Each overreach, unbalanced step or mistimed strike was met with a withering glare, and a shouted word that Cade now hated more than any other.

'Again!'

Tsuru's voice whip-cracked through the training ground. The five of them broke from the melee with a collective groan. Cade knew why they had been stopped – their mock-battle had devolved into a shoving match. Somehow, none of them felt like hitting each other in the face at this late hour, even if their spear-tips were little more than boxing gloves. Go figure.

'I said, again!'

With another groan, Cade, Amber and Scott shouldered their shields and formed once more, facing Quintus and Grace across the field of sand as the pair backed away and squared up.

'Brace,' Cade called to his friends on either side.

Three feet scraped in the sand, cutting a furrow against the coming impact. Three shoulders set against inner shields, and three arms raised, spears aloft and poised. Quintus and Grace charged.

The pair hit the shields like a freight train, the clatter of wood against wood, shield-boss on shield-boss reverberating through Cade's entire body. Yet, even as he scraped an inch back, Cade stabbed his practice-spear forward, the softened end catching Quintus in the crook of his neck.

The Roman fell away, but not before Grace delivered a strike of her own, only for it to be caught on Amber's shield, swiftly raised at the last moment. A riposte from Scott took Grace's belly, and then she too fell back, wheezing for breath.

A slow, almost sarcastic clap echoed around them.

'Very good,' Tsuru said. 'I would chastise you, Quintus and Grace, but then, you were imitating the enemy. Tell me, how would you have attacked, had I not told you to do so?'

Grace let out a low hiss, the wind knocked out of her. Quintus rubbed his neck and gave Cade a wry smile.

'I would not,' Quintus said. 'Charging an enemy of larger numbers, in formation and prepared for us. It is stupid.'

Tsuru smiled. 'Correct. You have earned yourselves a rest.'

They collapsed immediately to the sand, and to Cade's dismay, it seemed it was dinner-time once again. The ship's boy had already doled out their portions of gruel and now scurried forward to hand them their bowls.

Cade considered the boy as he spooned the oatmeal into his mouth, grimacing at the taste. It never seemed to get better.

His portion was always larger, but he wasn't sure if the boy did it because he liked Cade or because he didn't. And it was impossible to tell . . . because the boy couldn't talk to them.

Ishak had cut out the boy's tongue. It was Tsuru who had informed them, in the first training session following the assassination attempt. Told them of the stump at the root of his mouth, and the burn where they had cauterised it.

The boy couldn't write, nor did he understand any language they tried with him. They didn't know who he was, or where he had come from. The Codex told them only that he had been born on Acies and they knew nothing else about him. They didn't even know his name.

But the small boy had found a friend in Quintus. The pair hadn't had much time together given all the training, but Quintus had already begun teaching the boy a rudimentary sign language. It was Quintus's hope that eventually, the boy would learn enough to tell them who he was. For now, they called him Sprog, a nickname that Grace had come up with, and it had stuck.

'A second helping, I think,' Tsuru announced.

Their lack of enthusiasm made her chuckle.

'Perhaps not today, if only because we are short on time. Now, off to the baths with you.'

Sighs of relief followed, but not from Cade or Amber. Because their evening wasn't over yet. Tsuru's duel training was about to begin.

FORTY-THREE

Over the past few weeks, Amber and Quintus had taken it in turns sprinting at Cade across the sand, equipped with a spear haft to swing in his direction. It had been a . . . painful learning curve.

But it had been worth it. Cade had become adept at countering these attacks, even succeeding in hitting them with his practice sword as the spear pole whipped over his head and they stumbled past him in the sand. It was all a combination of timing, angles and agility. Backing away and to the side limited their angle of attack, while opening up the area in which he could safely dodge aside.

Soon enough, they struggled to hit him at all. Training for the duel had gradually evolved over the weeks from the act of evading and countering a charge to the exchange of blows. After all, Cade could only use the beast's strength and momentum against it so many times before it approached too slowly for that to be effective.

Tsuru was less sure how to deal with this. She had

primarily dealt with training gladiators to fight creatures that usually bit their opponents, like carnosaurs. Those with claws tended to be of the four-legged variety.

Her hope was that the battle would be over quickly, with Cade killing it in the first blow as its momentum carried it onto his blade. But failing that, Cade would need to learn to stand toe-to-toe with a giant.

Unfortunately, Amber was not an eight-foot, muscled monster with sickle-shaped claws. Tsuru's solution had been to give Amber a pair of stilts, ones used by circus performers at the emperor's palace. She had also attached training spears to each of Amber's forearms, giving Cade a better approximation of what he would be facing.

The result was comical and cumbersome. Cade found it relatively easy to block or dodge the awkward, slow swipes of Amber's makeshift 'claws'. He danced effortlessly out of range as she tottered about the arena.

Today, Tsuru had handicapped Cade by attaching weighted bags of sand all along his arms, legs and torso, slowing him down and giving him a workout to boot. This, it seemed, was working.

He struggled to meet her blows, or stagger out of range. But he managed it all the same, and Amber grew more frustrated as she thrashed at him with her arms.

'I've had enough!' she yelled. 'This is pointless!'

She stepped away, and Cade collapsed to his knees, taking in deep, heaving breaths.

'The alpha will never be as slow as this,' Amber said.

'Cade is learning the technique,' Tsuru snapped from her

stool on the sidelines. 'How to block a blow from above, how to dodge a weapon that can bend at the elbow. We cannot prepare for his speed and strength, but in this, there is worth.'

'Then he's learned enough,' Amber said. 'I can't even touch him.'

'You almost have him,' Tsuru said, clicking her fingers. 'Again!'

But Amber ignored her, crouching and falling onto her backside so she could untie the contraption from her limbs.

'Did you not hear me?' Tsuru demanded. 'I said again.'

Amber muttered under her breath, struggling with the knots that held her stilts in place. Cade couldn't help but feel relieved. Another minute and he would have been too exhausted to continue.

'Are you scared of me, girl?' Tsuru asked.

'No,' Amber said, her voice sullen.

'Then why do you whisper your insults, instead of speaking them for all to hear?'

Amber abandoned the knots and growled in frustration.

'I said, what do you know about duelling?' she met Tsuru's eyes with a defiant gaze. 'You won *one* bout, almost a lifetime ago. I say you got lucky. I think you're a fraud.'

Cade knew Amber didn't mean it. It was an explosion of emotion, lashing out like a cornered animal. The months of the great responsibility they bore had been compounded by the knowledge that they might die a violent death, and soon. It was a wonder none of them had suffered a nervous breakdown yet.

Tsuru got to her feet and made her way closer. She stood

beside Amber, meeting her defiant gaze, as tears began to form in Amber's eyes. The old woman lay a hand on Cade's shoulder and leaned upon him as she settled beside them, her face unreadable. She brushed a tear from Amber's cheek. Then, slowly, she began to unpick the knots at the girl's feet.

'I was your age when I killed my first man,' Tsuru said in a soft voice.

Amber's brows furrowed, her tears stopping almost as soon as they had begun.

'I was the high priest of my temple, as my father had been before me. It was my home, and a shrine where the weapons of Japan's greatest warriors were kept safe. I and my fellow priests trained in Budo, the martial way, as its protectors. So prized was this shrine, all the warlords of our nation wished to take it for themselves.'

The old woman's gnarled hands made short work of Amber's knots, but neither moved. Instead, Amber seemed transfixed by Tsuru's story.

'The warlord Yoshitaka was one such man. My two brothers had already died at his hands on the mainland, a defeat that killed many of our warriors, and now he came to our island with armed men and ships. It fell to what was left of my clan to protect it, and I, their priestess, as leader.'

'You were sixteen?' Amber whispered.

Tsuru smiled, a faraway look in her eye.

'In those times there were many *onna-bugeisha* – women samurai. We fought alongside the men as equals. In this time of warring states, many leaders would die in battle, leaving their young heirs in their place. Sixteen was young, yes, but

256

there were many commanders even younger than I.'

She allowed herself a chuckle.

'Of course, there were many old men left in the village who doubted my right to lead, but being a priestess came with its own advantages. I told them I was the divine avatar of the shrine's *kami*, its god-spirit. That shut them up soon enough.'

'Like Joan of Arc,' Cade breathed.

Tsuru shrugged, not understanding, and continued speaking.

'We ambushed them the first time, as they marched through the forest to our shrine. Sent them running back to their ships. In that time I met my betrothed, Kurotaka. A good man. Kind, and brave. We were to be wed, but Yoshitaka sent his men once more, four months later.'

The old woman's eyes shone with emotion, and only then did Cade realise how hard it was for Tsuru to tell her story. Who else knew of her origins here, in New Rome?

'I attacked their general's ship myself. Climbed its very side with metal claws, my soldiers and I dripping with sea water. I could not stand more bloodshed. My people had suffered enough. So while the battle raged across their fleet, I challenged their general, a man named Ohara, to a duel. He laughed, seeing but a little girl. We fought . . . and I killed him.'

There was no pride in her voice. Only suffering.

'Yoshitaka's fleet left after that, cowed by the loss of their war-general. But fate is a cruel mistress.'

A twisted expression touched the edges of her mouth, the hint of a bitter smile.

'Ohara returned two years later, and Kurotaka died in the

fighting. I could not bear the pain of it. Once the invaders were defeated a final time, I threw myself into the sea. Only to be washed up on the shores of this island.'

Amber stared at her, for once speechless.

'So when you ask if I have experience in duels and the martial way,' Tsuru said quietly, 'believe me when I say that I do. Do not doubt me again.'

Tsuru stood and trudged back to Sprog. The boy took her hand, and the old woman turned her back on them.

'Come on,' Cade said, helping Amber to her feet. 'We'll pick this up tomorrow.'

FORTY-FOUR

'You also,' the guard snapped, pointing Amber in Cade's direction. He had just shoved Cade towards the men's baths.

'I beg your pardon?' Amber asked.

The guard stared at her blankly, then said in stilted English.

'Girls still in other *thermam*. You go this one now.'

Cade could hear the sounds of splashing and voices in the girl's baths across the hall and realised that their early departure from Tsuru's lessons had meant they had clashed with the bathing time of the girls from the other teams. After what had happened last time, and the guards responsible being whipped, Cade was sure this man didn't want to risk a repeat incident.

'It's fine, you go in,' Cade said.

'And leave you to stink up the whole prison?' Amber asked, flashing him a smile. 'We'll both go.'

'Are you sure?' Cade asked.

'It's better than bathing on my own, like I usually do after

259

extra training,' Amber said, glancing over her shoulder. 'I keep worrying someone's going to . . . come in. Maybe I'll spend more than one minute washing this time.'

Cade blanched, realising what she meant. He felt ashamed to not have considered that side of things. She'd risked a lot more than sleep when she had chosen to help him train.

'Go,' the guard barked.

They stepped through, and the doors slammed closed behind them.

'Turn around then,' Amber said, walking past him.

Cade spun on his heel, his face reddening as he heard the rustle of cloth. Then the splash of water as she entered.

'I'm turned around too,' Amber called.

Cade had never got undressed so quickly. Within moments he had waded into the pool, and he was desperately glad of the bubbling water that blurred everything below his upper chest from view.

Even so, as their eyes met across the water, Cade could not help but blush. For once, he was glad that his darker skin helped obscure his feelings. Her own flushed face could only be a result of the hot water though.

'You've filled out,' Amber commented, prompting a fresh wave of heat to his cheeks.

'Th-thanks,' Cade stuttered, unsure of what to say. 'You too.'

Amber grinned, and lifted an arm from the water, tweaking her bicep. Cade averted his gaze as the movement revealed slightly more than it should, setting his heart beating twice as fast. She noticed his eyes flick away and lowered her arm, her expression inscrutable. A silence followed, one that felt devastatingly quiet, though it was helped along by the bubbling of water.

'Tsuru's story,' she said. 'That was something, wasn't it?'

Cade latched onto her words with relief.

'She's a hero. A legend. I'm surprised I've never heard of her.'

Amber smiled at him.

'The Japanese Joan of Arc,' she said. 'I really put my foot in it, didn't I?'

Cade smiled back.

'Well, we both have a habit of doing that. If I hadn't goaded Abaddon, we might not be here right now.'

'If you hadn't goaded Abaddon, he might have waited another few weeks to start the game back up. Imagine if he'd only given us a few days to prepare? The world wouldn't have a chance.'

'But we might have never been captured,' Cade said.

'If you got mugged one evening, would you feel guilty about the time you decided to leave the house? Or that you left the house that night at all?'

'No . . .' Cade said, confused.

'Then you shouldn't feel guilty now. Bad stuff happens, whatever you do.'

'Right,' Cade muttered but he didn't really get it. Amber rolled her eyes and moved closer.

'Look. You gave us the gift of time, and it's you who has to fight the monster. Don't you dare think we're upset with you. Without you, or Quintus for that matter, the girls and I would have ended up here long ago.'

She took his arm, forcing him to meet her gaze.

'You've kept us alive. Kept Earth alive. And you don't even realise it. It's what I like about you.'

She caught herself, and let her hand slip back into the water. Cade was at a loss for words, and once again the silence stretched out between them.

'Hey,' Cade said, 'Maybe if we'd left later, we'd be fertilising some plant in a pile of dino-dung instead.'

Amber's brows furrowed for a moment. Then she laughed aloud, and Cade let out a laugh of his own, the tension dissipating. It hadn't been a great joke. But he'd be damned if he could remember the last time he had laughed.

'Right,' Amber gasped, 'or lugging some rusted armour that smells of dead Polish king through the jungle. Maybe old Caesarion did us a favour. It's a shortcut really, and we get a nice stay at this resort.'

'The food's pretty great,' Cade added. 'Local cuisine, and plenty of it.'

'And the spa facilities are to die for,' Amber said. 'Not to mention the *great* security – there's guards everywhere.'

'Except for the assassins,' Cade said.

'Well, nowhere's perfect.' Amber winked.

'We'll complain in the guest book.'

Cade grinned at her. It was strange to be alone with Amber. They had spent a lot of time with each other over the past few months, but never alone.

Amber dipped beneath the water, and Cade could see the dark cloud of her hair as she ran her fingers through it. He hoped that she was keeping her eyes closed.

'I will say, the warm water is a real perk of this place,' Amber said after she emerged. 'I hated the freezing water at the Keep.'

'You didn't seem to mind the waterfall last time,' Cade said. 'Remember that night before the battle. That wasn't so bad.'

Amber narrowed her eyes in mock-suspicion. 'You're right. This is the *second* time we've bathed together. If I didn't know any better, I'd think you'd bribed that guard.'

'I would never . . .' Cade spluttered. 'I mean . . .'

Amber laughed. 'You're so *easy*. Relax, Cade, I'm pulling your leg.'

'Thanks,' he groaned.

Amber poked out her tongue and pushed away, doing a small lap of the pool. Cade took the opportunity to douse his head beneath the water, hissing his embarrassment into the bubbling water.

'You know, I'm surprised Tsuru doesn't have us doing laps somewhere,' Amber said as he lifted his head. 'We used to do water aerobics after hockey practice. Great for stamina.'

She demonstrated, pressing her back against the side and kicking her legs above the surface slowly. Cade felt himself redden at the glimpse of her calves.

He saw them all the time . . . so why did they seem so interesting all of a sudden?

'Maybe she's scared of water,' he said, forcing himself to stare at the ceiling. 'What with her fiancé and all.'

Amber stopped and scooted closer.

'You could be right,' she said. 'But hey, they probably didn't have water aerobics in the . . . what century is she from again?'

Cade brought his eyes back down. She was awfully close. Well . . . not *awfully*.

'She didn't say,' he said. 'Codex, what period did Tsuru live in?'

'*Ōhōri Tsuruhime was born in 1526 and was declared dead in 1543. She lived during the the Age of Warring States, and was responsible for the death of famed general Ohara Takakoto following a duel by single combat.*'

Amber blinked in astonishment. Likely in part because of the Codex's sudden appearance above Cade's head.

'She wasn't lying,' she breathed. 'It really happened.'

'Such a sad ending though,' he said. 'Can you imagine loving someone so much that you can't live without them?'

Amber considered it for a moment. 'I guess . . . I just hope I get a chance to.'

Cade felt the same bitterness she did. It was not just their futures that Abaddon had stolen from them, but their present too. Cade had never even kissed a girl.

'We will,' he said firmly.

Amber forced a smile. 'Well, on that note, and in the full knowledge that the creepy Codex is listening to everything we're saying . . . I'm going to get some shut-eye.'

She stared at Cade expectantly.

'Turn round then,' she said.

'Oh . . . er . . . right,' Cade stuttered.

He turned round, instead staring at the Codex, which had returned to its countdown.

10:23:32:41
10:23:32:40
10:23:32:39

There was a splash, and the slap of wet feet on the ground. The dry rustle of her towelling off, and the huff of her breath as she pulled on her clothes once more.

Then, finally:

'See you later, Cade.'

Cade relaxed as the door slammed shut, allowing himself a brief moment before getting out. It was hardly the time to be thinking about Amber like that. He hadn't even allowed it to enter his mind during their slow recovery back at the Keep.

If he survived the duel . . . well that was a different matter. But for now, it could only do harm.

'See you, Amber,' he sighed.

FORTY-FIVE

There was no weight training leading up to the games. Their bodies could finally rest, the endless cycle of torn and regrown muscle fibres cut short. It was a relief to finally sleep without the constant ache, and their mock battles were replaced with more formation practice to allow their bruises and assorted injuries to heal.

And before they knew it, it was the night before the tournament. There was no speech from Julia, nor from Tsuru. It was like any other evening, though he and Quintus were waved away from duel training.

That, at least, had been going well. Cade's sword was now almost an extension of his arm, his form effortless as he blocked the blows that rained down upon him, and Tsuru now nodded in approval rather than pursed her lips. How he might fare in a full suit of armour against the stronger, faster foe was yet to be seen, but he could now fight an opponent taller than himself.

Yet despite this new confidence, the knowledge of the first

bout's impending arrival hung over Cade like a cloud. Sleep did not come easily that night for any of them. Instead, they talked into the late hours. Of good food and better times. Of family and childhood memories.

What little sleep they had was snatched in bursts, even though they were allowed to sleep in and the morning light filtered in from beneath the prison wing's doors. In the morning, they checked the timer, ominously ticking down.

05:09:57:12
05:09:57:11
05:09:57:10

Their breakfast, taken in their training arena, was not their usual protein-and-fat-heavy fare, but instead starchy, unleavened breads, root vegetables and greens that would keep their bodies energised through the long battle ahead. It was a welcome change, though the meal sat heavy in Cade's stomach as Tsuru made them hydrate, empty their bladders and then hydrate again. It was almost a relief when the guards finally came to get them and led them to the courtyard of Julia's *ludus* where their carriages waited.

They were the same type as the carriage that had brought Cade there. The other teams were already loaded, much to Cade's relief. He didn't relish looking into the eyes of the young men and women he might be forced to kill in just a few hours.

The five of them bundled into their carriage, and to their surprise, Tsuru followed them in, along with Sprog. The guards loaded their weapons too, and they found themselves rather cramped, travelling with their feet resting on chests of shields, swords, spears and armour.

'You're coming too?' Cade asked.

'Of course,' Tsuru said. 'I will be with you until the arena gates open. Then I shall take my place in the trainers' box, just below the emperor's.'

She caught Amber's raised eyebrows.

'The job comes with *some* perks,' she added drily.

The carriage wheels began to turn, and they juddered from sand onto cobbles, the equipment rattling in time with their chattering teeth. The others, having hardly seen New Rome beyond their initial journey to the *ludus*, pressed their faces against the bars at the carriage's back. Behind them crowds of children scampered and laughed, as if it were little more than a day off from school. Yet Cade found his attention drawn to his hands, hands that trembled more than the cart's vibrations would make them.

When he had fought the vipers, there had been no time for nerves. Getting everyone to the battle itself had been so difficult, it had almost felt like an achievement when it started. This time though, he'd had a month of anticipation.

A small hand grasped his wrist, and Cade found himself looking into Sprog's eyes. The boy flashed him an encouraging grin, and dropped something small and stripy into the palm of Cade's shaking hand. Zeeb.

The kid must have gone back to get him, knowing how much Cade loved to cuddle with the little beast. He supposed the boy didn't hate him after all.

'Thanks,' Cade said, as the creature preened. He ran a finger along Zeeb's spine, just the way he liked it. For now at least, it was a distraction. There was something about stroking a grateful pet that made the world seem a little less dark.

Soon enough, the sounds of the children had been replaced by the noise of a crowd, and their passage slowed as the drivers on top cracked their whip to clear a way through the masses. A few minutes later and the carriage rumbled to a stop. Cade passed Zeeb back to Sprog.

'You take care of him until we get back, OK?' Cade said.

The boy nodded, understanding the intent if not the exact words, and slipped Zeeb into his pocket to the sound of a disgruntled squawk.

'It's time,' Tsuru said, struggling to her feet. 'Walk tall, for this is the emperor giving those who could not afford a seat a chance to see you. The world will be judging you, and we will need their support. The cheers of the crowd can make all the difference.'

The carriage's barred doors swung open, and they stumbled out into the light. Cade saw the other boys blinking after their gloomy journey and stumbling from their own carriages, as loincloth-clad servants scurried to gather the equipment from within.

The noise increased threefold as the people in the crowded plaza around the Colosseum caught sight of the gladiators. Guards surrounded them with a semicircle of shields and reversed spears that they used like batons against the encroaching crowd. They looked almost like riot police, but the cries from the crowd were of wonder and fascination rather than protest.

Cade supposed they had never seen gladiators as modern as them. Though if that would play well to garner the crowd's favour was yet to be determined.

Still, it was not the baying masses that caught his attention, but the grand statue that shadowed the clearing he had just stumbled into. A colossus, as it was known, the Colosseum's namesake. Green as the Statue of Liberty and her equal in height, a man stood in that same pose, with a crown and uplifted torch. But this torch belched out a dark smoke, real flames flaring from its base, visible even against the hot sun above.

And the Colosseum itself was breathtaking. It had seemed almost unreal when he had seen it from the palace's balcony, like looking at a painting. But here, its stark facade towered high as any modern building, dwarfing anything nearby. It was made of the palest white stone, and it almost glowed in the sunlight.

The first three levels were made up of hundreds of towering archways, with a final storey of golden plaques and windows. The arches of the second and third storeys were populated with coloured statues looking out across the surroundings, depicting nobles, emperors and kings of days gone by, if Cade had to guess.

But there was little time for the gladiators to admire the place that was to mean death for nearly all of them. More guards streamed out from the Colosseum's interior, their spearpoints lowered. Shoulder-to-shoulder, they stamped forward in unison, herding the gladiators to what would be, for many of them, the last place they would ever see.

It was time.

FORTY-SIX

For some reason, Cade had expected to be taken directly to the arena, but of course they had yet to unpack their weapons and armour. So instead, they found themselves forced down a stairway, jostling each other as they felt their way down in the gloom.

Cade felt Tsuru take his arm, and he did what he could to give her space in the cramped stairwell. But it was not long before they found themselves beneath the Colosseum, and Cade could not help but stop and stare at the network of pillars and corridors that lay below the arena itself.

Heat hit him like a physical force, the walls damp like the confines of a sauna. Men bellowed orders, and slaves scurried back and forth like ants, carrying baskets, bundles and buckets of water.

The steamy air was tinged with the acrid stench of smoke, dung and sweat, and Cade could hear the screech and rumble of living creatures in among them, though they were out of sight.

What little light there was came from clay oil-lamps ensconced in the walls, but the gloom seemed not to trouble the weak-chinned man who stood in front of the stairwell, ordering the teams in separate directions. With each team, he glanced up from a scroll and barked a number, and guards would peel off, taking them to their place.

Cade caught a glimpse of Finch, the boy's face tense and unreadable, as he and his team were funnelled to the left, while Cade's team was directed to the right. Frog-marched deeper by a pair of guards, Cade could only stare at the vaulted ceilings that must have held up the sandy arena above, and try to catch a glimpse of what else lay within the dark confines of what he knew to be called the *Hypogeum* . . . the underworld.

On they went, through the guts of what now felt like a living, breathing beast. Cade could hear the roar of the crowd above, separated only by the thin layer of wood and sand that made up the arena floor. A chant, rising and falling to allow a raucous applause . . . and interspersed with the clang of metal.

'The entertainment before the bout,' Tsuru said, catching Cade's expression. 'Criminals to be executed.'

A scream of anguish tore through it all, suddenly cut short. The approving clamour of an adoring audience followed.

They were halted then, and forced to stand on a sandy wooden platform barely large enough to accommodate them all. Pulleys and counterweights hung from the ceiling, and Cade knew this was a primitive elevator. They were to be raised directly into the arena.

Stranger still, he could see another level through the gaps at the edges of the platform beneath them, and an animal stench emanated from there.

The chests containing their equipment were laid beside them, and the guards beckoned at them to arm themselves, and quickly.

'Slowly, now,' Tsuru said, as Sprog threw open the chests and began to hand out the armour. 'There is still time. Do it right.'

Cade felt a sudden wave of compassion for the old woman. They were more than a job to her. She cared.

'Thank you, Tsuru,' Cade said. 'For everything.'

Tsuru looked up at him with that same, inscrutable expression she usually had.

'You can thank me when you come back,' she said, 'and I expect *all* of you to come back. Now, put on your damned armour.'

Cade helped Amber strap on the metal plates, as they always did before training. His hands shook as he started, leaving the knots loose and tangled. Cade pawed the sweat from his eyes and took a deep breath of fetid air, then began again. Once done, Amber returned the favour.

'You OK?' she asked, laying her hands on his shoulders.

Cade nodded, though he had never felt less prepared for anything in his life. For all Tsuru had done, their training had felt like a game. This was real.

And it was made all the more apparent as Sprog opened that box that had remained locked for most of their training, and handed them each their spears. Weapons that they would use to kill. And not so far away, scores of other gladiators would be preparing to do the same to them.

The team stood ready in the sweltering heat, their helmets held under their arms, shields at rest against their waists. Tsuru checked and rechecked every knot.

'You are ready,' she said.

She stepped back, pulling a reluctant Sprog behind her. The boy looked at them intently, then threw a hurried hug around Cade's chest. Cade patted his head, and the boy released him, wiping tears from his eyes. Tsuru took his arm.

'I must join the other *doctores*,' Tsuru said. 'But hear this. Each one of you is as fine a fighter as I have ever trained. Know that you are the best team to set foot upon those sands today. Trust what you have learned, and do not let fear rule your choices. Fight well, my children.'

She turned, pushing her way past the guards. And then, she was gone.

Cade stared after her, even as the roar of the crowd grew louder, impatient for the bout to begin. Almost a hundred thousand people, waiting to watch blood spill across the white sands below them.

Still, the gladiators waited. Listening.

Cade saw it then. A slave, dragging something behind him, down the corridor. A bloodied body, nearly unrecognisable thanks to the butchery it had been subjected to above.

He threw up on the floor.

A hand rubbed his back, and he looked up through watery eyes. Quintus.

'Waste of good meal,' the boy said.

He winked. Cade was almost taken aback by the legionary's nonchalance. After all, even as a soldier, Quintus had only ever taken part in one real battle.

But as the others helped him stand straight once more, he saw their smiles, felt their hands on his shoulders and back. They were being strong for *him*.

His friends had grown in that long month. And not just in body. There was a strength there, one born of purpose. No longer were they the human husks that had eked out an existence back at the Keep.

They had a chance now. And with that hope came the courage needed to seize it. Cade gritted his teeth as the crowd's roars reached a fever pitch above them.

The world lurched as the platform began its slow creak up, the chains that held it rattling in their brackets. Above, the trapdoor fell open, showering them with sand and blinding them with light.

Cade put on his helmet.

FORTY-SEVEN

Light.

Noise.

Birthed from the hot confines of the labyrinth below, they blinked in the dizzy space above. The sun beat hot and heavy upon them, beaming through a hole in the broad rim of awning in the roof that gave shade to the crowds. No such reprieve for them.

Cade had expected the arena to be a barren circle of sand, but he was mistaken. Four enormous pillars had been erected there, decorated to look like trees. Branches had been stuck there, though they bore no leaves to obscure the view of the onlookers. Patches of long-grass had been scattered around, to give some semblance of a real-life battlefield. These did not hide the streaks of red in the sand, left over from the earlier 'entertainment'.

At the centre of the arena, a square had been marked out with stones and white paint, its four sides made up of inward-facing crescents. What purpose it served was not apparent, but Cade knew it was likely the worst place to be, assailable from all sides.

If anything, Cade and his friends would head straight for the raised wall beneath the masses and form a shield wall there. He bet the others would do the same.

Eleven other teams were spread in equal distances midway between the arena's centre and its edge.

Those on either side of Cade had more armour than they had, and one group lacked shields. They wore chainmail instead, by the looks of it. He could not begin to guess at their origins, though they were just as young as he was, it seemed.

The other group were Danes armed with swords and shields. Finch was not among them.

And then, just like that, the crowd silenced. Confused at what sudden signal could have caused such a change, Cade spun round, only to see that his team was directly in front of the emperor's box. There was Caesarion himself, standing with his arms outstretched, his garish purple toga stark against the dark interior behind him.

Beneath him, Cade could see the *doctores* and the *lanistae* in another box, Tsuru's face just visible over the balcony, standing beside Julia.

'*Begin!*' yelled Caesarion.

Standing so close, Cade heard the words himself, but the order was repeated in a single, simultaneous bark from the guards that stood in menacing lines along the crowded seating of the amphitheatre. The sound of a horn accompanied the order, so loud that it temporarily drowned out the scream of the riled-up onlookers.

For a moment, Cade stood in shock. Did they expect them to start slaughtering each other right then? Because if so, they were in for a disappointment.

'The walls,' Cade shouted. 'Hold there!'

He led the way, heart thundering, scattering sand with every step. He glanced to his left and right, saw the others had not moved and the ground opened up in front of him. He teetered, nearly losing his spear as he flailed for balance, and a hand yanked him back.

But not before he saw what was rising from below. A monster.

'Go!' Cade yelled.

They split in two, running around the great hole, as a monstrous feathered head emerged, a single beady orange eye catching his gaze. Then they were past and at the wall, slipping into formation.

'*Testudo* formation!' Cade called, but the others were already moving. He knelt, Amber to his left, Quintus to his right, and Scott and Grace behind with their shields propped above, resting on the soft crest of his helmet's mohawk.

He gazed through the gap between the shield rims, as the dinosaur took its first tentative step onto the sands. And across the arena, three other dinosaurs did the same.

'No,' Cade breathed.

They looked like feathered *T. rexes* – carnosaurs of varying sizes and colours. All towered well over twenty feet in height and looked capable of swallowing a man whole.

'What do we do?' Amber hissed.

Cade didn't know. Now he could see the chain wrapped about the neck of the beast opposite like an attack-dog's leash. It was one of the larger specimens, with a black-fuzz plumage, and a red-blue wattle beneath its yellow-toothed mouth.

And then, movement. The Danes ran for the arena's centre, and Cade's heart soared with guilty relief as the beast saw and gave chase. A lumbering run that covered ground quickly and matched the pace of the terrified boys.

They reached the square, just as other groups did the same, suddenly finding themselves surrounded by enemies. But as the carnosaur closed behind them, it stopped short, nearly falling as the chain tightened around its neck. A choked screech of anger followed, and the crowd roared with delight at the game masters' cleverness.

Cade realised then the purpose of the square at the arena's centre. It was where the carnosaurs could not reach, for their chains were too short. The gladiators' choice was simple. Face the carnosaurs or each other.

The space at the centre became more crowded, and two carnosaurs strained against their leads, snapping at the fighters within. And then the butchery began. The first swords rose and fell, shields clattering together as warriors fought for space in the small island of dubious safety.

Cade watched as a girl staggered back, clutching at a wound, and an enormous head snatched her from the ground. She was shaken left and right, like a dog's chew toy, and the starving animal had its first taste of blood. Cade looked away. The crowd leaped to their feet, roaring with fists in the air.

'Incoming!' Grace shouted.

Cade's eyes widened as he saw the team to their right approaching in a shambling run.

'Shield wall,' Quintus called.

They moved as they had trained to, standing and spreading in one fluid motion, their spears poised, shields raised. It took only two seconds, and Cade's heart thundered as the boys approached.

But they did not slam into them as he had expected, instead stopping just beyond their formation, chests heaving. The first to arrive was only a little older than Cade, and he was clearly Asian, as were the others. His sword was lowered, and his eyes seemed to plead with Cade rather than challenge him, and words tumbled from his mouth in a rush of garbled words.

Cade didn't understand, though the language sounded familiar. The others arrived, looking frantically over their shoulders. The leader repeated himself, pressing the backs of his hands together and opening them in a parting motion.

Cade was about to call to the Codex, when Amber spoke.

'They want us to let them through. They don't have shields or spears. They want to join us.'

Cade's breath choked in his throat. This was worse than a fight.

'We can't,' Grace said. 'There will be gaps in the wall. Or they'd be behind us . . . they could stab us in the back.'

'You said you speak Mandarin with your parents, right?' Cade hissed to Amber. 'Maybe ask them to drop their weapons?'

Amber didn't answer, instead rattling off a string of words

that Cade guessed must have been Mandarin. The leader shook his head, repeating the motion with his hands.

'He won't,' Amber said. 'They don't trust us.'

Cade cursed under his breath. Beyond, the carnosaur was still snapping at the maelstrom of fighters, the scent of blood likely driving the starved beast mad. But if it turned . . . the other team would be helpless.

'Tell them if they drop their weapons they can stand behind us, or lie down beneath us,' Cade said. 'But that's all.'

Again, Amber shouted over her shield, and again the leader shook his head, yelling back in desperation.

'He won't,' was all Amber said. 'Looks like either we trust them, or they trust us.'

'Idiots,' Scott snapped. 'We're the ones with the spears.'

'If they join us, we are weaker,' Quintus said.

'We don't even know who *they* are,' Cade said. 'Codex, tell us.'

'*According to Chinese Colonel Li Fu Sien, 2,988 of his soldiers disappeared without a trace overnight. This event took place in 1939, after the Japanese invaded the city of Nanking.*'

Soldiers then. But did that mean they could be trusted?

'Maybe we should let them in?' Amber asked.

'No!' Cade snapped.

'They'll die. *We're* killing them,' Amber hissed. 'You know that, right?'

Cade gritted his teeth and shook his head.

The teen in front was becoming more agitated, snatching glances over his shoulder every few seconds. Now the others joined in the shouting, clasping their hands together as they

282

begged. One even threw down his sword.

Then it happened. The carnosaur in their section backed away, the chain slackening from its neck.

It took a few seconds to turn its head and snap at the chain that constrained it, as if it were a snake encircling its neck. And as its head turned, it caught sight of the soldiers.

The leader panicked. Cade saw it happen, the terror forming a rictus in the man's face.

'Get away,' Grace hissed.

The boy charged, sword raised. Four steps taken in what seemed the blink of an eye, and Cade hardly had time to think.

The sword swung, and instinct took over. His shield snapped up, knocking the blow up. And his spear whipped forward.

But this was no training spear. No padded sacking to knock the man away. It was a razor point that took the boy's throat and spun him away and the others scattered in terror.

No time. No time to regret, no time to think.

'*Testudo!*' Amber cried.

Cade knelt in the blood he'd spilled. Unseeing eyes stared accusingly at him, and beyond, the dark form of a primeval monster barrelled towards them.

No time.

FORTY-EIGHT

Spear grounded, back-spike screwed into the wood beneath the sand.

Point angled up, shield braced against shoulder and knee.

Eyes up, grip tightened.

Breathe. Wait.

The carnosaur came. It was the blood that did it. The starving beast, mad with hunger, did not chase the difficult quarry that was the Chinese soldiers. It came for the meat.

Footsteps shook the ground; the boards beneath the sand creaked with its weight as it lumbered closer, the long plume-spiked tail lashing lazily behind it.

Cade stared through the gap above his shield, knowing all that separated them was a thin barrier of wood. The massive feet stopped in front of him, black-taloned and three-toed.

A giant head lowered, followed by a snort that sprayed sand as it nudged the dead boy with its snout. Then, almost gently, it took the corpse in its mouth and lifted it out of sight.

Blood showered down, dripping through the cracks between their shields. It was a strange sound, as the beast chewed through the metal of his chainmail and into flesh and bone. A crunch and squeak, methodical as the jaws worked up and down.

The body fell, landing on their shields with a thud. Then the weight was lifted and the chewing renewed. Somewhere beyond, the crowd continued to cheer, yet Cade's world was reduced to that narrow view of the carnosaur's feet.

'Why isn't it over?' Scott whimpered. 'Surely half the teams are . . . are gone by now?'

Grace hushed him.

And then the body fell again, in front of them. Cade tried to avert his eyes, but it was too late. Mangled, bloodied chainmail, wrapping the lion's share of the meal. It seemed the carnosaur could not handle the metal.

Something nudged Grace's shield above him. Then again, scraping along its surface, as if seeking a gap. Another snort, and the stench of carrion filled their world.

Then a thud, slamming Grace's shield onto Cade's head and shoulders.

'Brace,' Cade called, as it came again. Light burst through as the shields were forced aside. For a single, terrible moment, that giant snout pushed between Amber and Cade, bloodied feathers scraping along Cade's shoulder.

Quintus struck. His blow was weak, with no room to backswing for his rusted gladius. Still, the jab sliced along the beast's snout above its eye.

Blood sprang forth, and the carnosaur reared. Their spears

285

jabbed up as the shields closed once more. Again and again, Cade blindly pumped his spear up and down, feeling the catch of a hit, and hearing the screech of anger and pain.

Then the snout came again, bursting between them like a giant sledgehammer. Teeth snapped, and they scrambled back, their formation breaking until it pulled back.

Even as they threw themselves together and upheld their shields once more, Cade knew they were on borrowed time. Their blind stabbing was too easily avoided, their shields no more than a temporary annoyance.

He stared at the monster's feet, at the corpse and the trailing chain behind it. An idea came, half-formed, and he acted even before he knew what it was. He broke ranks, hurling his shield aside and diving forward. It was a frantic, awkward move, and as he did so, he stabbed his spear up, punching through the plumage and letting the spear dangle as he rolled between the carnosaur's legs.

A monstrous foot stomped down, crushing the soldier's corpse and missing him by an inch. But then the soldier's blade was in his hand, a simple sabre that he swung as he staggered to his feet, carving a notch in the carnosaur's leg before sprinting past a thick lashing tail.

He snatched a glance over his shoulder, his feet scattering the sand. It followed a roar of fury that told him this fight had become personal. All he could do now was race it to his target. Not the square. Not another section. But the pillar, planted not far from where Cade's team had emerged.

There was no chance to look back again. He could hear the thudding footsteps, practically smell its breath. Every second, he expected to be knocked from his feet, or his world to disappear down a monstrous gullet.

But it didn't. He reached the tree and rounded it in a wide circle, heard the rattle of the chains, and continued on, now sprinting back to his friends. His heart thundered in tempo with the pulse at his temples, and his breaths were snatched and ragged. Still, he ran.

A weight smashed into his back, throwing him head over heels. He scrambled to his feet as a pink maw opened wide in front of him . . . and snapped an inch from his face.

The carnosaur lunged again, and Cade scrabbled back in the sand, watching as the chain tightened so snug around the monster's throat, he could no longer see it. Behind the beast, the chain's remainder stretched from the trapdoor to the pillar, then back again – an anchor in the sea of sand.

Half-stumbling, half-crawling, Cade made it back to the others, collapsing among them as the carnosaur heaved and choked. But the tree held firm. Whatever rooted it to the spot was sturdy.

Still gasping for breath, Cade looked beyond the dinosaur to the square in the centre of the sands. And there, he saw slaughter. Swords rising and falling, gladiators screaming in fear, fury and agony. There seemed to be no rhyme or reason to it, only a frenzy of desperate blows and scrabbling feet.

A horn sounded, long and deep. The note reverberated through Cade's chest, and it silenced the crowd in an instant. The gladiators paused. With a jerk and a clinking of chains the carnosaurs were dragged back.

Cade fell to the ground, letting the sabre fall from nerveless fingers. They had done it.

The first bout was over.

FORTY-NINE

They were led through gates in the arena walls back down to the *hypogeum*, each group cordoned from the other by a handful of guards.

Cade had thought there would be half the number of gladiators walking with them, but it seemed far fewer. Of the teams that had survived, many were missing members. Others could not walk, their injured bodies carried on stretchers by slaves.

They pressed on through the vaulted corridors below and into a larger room, and it was there that Cade saw the full horror of what had transpired above.

Men, dragged along the ground by hooks, like meat at a butcher.

Some were still alive, their eyes fluttering in delirium, covered in grievous wounds they had no chance of surviving. Each was stripped swiftly by a pair of waiting slaves, businesslike as they tugged off armour and collected weapons to leave the bodies, alive and dead, nearly naked beneath.

Cade's own weapons and armour were taken from him and placed in waiting chests; he expected they would go back to their *ludus*.

He had to look away from a pile of bodies, but he could not block out the buzz of flies, and the rotting stench.

Walking on with eyes half-closed, he saw a man wearing a dark hood that must have been stifling hot in the heat. False wings adorned his back, a parody of some god or mythical creature. He held up a hammer, and beneath, a dying gladiator stared up in dull acceptance of his fate. A Dane.

Behind the man, more bodies lay in a macabre mound, the results of his actions plain to all. He was the executioner, putting the mortally wounded out of their misery. Was it kindness? Or cruelty?

Cade closed his eyes as the weapon swung down, allowing the guards to herd him forward. There were no carriage rides back this time. Instead, they walked through a dank tunnel beneath the earth, their ankles submerged in grey water, droplets dripping from the ceiling.

The passages split in four, and soon Cade found himself alone with the surviving Danes and girls, plus the guards that separated them. He saw Finch was still alive, and did not know how to feel. Was Finch so bad that he deserved the same fate as . . . the Chinese soldier?

That thought twisted Cade's chest. He had killed someone. Killed them like it was nothing.

He fought for breath as he remembered the spear sinking into flesh, so easily he had hardly felt more than a tug as his opponent fell away. The panic on his face as life left him.

And then, as the light had faded from his eyes, the blank stare of accusation.

Panic seized Cade's throat like a vice, the walls seeming to close in on him. He could only walk, even as the world swam in front of his eyes. He heaved, and the acrid burn of bile burned his throat.

The guard behind shoved him when he slowed, and Cade let his hands guide him along the slime-slick walls. He could see the dim glow of light ahead, and he focused on putting one foot in front of the other. Steps came, and the light grew brighter.

He staggered between open doors into the sands of the *ludus* courtyard and fell to the ground. Felt tears run down his face, hot and caustic. Sobbed into his knees, holding them close to his chest as he rocked back and forth.

And then Amber was there. She held him, as feet trampled past and the guards laughed. Like a dam bursting, he sobbed out the anguish that had built inside him. All the fear, the anger, the hurt. Nobody stopped him.

It seemed like an hour before he was all cried out. A single guard watched over them. Only Amber remained, sitting with him in the shade, her hand rubbing his back.

'I'm sorry,' Cade said, wiping his nose.

'Don't you say sorry,' Amber said. 'Don't you dare.'

She hugged him close, and lay her head on his shoulder.

'He was just like us,' Cade said. 'He could have been me.'

'I know,' Amber said. 'I know.'

It didn't feel wrong, to be so vulnerable in front of her. He realised now that he had always trusted her. Amber did not judge. She saw the good in people. Saw the good in him, even when he could not.

'It wasn't your fault, Cade,' Amber said. 'None of this is. We do what we have to, and nothing more.'

He knew what she meant. Even agreed with it. But as he looked at the blood that spattered his clothing, he could only feel the guilt of what he had done. The word murderer twisted through his mind like a knife, repeating over and over.

'Come on,' Amber said. 'You need rest.'

So they went. But before they could return to their cells, Tsuru stepped forth from the shadows.

'You fought well,' she said, her hands clasped in front of her. 'Of all the teams, only one of Lucretia's saw so few casualties or injuries as yours. It is they you shall face tomorrow.'

Cade stared.

'Tomorrow?' he rasped. 'They can't possibly expect—'

'People have come from all across the land, abandoning their crops and homes to watch the games,' Tsuru told him. 'Any delays will cause unrest and displeasure – the exact opposite of Caesarion's intentions. The games will take place over three days, as planned.'

Cade could hardly imagine walking out onto the sands so soon after the horrors of that morning. And he knew they had been lucky. That he had only been forced to kill one man in self-defence, while the others had been forced into a slaughterhouse at the arena's centre.

But tomorrow . . . he would be forced to kill again.

'Sleep,' Tsuru said. 'Rest. Eat. There is nothing more to be done now.'

Cade allowed Amber to pull him back to the cells. Dread clutched his heart with an icy hand. Tomorrow they would fight again.

FIFTY

Waiting was the bane of Cade's existence. The weight of what was to come settled over the five of them like a heavy cloak, stifling conversation beyond small kindnesses – checking how each other was feeling, if they were injured.

Nobody wanted to relive the morning's horrors. They washed their clothes and bathed. Basked in the sun in their small training ground. Tsuru treated them to a meal of meat-and-potato stew, and it tasted heavenly.

It was a slow transition that day, from terror to acceptance. There were moments of dread, but these faded as they made the most of what little pleasure was left to them. In the knowledge that they might die the next day, and now having experienced the reality of that fact, the world seemed more real again. Tastes were more intense, colours more vivid. Even the sensation of the wind set his skin in gooseflesh. And the girls . . . well . . . they were more beautiful.

What had seemed to matter so much before didn't any more. Amber, in the glow of the setting sun, looked radiant.

He took her hand. It did not matter if it was the action of a friend, or something more. It felt right, and no one commented as they sat in comfortable silence.

But Tsuru had one more surprise in store. Edging from the shadows, she ordered them to bed. But not before pulling Cade aside.

'Cade,' Tsuru said. 'Stay a moment.'

Amber shot him a worried glance, but Cade waved her on with a forced smile.

'Go on,' he said. 'I'll be right behind you.'

Tsuru waited until the others were gone, then beckoned Cade to follow her. A pair of unfamiliar crates lay at the edge of their training ground. She asked him to open them, and Cade cracked open the lid of the first.

Within sat a weapon. An axe, one so large he struggled slightly with its weight as he hefted it. And as Tsuru opened the next one, he saw more armour. A chest plate and other pieces, which Tsuru wasted no time in strapping to his body.

'What is this?' Cade said, unable to hide the worry from his voice.

Tsuru ignored him, continuing to armour his body.

The axe was in poor condition, rusted to the point of being nearly useless, and Cade could see the holes within the armour itself.

'We haven't trained for this,' Cade said. 'I don't know how to use an axe.'

Tsuru smiled, putting the finishing touches to him.

'You do not need to,' she said.

Now, Cade was clad head-to-toe in rusted armour, though

he had little confidence in its quality. A single well-placed blow would punch through it in an instant. As he moved, the metal screeched.

'Be still,' Tsuru hissed. 'He is almost here.'

And it was then that Sprog arrived, with someone else in tow. Strabo. The tongueless man. Lucretia's spy.

'*Help clean this up*,' Tsuru ordered dismissively, motioning at the dirty bowls that Cade's friends had eaten their meals from.

The man did so, but slowly. Cade stood in the shadows, half-out-of-sight, but he could still feel the man's eyes on him. He tried to back away, but Tsuru's hand held him in place at the small of his back.

After a minute, it was done. Strabo bowed to Tsuru, before making for the doors with far more speed than he had taken to clean up the bowls.

When he was gone, Cade rounded on Tsuru.

'What was that?' Cade hissed. 'You give us new weapons and armour, then let our enemy know exactly what we are using?'

Tsuru grinned.

'Exactly. Now, Strabo will send word to Lucretia that at least some of you will not be fighting in light armour with shield and spear, but heavy armour and two-handed axes.'

Cade went to argue again, then understanding caught up with him. 'But . . . we won't be,' he said slowly.

Tsuru prodded Cade's armour, and showed him the rust there.

'Of course not. I bought this set for hardly anything at all

– it was going to be melted down as scrap. It would hinder you more than help. Useless. But in the darkness Strabo saw only the armour and weapon, not its condition.'

Cade's eyes widened.

'What will they do?' Cade asked. 'If they think that we've switched strategy?'

Tsuru shrugged. 'Lucretia's soldiers wore no armour at all, and carried bows. They survived this first bout unscathed by being faster than everyone else – avoiding the beasts by being unencumbered and loosing arrows into the square from afar.'

Cade had hardly seen what had happened beyond his own section of the arena, but the strategy surprised him.

'I don't understand,' Cade said. 'No other weapons?'

Tsuru nodded.

'Lucretia has better spies than I – she must have known exactly what the first bout entailed and planned accordingly. She purchased no weapons beyond the bows, and no armour at all. It leaves her with money to burn for the second round. And now, she knows what her opponents will be outfitted with, and can purchase the correct weapons and armour for them. A risky strategy, but one that has paid off for her, it seems.'

Cade thought for a moment.

'What if she's already purchased her weapons?' Cade asked. 'What if Strabo is too late?'

Tsuru shook her head.

'She will wait for his report before doing so. It is not uncommon for *doctores* to buy a new set of weapons and armour between bouts – of poorer quality, yes, but allowing them to surprise their opponents with a new strategy in the next. That is what she will think we have done.'

'I just hope it works,' Cade said. 'Do you know what we will face tomorrow?'

Tsuru smiled.

'The best counter for heavy infantry is a lightly armoured opponent, most likely armed with a long weapon, such as a spear, and a shield to trap their axe. So tomorrow, we may face our mirror opposites, albeit ones armed with bows.'

'Only, we've been training with spear and shield for much longer,' Cade said, realisation dawning on him.

'Indeed,' was Tsuru's only reply.

Yet, there was a strain to her voice. Was it worry for them . . . or something else?

'Tsuru,' Cade said, an idea coming to him then. 'The assassin's javelin. I still have it. Could we use that in the battle tomorrow?'

Tsuru froze.

'You have a weapon in your cell?' she hissed.

'Well, yes,' Cade said, confused. 'If another assassin comes, I need to be able to defend myself.'

'You fool,' Tsuru growled. 'You are lucky it has not been discovered. The punishment for hiding weapons is death. No exceptions.'

She shook her head.

'I shall collect it tomorrow, before the guards come to fetch you. And of course we cannot use it, there is no proof of purchase. Do not do something so foolish again.'

'I'm sorry,' Cade muttered. 'I didn't know.'

Tsuru sniffed, and began to remove his armour.

Cade stared up at the star-studded sky. It could be his last night. The last time he might see the stars. But now he made a vow.

They were *all* going to see the night sky together again. And he would kiss Amber beneath it.

FIFTY-ONE

The crowd roared overhead, and the five of them sweated in the underworld. The long journey through the tunnels had felt like the walk to an executioner's block, and now they listened as the fighters above killed each other for the pleasure of the mob.

Six teams of the twelve had survived, and now the second bout would be completed in three rounds of paired teams fighting to the death. Their team and Lucretia's were to be the final pairing. Saving the best for last, Tsuru had said, before bidding them farewell.

Saving the most unscathed for last, more like. Cade had witnessed the injured limping to their places in the *hypogeum*. Saw the blades tied to their limp hands, and splints surreptitiously holding their legs straight. Watched the bandages torn free as the elevator lifted, so that the crowd would not see how pitiful these sacrificial offerings were.

And now, as the crowd silenced and the bodies were dragged by, the five stood on their platform, waiting for their

300

turn. Would there be carnosaurs this time? Raptors? Some other horror?

One thing was certain: there would be no avoiding the fight this time. Unless some beast did the killing for them, there would be at least five deaths at human hands that day. And though he hated the thought of it, Cade's only hope was that *they* would be the killers.

The elevator lurched, in tandem with Cade's stomach. But he did not throw up this time. He had a vow to keep. Instead, he gritted his teeth. Anger would serve him better than fear, however misdirected it was.

'Shield wall,' he growled.

Light and sand fell in equal measure, and they crouched in preparation for what they would face above.

'Oh . . . shit,' Scott muttered.

There was their enemy. And they were armed to the teeth.

Shields yes, but small buckler-sized ones that strapped to their wrists. Bows, ready drawn. Swords, and spears too. And armour. More than theirs. But not so heavy as to slow them down too much.

Thunk.

The blow reverberated through Cade's shield, and he saw the arrow-head burst through its interior. Just the tip, but enough to nick his wrist. Blood twisted down his arm, as another hit home, this time near his feet.

'Kneel!' Quintus bellowed.

They did so just in time, another arrow skittering low along the sand to splinter Amber's shield's lower edge. More followed, the staccato *thud thud thud* like a drum roll.

'We trained for this,' Cade growled. 'Forward, double time.'

They moved as one, their feet padding in sync along the sand, as the archers ahead of them scattered. This was not good – the field of fire for the enemy widening. Their sides were exposed, then their backs. Just as they had been trained, their formation changed from a crescent to a ring, slowing them as Scott and Grace were forced to move backwards, and Amber and Quintus to crab-walk sideways.

And now, they were stumped. Even the archer in front could outpace them, and still the arrows whipped home, leaving their shields pincushioned with the weight of the projectiles.

'They won't stand and fight,' Cade said. 'So we wait until they run out. To the wall, quickly.'

They hurried, even as the enemy opposite skipped out of spear-range, lancing another arrow into Cade's shield. He winced as the dart burst through halfway, stopping a mere inch from his mouth.

At so close a range, the shots were more powerful . . . and the enemy knew it. As Cade and his team backed up against the wall, their opponents came closer.

'Double up,' Amber hissed. 'Layered shields.'

They had practised the manoeuvre only once. But with the wall protecting their rear, it was as good a move as any. Amber and Quintus slipped their shields tighter behind Cade's, meeting in the middle. Grace and Scott moved half of their own shields behind Amber and Quintus's, huddling closer.

Now, there were two layers of shield between them and the enemy, except for the very edges. Arrow after arrow thudded home, pinning their shields together. But for the moment, they were safe.

It did not take long for their enemies to slow down the rate of fire. Cade peered at them, seeing they were standing only twenty feet away, arrayed in a spaced-out group of five. They were at a stalemate, it seemed.

'Who are these guys?' Grace hissed. 'They know what they're doing.'

Cade saw a flash of blue. In the bright light of the sun, it was hardly visible, but he knew the Codex had scanned their opponents.

Soon enough, a dull voice above them answered Grace's question.

'Colonel Sherod Hunter of the Confederate Army was last heard of attempting to found a Confederate colony in Vera Cruz, Mexico with other fleeing soldiers in 1866, following the American Civil War. What later became of him and his fellows is unknown.'

Cade gulped. He noted their leader, a man in his thirties, with a red handlebar moustache. Hunter.

'Fighters then,' he muttered. 'Experienced ones.'

'They used guns?' Quintus asked, glancing sideways to read Cade's lips.

'Yes,' Cade muttered. 'But bayonets and swords too.'

'We can take them,' Amber said. 'They've been training with their bows, that much is obvious. But Tsuru tricked them into using spears, which we're better with. If we can get into melee range—'

She winced as another arrow thudded into their shield-wall. The crowd had begun to boo at the lull in action. As Cade watched, he saw the purple figure of Caesarion opposite, and a slave waving a red flag beside him.

It did not take Cade long to see what the flag was signalling. Men suddenly appeared at the walls, some directly above them. Holding crossbows.

But not just any crossbows. These were artillery pieces, as wide as a man was tall, with bolts the size of javelins. Cade recognised them for what they were: Roman scorpions, powerful enough to pierce a wooden palisade, let alone flimsy shields such as theirs.

The weapons were turned upon the gladiators below. Silence, as deafening as the crowd had been earlier, slowly settled across the arena. Then, a chant.

'*Viginti! Undeviginti! Duodeviginti!*'

Cade's breath caught in his throat. They were counting down from twenty.

'Cade,' Scott called. 'What are they saying?'

'We have fifteen seconds,' Cade called.

'What do we do?' Grace asked.

Ahead, the Confederates stood firm, and Cade heard Colonel Hunter call the words he had been dreading.

'Hold, boys. We've got 'em now!'

It was a game of chicken . . . only the others weren't going to move. If they charged Cade's shield-wall, they knew they would lose.

'*Decem! Novem! Octo!*'

'We run at them with our shields up,' Cade said. 'Take the closest man.'

'Cade . . .' Scott began.

'There's no time,' Cade snapped.

He took a deep breath, watching the enemy's eyes. The spear was slippery in his hands.

'*Quattuor! Tres! Duo!*'

'Now!'

They broke, wrenching their shields free from each other in a rush of pounding feet. Cade heard the thud of arrows, heard Grace cry out. But there was no time to look. Nothing but Hunter, who stood with arrow drawn as Cade bore down on him. Ten feet. Five.

Thunk!

Pain flared in Cade's fingers, the arrow slicing between them as it punched through his shield. He released the handle, the wooden barrier tangling in his legs, and Hunter backed off, reaching for another arrow.

Cade fell. Even as the world spun, he launched his arm forward with all the strength he could muster, letting the haft slip from his hand.

They had never thrown their spears before, but at this close range he could hardly miss. The blade took Hunter in the belly, sinking deep and spinning the man away as the bow fell from his grasp.

Grace screamed again, and Cade saw her to his far left. Her shield was pinned to her leg by an arrow, and then a second knocked her onto her back, though he didn't see where it hit.

An enemy soldier rushed forward, his spear raised, shrieking with fear and anger. Cade snatched up Hunter's bow and the fallen arrow along with it. His hand flared with pain, fingers slippery with blood.

He knocked the fletching, heaved back and loosed it as Grace's opponent raised his spear. The arrow whipped through the air . . . and missed, tumbling by the man's face in a parody of flight.

But it was enough to slow him, his face turning in shock at the apparent betrayal by a teammate. Enough for Grace to rear up and strike, the spear lancing up through his armpit and into his chest.

A groan from ahead made Cade turn, only to see Hunter pulling himself along the ground, then falling still, a bloodied streak left behind him. Beyond, he saw Scott's opponent staggering with a spear in his throat, and Quintus stabbing down to finish an opponent.

Amber, her own opponent finished, crouched beside Grace. He heard her let out a cry of anguish.

Then the horn, sounding their victory.

FIFTY-TWO

There was no triumph. No relief, no joy. Not as Grace was carried through the tunnels on a stretcher, an arrow buried in her belly.

They trudged beside her, Amber holding Grace's hand. The slaves had tried to carry the stretcher, but Amber had sent them away with a snarl. It would be Grace's friends who carried her back to the *ludus*. No other could be trusted with such precious cargo.

'I'm sorry,' was all Cade could say.

He said it over and over like a mantra, but it did little to help. Grace's breathing was ragged, eyes glassy as she stared at the ceiling.

'Water,' she begged, her tongue darting for the droplets that fell from the ceiling.

But they had none.

It felt like an eternity, that long walk back. But at least, when they arrived, the doctor was waiting for them.

'Quickly,' he said, as they emerged into the courtyard.

'Bring her to the *saniarium*.'

They followed, back to the room where Cade had first been examined upon arriving at the *ludus*. Grace was laid carefully on the long table, as the doctor splayed out his tools beside her.

'Hold her,' the man said. 'This will hurt. I would push the arrow through, but it is in her belly. It will have to come out the other way.'

Tears streaming down her face, Amber took an arm, and the others followed her lead. A leather strap was pushed between Grace's teeth.

'Bite,' the doctor said.

Grace blinked, delirious, but seemed to do as he asked. Meanwhile, the doctor pulled an amphora from the room's corner, and Cade smelled the strong scent of alcohol. The man splashed some onto his hands and rubbed them like disinfectant, then reached for a strange pair of forceps that looked like salad tongs, with twin spoons on each end.

'Hold,' the doctor repeated. 'Bite.'

The man placed the spoons on either side of the shaft's entry point and sank them into the wound. Grace's eyes widened, and she bucked on the table in agony.

'Hold!' the doctor growled, and Amber sobbed as she placed a calming hand on Grace's forehead.

'Got it,' he hissed, gripping both the tool and the arrow shaft in each hand and pulling slowly.

Inch by inch, the blood-slicked shaft lengthened, until the spoons emerged, the arrow's head ensconced between their hollows.

The doctor lifted the metal head and examined it, and Cade saw the barbs there. The spoons had covered them, allowing the cruel point to be withdrawn without catching on her tender flesh. Ingenious.

Blood spewed from within, but instead of putting pressure there, the doctor leaned forward and sniffed at her stomach. He nodded with approval, then drew forth a needle and thread. Cade looked away, feeling nauseous.

'You,' the doctor said, nodding at Amber. 'Press here.'

He placed a folded white rag over the wound, pushing his weight on to it. Amber took over as he said, and the rag soaked red while Grace kicked her feet in pain.

'Almost done,' the doctor said, placing a hand on Grace's forehead.

He turned and fetched a pot from another table, and removed its lid. A strong odour of raw garlic and onions filled the room.

Cade would have thought it was some kind of poultice, but he was mistaken. Instead, the man brought it to Grace's lips.

'Drink,' he instructed.

Grace turned her face away.

'Drink,' the doctor insisted. The girl pursed her lips.

'What are you *doing*?' Amber snapped. 'We don't need her to drink some medieval potion. Unless it's antibiotics, you can chuck that in the bin.'

The doctor stared at her blankly, then sighed.

'It is in her belly,' he said, pointing at the wound. 'If it has cut her intestines, she will die. This will tell me if it has.'

Amber stared at him, mystified. Cade lay a hand on her shoulder.

'He's the best chance she has,' Cade said. 'Let him do what he has to.'

Amber sniffed, then leaned close to Grace.

'Drink up, Gracie,' she said, kissing the girl's brow. 'It'll make you better.'

Grace's eyes fluttered, and she nodded. This time, when the doctor brought it to her lips, she swallowed half of it down, before coughing and turning her head away.

The doctor seemed to think it was enough, next bringing a flask to her mouth and giving her water to wash it down. This she gulped greedily, and Cade took it as a sign she might live. But the doctor's words had scared him. It was a deep wound.

'And now?' Amber asked, as the doctor stared down at her.

'We wait,' he said, 'and I tend to the other wounds. Cade, let me see your fingers.'

It surprised Cade that the doctor knew his name, but he offered his hand. He had hardly looked at it. Luckily, the wound was not deep, nor had it severed the delicate tendons of his fingers. Still, Cade almost threw up when the man stitched each deep cut closed, and it was pure agony when the man poured alcohol on them for good measure.

He did the same for Grace's injured leg, the arrow mercifully having fallen out, and bandaged other lighter cuts and grazes on the arms and hands of others. This took a few minutes, but still the man made them wait.

'How do you know my name?' Cade asked.

The doctor grinned. 'I have money riding on you. A great many people have bet that you will win.'

Cade furrowed his brows. 'Why? What's special about us?'

'Someone was offering good odds against your team, before the first bout. Betting big that you would not win the tournament.'

It dawned on Cade then.

'Ishak,' he muttered.

But before he could pry further, the man motioned for Amber to remove the compress from Grace's belly.

With wrinkled nose, he sniffed at the wound. Only then did Cade understand what the man was doing. If her intestines had been cut open, the strong smell of the minced onion and garlic would have seeped through.

He held his breath as the doctor snorted again, massaging her belly as if to push the scent forth.

Then he looked up and smiled. 'With luck . . . she will live.'

FIFTY-THREE

'We should have split up from the beginning,' Cade said, clutching Zeeb close to his chest.

They were in their cells, trying to sleep. But none of them could. The battle replayed over and over in Cade's mind. An endless cycle of possibilities. What could he have done differently?

'Cade.'

Quintus rolled from his bed to face Cade, and the two met each other's gazes in the gloom.

'We alive. The others – not all.'

Cade forced a smile. 'Yes. But tomorrow, they'll still force Grace to fight. If she can't . . . the man with the wings will kill her.'

'The executioner.' Quintus nodded grimly. 'He wears the costume of Charon, the ferryman. He guides the dead across the Styx to the Underworld.'

Cade shook his head. Did they honour the dead with such a costume? Or did they mock them? He couldn't decide.

'Grace is strong,' Quintus said. 'She will walk tomorrow.'

'That she will,' came a voice.

Cade turned in surprise to see Tsuru crouched in the darkness. They had not seen her that day since leaving the arena. Cade had thought maybe it was out of shame that she had not come to see them, but now he was not so sure.

'I have been to see her in the *saniarium*. She is recovering well, though Julia has doubled the guard on her regardless.'

'Julia thinks she's going to try to escape?' Cade demanded. 'Is she crazy?'

Tsuru shook her head.

'No. She believes that Ishak will try for your team again. You see, I have been making inquiries. Ishak did not bet against Julia's teams. He bet against *yours*.'

Cade stared. Of course. The doctor had said as much.

'The man has wagered everything. His ship, his savings, his slaves. He will be desperate. We expect . . . something.'

His eyes strayed to the open doorways at the end of his cell block, protected by a single guard each. In the face of Ishak's crew, it felt like very little.

As if she could read his mind, Tsuru spoke again.

'Julia will have two of her teams fighting in the final bout, but there is a third from House Cornelius – Atilius's. So it is in her interest to keep you alive.'

Cade wondered absently if Finch's team was the one that had survived. He had not seen the winners of the other bouts yet.

'Now, I have an important question to ask you all. Otherwise, I shall have to remove you from your cells and train you overnight.'

Cade licked his chapped lips and nodded, anxiety twisting in his belly. What fresh horror could they have prepared?

'Can all of your team swim?'

It was not the question he had expected.

'Swim?' Cade asked. 'What does that have to do with anything?'

'Answer me,' Tsuru snapped.

'Yes,' Cade said, thinking back to their occasional dip in the waterfall's plunge pool. 'Well enough. Scott is more of a doggy paddle, but he gets by.'

'Hey,' Scott called in the darkness. Then he paused.

'Yeah, all right,' he said. 'It's true.'

Tsuru breathed heavily and leaned on the bars of the cage.

'Thank *Ebisu*,' she sighed. 'All would be lost otherwise.'

'Tsuru, what does that have to do with the fight?'

The old woman did not answer him immediately. In the red-hued light of the moon, she looked fragile. And so tired. In fact, it looked like she had barely slept at all.

'I have called in every favour,' she said. 'Begged or bribed every contact I have. And still, the details of the final bout elude me. But I do know one thing. That the *hypogeum* has been evacuated, and the arena floor removed. They are going to flood the arena, at least in part. This is to be a water battle. *Naumachia*.'

Cade was almost speechless. It was hard to imagine it at all. Such a feat of engineering would have been beyond belief, had he not known that the Romans had done the very same with their Colosseum, all those centuries ago. Or at least,

314

many historians had believed it to be so.

'We have to fight while swimming?' Cade asked. 'That can't be much of a spectacle.'

Tsuru shook her head. 'In the past, the gladiators would re-enact ship battles. I expect the same tomorrow, which means our formation training will be useless. And beyond that, I know nothing.'

Cade closed his eyes. 'Well, it's not like there's much else we could have done to prepare anyway. Got any money left over for new weapons?'

'Your spears are already the best weapons for a ship battle,' Tsuru replied, shaking her head again, 'though we will wear no armour in case you fall into the water. Smaller shields might also have been better, but there is no money to buy new ones. It shall have to do. Now . . . you must rest. Tomorrow shall be the ultimate test.'

With that she swept away, leaving them to their thoughts.

Across the corridor, Amber stirred, and Cade saw her press her face between the bars. She was alone in her cell now, and Cade couldn't help but wish he was in there with her.

'There's one good thing about tomorrow,' she said. 'Grace will be easier to protect if we're all in the same boat.'

Cade hated seeing the worry on Amber's face.

'We'll get her through this,' he tried to reassure her.

She forced a smile and moved back into the shadows, but her eyes never left his face. He had promised himself he would kiss her some night.

And yet, in the misery of Grace's injury, nothing could have been further from his mind. But he did want to hold her. Wipe the still-drying tears from her face.

The gulf of that corridor stretched between them. It might as well have been an ocean.

FIFTY-FOUR

The carriages awaited them. But this time, there were two for Cade's team, and two for Finch's, who had indeed survived the battle. It was more than they needed. But carriages it had to be, for the tunnels to the *hypogeum* were flooded.

Finch's team only had three warriors left, and all bore the bandages that spoke of the cruel violence of the earlier bouts. Among them was the girl, Mary Seward, and the big Dane, Bjorn, who eyed Quintus with hatred, his expression all the more twisted by the scar that adorned his face. But it was Finch's gaze that scared Cade the most. There was no emotion in the boy's expression as he watched them with cold calculation. Meeting Cade's look with his own, the boy's eye twitched, as if holding back madness just beneath the surface.

'Why so many carriages?' Cade asked Tsuru, who would accompany them to the Colosseum.

'As a diversion for Ishak's men,' she replied drily. 'Though I doubt they would have the audacity to attack so brazenly, in broad daylight. No, their chance has passed. It seems Ishak

317

can only pray for your deaths.'

She let out a laugh, though it felt forced.

'He seems to have only done us good, the fool. Why, we would not have Sprog were it not for him.'

The boy perked up at his name, pausing from loading their weapons into one of the decoy carriages with Strabo. The two made quite a pair, neither able to communicate beyond signalling with their hands. As Cade smiled at the young boy, Strabo smiled back. Cade turned his gaze away, confused.

It seemed he was not aware of the trick they had pulled on him, or the danger that put him in with Lucretia. Cade could only pity the poor man.

'And half the crowd will be rooting for us, having placed bets against him,' Tsuru went on.

Cade did not put as much faith in the support of the crowd as Tsuru did. Beyond their petty bets, he knew they only wanted one thing. Blood. It did not matter who shed it.

'Grace,' Amber called out.

Cade turned, to see Grace limping towards them, a crutch beneath her arm and the doctor at her side.

'She has the spirit of a bear,' the doctor said, patting Grace on the shoulder. 'But she will not fight today.'

'I can speak for myself,' Grace grumbled, shaking her shoulder free. 'I refuse to be dead weight – I'm fighting.'

'Grace, I don't think that's a good—'

But Cade was met with a glare that cut his words short. The doctor smiled anxiously.

'My apologies,' he said. 'Know this: the crutch cannot be

taken into the Colosseum – you must walk unaided.'

Grace stopped, then let the crutch fall away. She took a faltering step. Then another.

'You will tear the stitches,' the doctor warned.

Grace ignored him, instead wrapping an arm around Amber's shoulder. Together, the pair entered the carriage.

With the last of the weapons loaded, the guards herded the rest of the team aboard, along with Sprog and Tsuru. Cade took a last look at the *ludus*. Whatever happened, it would be the last time he would see it.

Soon they were rumbling along the city streets once more.

'Grace,' Cade began, but the girl held up a finger.

'Not a word, Cade. You'll treat me just the same today.'

Cade shook his head. 'I just wanted to say I'm sorry. If we'd . . .'

'If nothing,' Grace said. 'I'm here, aren't I?'

She looked him in the eye with an intensity that he had not seen before.

'There is no room for doubt today,' Grace continued. 'Winning is *everything*. Keeping us alive is not.'

'You don't know what you're saying, Grace,' Amber said, laying a hand on her shoulder, but Grace pulled away gently.

'I've thought a lot about this. The most important thing is to *get Cade back*. It's not me we should be protecting, it's him.'

Cade couldn't believe what he was hearing. But Grace wasn't done.

'If it was you who caught that arrow,' she said, 'all of this would have been for nothing. You'd not stand a chance against the alpha. Getting you back to the Keep, uninjured, is our only priority.'

'You think I'm just gonna stand back and let you guys do the fighting for me?' Cade asked.

'Didn't you just expect me to do the same?' Grace snapped back.

Cade had no answer for her. And he saw the others nodding in agreement.

'You're seriously going to side with her?' Cade asked. 'If we're going to win, we need all of us fighting. Our advantage is that we outnumber them.'

He turned to Tsuru for support, but she shrugged.

'I have no dog in this fight,' she said. 'But I'd rather all that extra training not be for nothing.'

Cade hissed out a sigh of frustration, unable to meet their eyes. If he ignored them perhaps they would not push the issue. But as he stared out of the backdoors of the carriage, his eyes widened.

Crash.

The decoy carriage slammed into another, one that had careened out of a side street.

'Go!' Tsuru yelled, and Cade heard the crack of the driver's whips above them. 'Take the side roads!'

They sped away. Cade and his friends held their breaths, but nothing happened.

In fact, after a few minutes, Cade saw that their decoy carriage was not far behind, catching up to them. If it had been Ishak, he had failed, his men likely abandoning their attack once they saw the carriage held no gladiators. Julia's idea had worked, it seemed. For that, at least, Cade could be thankful.

Now he could hear the chanting of the crowds, and before long their carriage had stopped and they were being herded into the Colosseum once more. Finch and the other team were nowhere to be seen, and Cade assumed they had stopped on another side of the building.

For a moment, Cade felt his heart in his throat as Grace staggered on her own towards the entrance under the watchful eye of the guards. But she did not falter, even as the sweat beaded on her face. Cade was proud to have the fierce warrior at his side. He'd take an injured Grace over any seasoned gladiator.

This time, there were no crowds to greet them. In fact, the streets were near empty – the new route they had taken there must have made them late.

They were not taken to the stairs this time. Instead, they were moved into a passageway, one that took them beneath the seats that held the chanting crowds. And then, just like that, they were at the arena's edge.

The sand was gone. The floor was gone. And in its place, a sea of water. Water as clear as a mountain spring, such that Cade could see the *hypogeum* and its many pillars beneath. But that . . . that was not all he saw.

Dark forms, circling below like sharks. Only these were much, much larger than sharks. Too deep to see . . . he hoped they stayed that way.

Worse still, he now saw the vessel they would be floating in. It was hardly bigger than a rowboat, with four oars lying inside and a tiller at the back.

'We're going to need a bigger boat,' Cade muttered.

'Hey, I get that reference,' Amber said, forcing a smile.

Inside, there were no seats, just a hollowed-out interior with a flat bottom. At the head, a five-foot iron spike protruded just below the waterline, which Cade took for a battering ram.

Two other vessels lay at equal distances away from them, and now Cade saw Atilius's team for the first time. Two men, both hardly able to stay upright. They leaned on each other like drunken sailors, and Cade felt sickened that people in such a state were forced to fight.

But he was also glad of it. Even if the opposing teams joined forces, Cade's would still have the advantage.

The thud of their weapons and armour being unloaded jarred him from his thoughts. The decoy carriage had arrived just in time it seemed; he could see the flash of weapons across the way, and the opposing teams clambering into their vessels. Cade's team were the last to arrive.

And in the crowd . . . he saw him. Ishak, resplendent in his robes, seated in a box close by where Cade stood. A cruel smile had twisted the man's face, and Cade grinned back in defiance. He only hoped that Ishak's galley slaves would be freed when it was all over.

The chanting of the crowd rose, eager for the fight to begin.

'Quickly now,' Tsuru said, throwing open the first crate. 'Get . . .'

She stopped. Cade turned, and saw the old woman's face

draining of its colour. For a moment he thought she had been injured, so stark was the difference.

But then he saw what she did. It was their weapons crate. The box was empty.

'No,' Tsuru croaked in a hoarse whisper. 'They were . . . they . . .'

And Cade knew then. The decoy *had* been the true target. Ishak's men hadn't been after *them* – that would be too obvious, too daring.

But this . . . it was cruel genius. They had stolen their spears. And now, they had no time to call for new ones. Not with a bloodthirsty crowd, impatient for the game to start.

'*Fetch the game masters,*' Tsuru cried, pointing at a nearby guard. '*The games have been sabotaged!*'

The guard flicked her an impatient glance.

'*Quiet, slave,*' he growled. '*Get them on that boat or I'll beat you until they do.*'

The crowd's chanting became more frenzied. Some stood and shook their fists, and Cade felt a spatter across his face as someone threw a half-eaten fruit at their team. More followed, one by one, and the guards lowered their spears and stepped closer.

'You have one minute to get on that boat, or we will throw you in the water,' another barked, this time in English.

Cade saw Ishak in his box. The man raised his goblet, a sarcastic salute that filled Cade with anger.

'Bastard!' he yelled.

'I'm sorry,' Tsuru whispered. 'There . . . there is nothing I can do. He played us perfectly.'

Desperate, Cade threw open the box that usually housed their armour, hoping there had been some mistake. It was empty too.

'*I said move!*'

The guards' spears jabbed them towards their boat. For a mad moment, Cade was tempted to grab one of the weapons and leap for the boat. But he pushed it from his mind – such an act could get his friends killed.

Instead, he staggered onto the boat, and the others came with him.

'We'll fight,' was all Cade said, as the others followed him aboard. 'And we'll win.'

FIFTY-FIVE

The boat dipped low as they piled in – so low that Cade wondered if it had been built for five at all. Water slopped over the gunwale as it tipped to the side. And even before the last of them jumped in, the deep horn sounded that announced the game had begun.

'What do we do?' Amber yelled over the noise. 'We've nothing to fight with!'

Cade pointed at Atilius's pair of fighters. 'We need weapons,' he shouted back. 'And those two have some.'

But to his dismay, he was not the only one zeroing in on the injured pair – Finch's team was paddling towards them with frantic speed.

'Go!' Quintus yelled, snatching up an oar.

Cade followed his lead, water splashing as he thrashed his oar into the lake's depths, ignoring the dark shapes that had begun to circle beneath them. Whatever creatures lay below, he knew they would be half-starved and desperate. But there was nothing he could do about them now.

'Come on,' Amber groaned.

They were slow, their boat sitting deep in the water, in stark contrast to Finch's with fewer people within. The enormous Bjorn knelt at the prow of his boat, paddling left and right with bulging muscles. No matter how hard Cade rowed, their opponents pulled even further ahead.

'It's no use,' Cade called, after a few more strokes. 'Save your strength. Maybe they'll take each other out.'

'Here's hoping,' Amber hissed.

They stopped, now near the centre of the lake, as Finch's boat closed on the other one. The two men had turned their boat side on, and now stood at each end. It was a clever move, allowing them the greatest range of movement and balancing the boat. Even so, they swayed on their feet, and Cade suspected it was not just the water that made them so unsteady. These men were on their last legs.

Cade had expected Finch's team to ram their opponents, but instead, they slowed at the last moment, facing the men across five feet of water.

It was Mary who moved first. She was armed with a sword, like Finch, and she extended an arm across the channel of water that separated them from their enemy. It was a strange motion, as if reaching out for them, leaning as close as she could. She would never reach.

Then, she extended her sword . . . and sliced it deep into her own outstretched palm.

'What on earth . . .' Amber breathed.

The girl clenched her hand into a fist, and the blood splashed into the water like liquid squeezed from a sponge.

For a few seconds, Cade thought it was some ancient ritual, an attempt at blood magic from a forgotten time.

But then, as Bjorn and Finch back-paddled the boat away and Mary used strips of cloth to bind her cut, Cade saw the blood's true purpose.

He saw it in the water itself, shadowy forms rising like demons from the abyss.

Dark humps crested the water and headed directly for the men. Men who were realising too late what had happened. Too late to sit down. Too late to paddle away.

It happened all too fast. A jolt through the pair's boat. The vessel lifting from the water, the men pinwheeling their arms. One fell in the water with a scream and a splash, hardly heard above the howl from the crowds. The other hung over the side, the wind knocked from him.

Cade almost closed his eyes. But the contender in him kept them open. He had to see . . . had to know.

A leviathan rose from the deep like the sea-monster it was, snatching a dangling arm in its mouth and pulling the winded warrior in after it. For a brief, desperate moment, the man gripped the boat with his knees, towing it behind him. Then he was yanked below the surface, and his companion soon with him.

In the depths, Cade saw thrashing, dark shapes, swimming in a red cloud. And yet hardly a ripple disturbed the surface . . . as if it happened on another plane of existence.

But Cade had seen the beast in all its horrific glory when it had erupted from the water. Like a giant, smooth-skinned crocodile with paddles for limbs. As large as a killer whale,

327

and far more worthy of the 'killer' epithet.

'What . . . what are those things?' Scott croaked.

'Kronosaurus *was a marine reptile, specifically a short-necked Pliosaur that lived approximately one hundred million years ago,*' the Codex dutifully intoned. '*These carnivorous predators averaged ten metres in length.*'

Finch's crew watched from afar, and despite the swelling noise of the crowd, Cade could hear the triumph in their voices. But they did not paddle again, even as the crowd began to quieten. Instead they watched, and waited.

'Did you see the swords?' Amber asked. 'Did they fall in the boat?'

'Maybe one of them,' Cade whispered. 'But do you want to go over there?'

Amber bit her lip.

'If we stay seated . . . they can't knock us in. And a sword gives us a chance.'

Cade shifted for a better look and shuddered as the boat rocked with his movement. Their vessel was so deep in the water, he imagined they were more likely to be swamped than be pitched in.

'OK,' Cade said. 'Slowly.'

And, after a moment's thought, he added.

'Don't splash.'

The group took hold of their oars and dipped them into the water. As they did so, Finch's crew made the same move.

'Stop,' Cade groaned. 'Save your strength.'

With bated breath, Cade watched as Bjorn thrust their

skiff back towards the empty vessel. Dark humps crested the water nearby, but a prod from Finch's blade dissuaded one from approaching too closely. And beneath, their meal was still being fought over. Soon enough, the enemy team was alongside the empty boat. Cade had thought they were only going there to prevent his team from gaining access to it. Now he watched in trepidation as Bjorn rolled into the boat himself.

'What are they doing?' Amber hissed.

'I don't know,' Cade murmured. 'But it's not good.'

He had no idea what their plan was, but the fact that they had one was what worried him. Because at that moment . . . Cade didn't.

'We don't need spears,' Quintus said.

Cade looked at him, confused.

The boy held up an oar. 'We have these.'

'Oars?' Scott said. 'Really?'

Cade hefted his own oar, but his heart dropped as he attempted to swing it from a sitting position.

It was unwieldy, pitching the boat as he swiped it through the air. The wooden handle was thicker and shorter than he would have liked, only slightly longer than a sword, yet somehow heavier. The tapered end was flat and thin, making for a poor club.

'We don't need to kill them with these,' Cade said. 'Just knock them into the water.'

'While they chop at us with swords?' Scott asked.

'You have a better idea?' Amber snapped. 'Because if you do, spit it out. They're moving again.'

Finch and Mary were paddling in one boat, with Bjorn in the other.

They were coming.

FIFTY-SIX

Cade understood their plan almost as soon as it was set in motion. He saw the two skiffs angling around, parting and travelling towards them on opposite curves. A pincer manoeuvre.

'They're going to ram us!' Cade shouted.

Any attempt at ramming could be thwarted by simply turning the boat to face the enemy – the spikes at the front of each boat guaranteeing mutually assured destruction. But by attacking from two angles . . . Cade could only face one at once. The other could smash into their side or back, sinking them.

'They knew,' Amber hissed. 'This is too smart a play for them to figure out on the fly.'

'What's *our* play?' Grace asked.

Her voice was faint, and Cade turned to see her stitches had torn – her clothing was spotted with blood at the belly. She was manning the tiller, so there was no need for her to row . . . she would not be fighting any time soon.

'We head for Bjorn,' Cade said. 'They've divided their forces . . . let's go five on one.'

'Finch will ram us from behind,' Scott said.

'Then we move onto Bjorn's boat once we've beaten him,' Cade snapped. 'Now row!'

They heaved on the heavy oars, sweating beneath the unforgiving sun. He heard Finch yell out, his words garbled beneath the rising noise of the crowd. He ignored them. All they could do was push on, closing the gap between Bjorn's boat and theirs.

Cade saw Bjorn's eyes widen as they approached him, but the Dane did not waver from his course. It was a game of chicken now. If they rammed each other, both would sink. If one turned aside at the last moment, they would be caught. But if both slowed and pulled up alongside . . . they would fight.

Only, Bjorn was not slowing. The big Dane's muscles bulged as he rowed towards them, and Cade had the panicked notion that he would sacrifice himself to give Finch and Mary the win. Then, as the boats neared, Bjorn let out a bellow of frustration. He let the oar fall, and pulled up two swords from the bilges. With one in each hand, he roared a challenge across the water.

'Grace, put us on his left,' Cade ordered. 'Scott, you keep rowing. Get in close, quickly!'

He moved to the right side of the boat, where Amber and Quintus were already waiting. As he joined them, the boat tipped towards the water, its rim precariously close to the surface.

'Scott, Quintus, get to the other side,' Cade said.

Scott moved from beside Grace to balance them, but Quintus shook his head.

'You go,' Quintus said.

'There's no time,' Cade growled, but Quintus set his jaw, staring at Bjorn instead.

Cade fell back when the boats met. Two oars swung, and Bjorn scuttled back, crouching in the boat's centre. It would be hard to knock him into the water.

'Behind us!'

Scott's yell made Cade turn, only to see Finch's ship bearing down on them. Fifteen feet. Ten.

'Turn!' Cade ordered, thrashing at the water, monsters be damned. Too slow, the boat shifted. Cade saw the long five-foot spike coming for them, and shoved Scott aside as the blade punctured their ship's bottom, punching through the planking and springing water like a tap.

He risked a glance over his shoulder, and saw Quintus and Amber still jabbing at Bjorn, unable to dislodge the giant. The pair had boarded his boat, having pushed Bjorn to the back, but were unable to move closer as he swung his sword at them. If they couldn't take Bjorn's ship . . . then Cade would take Finch's.

'Help get Grace on the other boat,' Cade said to Scott.

'It won't carry six!' Scott said.

'It won't have to,' Cade said.

Then he turned to Finch, who crouched on the enemy boat's prow. Mary waited behind, her blade outstretched.

'Come on,' Finch snarled.

Cade could already feel the water pooling around his ankles. He heard a cry of pain from behind him, but he did not turn. The roar of the crowd faded, his world reduced to the thin gap of water between the boats, and the two enemies opposite.

He swung the oar, and Finch flinched. But Cade had not been aiming for him – instead he splashed the water, dashing it into the boy's face. It was the half second he needed as Finch blinked at the spray, carrying through his swing and thrusting at Finch's belly.

Finch fell back, and Cade leaped over the gunwale, falling into the enemy boat. The boy swiped down, half-blinded, but the blow splintered into the prow above Cade's head.

It gave Cade time to move into an awkward crouch, as Finch wrenched his sword free and swung again. Cade raised his oar two handed, and the blade sank into the wood between. Finch heaved back, his weapon stuck.

For a moment they kept up the tug of war, while Mary crawled to Finch's side, blade held in her bandaged hand. Cade changed his pulling into a shove, releasing the oar. Finch pinwheeled back, collapsing on top of Mary. The girl released the sword with a cry.

Cade snatched it up, just before Finch pulled his blade loose from the oar. The pair stared at each other across the boat, Mary sobbing behind him, Finch's face mad with rage. The boy charged.

He lunged . . . and Cade ducked beneath the blade, a hundred hours of training taking control of his body. He heard the thrum above his head, so close he almost felt it.

But as Cade went to riposte, he found Mary shoved in his way, the girl's arms flailing. Cade wrenched his blade up, refusing to kill the unarmed opponent. She fell in a heap at his feet, hands over her face.

Finch's eyes gleamed as he crouched at the back of the boat, but behind the usual bravado, Cade saw a hint of fear.

Even armed with little more than an oar, Cade had bested him over and over. Finch knew he was outmatched. And with no more than a thin stretch of boat between them, there would be no dirty tricks to pull.

But then, Finch's eyes flicked aside. Cade did not take the bait, knowing it would only be a distraction. And, a moment later . . . Finch mounted the gunwale, poised above the water.

Cade allowed himself a second to glance over, and his heart leaped to his throat as he saw Finch's target: Scott struggling with Grace at Bjorn's boat's prow, their own boat nearly submerged.

They would be sitting ducks.

Finch dived into the water, slipping in with hardly a splash.

'Scott!' Cade screamed, but the boy only glanced over his shoulder, nearly in the water himself, as he heaved at Grace's limp form. He could not see the danger.

Beyond, Amber and Quintus were occupied with Bjorn, holding him at bay with the length of their oars. He had no choice.

Cade closed his eyes . . . and leaped.

He plunged beneath the surface, resisting the urge to kick as the lukewarm water swallowed him whole. In the murky darkness, he could hardly see more than a few feet ahead.

Except Finch was no longer heading towards the other boats. Instead, he had turned, his sword outstretched in Cade's direction.

It had been a trick. With neither practised in fighting underwater, the odds had been evened.

Cade surfaced, taking in a gulp of air. At the same time, his mind raced, calculating his options.

If he returned to the boat, Finch would skewer him before he clambered in, if Mary didn't strike with an oar first. He had no choice but to face Finch, here and now.

Cade allowed himself to sink, the weight of the sword pulling him down. Finch made his move in the same instant, striking as Cade's eyes accustomed to the water.

The blow fell an inch short, the blade glinting as it flashed in Cade's face. He lifted his own blade to knock it aside, only to find his movements slowed to a crawl.

The blades clanged together ineffectually, and Finch lunged a second time. Cade barely managed to evade it, kicking away with a silent, bubbling scream.

Finch was playing a suicidal game. One drop of blood could spell death for both of them, inviting the circling monsters to feast. It was a wonder they had not come already.

Cade breached the surface, and Finch cackled as they faced each other.

'Not so quick now, are you?'

Cade did not reply, preferring to take in deep, desperate breaths. There was only one place that he would be safe. A boat.

Clearly, Finch's plan was to return to his own as soon as he had cut Cade. So Cade needed his own safe haven.

He had one move left to him. A mad, all-or-nothing move.

Cade lifted his sword aloft, as if it were easier to tread water that way.

'You're dead, Cade,' Finch growled. 'You've—'

Cade hurled the sword, a weak throw that he did not wait to see the result of. As the blade tumbled towards Finch, Cade launched himself towards his own floundering boat.

The world devolved into the frantic motion of Cade's legs and arms, his vision flashing between dark water and bright sun. His hand slapped the rim of the near-sunk vessel, and he rolled himself over.

By now, the boat was almost sunk, and he could only rest his feet on the bottom of the shell that hung just above the surface. He blinked water from his eyes, spotting Finch only a few feet away. The boy pointed his blade towards Cade, savage anger plastered across his face.

'Nice try,' Finch snarled. 'But it hit me with the wrong end. You're dead.'

Cade's submerged boat had drifted away from Bjorn's. There was no weapon for him now. Not even an oar. Finch had him at his mercy.

And yet, as Cade stared into the other boy's pitiless eyes, a slow trickle of red dripped from Finch's brow, just above his hairline.

The wrong end had struck . . . but it had still drawn blood. The first drops mingled with the water.

337

Finch didn't seem to notice as the dark forms swept in, rippling the surface. He only frowned as Cade's boat rose and fell.

Then he gasped, just before he was jerked beneath the water. Cade did not watch. Instead, he lay flat in the centre of his sunken vessel, praying the flimsy wood might protect him from the thrashing monsters beneath. Twice more he felt the scrape and thud of passing creatures, until the fight over Finch's body moved beyond his fragile haven.

But the battle was not over yet.

He looked to the side only to see Amber and Bjorn grappling, the girl gripping the Dane's wrists, the blades in each of his hands pointed at her chest. With each second, they inched closer.

Then Cade saw him, clambering from the water at the ship's back. Quintus had risked the waters to flank Bjorn, and now he punched out with a closed fist, smacking the boy at the fragile juncture of head and spine. Bjorn staggered as Amber butted her head forward, his nose spurting like a ripe tomato.

Together, Amber and Quintus shoved him against the side, the dazed boy's legs tripped up by the low gunwale. There was a splash . . . and the dark shapes glided beneath the water to meet him.

Somehow, Bjorn surfaced, and struck out for Mary's ship. But Cade knew it was hopeless.

A sob from Mary brought his attention back to her, only a few feet away from him. She knelt in the boat's centre, bereft of weapon or ally.

'Please,' she begged. 'I don't want to be here.'

Cade could do nothing as she stared at him through streaming eyes.

'Please.'

Now, the chanting had begun. The outside world had come back into focus as the crowd bellowed a single word, over and over again.

'Iugula! Iugula! Iugula!'

Kill. Kill. Kill. Cade refused to even consider it. They had won, and everyone knew it. He would not slaughter her in cold blood for the sake of such people. Condemned to die though she was, whatever this battle's outcome, he refused to do their dirty work.

By now, the others had paddled their new boat closer, and Cade risked the short swim to Bjorn's ship. Scott's outstretched hands pulled him to safety in a matter of seconds.

He heard Bjorn's screams as the monsters circled. The Dane was snatched below, once, then came back up, even as crimson stained the water beneath him. Laughter pealed from the crowd, their attention divided between the girl they wanted put to the sword, and the boy to be devoured.

Mary moved.

'Wait!' Cade yelled.

But it was too late. Mary was in the water, swimming for the arena's edge. She even got halfway there, before the first shadows rushed towards her. Cade closed his eyes, and covered his ears.

They had won, and he had never felt more ashamed.

FIFTY-SEVEN

'I *am* impressed.'

Caesarion lazed on his bed, eating olives from a bowl. He offered one to Cade, who shook his head. Cade could hardly stomach being in the man's presence.

'And what a show you gave us. The best tournament in New Rome's history, so they say. You were right . . . a chance at freedom makes gladiators fight all the harder. We shall have to do it again.'

Cade did not reply. Despite it all, his mind could only focus on one thing. Finch's face. Those blue eyes, widening in horror as he was dragged beneath the water.

The first men he had killed were strangers. But he *knew* Finch. And though Cade hated the boy, that did not make the fact he had killed him feel any more justified.

Caesarion lifted his head to meet Cade's eyes.

'Why so glum? You won.'

Cade wondered if Caesarion wanted him to smile, but he could only lift his chin.

'Who knows, maybe we'll send all our winners to your "Keep", yes?'

Cade stared.

Caesarion grinned and rolled from the bed.

'That got your attention, didn't it?'

'Why would you do that?' Cade asked.

'Let's just say I have a soft spot for you moderns,' he said. 'You are far more fun to watch. And should the world end, why, who will bring me new books to read?'

He laughed at his joke, and sauntered closer to Cade, his jewellery clinking.

'Yes, I think I'll do just that,' he said.

'As long as they don't hunt in the lands close by,' Cade said.

The emperor flapped his hand in agreement, as if it were a given.

'My friends are outside,' Cade said, motioning to the doorway. 'Can they come in?'

'Bored of my company already?' Caesarion asked, a teasing smile upon his face.

'I need their help picking a remnant,' Cade said, gesturing at the glass cabinets that littered the space. 'There's so many to choose from.'

Caesarion tutted.

'Five gladiators in a room with the emperor? No.'

Cade's eyes flicked to the giant bodyguard, who watched Cade with hand on hilt. Somehow, Cade didn't think the five of them could take the armoured giant, but he supposed the emperor had a point.

341

'So . . . one item, wasn't it?' Caesarion said, shooing him with curled fingers towards the maze of glass cabinets.

'About that,' Cade said. 'Would you be willing to grant me a suit of armour instead? That's what I need.'

The emperor considered Cade for a moment, then chuckled.

'That was *not* the deal. These trifles mean nothing to me,' Caesarion said, waving vaguely at the items beyond. 'Clutter and more clutter. Choose, before I change my mind. You have five minutes.'

Cade hurried away, feeling the prickle of Caesarion's gaze on the back of his neck. The emperor could break his word at any moment. Best to take what he could now.

He had to make a choice, and quickly. They had three days until the battle with the alpha, and he refused to have survived all of this, just to return to square one, venturing into the jungle for the Polish king's armour a second time.

Armour was his priority, tempted though he was by the crossbows and javelins he saw there. But he knew that the weapons and armour they had used before would remain at Julia's *ludus*. They were lucky to keep their padded linen clothing.

There was so much to choose from. Too much, even. He would hardly have enough time to examine *half* of the remnants there in five minutes. Lucky for him, he didn't have to.

'Codex,' Cade whispered.

To his surprise, the drone materialised. It did not seem to mind Caesarion seeing it.

03:04:47:52
03:04:47:51
03:04:47:50

'I need you to scan every remnant in this room. Then, I want you to lead me to any that include armour.'

It was the work of a moment, the small machine's path visible through the flashing blue light as it roved back and forth along the rows. To Cade's dismay, it wasted a precious thirty seconds scanning the books as well, before finally returning to Cade and flickering into existence.

'*Two relevant remnants found,*' the Codex intoned. '*Please follow me.*'

'Two?' Cade whispered.

He had thought there would be more.

There was no time to dwell on that though. The Codex floated down the corridor of cabinets, turning once and coming to a halt opposite a glass box containing what looked like a combination of breastplate and skirt, both made of the same material – squares of dark, wrinkled leather, held together by loose threads.

The armour looked to be of Asian origin, though it seemed almost rotted rather than rusted in appearance. Mildew had eaten at its edges, and there were gaps where the squares had fallen away.

'What is it?' Cade asked.

'*This armour belonged to a pre-samurai Yamato warrior from Japan, though no specific record of this individual remains. It is known that he fought in the Battle of Baekgang in 663 AD,*' *where over four hundred Japanese ships were sunk by the Chinese Tang dynasty in the Geum River.'*

Cade was hardly listening, his heart sinking fast. This was leather, and in poor condition at that. Not to mention that it would cover only his chest and upper thighs. Hardly enough to protect him from the alpha's claws.

'Next one,' Cade whispered, crossing his fingers. 'Quickly.'

The Codex shot away, and Cade hurried after it. This time, it took him down a winding path, until Cade found himself standing opposite one of the largest cabinets of all. But it was not armour propped up on a wooden crosspiece, as the last remnant had been.

This was a dark metal box, as long as a man was tall. The outside was covered in what looked like barnacles, though these had long dried out.

'I thought I asked you for armour,' Cade hissed. 'A metal box doesn't count.'

'This remnant contains the body of Sir Francis Drake, who was buried at sea off the coast of Panama in 1596. Famously, he was dropped from the side of his ship, the Defiance, *in full armour, within the confines of a lead coffin.'*

Cade's eyes almost popped from his head. A full suit of armour? That was exactly what he needed. The only problem was, he had no way of checking what condition it was in. Who knew if the coffin had filled with water, eating it all away to leave only a brown paste of rust inside.

The other armour was better than nothing. But at the same time . . . Cade knew that better than nothing was not good enough. He would have to roll the dice.

'This one,' Cade called. 'I want this.'

Even as he said it, uncertainty rippled through him.

Caesarion wandered over, his hands clasped behind his back.

'Ah, the Drake coffin. Very good taste. I shall have it sent to your ship.'

Caesarion turned on his heel and walked away.

'Thank you . . . ?' Cade said.

But the emperor seemed to have forgotten he was even there, disappearing into the rows of bookshelves.

The bodyguard took hold of Cade's shoulder and propelled him back towards the double doors.

And just like that . . . Cade was free.

FIFTY-EIGHT

His friends waited on the palace steps, enjoying the sunshine. Tsuru and Sprog sat with them, having joined them in their journey there, travelling in one of Julia's carriages.

'This is the last time we shall see each other,' Tsuru said. 'Or at least, I hope so.'

Cade impulsively hugged the old lady. When he pulled back, he looked her in the eye.

'Without you, we would've never had a chance,' he said. 'How can we ever repay you?'

Tsuru flapped him away, for once flustered.

'You make much of very little, boy,' she said. 'Just you make sure to beat that monster.'

Cade nodded, and felt tears well in his eyes. He had not realised just how attached he had become to the crotchety old warrior.

'Before I forget,' Tsuru said. 'I have something for you.'

She motioned her head at Sprog, who had been holding Grace's crutch. The boy proffered it to Tsuru.

'Thanks,' Grace said, holding out her hand.

Tsuru ignored it.

'There is more to this than meets the eye,' Tsuru said, winking.

She held the crutch up. It was made from bamboo – a simple hollow thing of wood and twine. As Cade watched, Tsuru took hold of the top. The end came off with a twist, and Cade's mouth flapped open.

'The assassin's javelin,' Tsuru said to Cade, showing him the metal tip hidden within. 'It was all that would fit.'

She twisted the lid back on and handed it to Grace.

'Tsuru, you are a genius!' Cade cried.

He swept her up in a second hug, and this time, the old lady returned it.

'Thank you,' he said. 'I—'

'Enough of that!' Tsuru said, dabbing at one eye. 'I'll hear no more thanks today.'

'We're going to miss you, Tsuru,' Amber said, taking her hand. 'I wish we could take you with us.'

'To a cold ruin in the wilderness?' Tsuru asked, though her face reddened at Amber's words. 'My old bones could not stand it.'

'What about Sprog?' Cade asked. 'Julia would not notice if he came with us, would she?'

Tsuru shook her head. 'Even if she would not, the boy is safer here, with me. I will make sure he's well cared for.'

Cade crouched down beside the boy, who stared up at Cade with worry in his eyes.

'You make a good life for yourself here, OK?' Cade said.

347

'Ishak will never hurt you again.'

Sprog blinked, somehow understanding that this was goodbye. He reached into his pocket, and held out Zeeb to Cade.

Cade lifted the small creature and stared into its dark eyes. Zeeb had fattened over the weeks there, its wing entirely healed, and yet it had chosen to stay with him until the end.

But what fate would await it at the Keep, where that slow starvation would begin again? Cade wouldn't be able to care for it.

He gave Zeeb one last chin scratch, then turned back to Sprog.

'You know,' Cade said. 'I think you should keep him.'

He closed Sprog's fingers around the little beast, and the boy's face lit up with a smile. He wrapped his arms around Cade's waist, as a carriage pulled up alongside them.

'All right,' Cade said, prying the boy's arms free. 'That's it then.'

The goodbyes were all too fast. More hugs, hurried words of care and kindness. And then they were aboard, sitting among the cushioned seats and windows, rather than the barred interior of a prison-carriage.

'Kind of wish we could stay too,' Scott muttered, plumping the seating with his hands. 'Man, I'm going to miss those baths.'

'And live among these people?' Grace snapped. 'The ones cheering while I was dying in the sand?'

Scott lowered his eyes. 'Maybe not, then.'

The carriage rattled on along the cobbles, and Cade knew they were headed for the docks. He wondered absently where they would sleep in the ship on the return journey – as prisoners, crew members or honoured guests?

It hit him then. They were free.

It had seemed impossible, and yet here they were, trained by the best and with a suit of armour coming with them. They even had safe transport to the Keep itself. He had to wonder if it was all coincidence.

Tsuru an expert in both fighting beasts and Japanese swordplay. They had been fed and trained as warriors. A remnant had been handed to them, cherry-picked from over a hundred, preserved behind glass like an inventory to choose from. Could Abaddon have had a hand in this?

Except Grace's injury, they were in a far better position than they would have been, had Ishak not come across them in the jungle. Had that been supposed bad luck too?

If Abaddon had orchestrated it all, it was a risky move. But a risk that had paid off . . . they were as ready as they would ever be.

Once again, Cade was but a pawn in a much larger game, bound by the whims of a cruel overlord. The only silver lining was that Abaddon was on *their* side. A strange thing to think, after everything.

Cade was still deep in thought when the carriage stopped, ten minutes later, at the docks.

He leaped from the carriage, bumping into Amber who stood transfixed in front of the doors. 'Everything al—'

Cade stopped, as he saw what she had. Saw what awaited

them on the jetty.

It was the other slavers. The same ones who had captured Cade and the girls in the jungle all those months ago, with over a dozen men among them and a chain of rowers-to-be trailing in their wake.

He would know those at the front anywhere, from the pigtailed boy to the man who had knocked him unconscious. Their faces had been burned into his memory, even if they now wore the light clothing of sailors rather than the armour of before.

Pigtails stepped forward.

'Your items are already on board,' he said loudly, a thick, Scandinavian accent lacing his words. 'Now you are all here, we shall leave within the hour – the winds give fair sailing. You will obey our every command, or we shall kill you. Do you understand?'

Cade nodded.

'Come,' Pigtails motioned.

They followed.

As the men crowded down the jetty towards their ship, Cade's eyes were drawn to a familiar face amongst the chained slaves shuffling behind them: Ishak. Beaten to a pulp and stripped of his garments, the man now wore little more than a loincloth. He stood out from the other slaves, as his body was not coated in filth, but Cade saw those same hooded eyes staring at him with a hatred he hardly believed possible.

Then the chain jerked, and the rowers shuffled on, off to condemnation in the bowels of a wooden beast. It was a fitting end to the slaver, yet Cade felt no triumph in it. No man deserved such a fate. Not even one as evil as Ishak.

It was hell on Earth.

Or hell on Acies, anyway.

FIFTY-NINE

They were locked inside a nondescript room, with a single porthole, four narrow bunks, a bucket and little else. It was in the lower decks, where the stench of working men and the heat of the sun made for a muggy atmosphere.

Cade knew that they would spend only one night here, so he did not mind the accommodation. But when he tried to give up his bunk to the others, he was met with derision.

'You're about to fight for the fate of the world, and you think you're the one sleeping on the floor?' Grace chuckled, wincing at the movement.

'I suppose not,' Cade said. 'Being the sacrificial lamb does have its perks.'

So Cade lay down, groaning with relief. This was no straw mattress, narrow though it was. His back revelled at the chance to sleep on what felt like feathered stuffing. He had not slept on something this comfortable since he had arrived on Acies.

The pitch and roll of the sea lulled him to sleep. In a haze of exhaustion, Cade dipped in and out of slumber, woken by the shouts of the sailors and the creaking of the ship, only to slip back to sleep again.

Cade dreamed. Dreamed of tentacles and teeth, of Finch's face. Of blood and horror, and the oblivion of death. His parents, gone in a flash of white. Images, searing across his consciousness to set his heart pacing in tandem with a silent, internal scream.

Time slipped by. When he woke, jarred by a roll of the ship, he stared at the ceiling, trying to push the bad thoughts from his mind. But when he did so, little was left. The good in his life was restricted to the people in this room. Quintus, whose loyalty and friendship he was grateful for every day. Scott, who never failed to bring a smile to his face. Grace's courage and resilience that he could always rely upon.

And of course, Amber. He turned to look at her, as she slept peacefully on the bunk across from him. Watched as each breath disturbed her hair, and her button nose wrinkled as the strands tickled it.

That fierce, loyal girl. The rock that he could lean on when the world seemed to be collapsing around him.

Was there some piece of happiness they could carve out for themselves in this world? Romance was hard to come by in this crowded, sweaty box of a room, let alone in that slow starvation in the Keep itself. Perhaps he had missed his chance.

The rattle of a key in the door broke through his thoughts, followed by a light tap. The soft snores of the others told Cade it had not woken them, and he rolled from the bed.

The porthole had been dark for several hours, and Cade wondered who could be there, at this late hour.

With trepidation, Cade opened the door. Pigtails stood in his presence, an axe held in his hand. The boy's eyes darted nervously about. Was he not supposed to be there?

'I cannot tarry,' the boy said. 'But I come to warn you. My captain intends to return to the Keep, and recapture you again in a few months' time. And he is not alone in that intent.'

Cade's eyes widened, lethargy leaving him as fast as the words reached his ears.

'Why?' Cade asked.

'To return with the same warriors who had won the last tournament, ready to fight for your freedom again,' Pigtails said. 'The crowds would love it. You are worth more than your weight in gold.'

It was true. So true that Cade wondered why he had not thought of it before.

'It's against the rules,' Cade said.

The boy shrugged. 'Who would care? The emperor would want you for his games. He would ignore the slavers' lies to have you fight again, so long as he himself had fulfilled his end of the bargain by placing you on this ship.'

Cade stared in horror. It made sense. The emperor would not go against Abaddon and change the laws, but the slavers would have no problem breaking them, if the rewards were worth the risk.

'Why are you telling me?' Cade asked.

The boy lifted his chin. 'You and that girl could have

killed me. Twice. And yet you did not. I owe you.'

'I would've thought you'd resent us for capturing you in the first place,' Cade said.

Pigtails cracked a smile. 'I did, at first. But watching you fight in the arena . . . I saw your courage. I respect it.'

For a moment they stared at each other, and then Pigtails motioned with his head.

'I must leave. Know that you are no longer safe, even at your Keep. You have become the most valuable commodity in New Rome, and every slaver will hunt you to their last breath.'

He turned, then stopped and looked back. 'Good luck, Cade.'

Then, just like that, the boy was gone, disappearing through a hatch up to the deck.

'Wait,' Cade hissed. 'You didn't lock the door.'

But it was too late. He only hoped that nobody would notice when they came to get them in the morning. Cade went to close the door, when a sudden thought hit him.

He didn't lock the door.

Armour. These slavers had plenty of it. If Cade could steal some, perhaps some chainmail to hide beneath their clothing, or even stash inside Drake's coffin if he could find it . . . it was as good a back-up plan as any.

Holding his breath, Cade emerged from the room. He was feeling *déjà vu*, every sense screaming at him to get back in.

At the same time, he knew that they *needed* armour to win, and that Drake's coffin was a long shot. If he was captured and killed, another contender could take his place.

But if he found armour . . . he might just have a chance. It was a calculated risk, and he would take it.

He peered into the darkness and saw a barred gate, one with a keyhole. Clearly, *these* slavers worried about escaped slaves even more than Ishak did. No hope of getting through there.

To his left lay a dead end, and a step-ladder to the deck, where Cade knew men would be up and about. It looked like he would not be going for a midnight wander after all.

However, there *was* a door opposite him. Cade tested the handle, and was surprised to see it open with relative ease. He entered the room there as swiftly as he dared, knowing that a slaver could pass by at any moment. Inside, Cade had a momentary panic, seeing there were four bunk beds there too.

Fortunately for him, they were empty. It seemed to Cade that these bunk rooms were rarely used, if the dust within was any indication. Cade's groups' weapons. Strangely, other items had been stored there too. Statues and pottery, some silver cutlery. There were even muddied clothes. Artefacts from the jungle. Remnants.

Mostly, they seemed to be luxury items, the kind that the slavers might sell to wealthy collectors in the city.

For a moment, Cade was tempted to try to open the coffin there and then, see what was inside. When he looked closer, he saw nails and a wax seal around the edges that would make it a loud and lengthy process.

Frustrated, Cade turned to go. But something caught his eye. The Codex had flashed its timer.

02:15:56:49
02:15:56:48
02:15:56:47

He froze. He hadn't asked it anything. It was almost as if it wanted him to look at it. Even as he stared, the timer disappeared. What had it wanted him to see? He already knew how long they had left.

There was nothing near it, except for some folded sheets. They'd been given pride of place, folded neatly with an entire top bunk to themselves. Three swathes of golden cloth that seemed to glow in the soft moonlight filtering through the porthole. Clearly, it was something of worth.

He could hardly use it for more than a blanket, and its absence might be noticed when the slavers came to unload their things. But of everything in the room, he could most easily stuff one swathe inside his clothing. So he did, and returned to his room.

A small, petty victory . . . but he'd take it.

SIXTY

They were dumped unceremoniously in the late afternoon of the next day; yanked from their bunks and hustled down the gangplank to shore within the space of two minutes.

Not a word was spoken to them, and to Cade's relief, the coffin and their weapons were waiting for them on the bank. Moreover, they had been left only a hundred yards from the plunge pool of the waterfall, where the clearing of tree stumps met the edge of the forest.

It worried Cade that the slavers knew the Keep's location so precisely, but that was a problem for another time. As they stood watching the ship recede, the coming battle shifted to the forefront of his mind.

Perhaps unsurprisingly, the Codex flickered into existence as soon as the ship was out of sight. Cade kind of preferred it when it was invisible.

'So this is it?' Scott asked, nudging the coffin with his foot. 'I thought it might be a bit more . . . fancy.'

'As long as it has usable armour inside, I don't care if it's made of Silly Putty,' Cade replied. 'Let's get it back to the Keep so we can open it.'

When they tried to lift the thing, it was far heavier than it looked. They could only shuffle it a stone's throw at a time before having to lower it to the ground. Grace helped those walking backwards to navigate the tree stumps, hopping in front of them with her crutch.

'Lead is heavy,' Quintus grunted, after their third stop.

'Look, what's the point in wasting our time getting it to the Keep, if there's nothing but sea water inside?' Amber asked. 'I want to see if Yoshi and the twins are OK.'

'Let's open it here, and if there's armour, we'll take it out and leave the coffin,' Cade suggested. 'Unless one of you thinks a lead coffin is worth keeping?'

'Good plan,' Scott said, flexing his hands with a grimace.

Cade shrugged and hunkered down beside the coffin. The pale wax along the nailed lid was cracked, but had been lathered on so thick that Cade could not be sure it had been eaten through.

The team recovered their weapons from the ground, struggling to open the coffin with their bare hands. Cade drew the Honjō Masamune from its scabbard, now slung across his back where it belonged, and cut along the edges as best he could.

Then, he jammed in the blade and leaned forward, putting as much weight on it as he dared. Slowly, the lid levered up, opening with a slight hiss.

The others added their own blades, and soon the lid was loose enough for them to worm their fingers beneath.

'On three,' Cade said. 'One. Two. Three!'

They heaved, and the lid creaked off, the nails coming loose with a splintering screech. To Cade's surprise, the interior was made of wood, the lead layer but a coating.

But it was not this fact that drew his eye. It was the skull staring back at him. A skull so well preserved that he could see the wisps of beard still upon its chin. And below . . . armour.

Black metal, polished and oiled to a sheen, with two gauntleted hands crossed upon Drake's chest. A helmet rested between his legs, and a bed of straw lay beneath.

'Dude,' Scott breathed.

For a moment, the five stared down at the body. And then a voice.

'Amber!'

They spun, and saw three figures rushing from the tunnel. A trio of familiar faces, bright with smiles and shining with tears.

Cade had known he would be happy to see them. He had not realised he would break down crying. The relief, to see Yoshi, Bea and Trix, as alive and well as he had left them. Perhaps more so, their good health apparent as they drew closer.

His legs began to move, and soon he found himself crushed between seven sobbing teenagers, hugging each other for dear life. Words tumbled from their mouths, incoherent with joy.

'We saw you from the mountaintop,' Yoshi laughed. 'What the hell was that ship?'

'It's a long story,' Cade said, grinning.

'You made it, that's what matters,' Yoshi said, holding Cade at arm's length. 'And man . . . were you working out while you were away?'

'You guys don't look so bad yourselves.'

Yoshi had grown the beginnings of a beard, and his body had been baked tan by the sun. He held himself differently, with new confidence. And the gaunt appearance of his face was gone. What a difference a month could make.

As the others extricated themselves from the huddle, Cade saw the twins were also no longer the emaciated waifs he had left behind. Their cheeks were full and pink, eyes bright and lively. Food no longer seemed to be a problem.

'You hungry?' Yoshi asked. 'I've got a stew on the boil.'

'Real stew?' Grace asked, eyeing Yoshi with trepidation.

'Yes,' Yoshi said. 'And when I throw in more fish, it'll be enough for all of us.'

Cade raised his eyebrows. Had the three of them really become that good at fishing? As if reading Cade's mind, Yoshi grabbed Cade by the arm and led him to the riverbank.

'Look,' Yoshi said. 'A gill net. I made it with Bea and Trix.'

Cade peered into the green water, where he could see a log extended into the water, with a net hanging from the bottom.

'Fish get their gills caught in it,' Yoshi explained. 'We've been netting a couple of them a day.'

'Nice,' Cade said. 'Is that what you've been living off of?'

Yoshi grinned.

'You know, with the five of you gone there was enough to

go round. But we can put out a few more nets if we need; me and the girls have been getting pretty handy. We've even weaved a few baskets.'

'Hey, are we gonna take this dead dude out or not?' Scott called. 'I'm starving.'

Cade returned to the coffin. Somehow, he didn't feel like picking up the corpse with his bare hands.

'There's more of us now,' Cade said. 'Come on. We'll carry the coffin to the Keep together.'

SIXTY-ONE

Their story was long, but with close friends and warm food in their bellies, it made for a good evening. Though his battle with the alpha was two sleeps away, for now, Cade revelled in their success. Things could not be much better.

A chill descended as the evening came, and Cade revealed his looted cloth from the slavers, finding it to be immeasurably soft and light. It was a strange thing, decorated with the patterns of spiders and webbing, and shaped like an overlarge, u-shaped poncho.

Still, it kept him warm enough, not least because Amber joined him beneath it. Through the night, they sat around the crackling fire talking until their eyelids became heavy, and their stomachs could not fit another bite.

Reminiscing slowed. Talk descended into comfortable silence. One by one, the others peeled off, until Cade was left alone with Amber. For a while they remained there, watching the flames turn to embers and the first blush of sun peek through the horizon.

Their joy was marred only by the ticking of the timer, which had become a constant as soon as they had stepped foot in the Keep.

01:11:12:04
01:11:12:03
01:11:12:02

'It's cosy here,' Amber finally said. 'Good job with the blanket.'

'Pretty fancy blanket,' Cade said. 'You gotta wonder what the slavers were keeping it for.'

Amber yawned and shuffled closer to Cade, her thigh lightly pressing against his. Cade wondered if she noticed.

'Why don't we ask,' she murmured, sleepily laying her head on his shoulder.

The snug feeling of comfort fled, and suddenly Cade felt his palms sweat, despite the chill in the air. This was new territory. Amber seemed oblivious to his nerves.

'Codex,' Cade said, clearing his throat. 'What is this blanket?'

He had half-expected the Codex to tell him it did not originate from Earth. Instead, the Codex unleashed a torrent of information.

'*This item constitutes part of a set of bed linens that were displayed in 1900 at the Paris Exhibition. Made from spider silk from the golden orb weaver of Madagascar, the technique for harvesting the spider silk was developed by Father Camboué, a catholic missionary. It took millions of spiders and several years to create. Revered for its natural golden colouring, this one-of-a-kind set was lost soon after its début in Paris and has never been seen again.'*

Amber chuckled sleepily.

'I'm not sure whether I should be amazed or disgusted. Who knew spider silk was so soft.'

'It *is* soft,' Cade said. 'And I bet this is as expensive as hell. Being a contender has its perks.'

He tugged at the material, finding that it gave and stretched, like Lycra.

'Didn't Tsuru say silk would be better than linen for our under-armour?' Cade asked.

'That can't be right. When did anyone ever use silk as armour?'

The Codex spoke, and Amber groaned.

'Modern-day police in Thailand use layered silk vests to protect against small calibre bullets.'

Amber sat up, and Cade felt a pang of disappointment. At the same time, his own interest was piqued. And the Codex was not done.

'. . . the year 1893, a monk named Casimir Zeglen used silk to develop bullet-proof vests and material,' it continued. *'This was later sold to Tsar Nicholas II of Russia, Archduke Franz Ferdinand of Asutria and the King Alfonso XIII of Spain . . .'*

'Chinese Ming dynasty warriors would use layers of silk and cloth as their only armour as late as 1644.'

'Is this for real?' Amber whispered. 'Silk's not *that* tough.'

'. . . Japan, a silk kite known as a horo *would billow behind cavalry to catch arrows fired at them . . .'*

'I think it is,' Cade breathed.

'. . . *Genghis Khan had his best warriors wear silk beneath their armour so that arrows would be enveloped in the untorn silk and their barbs not tear the flesh*—'

'OK, enough!' Cade said. 'What about spider silk? Is it so different from normal silk?'

'*Spider silk is considered far stronger than that of the silkworm. It is five times stronger than steel and is even tougher than Kevlar. Its density is such that a strand long enough to encircle the Earth would weigh less than half a kilogram.*'

'It's *better*?' Amber breathed.

'Must be,' Cade said, feeling his heart quicken. 'I mean, I don't know if bed hangings are designed to stop bullets . . . but maybe it'll do a better job of stopping a claw.'

He examined the cloth with new eyes, squinting in the low light of sunrise. The stitching was tight enough, but a sharp point could probably push between stitches. Not to mention that with enough force, a claw would still rip into his flesh, whether it was encircled in cloth or not.

Even so, it was a godsend. Did he dare to hope? Who knew if this would work. It was a single layer after all.

'Don't you see?' Amber laughed. 'You're going to win this thing!'

She turned to Cade, her cheeks tinged pink with excitement. Her arms enveloped him, gripping tight. They held each other, disturbed only by the crackle of the embers and the soft sigh of the breeze.

A perfect moment.

Slowly, they parted, inches from each other. Amber

searched his face, her eyes drifting down to his lips. Nerves intermingled with hope in his chest, a heady mixture that threw his caution to the wind as he dared to lean closer.

Time slowed, and then their lips met, an electric softness that took his breath away. His fingers traced the curve of her back, as she returned his kiss with a fierceness belied by the soft clasp of her hands on his waist.

She pushed away, as suddenly as that same flare of passion a moment before.

'Cade,' she said, unable to meet his gaze. 'I don't know . . .'

'I do,' Cade breathed.

He touched her chin, lifting her face to meet his. There were tears on her cheeks, and he brushed them away with a thumb. She smiled through shining eyes.

They shared a last tender kiss. Then she stood, leaving Cade feeling bereft, even though she stood only a foot away.

'You need your rest,' she said. 'And so do I. Good night, Cade.'

She flashed him a smile, and then hurried away, back to the Keep.

Cade didn't know how to feel, but his face did. It had produced a grin so wide it hurt the sides of his face. He fell back, looking up at the sky. No stars . . . but a sunrise was far more romantic.

'How *very* sweet,' came a familiar, girlish voice. And a slow, drawn-out clap.

Abaddon.

Cade sat up, and there she was. Hardly older than a toddler, skipping daintily about the fire. The cherubic monster that was their overlord's avatar.

'I see you found my gift,' Abaddon went on, stopping in front of Cade and booping his nose. The finger hummed with static, and Cade flinched away.

'Gift?' Cade blurted.

The girl lifted the silk blanket from him and threw it about her shoulders like a cape. It brushed along the ground as she twirled.

'A little something I left for those slavers on their last trip. It took a thousand little nudges to place it within your reach. A whisper in the ear. A key falling from its chain.'

Cade swallowed, his mouth suddenly dry. Abaddon skipped closer, letting the bed hanging fall.

'It helps that you are *so* predictable.' The girl gave a tinkling laugh. 'As all you humans are.'

'Is this all you've done?' Cade demanded. 'Or did you orchestrate our capture? Have Tsuru train me?'

Abaddon smiled sweetly at him.

'This game that my siblings and I play is not for you to understand. Does the pawn ask the hand why it is moved?'

'So your siblings don't object to your meddling?' Cade asked, though he wasn't sure why he did.

'What occurs in my domain is watched by all, and they contest any disproportionate influence on my part. It helps if in the act of interference, your journey becomes more . . . eventful. Like fighting in an arena for instance.'

'We almost died,' Cade said, his shock at the alien's appearance giving way to anger. An anger that had been simmering inside him for so long, he had almost forgotten it was there.

'Almost,' Abaddon said, holding up a dainty finger. 'I admit, there were times I was sure you would die. Still, now you are here. A trained gladiator, armed and armoured. Believe me when I tell you, had I not intervened, your so-called plan would have been an abject failure.'

Cade seethed, but even he could not deny that they were better prepared for the duel now than he could have hoped to be when they had first set out from the Keep.

'So what are you doing here?' he snapped. 'To give me some more *help*?'

Abaddon sighed and sat cross-legged by the fire.

'Ever ungrateful. It's a wonder I don't just let you fend for yourselves. Were it not for me, you'd be long dead.'

'If it weren't for you, I wouldn't be here!' Cade snapped.

Abaddon's sweet face suddenly twisted into a mask of anger.

'Were it not for me, your *planet* would not exist. Speak one more word, and I shall tear you apart by the very atoms.'

Cade fell silent, and Abaddon shuffled closer.

'I came to tell you that my siblings are used to the clash of armies, not the petty skirmishes that a group of your size engenders.'

It took a moment for Cade to understand what Abaddon was saying.

'So . . .' he said.

'You shall not be alone much longer,' Abaddon said. 'More contenders shall be with you soon enough.'

Cade's eyes widened.

'Who?' he asked.

The girl tapped her button nose.

'Never you mind. You just worry about winning the duel. Should you lose, it will not matter. Earth shall be wiped from existence.'

The little girl's form began to fade.

'Sleep well, Cade,' Abaddon said. 'You have a busy day ahead!'

SIXTY-TWO

'Cade.'

The voice drifted through Cade's consciousness, and he felt the gentle shake upon his shoulder.

'Cade, you should wake up.'

He opened his eyes. Yoshi was hunkered down beside his bed, a worried look in his eyes.

'Oh man, I was worried there for a minute. You've been asleep for ages.'

Cade sat up and rubbed his eyes.

'How long?' he asked, swinging his legs over the side.

'Depends when you went to bed,' Yoshi chuckled. 'But it's late afternoon now. Here. Lunch.'

He held out a bowl, where the flaked flesh of a cooked fish sat. Cade grimaced and took it. There was something about eating fish after waking that didn't feel right . . . but he slurped it down regardless.

'Guess I should try that armour on, huh?' Cade said.

'That's what we were thinking,' Yoshi said. 'We took it off

the . . . dude . . . this morning. Buried him out by the river.'

'Thanks,' Cade said. 'That can't have been fun.'

Yoshi shrugged.

'When you've buried your friends . . . some ancient stranger isn't so bad.'

Cade winced. He had not been there for the burial of the others, after the qualifying round. His body had been too broken to make the climb to the orchards.

'Sorry,' he said.

Yoshi gave him a quick smile.

'Come on,' he said. 'It's waiting for you.'

Cade followed Yoshi down the stairs, and found everyone gathered outside. The armour was laid out on the cobbles, piece by piece. The spider-silk cloth was splayed out beside it.

'Morning, sleepyhead,' Scott called. 'Were you out partying last night or something?'

Cade saw Amber blush. She looked tired, and Cade guessed she had hardly slept at all.

'We've figured out how to attach the armour,' she said, 'And we've made a plan for the spider silk too.'

It was strange. To talk as if nothing had happened the night before. But what else did he expect her to say?

'You've been busy,' Cade said. 'Thank you.'

'Just stand with your legs and arms spread and we'll see if it fits,' Bea said. 'Drake looked a bit smaller than you. I just hope he shrunk while he was . . . you know.'

Cade grimaced at the reminder.

'I feel like I'm being measured for a suit,' he said, as the others went to work.

It was a strange set of armour. Black as pitch, with gold filigree traced along its edge in swirling patterns. The ensemble looked almost ceremonial, but as they began to strap parts to his body, it felt sturdy enough.

The helmet was perhaps his greatest surprise. Training with Tsuru, their faces had been open, their vision unimpeded. But this . . . it had hardly more than a slit. Though at least he could raise the visor to give him a better view.

One by one, the pieces were slotted into place. He sweated in the afternoon sun, wishing they had chosen a more shaded area to dress him.

The helmet was lowered over his head, and he thanked the heavens that it only smelled a little musty.

'So,' Amber said, slapping his shoulders with a clang. 'How do you feel?'

Cade took a faltering step.

It was heavy, heavier than he had expected. And tight too. Not so tight that it was hard to move, but he still felt a pinch about his groin and underarms as he stretched and sidestepped on the cobbles.

His world had been reduced to a narrow band of vision. It was a little better than he had thought it would be, but it seemed strange to not be able to see where he was stepping. He could only hope they would fight on even ground.

'Pass me my sword, please?' Cade asked.

He outstretched a hand, and felt its weight pressed into his palm. The gauntlets themselves were also a little snug, which did not help with the pain from the stitches in his fingers. Luckily, he found he could hold the sword well enough.

'Give me some room,' Cade called. 'I don't want to hit anyone.'

Sword in hand, he launched himself forward, slicing, ducking and dodging as Tsuru had taught him. He was slower, of course. His legs felt more strain, his range of movement tighter and more restricted.

With each step, the metal clanked and scraped. It felt . . . wrong. But when a juggernaut of muscle, claws and tentacles bore down on him, it would be a far better option than padded cloth alone.

He turned and lowered his visor.

'It'll do,' Cade said. 'But I wouldn't go for a hike in it.'

'Great,' Trix said. 'Now let us take it off and then you can strip down to your underwear.'

Cade stopped, confused.

'What?' he asked.

'We're going to stitch this silk onto your linen clothes,' Bea said. 'Can't exactly do it with you in them.'

'Oh right,' Cade said, suddenly intensely aware of Amber's gaze. 'Um . . . maybe I should get some more practice at moving around in this thing before we do that.'

'Better we do it now and you practise later than practise now and run out of time,' Yoshi said. 'You go take a bath.'

Cade thought of the cold waters of their bath below. They *did* sound tempting. Tsuru had been right – the armour was roasting him like an oven under the hot sun. Plus, it had been two nights in a row he had not washed, and he could practically taste the salt of dried sweat on his skin.

'I'm gonna go check the gill net,' Amber said, as if noticing Cade's hesitation. 'Cade's gonna need his strength for tomorrow.'

She hurried away, and Cade wondered if it was to save his embarrassment . . . or something else. He shook his head. He couldn't afford to be distracted right now.

'Little help?' he asked, outstretching his arms.

SIXTY-THREE

It took them longer than Cade expected to finish it, summoning him from the gloomy baths only when he'd had a thorough soak and his fingertips were wrinkled white. All the while, instead of thinking of his battle . . . he wished that Amber would come down the stairs.

But only Yoshi came, to tell him his new clothes were ready.

He dried off and wrapped himself in one of their towels, made from the rough sacking of the mattresses they had scavenged. Outside, his friends held up their handiwork proudly, and Cade could not help but be impressed.

It was not pretty by any standards. But the arms, torso and upper thighs of his linen outfit were now completely covered in the golden material, even if the stitching and cutting was haphazard, and overlapped in places.

'Do you have any idea how hard it was to cut this thing up?' Yoshi groaned, prodding at the golden suit. 'We had to saw it with your sword, thread by thread.'

Cade grinned.

'Means the alpha will have an even harder time getting through it,' he chuckled.

He looked around, noticing someone was missing.

'Where's Amber?' he asked.

Grace shrugged. 'She went up to the orchards,' she replied. 'Said she wanted to make sure we had enough for your breakfast tomorrow.'

'Oh,' Cade said, disappointed.

Was she avoiding him?

He knew he should not be worrying whether Amber had regrets about their kiss. The fate of his very species was at stake, not to mention his life.

And yet somehow, it was all he could think about.

Holding the towel to protect his modesty, he dressed awkwardly. Then the long process of putting on his armour began again.

'Dinner in two hours,' Yoshi said, as Cade flexed and stretched.

'About that,' Cade said, resisting the urge to glance up at the mountains. 'I think I want to eat alone tonight. It's nothing against you guys . . . I just . . .'

'You don't need to explain,' Scott said. 'We understand.'

'Yes,' Quintus whispered.

The legionary had been unusually quiet the past few days. Cade considered the boy, whose eyes looked sunken with worry.

'Hey, can you do me a favour, Quintus?'

'Anything,' Quintus said.

'I need someone to teach me how to throw a javelin. You learned how to throw a *pilum* in the legion, right?'

Quintus grinned at him.

'When do we start?'

They practised beside the waterfall, using an old stump as a target. Each time Cade threw the javelin, he walked over to get it himself, acclimatising to the weight and balance of the armour.

There was not much to throwing a javelin, at least at the range that Cade intended. To throw it as far as the Romans might have would have been a challenge, especially with a gauntlet and weighted armour.

Lucky for him, Quintus had helped figure out how far away the alpha should be before he threw it. They did this by having Quintus sprint at him, and timing how long it took for Cade to throw the javelin and tug his sword from the ground . . . with a substantial margin for error, of course.

Gripping the javelin was another problem. The wood found little purchase on his metal-clad fingers, and Quintus was forced to nail a wrap of leather where Cade would grip it, so it would not slip. With that done, Cade found it easy enough to hurl, and with slow practice, he began to throw it without the javelin turning over in the air . . . and eventually even hit the target.

When Cade's arm tired of throwing, they practised the duelling techniques he had learned with Tsuru, now completely armoured, and with a heavy sword in its scabbard to prevent him from cutting Quintus. To his surprise, it took only an hour before he hardly noticed the armour's weight.

Cade slumped to his knees as the sun set. He could hardly see, and exhaustion had set in. He hoped he had not overdone it, but getting used to his armour was his first priority.

'OK!' Cade groaned. 'I'm done.'

Quintus helped him to his feet.

'Thank you.' Cade paused. 'For everything. I don't think I've said that enough. You're my best friend, Quintus. The best I've ever had.'

He felt the prick of tears in his eyes and looked away.

'Not friend,' Quintus said, his words hesitant. 'Brother.'

The boy sat heavily on a stump and beckoned Cade to join him.

'I was called weakling,' he said. 'Idiot. I had no friends before you.'

Cade sat. Quintus hardly spoke about his past, beyond what had happened here on Acies. The boy stroked the streak of white in his hair, and pointed at his mismatched eyes.

'They said I was cursed. By Gods. Do you know what they did to children like me? The . . . imperfect?'

Cade shook his head.

'They killed us. Our laws say I should be stoned to death, but my mother followed custom. She left me on the mountain to die. No clothes, in wind and rain.'

Cade felt sick.

'Like the twins, Romulus and Remus, I lived,' Quintus said. 'But no wolf raised me. Old farmer and his wife. They had no children. They wanted me. My own mother did not.'

'I'm so sorry,' Cade whispered.

'I worked the land, and they grew older. But when they died, I was forced to leave. In grief, I joined the legions, to get as far away from Rome as I could.'

He paused, twisting his hands. It seemed clear to Cade that the boy had never spoken of this to anyone.

'I bribed them to join with money I save. I asked go to the . . . end of our empire. Britannia.'

A tear trickled down his cheek.

'But I was marked with curse from the gods, and soldiers said I bad omen. They spat on me, steal from me. I ate what I could hunt. I believe them. That my mother right. And then, we march to Caledonia . . . and I arrive here.'

Quintus looked up, his eyes shining.

'No one has been kind like you. You patient. Brave. Do not thank me. I thank you.'

Cade put an arm around Quintus's shoulders.

'Maybe we can thank each other,' he said. 'Brothers then?'

Quintus smiled back.

'Brothers.'

SIXTY-FOUR

Cade ate alone with Quintus that night, the others already gone to bed. He tried not to think of Amber, and how she seemed to be avoiding him. Though it seemed she had almost no sleep the past night. Was it so strange for her to go to bed without saying goodnight?

As he tossed and turned, it was the dread of the duel that was worst of all. There had been so much to do in the past weeks. The duel had seemed so far off, with his focus on winning his freedom. Then that journey on the ship, his reunion with the others. His training . . . that kiss.

Now, in the silence of the night, with the others sleeping downstairs so as not to disturb him . . . he felt utterly alone. No friend would accompany him onto the battlefield this time. Amber's shield would not protect his left, nor Quintus's his right. Grace's strong arm would not hold him steady, nor would Scott be there to whisper soft encouragement.

He knew death now. He'd watched enough men and women pass on, choking on their own blood, awash in misery and agony. There was no glory here. It would be an ugly thing.

Most of all, he asked a single question, one that had been at the back of his mind since Abaddon had revealed the origins of Earth. Was there an afterlife . . . or just oblivion?

Morning came too soon, spurred on by a fitful sleep. Cade took a cold bath to wake himself up, as the others lay in bed. He sunk his head beneath the chill waters and screamed. Fear, misery, anger – he released them into the world.

Then he lifted himself from the pool. He left those feelings behind. He had a task to do. What was his life, and an ugly end, when the very world was at stake?

When the others woke, he ate what food Yoshi put in front of him, hardly tasting the fish and root vegetables as they passed into his belly. He answered 'yes' and 'no' as they asked him if he'd slept well, if he was OK, if they could do anything. His mind was focused now. Running over the battle as he saw it happening. The steps he would take. The timing of the throw, the angle of the cut.

The questions petered out, and they dressed him. Yoshi had sharpened his blade, and Quintus refitted the leather grip of his javelin.

And Amber. He hardly looked at her as she tied back his hair, now grown so long that it hung over his eyes. The helmet fell over his head, and with it his world fell into focus.

00:00:00:30
00:00:00:29
00:00:00:28

The timer ticked on, and they watched from beside the fire. Would Cade vanish into thin air, to battle on some distant field of the Pantheon's choosing?

00:00:00:03
00:00:00:02
00:00:00:01

The digits disappeared. And then . . . they heard it.

A sound unlike any other – a chorus of screeching wails that set Cade's teeth on edge. A sound that came from the bone fields, beyond the wall.

They hurried up the stairs, Cade breathing heavily as he dragged his new weight up the flight. He raised his visor. And saw what had come to greet them.

Hydras seethed on the sands of the desert. Hundreds of them, tentacles wriggling from their conch-shell heads, as if tasting the very air for signs of life. From the bipedal turkey-like grubs, to the four-legged hunters, they covered the sands entirely.

But these, terrifying though they were, did not draw the eye. Not when there were a dozen alphas towering over the rest, and these still dwarfed by the elephantine matriarch at the centre of the masses.

A queen. Three times the height of a man, she knuckled the ground like a gorilla, walking on two short legs. The mouth was made up of four pairs of long hooked mandibles, differing her from her brood. But strangest of all was the forest of twisting tentacles on her back, and among them, orange egg-sacs that glistened in the sunlight.

Yet, not a single one had passed into their valley, blocked by the opaque wall of a forcefield.

'*Duel commencing. Will the contenders' champion please enter the battlefield*,' the Codex intoned.

Cade took a faltering step towards the stairs, but the Codex was not done.

'*No contenders may interfere in the duel. Such an action will result in the forcefield being lowered, and the subsequent battle determining the outcome of this round on the leaderboard.*'

'Now wait a minute,' Amber said. 'Let's think about this. What if we—'

'No,' Cade said. 'There's no way we have a better shot fighting all of them.'

'But the wall . . .' Amber said.

'That queen would smash through it in seconds,' Cade said. 'And then there'd be more than one alpha each for us to deal with, let alone the others. It's not worth discussing.'

He turned to the his friends. 'Even if I'm about to . . . don't you dare move. If the Earth is going to end, at least you guys will be OK here. Let me die knowing that, at least.'

He did not wait for an answer. Only went down the stairs, his sword in one hand, javelin in the other. Quintus ran ahead, and the iron bar that held the door closed was lifted. Then Cade was walking into the field, his iron-clad feet sinking into the moist soil beneath.

It was a field of bones. The ground was scattered with the remains of a thousand men and beasts, skulls half-buried like loose rocks. The ribcage of some giant beast lay nestled against one wall, a stark reminder of the monsters the Romans had faced – and killed.

'I can do this,' Cade whispered. 'I *can* do this.'

Ahead, the forcefield parted like a curtain. A figure stepped through, its arms splayed in challenge. The opaque barrier closed behind it, and then they were two, facing each other across a hundred feet.

Cade dropped his visor, and the alpha's form centred in his field of view.

The Codex spoke a single word, and it fell on Cade's ears like a death knell.

'*Begin.*'

SIXTY-FIVE

Tentacles writhed in the air, as if the beast was scenting his approach. One foot stomped forward, then another. But this was no mad charge. It was wary. Almost tentative.

Cade walked closer, giving himself as much room to manoeuvre on the battlefield as he could. This was not a fight where a back to the wall would be to his advantage. He needed room to duck and dodge.

It was a long walk. Somehow, he had expected everything to start at once – a clash of metal and claws as soon as the timer hit zero.

Instead, he felt like a batter walking up to the plate. On he trudged, and now he could see the alpha more clearly. It stood as a man would, broad-shouldered and muscled in the arms, legs and chest. The mass of tentacles at its mouth surrounded a sharp beak at the centre, while its head was shaped like a conch shell, studded with dark eyes.

Three large digits tipped its four limbs, and these in turn were tipped with razor-sharp talons. Its feet, in particular, gave Cade pause, for a much larger curved talon adorned the outer toe. The killing claw.

'Breathe,' Cade whispered. 'Breathe.'

The alpha was moving faster now. Stomping forward, its head twisting this way and that. It seemed to Cade that its sight was poor, for it did not seem to focus on him as he neared, now no more than fifty feet away.

The horror of its presence was almost a physical thing, forcing him back a pace. How could he defeat something so monstrous?

Now he was closer, he noticed the beast had fought before, though whether with humans or otherwise he could not say. The specimen was covered in scars, white against its grey-pink flesh. A veteran.

But Cade was a veteran too. He had fought the vipers and won. Faced down a carnosaur, even beheaded a raptor. And yes, he had killed men too, no matter how he felt about it. He was every bit the alpha's equal.

False confidence or not, Cade let himself believe it. He steeled himself.

The beast stomped forward. Forty feet now. Cade stabbed his sword into the ground, the movement increasing the alpha's pace as it noticed.

Thirty feet.

Cade drew back his arm, his breath coming thick and fast.

Twenty.

His fist lanced forward, the javelin sailing from his fingertips and spiralling towards the beast. He heard the dull thud of impact, saw the alpha's shoulder jerk back, tentacles flailing.

For a second, the javelin dangled from its flesh, the beast standing still as a statue. Then a massive hand lifted and snapped the protruding end in between its claws. Dark blood trickled from the wound, black as squid's ink.

And then, with a wailing screech . . . the beast charged.

Soil scattered in its wake, its arms pumping like pistons as it tore forward, faster than Cade had thought possible. He yanked forth his sword and jogged back, edging to the left, widening the angle of attack. Still it came, so close he could hear the hoarse breaths whistling from its maw and the thunder of its feet.

Thud. Thud. Thud.

At the last moment, Cade changed direction, lunging forward and to the left with twice the speed of his retreat. The beast's claw whipped round, but Cade's move made it mistime its blow, and talons swung over his head as he fell to one knee, his sword held out in line with the ground. He felt the jar of impact. Then he was sprinting on, distancing himself before turning to face his opponent once more.

But the alpha was already on him, and Cade could only dance back once more as blows rained down. For a few frantic moments, Cade reacted on instinct, ducking and blocking by muscle memory alone. Twice he managed to return the favour, desperate slashes that opened pink furrows on the alpha's chest.

The beast seemed to hardly notice, relentlessly pursuing him.

Encased in metal, Cade's arms throbbed with exertion, yet he dared not slacken, forcing the blade up again and again to meet the monstrous force of the beast's talon-tipped arms.

He couldn't hold out for much longer. Leaden limbs slowed of their own volition, and his lungs burned from dry, gasping breaths. A swipe screeched across Cade's chest plate as his armoured feet slipped on loose bones and soil.

In the same instant, Cade swung in a frantic counterstrike. Steel slashed an inch from the alpha's face, severing a tentacle; it dropped into the soil and wriggled like a living thing.

With a pained roar, the monster lifted its talons high and leaped forward.

Cade's sword countered the overhead blow, clashing steel on keratin, but the claws hooked the blade and held it still as the other forelimb smashed into his face in an open-handed slap.

He heard the clang of metal, his neck cracking as his head was slammed to one side. Dizzied, Cade staggered away, just as a kick thudded home in his chest, knocking him onto his back.

Pain flared across his stomach, but it was the dull pain of blunt-force trauma rather than the agony of disembowelment. He felt the breeze there, knew his armour had been opened up like a tin can. But the under-armour had held.

His vision filled with a wriggling mass, and then his head was enveloped by a beak snapping and scraping along his visor, pincering for his eyes. A massive weight fell on his chest, crumpling the metal. It was straddling him. Blinded, Cade stabbed his sword inward, felt the tip sink in a few inches before a weight slammed down on his arm, pinning it to the ground.

'No!' Cade screamed.

Saliva dripped from the beak as it tried to force its way inside his helmet, and now a tentacle wriggled through, and Cade felt the suckers ripping at his forehead. Blood trickled into his hair, hot and caustic.

He kicked his legs, only for a sharp pain to flare across his calves as the alpha's talons ripped through the metal and scrabbled beneath. It was agony.

Desperate, he shoved at it with his free hand. His gauntlet met the stub of the javelin, and he gripped it. Twisted, and tugged it free, eliciting a screech.

He stabbed, once, twice, into its head. Felt the weight fall away, the tentacle withdraw as he rolled to the side. He could hardly see for the blood and the crumpled helmet, and he yanked at his visor. But it would not move, and instead he pulled the whole thing away, gasping for breath as he used his sword to push himself to his feet.

The monster reeled, staggering and clutching at its head. Its eyes. That was its weakness.

But even as Cade stepped forward to press his advantage, his leg almost buckled from under him. He looked down, only to see his leg armour furrowed and torn, and felt the blood squelch in his socks.

He was injured. Badly.

The alpha wailed in fury, its tentacles flailing as it turned its head left and right, seeking him out. He could not go toe-to-toe with it, not with his legs like this.

But he was in an open field. There was no rock to hide behind. No tree to climb. No long grass to ambush it from. All he saw was bones. Bones and . . . he began to move.

Pain. It lanced through his body with every step, yet he knew that at any moment the alpha would spot him and charge. He forced himself on, until he reached his destination. The ribcage.

A dozen great curved spars of yellow-white, as large as a whale's, held together by sinew and half-rotted flesh. Enough to provide a barrier that Cade might use to his advantage.

Cade ducked through, just as he heard the hoarse breaths of the alpha approaching, dark blood streaming from its head, chest and side. It thundered towards him, and Cade crouched, his blade extended like a spear point between the great ribs of the long-dead giant.

Impact, in a blur of grey-pink flesh. Bone shards flew, yet the structure held, as the monster skewered itself on his blade. Tentacles wormed close, whipping for his face, and Cade was forced to release the sword as he fell out of reach.

The alpha staggered back, the blade deep in its chest, then lunged again. It clawed at him, talons grasping, and Cade could only cower as the monster forced itself closer, the ribs finally snapping and releasing the stench of rotting marrow.

But the beast was slowing. It sank to its knees, even as it edged into the ribcage, a trap of Cade's own making. Its clustered eyes fixed on his, full of animal hatred.

Like Finch's eyes.

A memory of the arena came unbidden . . . and his hand moved of its own volition, dashing soil in the alpha's face.

Blinded, the beast's claws swung for him, and he ducked and rolled beneath as he reached up and heaved on the sword.

Heart blood sprayed as it came free, dousing him in foul liquid. The beast's head dipped towards him. He felt the tentacles envelop his head, pulling him closer, the beak pincered once, twice . . . and then stopped.

Like a falling tree, the beast toppled forward, its great weight pinning him to the ground. Cade choked, the alpha's open jaws an inch from his face. Blood from its head dripped, spattering across his nose.

Cade's fingers hooked the earth as he pulled himself back, desperate to be away from the dying monster, its eyes still swivelling in its head. One by one, the suckers ripped free from his own head, and he sobbed at the pain of it.

The Codex was speaking, but he could hardly understand it as he scrabbled in the dirt, hauling himself over his broken ribs and the monster's twitching legs. He did not have the strength to go further.

'Help,' he croaked. 'I can't. I can't.'

Cade forced up his gaze . . . tried to look towards the Keep to find his friends.

But the edges of his vision blurred. He let his head fall, sobbing deep breaths into the soil.

I won.

The thought shone like a beacon in his mind, before the dark of unconsciousness stole it from him.